EVERY PIECE OF YOU

J. MORALES

Mom, thank you for your support. I appreciate it.
To my husband and kids: thank you for listening to me talk about my stories and always giving me ideas. Love you

To my readers: thank you for your kind support.

PLAYLIST

"Guilty as Sin" Taylor Swift
"Learning to Fly" Tom Petty and the Heartbreakers
"Fuck Up the Friendship" Leah Kate
"Wicked Game" Chris Isaak
"Feels Like" Gracie Abrams
"Rollercoaster" Bleachers
"Heaven Sent" Mr. Little Jeans
"What a Time" Julia Michaels, Nail Horan
"Breakdown" G-Eazy, Demi Lovato
"Waiting for Superman" Daughtry

You can find the rest of the playlist here:
Author J. Morales Playlist
You can also listen on your Spotify account below:

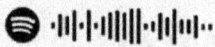

DEAR READERS

Every Piece of You is the third book of *The Delgado Brother Series*. I highly advise reading the first two books *Always You* and *Reckless You* first to become acquainted with the characters and backstory. Book Three cannot be read as a standalone. *Every Piece of You* follows the timeline, although <u>Part One</u> begins prior to *Always You* (Mila and Dominic's story), and <u>Part Two</u> continues with the present time with the end of the *Recklessly You* timeline. *Please note, if you read Book Three as a standalone, you might come across events that may raise questions that can be answered by reading the first two books.*

CONTENT WARNING

Please be aware that this book contains content that some readers may find disturbing such as: violence, sexual assault, miscarriage, mentions of childhood trauma and abuse, as well as explicit scenes and language. If you are a sensitive reader, please proceed with caution.

PART ONE

"Loving someone who's unaware of your feelings is depressing, but loving someone who is forbidden is even more excruciating." – *Rosaline.*

<u>Note to readers before proceeding.</u>

If you have read *Always You* the first book to the Delgado Brothers, <u>Part One</u> of Santiago and Rosaline's story is prior to Mila and Dominic's story. <u>Part Two</u> will follow after book two *Recklessly You. Present time.*

1

Past
Years Earlier

ROSALINE
Nineteen years old.

WITH MY FRESHMAN year at the Academy of Art in the books,
I'm finally home. As much as I loved Portland, San Diego has
my heart—and my room. I considered staying on campus for
the summer to take additional classes, but my aunt planned a
birthday party for me. And the other reason was to see Santiago, of course.

I toss my suitcase on the bed and start to unpack. I think
about Santiago and my brain revs like a race car. Just conjuring
his name, my stomach flutters. Will he see me differently this
time around?

Stop it, Rosa.

I try to think of anything but him as I unpack my acrylics and brushes. Art. Art is a much better passion to think about. Painting has always been my passion and helped me cope with my childhood trauma. When my mother tossed me to the curb at age three, my aunt took me in. Thinking of my aunt naturally led my thoughts to her son, Liam. That was a bad idea since they slid right past him to Dominic, Santiago's big brother. And there my thoughts go again. Dominic is Liam's best friend.

My hands itch to create art. Leaving the half-unpacked suitcase, I march to my stash of supplies and sit on my stool. I close my eyes and envision something to paint. Someday, I'll create expensive portraits and see them displayed in exhibits. I'm so close.

I sigh as the vision appears in my head. A tall, masculine man: muscles on top of muscles, tan skin, silk brown hair, dreamy dimples, a beautiful wolf tattoo with a forest landscaping decorates his back. Oh, and that smile is so gentle and perfect.

Rosa, get a hold of yourself.

Why can't I be eight years older

My phone buzzes. Setting the paintbrush down, I pull my phone from my jeans.

"Hello?"

"Rosie Posie, what are you up to?"

I chuckle at my best friend, Jasmine. "I'm about to paint. What else would I be doing in the hour since you dropped me off?" I tease.

Having Jasmine with me at The Academy of Art has been great, and even better since we get to drive home together for the summer. Inseparable since we were twelve.

She laughs. "I know, but I wanted to tell you about a couple of college parties with our old classmates. And my cousin just moved here—well, a year ago, when we moved to Portland. Maybe you two can hook up."

I scrunch my nose, and an *ick* sound slips out by accident. Her cousin is attractive, but he's not. . . a certain someone.

"Are you painting the man-god?"

"No," I say defensively.

She snorts. "Sure, I believe you. You only have a million paintings of him."

She's exaggerating—probably by half a million. She knows all my secrets. Like that I've had a crush on Santiago all my life and that I keep my paintings of him here at my aunt's. It's locked, so they can't have a heart attack. They would think it's creepy. I like to call it infatuated.

"I can't think of anything else to paint."

One long year without seeing him felt like an eternity. It's depressing to be in love with someone who doesn't see you the same way. For all I know, he might still see me as a kid.

"There are hundreds of different things to paint. Like animals or hot guys in college?"

"Sounds boring," I say honestly. They have no muscle, nor a deep, sexy, husky voice.

"You have it bad, Rosa. What are you going to do when he gets married? You can barely handle it when you see him with a woman."

Ugh, she's right. I would die of a broken heart. I don't know what he's up to. We've texted a few times this year. But when he texts, he asks how I'm doing and tells me to be careful and study hard. That's it. What if he's dating someone?

My stomach sours.

"I know, Jasmine. This sucks."

"You're not a kid anymore, Rosa. Maybe it's time you got his attention."

My brows rise. "How would I do that? I've never even kissed a guy, and I'm nineteen. How in the hell do you expect me to get his attention?" I blow hot air out.

"For one, Rosa, you're hot; you have curves, great breasts,

and an ass everyone drools over. And two, he hasn't seen you in a year. Flirt with him."

Cristo. Christ. I don't even know if I know how to flirt. However, my body has changed. My breasts have filled out. My friends developed at the regular age. I had been a late bloomer. I have always been on the heavy side, but now I have extra curves. My ass is still huge, and my belly fat is still there. That one is stubborn to get rid of.

"Well, I could give it a try," I drawl.

The problem is that Santiago Delgado is eight years older than me, and he's known me my whole life. We all grew up together. My *tía* worked two jobs to make ends meet, so I spent my days with Liam hanging out at the Delgado household. Or, more accurately, hanging out with Santiago. He always took the time to draw, tell me stories, and play dolls.

"Hell, it's worth a shot. What do you have to lose?" Jasmine asked.

I could lose him if he's not interested in me that way. The vital question is... Is it worth the risk if the result is him pushing me away forever? I'm not sure I could live without him in my life. He's been in it for sixteen years.

"*TIA,* CAN I BORROW YOUR CAR?" I ask.

She peers up at me from the cookbook she is reading. She surveys me.

"Look at you. You've grown into a beautiful woman. Yes, you can use *your* Jeep. Santiago fixed it for you a while back."

"That was sweet of him."

She takes her reading glasses off.

"He is very sweet. That boy is a hard worker. Ever since he was young, he's taken care of his brothers, and you, when I've needed a hand." She takes a sip of her coffee. "Someday, he's going to make a woman very happy."

My heart deflates like a balloon flying all over the damn city.

"I'll be back in a couple of hours. I won't be out long."

"Have fun, *mija*."

The metal screen door slams behind me. Now, I can't help but think about what Jasmine said.

Parties, in general, have never been my type of entertainment—not in high school or even college—because I'm not much for socializing. I've always kept my circle tight. Friends have never stayed friends for long, except for Jasmine. She's been my ride-or-die.

Jasmine, her boyfriend, Tank, and I walk into the party. Rock music is blasting, beer is flowing, and guys are man-spreading on the sofa with chicks on their laps. Hands all over the girls in places I've only dreamt of being touched. Although, I do feel cringy about it. I wouldn't want random guys being handsy with me. It makes me feel like an inexperienced woman. The dining room is a roiling mass of noise and bodies, with tables adorned with colorful cups and red plastic balls. Barking laughter and drunken cheers fill the air as guys and girls compete in an aggressive game of beer pong. Their competitive spirits shine through in their focused eyes and quick reflexes. Bottles of beer are precariously perched on the edge of the table, waiting to be consumed by the victorious players.

I tiptoe over spilled beer—or some kind of fluid. As much as I would like to jump in the car and head home, I promised myself I would get out more. I've only been to two parties in my life. Nothing compared to this one. I spin on my heels, and Jasmine is already sucking face with Tank. They have been together since high school, but making a long-distance relationship work after he took a football scholarship in New York has been hard.

"Hey, you're Rosa, right?" a tall guy with brown hair and a football jersey asks.

"Yes." I raise a brow.

"I'm Ryan, Jasmine's cousin." His gaze traces over my body, lingering on my lace tank top and then sliding down over my bandage skirt.

Jasmine encouraged me to try a new style, something other than my regular jeans and baggy shirts to cover my stomach. I'm trying really hard to work on building confidence. I'll admit I have my days. Not many, but I have them.

"Oh, hey," I blurt, lacing my fingers, being awkward.

"Jasmine has been talking about you for years. I missed meeting you when I moved down. She told me you were hot as fuck. I have to say I agree."

My face warms. Ryan is handsome, no doubt about it. But conversations are not my strong suit. The only guys I can keep a conversation going with are Santiago, Mark, Dominic, and Liam.

"Can I get you a drink?" He tips his chin toward the cooler.

"No, thanks, I have water. I'm driving."

His tongue swipes at his top lip. "Let's go talk where we can actually hear each other." He grabs my hand and leads us out to the backyard. Ryan's hand in mine has me feeling some kind of way. Like it shouldn't be him holding my hand. It's still noisy. There's a group in the pool and some in the hot tub having a threesome. Ryan doesn't react to it. Maybe he's used to seeing sex at parties. I avert my eyes, and my stomach lurches. I hope Ryan doesn't expect anything from me.

We sit on separate folding chairs, and I cross my legs, which only has his gaze lingering.

"This is better," he says. "Are you happy to be back?"

"Yeah, I missed home. It's been an interesting year. My family's having a birthday party for me, so that's one reason I came back."

He nods, then takes a sip of beer. "What's the second?"

"Huh?"

"You said one reason. What's the other?"

"Oh, to visit a friend."

He scoots his chair closer so that our legs touch. "Is this friend a guy? Do you have a boyfriend?"

Calling Santiago my boyfriend would be like winning the Olympics, considering I'm not athletic.

"No, I don't have a boyfriend."

"Yet," he adds with a smirk on his boyish face.

That makes me laugh. I relax, and we talk about his scholarship to play college football here in San Diego. He asks about what I'm majoring in. The conversation is a breeze. He's nice and funny, and his personality is like Jasmine's, making it easy.

And before I know it, it's past midnight, and I'm exhausted. It's been a long day. We drove from Portland to San Diego, which was long, with a night spent at a hotel.

Ryan's been doing most of the talking.

"I better head home."

He stands and takes my hand. "I'll walk you out. Soo, do you think I can get your number? I'd like to call you sometime."

"Sure," I say, walking into the house to look for Jasmine and Tank, but they're already waiting by the front door.

"Awesome. I'll get your number from my cuz."

"Okay, well, it was nice talking to you. Thank you for keeping me company."

His finger brushes my chin, and his gaze is on my lips.

Oh, God. No.

"My pleasure. Talk to you soon." Then he presses a kiss on my cheek.

Jasmine closes the door behind us. "My cousin has the hots for you."

I'm not sure I can reciprocate, even if I wanted to. I like them older, mature, and built. But most of all, I like them on motor-cycles. If only he saw me as a woman.

I still remember the day I met Santiago. A couple of weeks after I moved in with my aunt, Liam took me with him to play with Dominic, and my life changed.

Some might think three years old is too young to remember such minor details. It's like meeting the first person you find yourself curious to get to know. It's wild to think since I was so small, but something about him drew me to him. It could be because he made everyone around him feel safe.

Liam said I could come with him. I jump on the peg of his bike and hold onto his shoulders. When I step inside Dominic's house, an older boy is cooking tater tots. Dominic said his big brother, Santiago, is eleven. Their mama is not home. They have a younger brother, my age... three.

Dominic smiles so big at his brother that the little holes in his cheeks get bigger.

"Is dinner almost ready?" Dominic asks between breaths.

Santiago smiles. "Yup, but who are your friends?"

"This is Liam. He just moved to my school. We're going to be best friends," Dominic says.

My stomach gets really tight. I don't enjoy talking to people. So, I hide behind Liam.

"Hi," Liam mumbles.

"Who's that behind you?" Santiago asks in a soft voice.

Liam points his thumb behind him. "She's my cousin," he says.

I don't know why, but I peek to the side. "Rosa," I whisper so low.

"Like the flower?"

It's been a while since I've smiled or laughed, but he made me giggle.

I MIGHT NOT HAVE REALIZED I had a crush on him until I was eleven, but the memory has me swooning. Over the years, it turned into falling for him. I've never had a boyfriend. I've tried hanging out with guys and going on dates, but it never worked out. They're too immature for me. That's not the only reason. It's my lack of social skills. After my mom left me, I lost hope in people sticking around. My only long-term friends are Jasmine and the Delgado brothers.

Santiago has never been the type to have an official girlfriend. That didn't stop them from dropping by the house though.

One of them couldn't keep the rules though. Marissa. God, that girl was a bitch. She hung around like a leech from when Santiago was fifteen, up until his twenties.

When I was fourteen, we were all hanging out at Santiago's, talking about whatever random topic came to mind, when Marissa showed up. That girl was obsessed. When she heard me ask Santiago for a ride on his motorcycle, she called me a fat cow. Santiago kicked her out. Mila, Dominic's ex-girlfriend, defended me from her.

It was a godsend, but now he's been messing around with Monica, his best friend Reese's cousin. Monica is beautiful and has been his hook-up for around three years now. They're not dating, just screwing. Gross.

I know they're both other people. I listen to the guys talk.

I hate how my chest caves, how my soul hurts, knowing it will never be me. He's always called me "kid" and ruffled my hair. I wonder if he sees me as a little sister like Dominic and Mark do.

2

SANTIAGO

Twenty-seven years old.

IT'S TOO DAMN hot to wrench under a car. The AC in the shop doesn't blow all the way through. I add the last bolt and slide out to start the Chevy truck I'm working on.

She purrs like a kitten. Damn. Not to be conceited, but I'm a hell of a mechanic. That's what I get for fixing all my own shit since I was twelve. My father left us when I was eight. It gave me no choice but to learn on my own. Before he left, he taught me how to work on cars—not that I picked up on anything—but it planted a seed. It still irks me how a man could walk out on his kids—three little boys who needed their dad. Sure, if things didn't work out with my mom, that's fine, but to ghost his three sons as well? To force his eight-year-old to grow up too fast and be the man of the house? What man leaves that weight on a child?

I'm exhausted and frustrated. Not from work. From everything else. And I need a break from the constant grind of my life.

"Santiago!" Reese yells from the office.

"Yeah, what is it, bro?"

He peers at me from the computer. "You want to go for a drink?"

Being the boss' son, Reese gets to make those calls. I vigorously scrub at the grease coating my hands. The rough texture of the towel scrapes against my skin, erasing the grime of today's hard work. "You gotta yell to ask instead of getting your ass up?"

He shrugs. "Having a drink on a Friday night is an emergency,"

It *is* fucking hot. "All right, I could use a drink or two. It's been a long week."

He stands and pats my back. "Let's lock up and get the hell out of here."

Twenty minutes later, we walk into Rocko's Bar. The air is thick with the smell of sweat, alcohol, and faint cigarette smoke. The place is busy, as it usually is at the end of the week. The jukebox plays rock music and balls clack against each other on the pool table in the back. We pull out chairs beside Damian.

"What's up, man?" He gives me a handshake.

"Not much. Just working and the same old bullshit."

Reese sits on one side, and I sit on the other side of Damian.

"Same here. How are your brothers doing?" Damian asks.

I run my fingers through my hair. "Dominic is doing great—better than me. He opened a restaurant a couple of months ago and moved out. He's still hoping for Mila to come back. Also, Mark's done with his first year of college." Mila is Dominic's ex-girl.

My brother, Dominic, had cancer a couple of years ago. While he was recovering in a different state, his girlfriend left.

Since then, he hasn't been himself. They say grieving the living is just as bad as grieving the dead. I wouldn't know. I've never been in love. However, I'm proud of Dominic. He's come a long way.

"Oh, yeah. He graduated the same year Rosa did," Damian tells me.

Will, the bartender, saunters toward us. "What can I get you guys? Are you boys getting your usual?"

"I'll have a Corona with lime," I say.

"I'll have the same," Reese adds.

Will nods and walks away.

I turn to Damian to confirm. "Mark and Rosa are the same age."

"She's back for the summer. I saw her at a gas station. She was dressed for a party," Damian juts his chin. "I barely recognized her. She doesn't look like little Rosa."

The mention of Rosa brings back memories of that shy, toothy kid, and I can't help wondering how she's doing and how she's grown. She would never have gone to Portland if I hadn't encouraged and pressured her to chase her dream.

"What does she look like?" Reese presses.

I lean to the side of my chair to hear what they have to say. I've always been protective of Rosa. She was my shy little shadow until she hit her teenage years. She couldn't help it though. She was always an anxious little thing after what her mom put her through.

"She's grown up enough to look hot in that tight skirt she had on."

I punch him in the shoulder. "Watch it, man. She's just a kid."

"She's all woman, dude," Damian says, "And nineteen isn't a kid. I thought you'd seen her."

I shake my head, then squeeze the lime in the bottle of Corona Will set on the table. "No, I haven't seen her since last year. She texted me a couple of times, but that's about it." A pang of guilt eats at me for not checking up on her more than I have. Also, I know my boundaries. She's young, and I need to give her space to grow. Rosa has always been my best friend. Even though there's a gap between us, she can always hold a conversation with me. "And I know how old she is, but she'll always be a kid in my eyes. You two better leave her alone. She's off-limits."

"I thought you two were close friends," Reese says.

"We were when she was small. Liam and my brothers would play video games, and she would follow me around. We'd play and draw and she'd talk my ear off—even though she was usually quiet around everyone else."

The thought makes me laugh. Rosa always wanted my full attention. From the day Liam brought her to the house, she stuck close to me.

I take a swig of my Corona and remember one of those times when I was fifteen. I'd just whooped a guy's ass dirt biking at The Ring. High stakes, but I'd spent the whole summer cleaning yards to buy my dirt bike and fix it up I knew I'd beat his ass. That night, Reese, Damian, and I sat talking on the tailgate of Damian's truck.

Straight ahead on the road, reflectors drift toward us. Liam pedals over with Rosa on the bike's peg.

"What are you two doing out late? It's eight at night," I ask Liam and Rosa.

Liam huffs in annoyance and tips his head back. "Rosita wanted... needed to talk to you. She said it's an emergency. Mom is at work, and Grandma fell asleep." Liam brushes his hair to the side.

His brown-gray eyes always look sad. Liam lost his father at the young age of six. Rubbing the bud of the joint on the bed of the truck to light it out, I stand and walk toward Rosa.

"What happened, flower? Are you okay?"

She twists her finger in her pigtails. She's wearing My Little Pony pajama pants and a shirt. "I...I...don't know what happened to the prince. You didn't finish the story." She gives me those pouty lips and puppy eyes.

Damian laughs. I'm sure it's because he knows I'll give in.

"All right, kid, I'll tell you a story. No more having Liam bring you over when it's late."

She jumps up and down. "Okay. I...I just want to know if the prince got his ever after."

Not all princes get their happily ever after—not in this story, at least. But I'll always give those I care about their happily ever afters.

"WHEN YOU SEE HER, you'll know what I mean. Our little Rosita has grown up." Damian mouths into his cup of beer.

My jaw clenches, and my fists curl with the mention of Rosa as not a little girl anymore. I would tear down the world to protect her. Honestly, I don't know why he's talking about Rosa this way. He's madly in love with his girl, and Rosa is just a kid.

While the guys shift to talking about Damian's girl, I can't help but zone out into the crowd of couples walking in, sitting at tables, laughing, and smiling at one another. No one I know. Will I ever have that? I don't know when I'll catch that break or if I ever will. Among the responsibilities I have to my brothers, there's no chance for that, at least not until they start their own life and are in a good place.

"MARK!" I shout from the living room.

"What?" He stomps out of his room. His brown hair flops to the side, and he's still wearing pajamas. It's noon.

"First, get your ass dressed and go mow the lawn, then go find yourself a job. Give those video games a rest." I haven't given Mark shit about finding a job for months, but it's time for him to get himself together.

"Fuck," he grunts. "Fine, I'll be right out."

My shoulders slump, and I let out a heavy sigh. The kitchen is a mess. I've been so busy with work that I haven't had time to clean. I gave up waiting for my mom to do the cleaning. She hasn't been present mentally for years, maybe since my dad left. Dominic would help, but now that he's moved out, the load falls back on me. Like always. Now that it's the end of spring semester Mark needs to get himself a job. He quit his job after winter break to concentrate on school.

Now that Dominic moved into his condo, I wish I could move out. I've been saving money, but helping pay everyone else's bills hasn't left me enough to save. But Mom has started saving and is even considering buying a house soon.

After washing dishes, I go outside to work on my motorcycle. The sun is so damn hot and uncomfortably bright that I have to squint. I chuck my shirt onto the cement and kneel next to my Harley, then get to work unscrewing the bolts to fix the clutch.

The crunch of gravel pulls my attention up from the bike. Rosa pulls up the driveway. She hops out of the old Jeep she left behind and strolls toward me with a smile. I mirror the same expression, happy to see her. I hate to admit the guys were right. Rosaline is not the young girl I last saw a year ago. How can a person change in a year's span? She's beautiful, so hot, I'm afraid I'll have to be overprotective of her. The amount of men who will want to fuck her. . . My forehead creases at how annoyed I am to think the word hot.

"Hey, flower, you're back in town." I stand to draw her in for a hug.

"Yeah, *Tía* planned a party for me. Even when I told her not to. So I'm here for the summer."

"I'm glad you came to say hi. How is college life?"

She appears older than when she left. I guess one would say mature.

"It's good… I'm doing what I love. The school is amazing. It's everything I dreamt it'd be.

"There you go. That's all that matters. As long as you're painting, it's all good."

"What have you been up to?"

"I'm doing all right. You know, the usual. I'm still working at Reese's dad's shop and living at home."

I know it sounds like I'm whining. It just sucks when you've been putting everyone first, you're twenty-seven, and have shit to show for it.

Rosa pulls out a camping chair from under the porch. She sits, crossing her legs. She's wearing a short jean skirt and a tank top and appears older. This is what Damian meant. I guess she's dressed differently. Rosa always liked to wear a T-shirt.

"You'll catch your break. Patience is a virtue," Rosa advises.

"College is rubbing off on you since you're schooling me," I tease.

She waves her hand in the air. "It's the truth, Santi. Amazing things will come your way. Just wait and see. College is not rubbing on me. I'm still the same person who hates crowds and would rather be home." She shrugs.

"You sound like a fortune cookie," I tell her.

Rosa snorts.

Mark rushes out the front door. "Hey, *loca,* how's it going? Man, I've missed you. Look at you…you look smokin'." He hugs her then lifts her in the air and spins her around. She giggles. Mark and Rosa have always been close friends.

"I've missed you too."

"How's the college party? Are you getting banged a lot?"

"Jeez, Mark, you can't say that or ask it. This is Rosa." My gaze goes to Rosa, whose cheeks are red.

"She doesn't care. So…" He grins, waiting for her reply.

"Oh, yeah. So many, I can't remember what they look like."

A frown creases on my face. I'm not sure why it doesn't sit

right with me. Maybe it's because I've known her since she was young, and I've always looked out for her. I'm not sure if she's pulling our leg with her sarcasm, or if she's changed now that us guys aren't watching over her.

"Dang! Rosaline, I'm glad you're living it up. I gotta put gas in the lawn mower. I'll talk to you later." Mark pats her shoulder and walks to the backyard.

Tires screech on the driveway. Both Rosa and I peer at the car parking behind hers.

Monica steps out of the car. Monica has been my constant hook-up. She struts toward me swaying those sexy hips. We don't hit it often, but it's usually her looking for me.

"Hi, hun. You're looking hot." Monica wags her brow. She is wearing a pink dress that shows off her long legs.

Rosa stiffens . . . like always. She's never liked any of the girls. Especially Marissa. That girl was a bitch. I still get mad when I remember the day she insulted Rosa. I kicked her out so fast.

Whenever I asked Rosa about Marissa, she would shrug her shoulders.

"Hey, how's it going?" I ask. "I wasn't expecting you."

Monica leans in to plant a kiss on my cheek. Her hands rake over my bare chest. "I came to see if you wanted to hang out."

I jut my chin at where Rosa is sitting. "I can't right now. I have company."

Monica glances at Rosa and smiles at her. "Sorry, I didn't see you. How've you been?"

"Perfect. How about you?" Rosa asks Monica, her lips forming a straight line.

"Doing good. I just came to see this guy. I brought him some leftover food from the restaurant I'm working at. They just throw that shit away."

"Oh, how sweet of you," Rosa says with a tone of sarcasm.

"Yeah, it's a taco plate with rice and beans and an extra bean burrito."

"Darn. Too bad Santiago doesn't like beans." Rosa says, looking sweet but super forced.

Monica peers at me. I'll eat beans, but it's not something my stomach agrees with. I wasn't going to tell her. I shouldn't be a dick about it.

"Sorry, I didn't know. I'll toss it. Next time, I'll bring him something he can eat."

"That's okay," Rosa says before I can reply. "Here, I'll take it. Liam will love it." Rosa stands and grabs it from her, then sets the bag of food on the chair. "Santiago gets gas. We can't let that happen."

My lips twitch, and I try not to laugh. I don't know what's going on with her.

Monica giggles. "Well, now I know. I guess I better go. I'll leave you two."

I walk Monica to her car. When I head back toward Rosa, she has her arms crossed over her stomach and is tapping one foot.

"Is everything okay?"

"Yes." Her answer is short. That's not the girl I've always known.

"You're not acting like it."

"It's nothing. I better go. I'm sure you have to meet Monica later." She walks past me, making a beeline for her Jeep.

"No, I was planning on working on my bike."

She spins on her heels so fast that she gives me whiplash. She's right in front of me.

"What's going on?" She's so close that our chests touch.

"There's a bug on your cheek," she says, reaching toward my face.

I'm about to tell her to flick it off, but she presses her lips on mine. Her tongue enters my parted mouth, and it's like it has a mind of its own. My mouth moves in sync with hers, although my body is as hard as a stone. It takes me fifteen seconds to react. With ease, I put a hand on her shoulder to break her away. She almost topples over the chair.

"What the fuck was that?" I shout. I rake my fingers through my hair. My nerves go haywire.

Her face is pale. I don't know what that means. I can't think straight.

"Sorry," she says, grabs the bag of food, and speeds to her Jeep.

"Rosaline," I yell, following her to her jeep. "What was that back there?" I'm pissed now. She doesn't know what she just did. I'm disgusted with myself, and things will never be the same.

"Nothing happened," she fires back, cranking the Jeep and peeling out.

But something did happen.

She kissed me.

My stomach sours, knowing I responded to it, even if it was only for a minute. I had turned to stone. I never would have expected her to do something like this. An unknown pressure tightens in my chest. I'm not sure what it means. It's tainted.

3

ROSALINE

AT A STOPLIGHT, I reach for my phone and dial Jasmine's number. *Pick up. Pick up.*

"Hello."

"Oh, my gosh. Get to my house. This is an emergency."

"What happened?"

"I just left Santiago's."

"Okay, I'm on my way." I hear her scrambling for her keys and purse.

The line clicks, and I'm grateful my aunt's house is just a short distance away. My heart pounds in my chest, and the urgency is palpable.

I've hyperventilated before, but it was for an entirely different reason. A fountain of memories hits like a tsunami. *"Rosaline, go hide in the closet, okay? I'll let you know when to come out,"* my mother said.

The pit of my stomach knots.

Trauma exists—it fries your brain even at a young age. It

sticks to you like tar, and as much as you want to forget, it taunts you. Mom pushed me into the closet. The cold and darkness stung my skin, and I sobbed, clasping myself. I can't be sure how much time passed. It felt like hours as I held my breath in the dark. Anxiety surged through me. Suffocating me. Drowning me.

It was worse when thunderstorms hit, and she locked me in the closet. When her boyfriend showed up, my skin crawled with fear. I knew what it meant. Hide in the closet. He hated me. Because I wasn't his. When he left, I could come out. Then one day, she chose him. She packed my bag and dropped me at my aunt Andrea's house. I heard them arguing, and then my mom drove off, never looking back. Not one call. Ever. She married him, had a family with him, and forgot me.

I was second.

I was not important.

Kissing the man I love has stirred up all the same anxieties as being rejected by my mom. Those searing lips pressed on mine were so soft, and his tongue danced like a delicate melody. I didn't realize my body was starving until I tasted him. My lips tingle with his lingering flavor. Sweet, with a hit of nicotine.

"I'm here," Jasmine pants, shutting the door behind her.

"Finally. *Cristo*, I'm about to lose it."

She sits on my hanging egg chair, and I sit on my bed, legs crossed.

"I kissed him," I yell.

Her hands go to her chest. "What?" She gasps. "Tell me how it happened."

"God, the second I drove up, he was shirtless. Those ripped muscles and the sun on his skin were a chef's kiss. Everything was excellent, and then Monica showed up." I groan. "I've never felt this type of jealousy. I can still feel it in my gut. I know they've often screwed, but what if they're more now? She asked him if he wanted to hang out with her. He told her he couldn't because I was there."

"Okay, that says something."

"No, it doesn't. He just didn't want to be a jerk."

She groans, and I continue.

"Then she was like, 'I brought you food.' It was tacos, rice, beans, and burritos. It made me feral. I went bitch mode and told her he doesn't eat beans."

"Well, he doesn't," Jasmine admits.

"Yeah, I told her I would give them to Liam." Only because I don't want her feeding him. It would make things worse. Like she's his girl.

"Then?" she presses.

"So, the green monster in me took over when he walked her to her car. When he walked back, I got close to him. My tits were on his chest. He looked all confused and wide eyed. He asked what I was doing. I freaked out and told him there was a bug on him. But being that close, I couldn't resist his lips, and I kissed him. He kissed me back for a hot minute at least it seemed that long, then he freaked and pushed me back."

"Oh, fuck."

"Yes, his jaw was all tight and mad, and he yelled at me. Santiago has never raised his voice at me. He looked disgusted. *Cristo!* I ruined everything and broke my own heart. He'll never see me again." I sigh, twisting a strand of hair around my finger. "Thanks for your *great* advice."

She points at me. "I said flirt, not throw yourself at him. However, I get it. Jealousy makes you do crazy shit." She glances at the bag of food. "I can't believe you brought the food after running away."

I laugh. "Heck yeah, he's not eating what she brings." I lay back on the bed. "What should I do?"

"The best advice I can give you is to act like nothing happened. Date my cousin—as friends or more, whatever you want it to be. He's totally into you and would be game for whatever. That will show Santiago that it was nothing, and you're not head over heels for him."

Even though I am.

He looked like a dream.

I missed him.

"Your party is coming up. I invited Ryan, by the way. This will be perfect."

I lift my head to look at her with the sound of foil crinkling. "You're eating the damn burrito?"

She shrugs. "I'm hungry. You called when I was about to eat a late lunch."

I toss my head back on the pillow. "He's my first kiss. I wish it had been longer, maybe more intense, and he hadn't been so set to stone. Those lips were so perfect. He probably kissed me back out of shock, but I felt it. I should have rubbed his chest. His abs are like an oiled machine."

"Oh my gosh, did you just cum in front of me? The bed is wet," she says in a frenzy.

"It's water, you idiot. I spilled it earlier." I laugh.

"I was about to throw up."

"You're ridiculous."

"What scares me is that I probably ruined our friendship. What if he never looks at me or talks to me the same way? Oh, crap. I hope he doesn't tell Liam. He would have a heart attack if I kissed our best friend, especially since he sees Santiago as an older brother."

I LET OUT an audible groan as I examined my reflection in the mirror. I attempt to suck in my stomach, then push it out after trying on three different bikinis that Jasmine lent me, and I don't want my oversized breasts spilling out of the cups. I know

23

I should appreciate being well-endowed. Jasmine insists that it's a good thing that they pop out—it attracts more attention. But I'm unsure if I want that kind of attention since the rest of my body is far from perfect.

Ryan is going to be there as well. He texted me a couple of times and asked if I would like to have dinner with him. I agreed to it. Only to prevent me from thinking of Santiago.

It's been seven days, and there's been no word from Santiago. Part of me wants to hear from him, but another part fears the humiliation and rejection. I doubt he felt any real spark between us, anyway. He always called me kid, and Liam would say, "he's like a big brother to you." I always hated when he said that.

FINALLY, I decided on the red polka-dot bikini. I slip on a pair of jean shorts and a shirt and then grab my tote bag with sunscreen, a towel, and a cover-up. I jump in my beat-up old high school Jeep.

"Hey, Jazy!" I shout as I approach Jasmine. Ryan stands beside her and waves with a smile on his cute face.

"Hey, Rosie Posie," Jasmine chirps, pulling a grin out of me.

Jasmine wears her curvy confidence like a badge of honor. She challenged me to wear a bikini today.

"You look hot."

"Thank you, and so do you," I reply.

"He's here," she mouths.

I know who she's talking about. Perhaps if I had known Santiago was going to be here, I would have stayed home. Especially if I had known Monica was going to be here too.

I'd been avoiding going to Santiago's house, ever since Monica started hanging onto him like a clinger. I couldn't stomach seeing her around him. What if this was the kind of girl he was going to marry? She's beautiful. I asked him once, years ago, if she was his girlfriend, and he said no. But she's still around. I should probably ask Liam if they're together because she's here with him.

I figured Santiago would never be mine, and that it was best to keep my distance from him. But that kiss changed everything. I know what he tastes like now, and I won't ever be able to forget it.

"Hey, good to see you again, Rosa." Ryan pulls me into an awkward hug.

I don't check to see if Santiago has even noticed me.

"Yeah, it's nice to see you too."

His gaze trails over my body. "You're sexy, Rosa."

My cheeks burn, not because of the sun. No one as cute as Ryan has ever called me sexy. Especially with Santiago being within earshot. Did he hear Ryan and did he agree with him, or does he see me as a child?

Jasmine snorts. "Come on, you two, let's head to the volley nets."

We follow her. Ryan chats along the way about how much more he loves living in San Diego than Montana. I'm sure this weather is heaven for him—not a drop of snow unless you head to Northern California.

A group was already waiting for us. I drop my bag on the sand and kick off my sandals. My toes sink into the cold, damp sand, and I eagerly shiver. I take a deep breath and slowly peel off my shorts, then my shirt. Tossing them in my tote bag, I pull my hair into a tight ponytail, ready to face the world. I feel the need to grab my cover-up and throw it on to cover my exposed body.

"Damn, Rosa. You're hot as fuck," Ryan breathes, gazing at me.

I've never had a man look at me this way. Well, I've never entertained it or paid attention, I guess.

"Hey, so I was wondering if you would like to go out to dinner tomorrow."

My lips go into a straight line. How lame is it that I have never been on a date? "Is this a date?"

He peels his shirt off, revealing his six-pack and smooth abs. He's like a hairless cat. I know what my problem is. I'm used to being around older guys—or at least a particular man I won't name. He's dusted in chest hair. I've always wondered how it would feel with the palms of my hands brushing on his coarse-curled chest hairs.

"We can call it a date, Rosa. Is that what you want?"

"I think a date sounds exciting."

Okay, I don't know what I'm saying. I'm keeping my mouth moving to keep me from spinning around to see *him*. Is he all over *her*? Fuck.

Ryan chuckles. "I'm glad you find it exciting."

We all get into our teams. I'm on Jasmine and Ryan's team. As the ball flies across the net, I prepare myself in position. With a quick jump and a powerful swing, I spike the ball over my opponents' outstretched arms, earning us a point. Volleyball has always been my favorite—the explosive energy of each play never fails to electrify me. I'm not athletic, but I'll never pass up a game of it.

The ball comes flying back to us. The other team hit it too far, so I run to get it.

"Rosaline," Santiago shouts. He only calls me by my first name when he's angry or if there's an emotional reason behind it.

I pivot to look at him.

My breath catches in my throat. He's sexy. Brown hair dripping and water droplets running down his bare chest. The tattoos on his arm and chest stand out in the sun.

All I can imagine is kissing him.

"Yes?"

"What are you doing here, Rosa?"

Seriously? After the kiss and ghosting me, he's asking this?

"Why shouldn't I be here? The beach is a public place. I'm playing volleyball with my friends. What's it to you?" I snap at him, entirely irritated by how handsome he looks.

I glance behind him and see the guys. My heart warms when I see Dominic. He's cancer-free, thank God. But my gaze keeps traveling and lands on Monica. She's laying on a towel with her ass in the air and wearing a bikini bottom that would make Jasmine blush.

I don't wait for a reply. "Go on. Your girl is waiting for you."

He grabs my arm, and I yank it away. God, I'm acting like a jealous woman.

"My friends are waiting."

His gaze roams my body, and I suddenly feel exposed in front of him.

"You're fucking naked, Rosa." His hands clench to the side.

"I'm wearing a bikini, just like all the other women around here, including your girlfriend." I point at Monica's way-too-white ass.

"It's different—"

Before he can say more, I hurl back, "Why is it different? Because I'm not stick thin like the girls you screw or the rest of the women around here?"

He reels back like I'd shoved him. "Fuck, Rosa. No, it's not that at all," Santiago says in a soft voice. His hand feathers into his hair, slicking it back. "It's different because guys are looking at you, and not innocently. You know, we"—he waves at the rest of the guys–"always want to protect you from douchebags."

I don't care if it's to protect me. I'll never be more than just a kid to him.

The kiss meant nothing.

"I'm not a little girl. I don't need you to watch over me constantly."

"Babe, pass me the ball," Ryan shouts.

I toss it to him. "Tomorrow, I'm going on a date with Jasmine's cousin, Ryan, and I don't need you boys all up in my business anymore."

"The guy who is looking at you like he wants to screw you? That's the guy you're talking about? He only wants one thing. You're not that type of girl."

I rest my hands on my hips. He's not looking at me, but over my head. He's acting strange. Just because he knows me doesn't mean he knows everything.

"Stop worrying about what I do. I'm old enough to know what I want, and if that's what I want, then it's up to me if I decide to sleep with him." I point to Monica. "By the way, your girlfriend is all over a guy. Go worry about her.".

Santiago glances over his shoulder to see her then turns back to me.

"She's not my girlfriend. She's not looking for a serious relationship or anything, just like me."

Good to hear, I guess. Santiago has always said he never wanted to be in a relationship. I don't believe it though. I think it has to do with putting his brothers first. It's always others before his happiness. I hope someday he'll put himself first.

But he still has Monica around, and I hate that there's no question about the kiss. It's like it never happened. I'm not going to mention it after the look of disgust he gave me.

"It certainly looks that way. Monica has been around for a while now."

I spin on my heels and jog back to my friends. I've never argued with Santiago before, yet I felt I needed to. I know I screwed up by kissing him. However, it doesn't give him the right to treat me like a child.

4

SANTIAGO

WHO IS THIS PERSON? What happened to the little girl who had me wrapped around her finger so tightly that her tears tugged at my heart, and I would willingly skip out on dirt biking to play dolls and do anything to make her happy?

"You said you would draw with me, and you said you would play Barbies." She throws herself on my bed, making snow angels, and adds, "If you're going to break your promise, take me with you."

"Flower, I'm not taking you with me. You're only seven." I pinch her cheeks, and she swats them away.

She reaches for Liam's hand. "Let's go home. Santi is being mean." Tears stream down her cheeks.

I hate making her cry. Since the day Rosa walked into my life, she's been by my side. Liam and Dominic are always hanging out, so Rosa is always around.

I sigh and give in. "Okay, kid, thirty minutes."

She wipes her tears and runs to get her small backpack. "Thank you," she whispers as she lays out the dolls.

I tug on her ponytail. "I'll be Ken," I say, handing her clothes for her Barbies. She always has them naked.

ROSA WALKS toward her friends playing volleyball. This entire week has fucked me up. I'm so confused. Why did she kiss me? Is she having an emotional meltdown? Let's say it was any random chick who would have caught me by surprise and pressed her lips on mine. I would have ignored it, but this is Rosa, the girl I've known my whole life. My job was always to look out for her, not because anyone told me to. It was because she was a little girl, and that's what you do with girls: you look after them. So, now that my tongue has slipped into her mouth, what am I supposed to do with that? Ignore it like she did?

She acted like nothing happened. In contrast, I'm embarrassed and disgusted at even thinking about it all week.

She's got to be experiencing some kind of hormonal imbalance. That's all I've got. It's the only thing that makes sense. She's going on a date with Jasmine's wanna-be-football-player cousin. She impulsively kisses me.

"I'm heading out," I yell at the guys lounging on the chairs.

"All right, see you later, man," they shout.

As I walk toward my motorcycle, I can't help but think about what Reese said before I called Rosa over. *"Damian is right. She looks different. Older. She's hot."*

My instant reaction was to sock him one. Liam, Dominic, Mark, and I would kick anyone's ass who talked badly or sexually about her in school.

Yet, she's right. She's not a kid, but a woman. I had no business grilling her about being half-naked when half of the women here are. I'm just not used to seeing Rosa in a woman's body and not as a young girl.

"Santiago, wait!" Monica shouts, running toward me.

"Hey, what happened?"

"Nothing. Where are you going? We can take a ride. You've never let me on your bike," she says.

Opening the saddlebags, I take out a clean shirt. Slipping on my muscle shirt, I answer Monica. "I'm saving that spot," I say, pointing to the backseat.

She frowns. "For?"

"For the one. When I find her, that's her spot," I say honestly, not being a dick about it.

A romantic relationship has never been something I've pursued. I've always known it wouldn't fit into my life, with so much of my time and energy dedicated to raising my brothers. Having a significant other just wasn't a priority for me. Things changed the older I got. I want marriage, kids, family, and the whole nine yards with a picket fence. When you're deprived of it as a child, your priorities change when you grow into a man. Yet, I haven't tried dating or anything like that because *I* haven't found a woman who makes me feel. Rosa filters through my mind. Dammit, that's crazy. I shake my head.

"We've been messing around off and on for the past three years. We're friends.

I think I deserve a ride."

Monica is a pretty woman, but I don't feel any different around her. Hell, I don't get jealous when she screws somebody else. She knows who I hook up with too.

I'm looking for what Dominic once had, but with someone who will stick around.

"But we're not in a relationship."

WHEN I TIGHTEN the last lug nut, the old clutch finally clicks into place on the truck I'm working on. I step back, wipe my hands on a cloth, and breathe satisfactorily before slumping into one of the rolling chairs next to my toolbox.

"You've been out of it for days, man. What's on your mind?" Reese asks as he lubricates some springs.

I can't deny that things I shouldn't be thinking about have consumed my thoughts. "You wouldn't believe it if I told you."

"Now I want to know," Reese murmurs.

"Two weeks ago, Rosa kissed me." There, I said it. I've kept it to myself long enough. I trust Reese not to blab about it.

His mouth hangs open. "Like a kiss on the cheek or a kiss on the lips with tongue?"

"She was acting strange at my house when Monica stopped by. Once Monica left, she just stood in front of me then pressed those lips on mine. I froze. The only things moving were my lips . . . and tongue. For some seconds, I kissed her. What the hell? It shouldn't have happened. She hasn't mentioned it. I thought she would say, Hey, sorry about that. I was having an off day."

Reese stares at me, eyebrows raised, mouth still open.

"Then what did you do?"

"I freaked and pushed her away and yelled at her."

"Why would you push her away?" he snaps, like I did something wrong.

"Because it's wrong. I've known her my whole life. She's eight years younger and a best friend."

"Now I understand why she told you off at the beach. You just don't get it. She's jealous of Monica and any other girls. She's been like that since she was little. It was obvious, she's had a crush on you since she was barely a teenager. Now she's about to be a twenty-year-old woman whose feelings for you haven't changed."

I never noticed whether Rosa had a crush on me. I'm not some perv to watch for shit like that in my best friend.

"Assuming it's nothing, since she hasn't mentioned it, why are you still bothered by it?"

My mind is a battleground, torn between what I desire and

what I know is right. But despite my inner turmoil, I can't shake these forbidden thoughts.

"Because I can't stop thinking about how her lips felt," I admit. It's wrong to think about how she tasted. It's like the flavor of her mouth opened up Pandora's box.

"You feel guilty for thinking of her intimately?" he asks.

"Yeah, I do. It's gross to think of her like that. We've known each other basically all our lives. I'm not going to entertain it. It's best to forget about it."

It will be history in a couple of weeks. She's dating and going back to Portland soon anyway.

"There's nothing wrong with feeling desire. She's of age and going to college." He shrugs.

"Like I said, I'm not going to consider any of it. She's Liam's little cousin, and I have no business thinking of her lips." Or how she tastes.

"Oh yeah, why did you get jealous of seeing wandering eyes on her at the beach?"

"I wasn't jealous," I growl.

"Sure, you weren't." His lips twist into a smile. "I've known you for a long time, bro. This wasn't you being protective of her as a friend. You're pissed someone lusted over something you want."

I stand and head toward the restroom. "You're full of it."

"The sooner you accept it, the sooner she'll forgive you for pushing her away."

I freeze and turn around. "What the hell are you talking about? Forgive me for what? *She* kissed *me*."

"You're the one who yelled at her for it. I have a girl, man. I know how it works. You humiliated her. You rejected her. How do you think it made her feel?"

Damnit, I didn't think of that.

"She's not going to talk to you about it. She made it known at the beach she's going out with the football dude. I don't know how long it will take for you two to move past it, but if you don't want her that way, then forget it happened."

～

"HEY, BRO," Dominic says, strolling in. He slumps beside me on the sofa. It's been a week since I've seen my little brother. Now that he's twenty-two and living in his own house, we don't see each other as often as we used to.

"How's the restaurant going? Is it picking up?" I ask. Dominic opened his restaurant, Delgado's Steakhouse, a couple of months ago.

"Not too bad. It's picking up. How are things going here?"

I had to force our mother to agree to have weekend dinners as a family. How disappointing is it to arm-twist your mother to spend time with her sons by threatening to confess all that I had done for them over the years? She'll do anything to keep the status of a doting mother.

"As promising as it can be. Mark graduated last year, so now it's time to move on. I've been thinking of opening my shop."

He sinks into the old gray sofa, legs spread. "Damn! That's badass, dude. You should do it. You know you'd have a trail of cars," Dominic says with a smile. flashing the family dimples.

"Sup," Mark greets us, slamming the heavy metal door behind him and tossing his keys on the table.

"Where were you?" I ask Mark.

"Getting a job like you wanted me to."

My brows skyrocket. I didn't expect him to get a job that quickly. Dominic peers at him and juts his chin. "Where at?"

"Computer Squad. It's a new computer repair place that just opened." He smirks as he sits on the recliner. "It's up my alley."

"See, doesn't it feel amazing to have a job? Now you can buy your own shit, and it will also help you since you want to major in computer science," I say while flipping the channels.

"Can you stop by the restaurant to install my new computer and software?" Dominic asks Mark.

Mark nods. "Yeah, but I'm charging you," he jokes.

"I'm already giving you a lifetime of free meals, but I'll pay you if you need the cash."

Mark is talkative today. He's typically reserved, but today he's in a joking mood and seems pleased with himself for landing a job.

"Nah, bro, I'm messing with you. I'll stop by tomorrow. Anyway, are you guys going to Rosa's party this coming weekend?"

"I'll be there. She came to the restaurant the other night on a date. He introduced himself as Jasmine's cousin." Dominic unknowingly lays the dirty laundry out, and my chest caves. My head has been spiraling. How can one simple kiss bewitch you? Is it the year-long distance that changed so much for me? I see her in a different way. Is it me, or is it her? I struggle to make sense of my conflicting emotions toward her.

Dominic adds, "He seems like an okay guy. He's respectful, which is what I noticed from a distance. I went to check up on them a lot. Well, in reality, I was checking if he's enough for her, and he was talking about taking her out again."

What the hell!

"I'm going to the party," I say, irritated. I don't want to hear any more of Ranger or whatever his name is.

"I don't think Rosa would like you to go if you're going to be grumpy about it," Mark says.

"I'm not grumpy," I spit out.

"You have the face you made as a kid when we would eat all your Cocoa Puffs," Dominic adds to the fire.

"Yeah, your jaw is tight. Your teeth are probably grinding. What has you fuming?"

"Damnit, just thinking about work," I lie.

"Maybe you should take a chill pill because you're about to rip the armrest off the dang sofa," Mark adds.

I stand. "I'm going for a ride."

"Boys, dinner is ready. I made a roast in the pressure cooker," Mom says in her fake voice.

Sometimes, I wonder what would happen if she had been the one who left. Would life have been better if my dad had come back for us? Thoughts like that occur periodically. As much as I love my mother, I despise her as well.

"Great, have the guys eat. I'm going for a ride." I lean on the doorway, and my mom's eyes cut to slits.

"You need to have dinner with your brothers," she barks, her long brown hair in a bun.

"I'm always having meals with my brothers. I'm sure they'll be okay if I step out for a bit. How about you converse with them for once?"

The door bangs behind me. I pull the pack of cigarettes from my pocket and balance one between my lips. Being in the house is suffocating. My brothers will be fine if I'm not there. They know I need a breather.

Turning into an empty parking lot, I light a cigarette. When I'm done with the last puff, I toss the butt and twist my boot on it. My nerves are in a bunch, and my emotions are taking over. Now, I'm picturing her with Jasmine's cousin. Why do I care? Does my mind wander to when I saw her in a swimsuit? Fuck yeah, it does. I know it's wrong to think of her curves or how her top barely covered her pebbled nipples. Then when she spun on her heels, her sexy ass shook when she walked.

I'm horrified at where my mind is taking me.

Throttling my Harley Softail, I swerve into the busy major streets, gripping the ape handlebars, and head to the small back roads leading to the red cliff on the beach. The gentle caress of the warm breeze envelops my skin, sending shivers down my spine. The roar of the motorcycle reverberates through my body, sending waves of adrenaline pulsing through me. I can feel every muscle in my body relax and surrender to the thrilling ride. From a distance, the ocean waves crash onto the beach as I approach the spot where I have been coming to get away for years. The only sounds are the roar of the waves and seagulls squawking. It's peaceful and quiet.

I sit on my bike and enjoy the sunset. I could easily find Monica or any girl to obliterate Rosa's mark, but the thing is, she's venom coursing through my veins, hissing like a drug, but I don't want an antidote for it. I relish the thoughts I have of her —more than I can admit. If a fifteen-second kiss destroyed me, just imagine what the rest of her would do. She would ruin me.

5

ROSALINE

"I've been playing football since I was six," Ryan mutters, cutting into his steak topped with onions and mushrooms. "It's been my life. So, I'm praying I will get drafted."

"You're good. I saw you at practice when I dropped off your bag the other day. There's no doubt in my mind you will."

This is the second date with Ryan. To be honest, I wouldn't call it a date. We enjoy each other's company, but I'm not feeling any type of magical chemistry. When he gazes at me, my heart doesn't thump, and when his fingers brush mine, no tingles run down my spine.

"Thank you, by the way, for dropping it off. You're a life-saver." He winks.

The other day, he asked me to give him a ride to practice. His car had a flat, so he forgot his bag. I drove back to drop it off.

"No big deal." I wave my hand in the air.

He grins. "You're cute. I'm enjoying spending time with you and getting to know you."

I dip a fry in ketchup. "Yeah, me too," I admit, although it's not in the way he might think. I don't want to lead him on.

"Do you want to go for a walk after dinner on the pier?" he asks.

"Sure, that would be nice." Okay, I know I should say no and go home, but being alone in my head makes me insane. All I can think about is Monica running to Santiago, and Santiago telling me I'm dressed half-naked when Monica is in a thong bikini. I get it. He lusts over her while he sees me as a kid.

The moment I saw Monica standing next to his bike, I thought he would have her as his backpack. Santiago has that spot reserved for someone, *the one*. I know this because I've heard him when he talks to his friends.

Walking in the sparkling night sky with crashing waves resembles a romantic stroll between lovers. It would be magical if I were walking with the right person.

I keep my hands laced together as Ryan and I walk. I know he's waiting for me to let go of my intertwined fingers so he can slip his in mine. Ryan's constant gaze clarifies he's waiting for that moment.

"It's a nice night," I mumble, unsure what to say.

He smiles. "It is being here with you."

I should melt like butter with his sweet words. Ryan is gorgeous and built like a football player. We walk around the empty pier and return to his car.

"How are you and Jasmine related? You're sweet, and she's blunt."

His lips lift. "My mama taught me how to be a gentleman, babe."

"She educated you right," I say beside his car.

His smile drops, and he steps closer. "It's hard to be a

gentleman around you because all I can think about is sucking on those lips."

Oh, hell. The sound of a familiar motorcycle roars nearby.

My heart races like I took a dose of dopamine, but it's not Ryan who has it palpitating.

My gaze stays pinned on Ryan, ignoring the roaring of his engine next to us. Ryan's stare stays on me, not fazed by the rumbling. He tucks hair behind my ear.

"Rosaline!" Santiago yells.

I jump, spinning to face him. "What?" I bark. What the hell is he doing here? He loops a leg off his bike and then unclips his helmet. He shakes his head, fixing his hair in place.

Sexy. Hot.

The second he looks at me, I notice his clenched jaw.

"Oh, I'm sorry. Did I interrupt something?" Santiago's tone is annoyed.

Ryan looks at me and Santiago. I know he remembers him from the beach. He knows Santiago is older, and I've known him all my life. Of course, he doesn't know I have a crush on Santiago.

He's been a dick lately; I don't know what curled up his ass. No, wait, I do. I kissed him, and he's pissed and disgusted by it. I knew it would change things, but I didn't think he would be an ass. With anyone else, I'd slip under a rug, but with Santiago, I'm angry he's being this way.

So, to be a bitch, I say, "Yes, you were." I lie.

His brows knit together, then shrugs. "That sucks. It's a good thing I drove by and saw you. I'll give you a ride home."

He doesn't ask if I need one… he demands one. "No, it's fine. I'm going home with Ryan." Oh, God. Rosa, you're getting yourself into a mess.

Ryan looks at me, grinning like he's winning. "Yeah, babe, I'll take you home with me."

Santiago steps closer to Ryan. His fists balled up. "You just met her. What's this, a second date, and you want to take her to your place already?" Santiago growls.

I roll my eyes.

"No, I would never do anything she doesn't want to do. If that's what you mean. I respect her." Ryan stares at Santiago in the eye for confirmation.

"Either way, you have a flat tire. It looks like I'll be taking her home. Find yourself a ride."

Ryan and I look at the front tire, and sure enough, the tire is flat. He kneels. "Shit. I need to get new tires. I have a spare, but I don't want to keep you waiting since it's getting late. It's up to you if you want to stay or go with him. Either way Rosa, I had a lovely night."

Cristo, I just want to go home at this point. "Thank you for tonight, but I can wait," I state. As much as I want to ride in the spot that's meant for 'the one,' I feel bad at the thought of leaving Ryan, especially because he's Jasmine's cousin.

"You don't have to. It's going to take me a while."

"Oh, well, Santiago—" I was about to say Santiago can help him.

"Come on, Rosaline. He's got it. I'm sure he's capable of changing a tire." Santiago's voice booms.

Sighing, I peer up at Ryan. "Call me when you get home or text me so I know you got home okay."

Ryan walks to his trunk, and I stand in the dark night with my dark knight. "Was this necessary?"

He hands me his helmet. "It was. I'm saving you from embarrassing yourself since you have the newfound habit of throwing yourself at men."

My mouth gapes.

I hate how he knows me. I used to love it, but now it's torture. I hate how he thinks I throw myself at men, how he's disgusted with me or disappointed—probably both. Saving? Yes, he's always been the one to rescue me from my anxiety or the lack of socializing, pushing me to make friends. But this is different. He's being a jerk.

I slip the helmet on to cover my watery eyes. He straddles his bike, waiting for me to hop on. "Let's go," he commands.

"No!" I shout like a child with my hands on my hips. He can't see me with the full-face helmet and built-in shield. His brows rise. Santiago gets off his bike and lifts me like I weigh nothing and sets me on the back. I want to swoon that I'm on his motorcycle, where he doesn't allow anyone, but I know it means nothing to him. "What the hell?" I grumble when he leans back to reach for my hands and then puts them on his chest.

"Don't be a pain. Hold on."

I'll show him pain. I pinch his nipple.

He cries out, "Fuck, Rosaline. Stop acting like a brat."

"Then stop being a dick," I mutter.

He says nothing but starts the bike up and drives toward our part of town. I take the opportunity to allow the racing of my pulse and the beats of my heart to ricochet against my ribcage when I run the palms of my hands over his muscular chest. The vibration of the roar of the engine deepens my arousal. At full speed, his shirt rides up. Instead of keeping his shirt down, I slide my hands over his warm, bare flesh. I know I'm poking the bear and he's going to give me shit for it, but when will I ever get another chance to feel what I dreamed of?

We are close to the subdivision we live in, although the neighborhood is so vast that we don't live close.

He eases in front of my house, kicks the stand, and I jump off, handing him the helmet. Santiago scrutinizes me. I rock on my heels, my nerves jumpy.

"Why did you do it?" he asks.

I swallow. "Do what?"

"Kiss me, Rosa. Why?"

My breaths come in sharp, stabbing pains. "I never kissed anyone before. I kissed you so I wouldn't make a fool out of myself when I do with Ryan." Half lie, half-truth. I'm not going to make that mistake again, telling him the reason I did it. He'll reject me, anyway.

His brows furrow. "You've never kissed anyone before?" He gasps in complete shock.

What a way to make a girl feel like a loser. Then he combs his fingers through his messy hair. "That's the reason? To practice for another guy?" He laughs. "Damn, flower, you know how to fuck a person up."

He gives me his back, starts the roar of his Harley, and peels out.

TODAY IS my twentieth birthday party, but I'm not in the mood for it. I'll forever be grateful for my *tía* Andrea. She does so much for me. She raised me like her own after my mom abandoned me, even though her husband had passed and she had no one to help her. *Tía* never once made me feel like I was a burden in her life, but a treasure. She showers me with love.

I don't want to see Santiago, not after I felt him on the ride and not after how he left me. I know I messed things up between us, but I'll be going back to school. When I come back, maybe he'll forget, or he'll be in love with someone else. I'd move out of the country. It would kill me to see him with someone.

My painting hand moves in a steady, hypnotic rhythm as I hum softly along to the lyrics of "Try" by Pink. Something about the process soothes me, making my worries and stress melt away. With every added paint stroke, the picture becomes more detailed and alive. I feel as if nothing else matters but this moment and the painting on my easel. Every minute detail takes on a life of its own—the sparkle in Dominic's eyes, the angle at which Liam crossed his arms, my smile that radiates from the center of the canvas, Santiago's broad shoulders with tattoos decorating them, and Mark's mischievous smirk. Finally, after what seems like an eternity, I step back to admire my masterpiece.

My door swings open, and Liam, now a beast of a man, steps in, dancing to the music. A loud, vibrating laugh escapes from my mouth.

"This is an old song. I'm surprised you like it. I'm heading to the gas station. Does the birthday girl want anything?" Liam asks with his arms crossed, staring at my new masterpiece.

"No, thank you."

His head tilts as he studies my work.

"You like?"

"I love it, Rosa. You're so damn gifted. I can't wait to see what life has in store for your future. Three more years, and you'll be finished. Sooner if you do summer school, I guess. I missed you." He rests his arm on my shoulder. "We may be cousins by blood, but you're more than that. You're my little sister."

A tear rolls down my cheek.

He jerks his chin to my painting. "Those are some good-looking dudes." Liam smirks before walking out and shutting the door behind him.

STEPPING INTO THE KITCHEN, I'm greeted by my *abuelita*, *Tía* Andrea, and *Tía* Sugar. It beats me why they call her sugar. The kitchen looks like it's run by the army. They all move in sync, working on their tasks with aprons tied around their waists. My *tío* Ernesto, my *tía* Sugar's husband, walks inside, proud of the banners he hung. "Happy Birthday, Rosaline."

"What can I help with?" I offer since my party starts in three hours.

My *abuelita's* eyes expand as her old eyes travel down my body. "Rosa, why aren't you dressed? You're covered in paint."

"I'll shower and get dressed. I just wanted to help you all first. After all, it is my party. I should help you cook." Cooking and baking are my second hobbies. I can basically whip up anything. I'm a foodie, and my hips prove it.

"We got this, *mija*. You go get all pretty," my *tía* Sugar calls over her shoulder as she rolls corn tortillas to make flautas de pollo.

"Is your boyfriend coming?" Abuelita asks.

"I don't have one. Jasmine's cousin is coming, but we are only friends at the moment."

She wags her white, thin eyebrows.

"She doesn't need one right now. She needs to concentrate on school. The one will come around when the time is right," my *tía* Andrea says.

The one.

At the rate I'm going, I don't see *the one* happening anytime soon.

My tall, cinnamon-haired best friend bursts into the front door, rolling a suitcase behind her and clutching a garment bag in her other hand.

"*Hola!*" she shouts, walking past them.

"Are you moving in?" I snicker as she runs past me like she's on some mission.

"Follow me to your room. Time to bedazzle you."

I trail right behind her and her heavy-ass suitcase. What the hell does she have in there? Are we heading to the Kardashian wedding where we must look smitten?

Closing the door behind me, Jasmine tosses everything on the floor, and it lands with a thump. She clasps her hands together, giving me an overall look—like she's going to work some fairy godmother magic.

Jasmine digs into the suitcase, searching for gold. I stand

next to her while she tosses clothes out of the suitcase. Finally satisfied, she hands me red lace underwear and a bra with tags still attached. My eyebrows quirk in response as I stare at the undergarments in my hand.

"Rosa, it's time you show that hot body of yours just like you did at the beach. Come on, didn't you see how all the guys drooled over you, particularly a hulk of a man." She unzips the garment bag, pulling out a short black dress. "I'm positive Santiago will show. No matter what, he wouldn't miss your party. You're no little girl, Rosie; you're a woman. It's time you show him you're one. Make him want you."

I rumble in laughter. "One, Santiago was not drooling over me. Two, he will never see me as more than the little girl he's known. Third, I have been dressing up more."

"Oh, he wants you. Based on what you've told me, he's been acting strange, and I'm positive. I think that kiss got to him. It's your age and the fact you're Liam's cousin. He knows your aunt, and you're his best friend, which is what's pushing him back." Jasmine holds the dress up to my chest.

My friend is so optimistic and clearly blind. She must be going senile.

"Perfect," she mumbles, then lays the tiny black dress on the bed. She paces up and down my small bedroom, her thumb brushing along her lips.

Deep in thought.

My eyes volley side to side as she paces. I can't take it anymore and must say something before I go cross-eyed. "What the hell are you doing?"

"Thinking."

"Obviously."

"I think you should ignore him, say hi, and act like nothing. Ryan will be there, too. I know you're not into him, and I'm fine with that. But now and then, look over to see if Santiago is looking at you when Ryan tries to get close to you—"

"I'm not going to play games. It's not like Santiago is going to get jealous or anything."

"Fine, I'll keep a lookout. I respect your point, but I can't entirely agree with it. I think he's into you, and this dress will have him hard as a rock."

Thirty minutes later, my body has never felt so polished, like it just stepped out of a car wash. I scrubbed my body with vanilla body wash. Stepping out of the shower, I slip on a robe and pluck my eyebrows. Then try on the red lace strapless bra and thong. Mind you, I've never worn a thong, and it feels like something is stuck in my ass. According to Jasmine, I'll get used to it. I slip my arms into the off-the-shoulder black dress Jasmine brought me and look in the mirror. The soft fabric hugs my curves, accentuating and cinching in to emphasize my wide hips and perking up my chest. I notice how the low cut of the neckline shows my cleavage off, along with the hollow of my neck and my shoulder, making me look like a grown-up version of myself. I feel an unfamiliar confidence surge through my body.

Jasmine carefully applies false eyelashes to my eyes, ensuring the adhesive is just right, and the lashes blend in with my natural ones. She then applies foundation to even my skin tone, followed by a shimmering blue-green eyeshadow and mauve-colored lipstick. Finally, I slip on a pair of tall, black stiletto heels and wobble as I practice walking.

"You look stunning, my friend." A glimmer in Jasmine's eye sparkles with pride in her work.

I stare at myself in the long mirror I have in my bedroom. It's hard for me to believe what I'm seeing.

Confident.

Beautiful.

My family members emerge from the backyard door, each carrying a tray heaped with enough food to feed an entire army. The weather is amazing for an outdoor party. Jasmine comes out in a dress similar to mine. She always looks stunning. Jasmine glances at her phone before approaching Ryan, who is strolling around the backyard with a small box in his hand. He sees me and waves. I respond with a smile as I make my way over to him.

"Wow, Rosa…wow." He steps back and gives my body a run down.

My cheeks warm up at the attention everyone is giving me, including Ryan.

"Beautiful. Happy Birthday." He gives me a big hug.

Looking over his shoulder, I catch the Delgado brothers strolling in. They all look incredibly handsome. Brushing myself off of Ryan, I step back and thank him for coming.

Mark is the first to run to me. We always used to bump into each other at school. He whistles, opening his arms wide for me to take. "Rosa, you look amazing. Happy Birthday! I hope you have a wonderful day. Enjoy your party." I give Mark a kiss on the cheek, thanking him, and then Dominic welcomes me in his arms. Santiago continues talking to Liam, not sparing me a glance.

While everyone is conversing, I make my way to the rows of different drinks they laid out. Soft, warm fingers brush along my exposed shoulder. I know who they belong to—his scent is engraved in me, a mixture of spice and smoke. Closing my eyes, I steady my beating heart, the goosebumps scattering throughout my body.

"Rosaline," he breathes into my neck, making tiny hairs stand up.

We haven't spoken since the ride he gave me.

Spinning to face him, my pulse leaps in my throat. Santiago is the picture of masculine perfection. His denim jeans are tight against his strong, well-built body, while his broad shoulders make his shirt bulge at the seams. His legs are long and muscular, while his tanned skin glistens in the sun. His face is rough and handsome, with a strong jawline softened by the faint hint of stubble. As he flashes a charming smile, dimples appear on each cheek, adding to his rugged appeal.

I hope he's in a great mood.

My eyes stay pinned on his lips. I know how they taste. Santiago's gaze rolls over my body. He takes a deep breath as if he were about to dive in for a swim. A quick exhale leaves his body.

"You're breathtaking, Rosaline—" He shakes his head, maybe realizing what he just said. "Fuck," he mumbles. "Happy Birthday. I hope you have a great day," His face stays neutral, handing me a small black box.

Is he drunk? Breathtaking? Yeah, I'm going with "he has been drinking."

Squaring my shoulders, I lift my chin, not showing how much he affects me—what that kiss did to me—playing it off just as he's doing it.

"Thank you. You didn't have to—"

"Flower, it's your birthday. I hope you like it." His voice is raw and husky.

The uneasiness in the air is as thick as if I were running around a football field stark naked. He's always given me a hug for my birthday, just as the guys have. Given he wants us to return to what we had as friends, I should make the leap forward, letting him know we're good.

As I lean in to hug him, his stiffness then eases into the embrace. I peck a kiss on his cheek and then step back. "Thank you. I appreciate it."

Liam walks toward us with a smile that resembles a Cheshire cat.

He pats Santiago on the shoulder. "Guess who I bumped into

at the gas station? Monica, I figured you'd want her here, bro, so I invited her. She said she's going to go change, then head here."

Mother fucker.

Santiago gives Liam a curt nod. "Cool, man." He turns to gaze at me.

I give him the best fake smile I could muster. *Cool man, my ass.* He studies me, and I study him.

"Liam, I need your help, please. At the bar," I demand.

It's not technically a bar. It's a table full of liquor. The keg next to it. I need a margarita, possibly one after the other. I drop my gaze from Santiago to Liam. He looks confused. Grabbing him by the arm, I drag him to the table.

"Why do you need help?"

I roll my eyes at him.

"Will you make me or show me how to make a margarita?" I know how to make one. It's an excuse to get him by himself so I could yell at him. "Why in the hell would you invite Monica? Is it your party? Did you ask me if she could come? Clearly not. She's as horny as a dog in heat." He lifts his hands.

"Chill, Rosa. Did she do something to you? If she did, I'll kick her out. Not a big deal."

She's stealing my dream man.

"No. I just don't like her." She's nice, but I don't like her because she had him first. Now that I've had his lips, I don't want anyone to have him.

Liam grabs a wide-rimmed margarita glass and sets it on the counter. Taking a wedge of lime, he runs it around the lip of the glass before dipping it in coarse sea salt. He unscrews the cap of a lime tequila, pours a generous amount into the cup, and stirs it with a plastic spoon.

"If she gets annoying, I'll tell her to leave." He hands me my drink. "Don't get wasted." He quirks a brow at me.

I salute him. Oh, big cousin, I'm getting wasted. If I have to see that woman all over him, I'm numbing the pain.

Speaking of the devil, Monica walks in with her beautiful brown locks of hair bouncing as she walks with her long-toned legs in a blue flower dress. She walks straight to the guys in a group talking. She leans into Santiago for a hug. Monica smiles at him, and he smiles back. She loops her arm into his. He doesn't bother to move it. My heart slams full speed in my chest. My stomach churns with jealousy. Envy is an unfruitful emotion, but I feel it. Now would be a perfect time to show my WWE moves. I learned by watching it with Liam. I could get her in a headlock. I snort just thinking about it.

I grab my drink and walk to where Jasmine, Mark, and Ryan are standing. The music from the D.J. plays, filling the air with vibrating cumbia music.

"Hey, babe," Ryan says. In his hand, he has a foaming red Solo cup of beer from the keg. He places his hand on the small of my back.

I give him a wink and lean closer toward him. I can feel Santiago's eyes on me, and my heart begins to race.

6

SANTIAGO

EVEN IF IT meant joining the ranks of those who were condemned to hell for just looking at her or daring to touch her, I would do it without hesitation. I'd spent the last weeks replaying the kiss we shared. Who would think that, considering our age difference and the fact I've known her my whole life? The kiss was genuine and passionate, and I wanted more of it. At my age, I've never been the type to enjoy kissing women. However, when she kissed me, it was like riding my motorcycle with the wind in my face. It felt invigorating and refreshing. I wanted to press my lips on hers as long as possible, and I admit I didn't want the feeling to end.

I wasn't expecting her to say the kiss was practice for another man.

What the hell!

When I stepped into my front door, I was more pissed off than when I left. The messed-up part is I jerked off in the shower with her name on my lips, reminiscing about how her hands felt on my chest. I came to realize I've never thought of anyone like I've thought of her, which is crazy.

When I arrived at the party, I wasn't sure how Rosa would act. She gives me whiplash from a couple of nights ago. One minute, she's with Ryan, saying she's going home with him. Next, I have her on my bike. She's feeling me up like we're lovers. Then I mean nothing to her. I'm just a puppet who has his dick pulsing for her.

Rosa seems unaffected, like it never happened. One thing is, I can't stop staring at her. My gaze has volleyed toward her over the last two hours since I got here. Rosa has always been a beautiful person, but tonight, damn. She is all woman. The fabric of the tight, black dress molds to her body like a second skin, the soft fabric that creases each curve and emphasizes her generous bust, a hint of cleavage peeking out at the top.

Fuck.

Open. Close. Open. Close. Tap. Tap. Tap. My fists open and close, and then I tap my fingers on my knee in a pattern to contain my anger. The jackass wanna-be jock carries himself as if he's on a late-night talk show. Rosa sits next to Ryan, Jasmine on the other side, and Mark sits next to Jasmine, along with a couple of other people, some of her old classmates. He goes on barking about how he was the star quarterback at his old school. I highly doubt it. He crosses his legs and has one arm draped over Rosa's chair. Rosa sips her third margarita.

"Should we head back to my place?" Monica purrs in my ear.

She's hooked her arm in mine as often as I've unhooked them. Monica, all over me, doesn't feel right anymore. When Liam mentioned he invited Monica, it made me feel uneasy. I was unsure how Rosa would act since she's never been Monica's greatest fan. She seemed fine with it, a little aggravated, but I expected her to say no.

"I'm good. If you want to leave, feel free to," I clip, annoyed at Monica Even though I shouldn't be. It's not her fault I'm about to rip Romeo's arm off.

"Did I do something wrong?"

I shake my head. "No."

"Then what is it? You've been ignoring me since I got here." Monica turns toward where my gaze is at. She smirks.

"Oh, I get it now. When did this start?"

I can trust Monica not to blab about how I feel. She's not emotionally attached to me, and neither am I to her.

"What do you mean?" I say, taking a sip of beer from the red Solo cup.

Monica tilts her head up her chin, pointing toward Rosa. "When did you start seeing Rosa with new eyes?"

New eyes. Is this what it is? I peer at Dominic and Liam in their conversation, not paying us any attention.

I lift a shoulder. "A couple of weeks ago," I say flatly. That's all she needs to know.

"Hmm." Monica presses a finger on her lips, then turns toward Rosa and back to me. "No wonder you want to strangle her guy."

"He's not her guy," I snap, running my fingers through my hair.

She laughs.

"I'm not sure if she has feelings for him. However, it's better if she does because I can't do anything with what I'm feeling."

"First, you're full of excuses. I understand now why she's been hostile to me. It's clear she's always had a crush on you, but now she's of age, and you're seeing her in a new way...a woman. You wanting her doesn't make you some perv. It doesn't make it weird because she's your best friend. You're eight years older than her, and it's not that bad since she's in her twenties. She has been an adult for two years. You know her better than anyone, and vice versa. Sometimes, people are in our lives for a reason, a purpose. We just have to open our eyes and hold on to it because if we don't, we can lose them in the blink of an eye."

I suspect she's not really talking about Rosa and me. However, she is right in some ways, but I don't know about her having a crush on me. Reese said she was jealous, so that means she could have kissed me for that reason, not for "practice."

Taking another gulp of beer, I reply, "It's not an excuse. My feelings will fade. It's all just fresh. The last thing I want to do is ruin anything between us." Rosa deserves to be loved, treasured. Knowing her as a small child makes it complicated for me. I'm not sure how her family would react.

"Let's see how long you can keep your heart caged. Especially when she starts seriously dating."

I lean back in the flimsy camping chairs and gaze at Monica, who is staring up at the night sky.

"Who hurt you?" I ask.

She sighs. "I moved here because I was, and still am, in love with someone I've known for years, but he never wanted more. He's with someone else. I couldn't take it, so I moved." She stands from her sitting position. "I better go. It's not my place to be here, Santiago. She cares for you, and I'm positive I'm the last person she wants to see by your side. Say something to her. You've got nothing to lose."

She walks out, leaving me in my thoughts. I stand and stroll to the keg, pumping a cold stream of beer into my cup. When I look up, I catch Rosa staring at me. I do the unexpected, even startling myself. I blow her a kiss. Her ears turn a bright pink. She turns around, taking a huge gulp of her margarita.

Adorable.

I exhale and recline in my chair, trying to focus on the conversation with the guys about Dominic's new restaurant. But I can't ignore the tightness in my chest when the wanna-be jock leans in to plant a kiss on her cheek.

~

TWO HOURS later and close to midnight, everyone's wasted. Rosa's group of friends, including Ryan, are gone. Thank the fuck. I couldn't take more of the attention seeker who only talked about himself.

The music died down. It's just the immediate family, my brothers, and me. Rosa stands from where she's sitting with her aunt and cousin. She has not spared me a glance the whole night, except that one time.

How do I know this? I've kept my eyes on her. I've never paid attention to anyone as I am now. It's ridiculous.

Rosa grabs a flauta from the tray. She needs to sober up, as she's swaying back and forth.

"Hey, did you have a good time?" I ask. She dips her flauta into the container of sour cream, taking a mean bite. "Looks like you had a good time with your friends," I say dryly.

Her beautiful, big brown eyes gaze at me. "Uh-huh." She reaches for another flauta and dips it into a bowl of guacamole. "I had a great time. I saw Monica kept you company," Rosa grumbles, taking another angry bite.

My lips curve into a small smile.

She's jealous.

"Not really. We hardly talked." It's true. Monica and I only talked when we spoke about Rosa.

Rosa nonchalantly passes me, heading to the house. I trail behind her, noticing how she sways as she walks.

"I know…. you're behind me. You don't have to worry about me. I get it…I'm sorry I kissed you. I know you're mad. Don't worry about me, Santi. Go find your girl," she slurs on the last words.

Okay, so she's pissed off. Reaching for her elbow, I pull her to my chest, but she pulls away like an angry bull. She loses her balance and topples over face down onto the ground. With her ass in mid-air, her dress rides up, showing her red-laced thong.

Fuck.

"Rosaline, are you okay?" I ask, more to her ass. Shaking myself from my trance, I pull her up by the waist. She groans, shimmering her dress down and trying to steady herself—her body molds into mine. Our faces are only inches apart, and I can feel the warmth of her breaths as she exhales. The glimmering gold necklace I gifted her for her birthday hangs delicately around her neck. Its big, phoenix-shaped pendant rests against her chest.

Her eyes drift to my lips. "I'm fine, Santiago, thank you." She swallows, and her gaze draws back from mine, staring at a bush behind us. "You're handsome. I'm sure you'll find yourself a beautiful woman someday to be your wife."

I'm not sure where that came from. Maybe it's the liquor talking. Little does she know I could never see anyone in my future as I do this second. It's her. I see my flower. However, life isn't always fair. We could never be.

"Hey, what happened? I saw Rosita tumble over like she was trying out for the Olympics," Liam says behind us, and I take a step back from Rosa.

"She's fine, I'm going to help her get to bed."

He nods. "Yeah, I'm heading for bed too. Stay the night, man. Pull out the sofa bed." Liam walks in, leaving Rosa and me behind.

Once we enter Rosa's bedroom, I pull the comforter back. I point to the bed for her to sit. She huffs and sits on the bed. Without a word, I kneel and unstrap her heels off each foot. She watches my every move. Her feet curl in my hand. I'm sure she's hurting. Rosa has never been the type to wear high heels. I begin to massage her feet. The last time I massaged Rosa's feet was when she was maybe eight years old. She ran on the gravel driveway barefoot. She was in pain and had me massage her tiny feet. I remember she had pink nail polish on her toes.

Rosa lets out a sigh of pleasure as I massage her foot. The sound of her voice causes a surge of arousal to course through me, and my dick responds in kind. Rosa's back arches, her long dark locks spilling onto the bed.

"God, Santiago, that feels so wonderful. Can you do it a little harder?"

Why is my mind going somewhere else when she says harder? *Snap the fuck out of it.*

My thumbs press harder in the arch of her foot. Another moan, Jesus Christ, is she trying to have my dick explode with the amount of blood pumping into it? Setting her foot down, I grab the other one and continue massaging.

Once I'm done, I stand up. She gives me a lazy, drunk smile. "Thank you."

I give her a slight nod.

"Can you help me unzip my dress? Jasmine did it earlier for me, but she left early."

"Yeah, sure," I utter, forcing a smile, though I'm really wishing I could find her aunt Andrea to do this task for her. Because once I see what's behind the dress, my hands will itch with desire while I imagine many possibilities.

I delicately pull the zipper along, allowing my fingertips to graze her silken skin. She trembles at my touch, and I wonder if she has real feelings for me, more than a mere infatuation. My breath tickles her as I reach the end of the zipper, exposing her lingerie. I take a step back, resisting the urge to run my hands down her bare back. Instead, I run them through my hair.

"There," I say, clearing my throat. I'm about to say goodnight and head out, but she slips her dress down. It falls to the ground, leaving her in a laced thong and laced bra, giving me a glimpse of her peaked nipples.

Shifting myself to face anywhere but at her, I bite my fist as if that is going to help me from wanting to take a bite out of Rosa. I hear the drawers open and close. If she were sober, there would be no doubt she wouldn't undress in front of me. Rosa has always been self-conscious. I turn to glance at her. She tries to balance herself while slipping her shorts on. Rosa's curves are undeniably beautiful. But I must push these thoughts away and remind myself that Rosa and I can never be together for a couple of reasons. One, it's hard to look at the girl I used to call kid and babysat and now a beautiful woman I desire, and two, I have too much baggage, and I'm nothing more than a man not having his life put together living at home. Third, a small percentage is because of how her aunt and Liam would feel about Rosa and me. I know they love me, but being with her could be a different story. Her beauty, both inside and out, has the power to enchant me, but I cannot let it cloud my judgment. If I give in, there will be no going back.

7

ROSALINE

IF I HAD BEEN in the right state of mind, not entirely sober, but not too intoxicated to be unaware of my actions. I wouldn't be undressing in front of Santiago. As I change into my comfortable pajamas, the weight of his gaze lingers on me like a physical touch. Goosebumps erupt on my skin, and I quickly pull my pajamas on. I blame the margaritas for giving me so much bravery. Because sober Rosa wouldn't dare. I'm not thin like the girls he's been with. When I spin to gaze at him, he's staring at me. I'm not going to lie, but I like the way he's looking at me. Maybe it's the alcohol that makes me hallucinate. Once I sit on my bed, I pat the space beside me for Santiago to sit. He sighs as if it pains him to sit beside me, but he does.

"Tell me a story. One is way overdue. It's been years.... you never finished the story. Did the prince ever find his princess, or was she lost forever?" I flutter my lashes at him.

In return, he gives me a genuine, heart-filled smile. "It has been a long time, hasn't it? I think in fairytales, a prince always gets the princess, and a king always gets his queen, but in real life, it's far from the truth."

I frown at that. Does he think falling in love doesn't exist, or is it because he feels love is out of reach for him? Has he been in love, or is he in love? Maybe it's Monica. A pang of jealousy and heartache funnels through me like a dark abyss.

"I disagree. Fairytales become real when we bring them to life. It's only our power that can make fairytales a reality. The king has to flip the world around to find and claim his queen."

He tucks a piece of hair behind my ear. "You've always been a princess in your own story, Rosaline. Maybe someday you'll find your prince."

I give him a stubborn shake of my head. "I don't want a prince. I want the king. Tell me, in your story, did the prince find his princess?"

He gazes at the ceiling, his throat bobs, and he says, "He never thought he'd find one, but he found her. It turns out she bloomed into a queen. The problem is she's out of reach. He'll wait for eternity until he can reach her—maybe in another life."

My eyebrows scrunch up, and my heart breaks for the prince, now a king. "Such a sad story. Why is she out of reach?" I whisper.

He leans to kiss my forehead. He doesn't smile. He looks sad.

"Because he's known her his whole life and knows she deserves better than what he has now. He's unsure if he's good for her. Good night, Rosa. Happy Birthday." He stands and walks toward the door, but drunk Rosa wants to make him feel better.

I stand to rush to him. My fingers curl around his toned forearm, and I slowly turn him around to face me. Our eyes connect momentarily before I lean forward, pressing my lips into his. He doesn't hesitate as his hands slide up my sides, lifting me gently onto the dresser behind us. My heart races as our lips move in sync. His beard stubble, rough against my chin, only heightening my pleasure. This kiss is not like the last one. It's more intense, wild, rough, and full of lust.

All I know is his touch, his lips, his warmth, and the comfort of his embrace, which is my home. I long for him as a lover, not simply a friend, and by his passionate kisses, I know he desires me, too. His tongue thrashes like an intense wave, pressing firmly as if he never wants to let go.

I'll never let him go. I want him to be my other half, my equal, and I won't give up until he becomes mine and gives into the pull.

If I'm kerosene, he'll be the fire igniting us. Our lips part, but we're still touching, breathing on each other, panting lingering breaths.

"Rosaline," he groans. His hard-on pressed against my leg. "Does it make me a bad person to want to keep kissing you? Because if it does, I'm going to hell. You taste so damn good, but we're drunk."

Oh, my gawd. He wants this too.

"No, it doesn't, because I don't want this to end. I want you, Santi. And you're not taking advantage if that's what you're thinking," I mouth into his. He tries to pull away, but I pull him toward me.

His hand covers my neck as his tongue swirls in my mouth, kissing me passionately. Santiago is kissing me. He wants me just as much as I want him. I must be dreaming. My fingers slide into his thick, brown, slick hair.

The sound of chatter coming from downstairs interrupts our moment, causing Santiago to pull away. I already miss the feeling of his touch and the warmth of his body against mine. His dark brown eyes roam hungrily over my figure, filled with an intense desire that seems to radiate from deep within him. His lips are now swollen, evidence of our passionate kisses. He runs his long fingers through his tousled hair, a sign that he's agitated or lost in thought.

"This can't happen again. Rosa—"

I hop off the dresser and shove my fingers against his hard chest.

"You regret it? Is that what you were going to say? It's a mistake?" I run my fingers into his hair, then trail them down his cheek. Santiago is gorgeous, with his olive skin, long eyelashes, and perfect dimples. "Because if you're going to say that. I'm going to call bullshit. You feel it, and you want it. Admit it."

He shakes his head, and the pit of my stomach churns. I'm suddenly feeling sober. Maybe he doesn't.

"Rosa, we've both been drinking," he throws out as if we're both wasted to the point of not being coherent.

I run my nails up and down his chest. "Seriously, are you blaming the alcohol? I'm sober now, and I know you didn't drink enough to use this as an excuse."

He sighs. "Rosa, you know we can't do this again. Nothing can come of this 'us.' Liam is my brother's best friend, and he's like a little brother to me. Knowing you since you were a small child in pigtails makes it seem wrong. Plus, Liam always says you're like a little sister to all of us." He kisses the tip of my nose. "I don't want to ruin anything between us, Rosa. Besides, aren't you practicing for Ryan?"

I drop my hands from his chest and step back. He's having a hard time separating the little girl from the woman. I can see that now.

"I lied. The kiss was for you. Maybe we can talk to Liam or your brothers about the reassurance you need." I'm somewhat worried of what my aunt and Liam might think, but that's a small part of it. "You see me as a child in the back of that head of yours, and you feel it's wrong to want me," I suggest.

When he shoves his hands in his jeans pockets, his arms flex tight around his biceps. "No, flower, we would never work. I've never had a girlfriend, and I'm not made for one.

You're too pure and beautiful to be with someone like me. You're young and have too much going for you. I'd ruin us... you. It's better this way. I come with baggage you don't need, and I could never hurt you." He steps closer. Santiago wraps a finger in my hair. "Date, Rosa—have boyfriends." His jaw clenches with each word. "I'll always be here as a friend." He steps away, opening the door and closing it behind him.

I toss myself on the bed. I can't help but release the tears stinging my eyes. He wants this for us, but the problem with Santiago is he'll always put others before himself. Santiago has never known how to give himself happiness. I can't force him to want me...us. Maybe it's best I do as he says and move on from him. We can never be.

LIAM CALLED and asked if I could pick up his coat and badge at Santiago's house. So, here I am, unlocking the door with the key Rachel gave Liam and me.

I'm surprised to find Rachel sitting at the table drinking coffee. She adds liquor, then stuffs the miniature bottle in her purse. Have I ever mentioned the deep-rooted suspicion I hold toward Santiago's mom, Rachel? There's something about that woman that sets off alarm bells in my head. When I visited as a child, she never acted like a mother. She was never mean to us, but she had an unsettling vibe.

"Hi, Rosa, how have you been doing?" she asks.

"Good. How about yourself?"

She takes a slow sip of her spiked coffee. "Better than ever." She grins. It's a smile that would make you want to sleep with one eye open.

"Great. Umm, so I came to pick up Liam's jacket. He left it here."

"It should be in Santiago's room. I found it in the garage and placed it there." She winks.

Okaay.

"Nice talking to you." I spin on my heels and walk toward his bedroom. The quaint house stands tall with three spacious bedrooms, each adorned with large windows that let in natural light. Mark and Dominic shared a room since they were young, and I remember toys and clothes scattered across every available surface. As they grew older, the lack of privacy likely led to Dominic's decision to move out and find his own space. The walls still hold echoes of their childhood laughter and arguments, a tangible reminder of the bond between brothers.

Santiago's door is closed. I'm a little nervous to see him after what happened the other night. He rejected us. I know he wants this—us. He's too worried to put himself first. I don't knock. I walk right in, and he's asleep.

My throat tightens, and I salivate at the sight before me. He lays shirtless, revealing his chiseled chest and defined muscles. A pair of well-worn jeans clings to his hips. One arm is nonchalantly propped behind his head, accentuating the toned lines of his body. My gaze drifts over every inch of him. I'm captivated.

Quietly, I pull my sketchbook from my purse and sit on a chair. I know I should split, but I can't help it. The artist in me has to draw this sculpted man. I trace the outline of his strong arms. My gaze moves to his handsome face, taking in every detail of his sharp jawline. Continuing down his body, I add the dusting of hair on his toned chest, following the line down to his V-shaped abs. The only sound breaking the stillness is Santiago's small snores, accompanied by the soft squeak of my pencil on the sketchpad. I move on to the waistband of his jeans, one button undone. It stirs my imagination.

What's under those pants? How would he react to my touch?

"Are you sketching me? What are you doing here?" Santiago's voice rumbles.

Startled, I drop my sketch pad and pencil on the floor.

"*Cristo,* you scared the hell out of me." I hurry to get my things off the floor before he sees. "No, I'm not."

"Go ahead and finish sketching me, you little liar. I'm feeling like a Calvin Kline model right now, flower."

You certainly look like one.

"I'm drawing a kitty," I answer nervously. He doesn't seem angry that I'm here. It was like the argument didn't happen or maybe sleeping on it helped change his perspective of things. I'm hurt he rejected us, but I'm trying to understand where he's coming from. Maybe he needs more time to soak it up and give in.

He snorts. "You're telling me you came and sat in my room, in my chair, to draw a kitty? Now I know you're lying." He tsks.

He sits up, giving me a full view of the wolf tattoo on his back. I've been a fan of wolves since I was small.

"I came to pick up Liam's jacket, then an inspiration hit, so I took the opportunity to sketch before I forgot. Sorry to barge in on you."

His brows rise. "Let me see your kitty." He extends his hand, but instead, I shove the notebook into my purse.

"No, I'm not done."

"Since when? You always let me see everything." He idles in front of me.

Yeah, right. Like I'm going to show him. I drew him all sexy.

"Not this time," I argue.

His intense gaze goes to my purse. He's so damn nosy.

In a flash, I dash to the other side of the room and jump on his bed when he tries to catch me.

"Come on. You're being insane…Did you draw me with a beer belly?"

"No!" I hop up and down on his bed. "Now leave me alone —" I laugh, then squeal when he grabs my leg, pulling me down. I land on my stomach, and he's on top of me, reaching for my purse, which just slid on the floor. The notebook falls out and opens right on the page.

A deep groan comes out of my mouth, and I bury my face in his scented comforter. He stays still, half of his body on mine. What does that mean? Is he mad? Is he happy?

"Rosaline...holy shit!"

Here it comes. He's mad.

"You make your portraits come to life. You've always been amazing, but I guess school sculpted you. I look hot." He slides the rest of his body off, and I lift my head to peer at him. Now, he's going through the rest of my drawings. I snag it from his hold before he sees the one made of us making out in my room.

"That's all you get to see."

"Don't I get to keep my picture?"

I shake my head. "No, that's for me," I admit, not like I don't have a gazillion portraits of him. He's my muse.

Heat floods my cheeks when I catch his gaze lingering on my lips. All my teen years, I wondered if, in my adult years, he'd look at me like he is now.

"You changed everything. I mean, we've always been close, but I can't get you off my mind. You're like a tempting fruit, just out of reach, but my desire for you feels forbidden." His thumb caresses my cheek. "It's wrong to want you."

"We're not blood related. Yeah, you took care of me when I was little. But that's what makes us so close now. And I'm not that little girl anymore. You have to stop seeing me that way. It's only forbidden in your mind. I've wanted you for so long, Santiago. Let me make you happy."

I wouldn't dare pour my soul out to another man like this, but with him, it's different because he knows me better than anyone else.

"It's not that simple."

"Why? Because you're fucking in love with Monica?"

He flicks his brows up, leaning on the wall. "No, she has nothing to do with it."

"Oh, I get it. It's because I'm too young—"

"I'm eight years older than you, but that's not the main reason. I'm having a hard time. In my mind, it's like I'm doing wrong by you." He stares at me as if I should be shocked by the age difference.

"I don't give a shit about our age either. What I'm trying to ask is if you don't even want to try because of my age? Is it because I'm inexperienced, and you want someone your age?"

"It has nothing to do with experience. But I'm not going to lie. If you were my age, it'd be different. I wouldn't see a small child I cared for and other reasons."

I gulp and fold my arms tightly, not sure what else to do.

"Come on, flower, I had to cut your pancakes." He smiles as if he's remembering it.

"You act like you had to change my diaper. You're making it more complicated than what it is."

He never admitted if he loved Monica when I asked.

"It's just not going to happen. Not now at least." He's not even willing to try.

I don't even know what I'm asking.

Would I want him to be my boyfriend? Would I still want to be with him even if he isn't my boyfriend? Do I want to sleep with him while he sleeps with other women?

I stand up as tall as I can and try to look nonchalant. "Your loss. I'm not going to chase after you anymore. I'll do what you said. Ryan asked me to be his girl, but I haven't answered him yet. Maybe I should give him a chance." I reach for Liam's jacket on the armchair, and I spin to open the door.

Santiago grabs my arm. "I-I—"

"Hey bro, are you here?" Dominic calls out from the living room.

Santiago lets go of my arm and steps back. "In here," he answers.

"Hey, Rosa." Dominic kisses my forehead as he walks into the room, then ruffles my hair like always.

"Hi. I just came to pick up Liam's jacket. I'll see you two later."

"See you later," Dominic says.

Looking over my shoulder at Santiago, I notice his gaze is on me. It would be delusional to assume he's going to give in to our chemistry.

8

ROSALINE

"Can I get one large macchiato with extra caramel drizzle, blonde espresso, and substitute caramel syrup?" I ask the barista girl at the register, tapping my nails on the counter. I add, "Also, a large lemonade with two pumps of raspberry, passion tango on top with a dragon fruit infusion. That's all," I say to the girl typing it all in.

She gives me a sour lemon face.

I had to make excuses to get out of the house. I've been bored, and it's only been four weeks since I've been home. It occurs to me to head back to the dorms, but Jasmine is not ready. She wants to spend more time with Tank before he heads back to New York. Football practice will start soon.

When the girl calls my name, I take my drinks and drive past Santiago's work. We haven't spoken since I went to his house. Not that I expected him to call, but a girl can wish. I'm not going to beg him to want me. When I glance out the window to see if his black pickup truck or red Harley is parked small shop, a single light flickers inside. It's close to five should be getting out soon.

Santiago's commitment to being a father figure to his brothers has always been admirable, but it can be suffocating. While I appreciate his dedication and hard work, it's obvious he neglects his needs and desires. It's a delicate balance that leaves me torn between admiration and concern.

I slam my foot on the gas pedal. My old, rusted Jeep lurches forward and speeds away. I can't risk him spotting me. I'm worried that we ruined our friendship—so many years of knowing him and being his shadow. I'm afraid I've lost him forever. I miss our conversations and the way it was between us. It's always so easy for me to talk with him. Will it be awkward now?

"Rosaline, you're home," my *tia* calls out from the kitchen as I enter, the metal door slamming behind me.

As soon as I step through the front door, the smell of baked cookies wafts through the air. The walls are adorned with family photos and the colorful paintings I've created. In the living room, a plush couch sits in front of a fireplace, inviting me to cozy up and relax. This three-bedroom house offers warmth and comfort, thanks to my aunt's loving touch. Despite the life she had to live when my uncle passed, she's never been bitter about it.

"*Hola, Tia!* Yes, I'm home." I lean in to kiss her cheek and hand her a drink. "Smells so delicious. What kind of cookies are you making?"

She gives me one of her signature beaming smiles. "*Polvorones.* One of my mom's recipes I kept."

I reach for one cooling on the rack. A happy groan vibrates from my mouth as I bite the soft, warm, pink cookie. My *tia* has it down when it comes to cooking and baking.

"So good," I mumble.

"Thank you for the drink." She smiles, pulling out a tray of cookies from the oven.

"You're welcome," I say in a sluggish tone. Her sharp ears don't miss my irritated response as her brow furrows in concern.

"Rosaline, my love, is everything okay? Are you having boy trouble in college?" she asks sternly.

"No boy troubles. I don't talk to any guys at school. Actually, Jasmine and I met some new girls, and they're pretty cool. I'm trying to socialize more, but it's taking time. Jasmine helps." I lean against the island, tempted to munch on another cookie, but my hips and butt don't need the extra padding, "We're actually going to a party tonight."

"Oh, yeah, honey? Sounds like fun. Remember, no drinking and driving."

I nod and grab a spatula, helping her transport the cookies from the pan to the cooling rack.

"I know you want to become more outgoing, but remember to take it slow and not force yourself into anything. By the way, are you still seeing Jasmine's cousin?"

"We're only friends for now. Why?"

"He doesn't give me the impression of the type of man who would put you first or the type of man who would tear the world apart to make you happy. I could be wrong. He just gave me that vibe." She rubs my back in a motherly, comforting way.

She's not wrong—maternal instincts, I suppose. I know more about him than he knows about me.

"You could be right. Ryan's not exactly my type." I look at the clock on the stove. "I should probably get dressed. Jasmine will be picking me up soon."

Her lips curl into a proud smile. "Take another cookie. A kind man never minds a woman with a little more padding on the hips."

I take the cookie from her hand and run upstairs without a second thought.

It's close to eight as I descend the stairs. I am greeted by a man's boisterous and throaty laughs that reverberates throughout the house from the outside, since *Tia* always has the screen doors closed and exposed. Goosebumps prickle my skin. My heels click on the tile floor as I make my way into the living room where my aunt sits. Her feet are kicked up on the recliner, dipping a cookie in her coffee. She's so hooked on her *telenovela* that she hasn't noticed me.

"*Tia*, I'm going now. Jasmine should be here in about ten minutes." Her head jolts up as she scrutinizes me. She sets her coffee mug down and then clasps her hands.

"Rosa, you look gorgeous. I'm loving all your new outfits, but remember, you look beautiful in anything," she says with a glimmer in her eye.

"Thank you, *Tia*."

"Have fun and be careful."

I blow her a kiss, stepping out the front door.

As I strut down the front yard's pathway, admiring my reflection in the living room window, I can't help but feel grateful for Jasmine's suggestions. A short black skirt hugs my curves perfectly, while a bold red off-the-shoulder blouse adds a touch of daring. My nerves kick in when the chatter stops as light whistles fill the air. I know he's here. I heard his beautiful husky laugh. My stomach coils in knots. I turn on my red heels to face them, and Reese whistles again. Liam punches him on the shoulder.

"Ow," Reese moans, rubbing his shoulder. "Rosa, you look beautiful. Where are you off to, hmm? Hot date?"

I don't miss how Reese smirks at Santiago. I wonder if Santiago said anything about what happened.

I don't turn to see Santiago's reaction. It's been weeks—two weeks, to be exact, although it feels like months since we've seen each other.

"Jasmine's picking me up. We're headed to a party," I say to the guys, Reese, Dominic, and Mark. "Are you going to the party, Mark?" I ask, since he knows them.

He raises a cold can of beer to his lips, taking a swig. The guys sit on foldable lawn chairs, and Mark tilts back to admire the glittering night sky above. Their faces glow in the moonlight, each one handsome and unique in their own way.

I can sense the desire in Santiago's heated stare. Damnit, Jasmine needs to hurry her ass up.

"No, not tonight," Mark replies.

"You should go with her, Mark. Keep an eye on fuckers who mess with her," Dominic adds.

An angry growl leaves my lips.

For God's sake.

"I don't need a damn babysitter." Anger makes my voice rise. I turn to face Santiago, who's watching me. His long gaze rolls over my body. Without liquor, I'm feeling self-conscious. However, he's not looking at me with disgust, but almost as if he wants to rip my clothes off. A shiver ghosts over my skin, and my body heats at his appraisal. An unlit cigarette dangles on his lips. I don't know why I find that hot.

"I think that's a great idea, Dominic. Mark, go with Rosa," Santiago orders with a stern command.

Idiota.

His eyes dart over mine in a challenge. Santiago's jaw tightens when my lips flatten in anger. He knows I'm not giving in.

With one hand on my hip, my gaze snaps to his, and lifting my chin, I say, "No! I can care for myself. Besides, Ryan will be there."

Santiago's nostrils flare. If he's jealous, he can shove it. And that's a big if. He made it clear I should move on from him, and that we would never happen.

Luck is on my side. The car horn honks, and Jasmine and her boyfriend drive up. I spin on my heels when Dominic shouts, "Rosa, don't let anyone serve you a drink. Water only."

I huff, my lips curl a smile. "Got it, Dad, thanks."

OUR CAR ROLLS to a stop in the expensive brick driveway of Elie Branson's home. The towering columns and grand entrance reek of wealth and privilege. From what I've heard, his father is a prominent doctor, but Elie has lived with his mother since they divorced. This explains why he throws wild parties every Friday night while his father is away for work.

As soon as we push open the wide double doors, the booming music reverberates through the walls. It's a typical college party. The scent of alcohol, sweat, sex, and vomit fills the air. I spot a table set up for beer pong with a couple of guys and girls already playing. In the large dining area, there are loads of liquor bottles, beer, and kegs. The crowd is overwhelming, and there's definitely some groping and making out going on.

"I'm so excited we came," Jasmine squeals. She missed partying with her guy.

"Me too," I shout over the music.

Tank walks toward us with two plastic cups and a bottle of beer for himself. He hands us our drinks, and I sniff into the cup.

Tank lifts his half-shaved brow. "Promise I didn't spike it. I double-checked if it's all good."

Jasmine takes a drink. Her face scrunches up into a sour lemon face. I take a tiny sip. Holy fuck, it's straight-up Vodka.

"I think I'll just have a beer instead," Jasmine hands Tank the drink. He gives her a nod, takes her hand, then guides her to the booze table. She yells, "I'll be right back."

I sigh and look around. I spot Ryan leaning against the bathroom door, making out with some girl. My hand goes to my chest. No racing heart, no jealousy. Nada. He texted me last night if I wanted to come to the party with him. I said yes and that I'd meet him here. Turns out he's already getting to know someone else.

I clear my throat and shout, "Hey, Ryan." His eyes go wide when he pushes away from the chick with her one boob hanging out.

"R...Rosa, I didn't know you were here," he stutters, clearly drunk with his red eyes confirming it.

I keep my face stoic. He looks scared as hell—poor guy.

"Don't mind me, Ryan. Continue," I say, turning to walk away. I'm not pissed at all, but if he were a real man, he wouldn't continually call me then tell me to meet him here for him to suck face with someone else.

I decide to tour the mini mansion. It's quiet in this area of the house—more private. I'm sure I shouldn't be here, but I'm in awe of Lacy Vanfreud's expansive painting collection, which is a renowned artist whom I've never had the chance to see up close. Lacy Vanfreud is based in London and is my ultimate role model. I dream of studying for my master's in one of her classes there.

"You like, beautiful?"

I'm startled by the husky voice. My eyes go wide when I see who it is. James, Elie's twin brother. His sandy blond hair falls to the side. He's always been the unhinged brother. I've never spoken to him before.

"Rosa? Isn't that your name?"

"Yes," I reply, voice above a whisper. James knows my name?

"Come on, let me show you the paintings in the study. You'll love these."

He grabs my hand and pulls me into the room. I should pull away and leave. The door slams closed, and the lock twists behind me. I spin to face him, panic settling in my stomach. He gives me a full-blown smile that would make most girls' panties melt but, to me, it's like Jack Nicholson's smile in *The Shining*.

9

ROSALINE

THE SPACIOUS ROOM is lined with towering bookshelves that seem to stretch on endlessly. In one corner, a cozy reading nook sits, complete with a worn floral sofa and a small side table stacked with books. The atmosphere here is dim and stifling, or maybe it's my anxiety rising.

"Why did you lock the door?" I turn to ask.

He ignores my question, pointing to the wall. When I spin to see what he's pointing at, I gasp. It's a rare painting of Lucy's. It sold for one hundred million. *Holy Shit.* It's authentic, signed by her.

"Wow, James, thanks for showing me this. I feel like I'm in a dream." I whip my head around, scanning the room for James. He stands at the bar and pours rich, amber liquid into a sparkling crystal glass. He expertly stirs it with a flick of his wrist, a small grin playing on his lips.

"Want a drink?" he asks, his blue eyes fixed on my breasts.

"No, thanks."

James's lips press on the glass of bourbon, his eyes not leaving mine. Any other girl would fan themselves silly, but he's not my type.

"I'm glad you love it. Many girls wouldn't know who Lucy is." He saunters toward me and dips his tall frame to whisper in my ear. "Let's sit and talk about what you owe me for showing you such a gorgeous piece of art."

My body stiffens at his proximity. The scent of spiced bourbon fills the air. The palm of his hand rests on the small of my back, guiding me to the soft, worn-out antique sofa.

The hairs on the back of my neck rise like a cat preparing for a fight. What does he mean by owing him? Taking a seat, I scoot close to the arm of the chair, and James sits closer to me. "I wasn't aware there was a cover charge for the viewing, but I could probably swing a lunch." My tone is soft and shaking, twiddling with the ends of my skirt.

He grins. "I had something else in mind. You see, you landed in my lap, Rosa. I know who you are because there's been talk about Rosa, the shy girl who doesn't get out. Rosa the virgin. It's no mistake you landed in the lion's den."

My stomach sours at where his mind is going. His hand drops on my bare thigh. I gently lift his hand off me.

"My reward is you," he purrs.

He's out of his damn mind if he thinks I'm going to give myself to him.

"I'm not sleeping with you. Sorry if you misread it. I was just walking around and landed where the paintings were."

"Don't worry Rosa. You'll love being worked over by this artist." He smirks.

It's clear that he's never been turned down before. Women always seem to fall at his feet, charmed by his good looks and wealth. Fear creeps over me. I'm here alone—no one from the party will hear me. I try to stand up, but he pushes me down with his body weight on the sofa. He grabs my leg, sliding me to lay long ways on the sofa. I kick and thrash. His body slams into mine.

He gropes my breast. "Stop!" I shout. "Get off of me, please," I plead, kicking and fighting.

"Rosa, come on, quit trying to play hard to get." He chuckles as if this is a game, and I'll give in. I dig my nails into his forearm. "You bitch." He shifts, and I knee him in the balls.

He groans and slumps off me. My heart races, and my breath quickens. I clutch at my chest and feel the familiar tremors of fear and anxiety. I grab my purse and stagger toward the door.

He groans. "I'm only fucking with you. It was a joke."

I unlock the door and run. My heels echo on the tile floor. I keep peering back to see if he's chasing after me. He's not. Was he going to…rape me?

Keep it together, Rosa, until you're out the front door.

The party has grown. More bodies. More strangers. More noise and smells. It's too much. I keep running until I'm out the front door and past the metal gates. Tears begin to flow. I dig into my handbag, pulling out my phone. I didn't realize I put my phone on silent mode. I have ten missed calls and messages from Jasmine. I haven't responded yet, but I know I need to leave this place.

First, I dial the only person with whom I feel comfortable.

"Rosa?" Santiago's husky voice comes from the other end. The sound of his voice washes over me like a warm blanket. I can't hold back the tears.

"Santi—"

"Rosa, why are you crying? What happened?"

"Can you come get me? I'm at the party, waiting outside." I cry, hiccupping between breaths.

"Yes, of course I'll come get you. Did someone hurt you?" His voice rises.

I don't answer.

"Who do I need to fuck up, flower?"

Another sob. I text him the address but keep him on speaker, constantly looking over my shoulder.

I don't want him to fight, but hearing that tone, that concern, and that protectiveness has my heart soaring. He's always been my protector, and I've always been his shadow.

The truck's rumbling tells me he's on his way. "I'll tell you what happened when you get here," I say, fighting not to let my voice break. I can still feel James' hands on me and the weight of his body. I'm disgusted.

My heart rate quickens.

My breath becomes shallower.

The familiar sensation of panic floods through me and brings a memory with it.

Trapped in a small, dark space, unable to move or escape. Fear and isolation consume me as I struggle for air. Tears well up in my eyes.

I know he can hear my breathing through the receiver.

"Rosa, look up. There are lots of stars out tonight. Come on, flower, do you see the one bright star shining among the others?"

I look up. Stars glitter in the night sky, but one bright star stands out. "I do."

"We are both looking at the same star at the same time. You're not alone."

The truck comes to a stop. I can hear the signal light click. He's turning.

"Whenever you need me, look up at the bright star, and I'll be looking at it too. I'll always be there with you, even when I'm far away."

My throat tightens. He always has a way of making me feel better. Just then, a falling star shoots so close, it's as if it were meant for me. I close my eyes and make a wish. I wish for him to be my forever.

~

Santiago

I CLENCH the steering wheel so tightly that my knuckles turn white. My pulse quickens, and a surge of anger bubbles up from deep within me. The road stretches out as, I navigate through the traffic with a dangerous edge to my driving. The sobs and heavy breathing on the phone break my heart.

When I finally turn into the damn house, I see Rosaline sitting on the sidewalk, looking over her shoulder. I hang up the line, put the truck in park, and jump out. She runs and wraps me in a hug. Her head rests on my chest, and she sobs uncontrollably. I draw her closer with one hand and gently stroke her hair from the top of her head to her back. The party continues, and the music pulses in the background.

"I'm here, Rosa," I whisper, pressing a kiss to her temple.

"I should… have listened and brought… Mark," she muffles in my chest.

My index finger slides under her chin, lifting it so I can inspect her. I don't see any scratches or bruises, but her mascara is smeared. With my shirt, I wipe her tears, cleaning off the makeup with it.

"Give me a name, baby. *Who* hurt you?"

I'm ready to rip all those assholes to shreds. If it was the cock sucker, Ryan, I'd strangle him by his neck. Rosa's chin trembles, and her mouth opens and closes. I'm unsure if someone said something hurtful. So I ask again after the minutes of silence she's giving me.

"Who hurt you, Rosaline?"

She hesitates. Her beautiful, wet eyelashes flutter at me. What breaks me is what reflects in those gorgeous brown doe eyes—pain and fear.

"He... he grabbed me. I tried to get away. He forced himself on me. God, I can still feel his breath on me—"

He forced himself on me. Those words echo in my head as if I'm trapped in a tunnel, hearing the echoes bounce off the walls. My body roars with rage. My heart races, my muscles tense, and my hands tremble as I clench them into fists.

"What's his name, baby? Was it Ryan?" My heart fucking bulges like it's going to explode.

"No, not him. Get me out of here."

"I will, Rosa. Once you give me his name so I can beat him the fuck up." Tears leak down her beautiful face like dew dripping off a rose early in the morning.

"Did he hurt you?" The words stumble out of my mouth, not sure how to ask—how far did the asshole go? "Did he ra— What happened?" I can't even finish the word.

"He pushed me down and was on top of me. He groped my breast, then I kneed him in the balls and ran."

My grip gets tighter around her waist, holding her in place.

"Can we go?"

"We will. Who was it, Rosaline?"

"James."

I clench my jaw. The monster inside wants to erupt, taking out anyone in its path.

For her.

Always for her.

As soon as Rosaline entered my home, her tiny fingers gripped a bag of colorful crayons and a spiral notebook. Her brown eyes widened with uncertainty as she surveyed the room, taking in every detail. She's like a little angel, all bundled up with innocence. From that moment on, I knew I would always protect her, no matter what.

I lift her, carrying her to the truck, her arms wrap around my neck. Her head rests on my chest, and I dig my nose into her neck, letting her sweet scent calm me. Opening the passenger door, I sit her down, kissing a tear on one side and then the other. Gently, I take her trembling hands in mine and place a kiss on them.

"I'll be right back, sweetheart." She holds onto my shirt. "I'm not going to let that fucker get away with it. No one lays a hand on you…no one, you hear me?"

She sniffles. "I don't want anything to happen to you."

I give her a small smile. "That's impossible." I shut the door and lock it.

The lame music ricochets through the entrance as I open the door. It's been years since I've stepped foot into a college party. Yet, nothing has changed, lame as ever. The Bransons are infamous for their weekly parties.

They're wealthy, entitled fucks who couldn't care less about anyone else but themselves. Elie and James are spoiled shits. They use money to get what they want. I only know who James and Elie are because they have a half-brother who's my age. We went to school together, and he would always talk shit about them. Even now, when I run into him, he says they get away with so much. It doesn't surprise me that James would try something with Rosa. The bastard is used to girls throwing themselves at his feet. Why? Because he's rich. Those girls are only looking for status. So, he forces himself on her and thinks he can get away with it. He does not know what he has coming.

My boots hit the floor with a thud, one right after another, surveying the place—scanning each and every person.

When my gaze finds Jasmine backed into a corner with her boyfriend sucking face, my angry steps move straight toward her. Then I hear a group of girls talking about James being in a room with their friend. I head down a long, vast hall splashed with color. This looks more like a museum than a home where a family lives. The farther I walk down the narrow hall, I notice a gallery of paintings decorating the wall. Looking at the paintings assures me I'm going the right way. Rosa must have trailed off in this direction.

I'll check here first, then make my way upstairs.

Anger boils under my skin, and the wrath I feel is molten in my very veins. The fear, anxiety, and sadness Rosa funnels into a tornado, takes her down a dark path, and bleeds out of my veins. The sense of suffocation and panic she experienced served as a haunting reminder of the time she was trapped in the closet for hours.

My fist tightens around the doorknob. When I push it open, it's empty. Only a desk, a safe, and a cart of alcohol. Disappointment bubbles in me. I go to the second door next to it. Empty. The long hall wraps around in a circle. The music dies. From where I'm at, the thick red walls block any noise.

"Take it off, doll," a husky voice orders.

I slam my body against the door to break through. Chips of wood chunk off. The rich prick lifts his head up from the girl underneath him. His blond hair shags down. He had Rosa on that same couch minutes ago. Forcing himself on her, and like it was nothing, he's here with another girl who's drunk and half-naked. His eyes go wide when he sees it's me. Perfect, he recognizes me. Grabbing him by the back of his shirt, I yank him off the girl. He falls on his side with his pants hanging loose, and his dick goes flaccid.

"Get going," I tell the girl, handing her a shirt.

She jolts off the couch and runs off. James balances his footing as he straightens up, tucking in his flaccid dick. I don't give him time to zip his jeans. My fist hits him right in the face. He stumbles back, blood smearing his mouth.

"This is for touching Rosa against her will." My teeth grind with wrath. My fist scrapes his cheek when I pound another blow to his face. "That's for touching what's not meant for you to touch."

He groans in response.

"I…I wasn't—"

I don't let him talk. He doesn't deserve to be heard. He leans into the side of the sofa, massaging his cheek. With a clenched fist, he lunges at me, but I easily sidestep and grab his arm. Using his own momentum against him, I throw him across the room like a rag doll. He collides with a sturdy end table of dark mahogany, splintering it on impact.

"Fuck," he shouts, groaning in pain.

Good.

Let him feel the pain he caused Rosa. After I'm done, he'll never glance her way or even breathe in her direction.

"I wasn't going to force her, man. I was only messing with her. When she said no, I was a little ticked, I admit, but I wasn't going to hurt her. It was just a game."

A dark laugh erupts from me. *A game, he says. Oh, I'll play a game with him.* James leans against the wall, grasping onto it for support. Blood trickles down from a gash on his forehead. He's got scrapes, bruises, and a busted lip. One eye is swollen and discolored. A wicked lick of gratification swells inside me for fucking up the rich prick's face. But I'm not done.

"A game?" I cock my head. "You forced yourself on her… groped her without her consent."

My boots pound on the wooden floor with every step toward James. He shrinks, covering his face. I smack his hands away, then wrap my hands around his neck to cut the oxygen with a tight squeeze.

"You see, James, you touched what is *mine*. I don't take it lightly. You hurt what is *mine*, and I hurt the person responsible."

His hands claw at mine. When his lips turn blue, I toss him to the ground. He gasps and whimpers. Pussy.

I press my boot on his neck as his long, thin legs kick in the air.

"Get off of me," he gasps.

I chuckle darkly, like a villain. "Get off of you? Rosa asked you to get off of her, didn't she?" I tsk. "Let's play a game, James, since you thrive on games. I'm going to press my boot until you're gasping and thrashing for air. Let's see how long it takes until you pass out."

His head stretches to look up behind me.

I turn to see what he's looking at. A camera. Something tells me this sick fuck brings chicks here to screw, and he looks back at the footage. If he thinks he can use this surveillance to blackmail me, he has something else coming. His rich ass won't be able to get him out of this because the name stamped on the security camera is none other than Maximilian's Enterprises. A friend of mine I met in passing when he stepped foot at the boxing club where I sparred. He's a badass fighter and owns a growing security company.

Putting a little pressure on his airways, I pull out my phone.

"Hey, my man Santiago," Max's gruff voice vibrates. He's training.

"Hey bro, I know you're busy training. I wanted to ask you for a favor." When James dares to try to remove my foot, I push harder. Push. Release. In a pattern.

"Of course," he says. Max is a man of few words, gruff, and reserved in his demeanor. But once you gain his trust, you are part of a select few in his inner circle. His loyalty is valued among those he lets in.

"Can you pull security on The Branson's home on Blueprint Street? I need today's recording erased on their end and the footage sent to me." I wink at the lame ass on the floor, gasping for air.

"Leverage?" Max asks, and his wicked laugh thunders like a storm on a dark night.

"You know it."

"I'll let my team know and send you the footage."

"Thanks, man." I end the call and drag James onto the sofa.

He's holding his neck, gasping for air, and looking like what he deserves. If consequences weren't a thing, I'd end his fucking life. "Never again," I say, then walk out.

Walking out of the house, I light a cigarette, inhaling the taste of nicotine, and make my way to the woman waiting in my truck. She's mine, and she'll always be mine.

Just not mine to make forever with.

10

SANTIAGO

THE STARS SHIMMER above the night sky. The truck's headlights cut through the darkness, approaching the looming cliffs ahead. We've been driving for fifteen minutes. The night is calm, with only the whispers of the waves slapping against the massive cliffs. The moonlight ricochets on the ocean.

When I was sixteen, I took a drive on my motorcycle, needing an escape from home. My mom inflicted a heavy weight on me at such a young age. It left me deprived of my youth. As a child, I'd gaze out the window, searching, hoping, and praying my father would return to us. Days turned into weeks, months, and then years. Life was so much different when he was around. Working on cars was a hobby of his. I would lay on the floor, mimicking him doing an oil change. Maybe that's where I gained the love of fixing up vehicles.

When I discovered the remote spot on the cliffs, it became my sanctuary, a place I could wind down.

We make it to the cliff's edge. Rosa has been quiet, staring out the window. I've held her hand the whole way to assure her I'm here for her. When I jumped in the truck after kicking the bastard's ass, she scanned me for injuries. Seeing my scraped knuckles, she tenderly pressed her lips on each one. The urge to hold her, touch her, and taste her overrode my good sense. It's wrong to want her. So I'll shut it down and be there for her. Just like I've always been. She asked me to take her somewhere, anywhere, but home. This is a place I can share with her. A place where I have spent hours dreaming, wishing upon falling stars, and clearing my head.

"Wow, it's so beautiful." Her eyes glisten like the moonlight shining down on the water.

"It is," I respond as I open the door, then go around, opening hers. Luckily, I have a blanket in the back that I use for my seats. Pulling down the tailgate, I extend the red throw blanket. Rosa stands, gazing at the ocean, her arms wrapped around her middle. She hasn't looked at me since we pulled out of the party. Knowing her this long, I know she feels embarrassed about what happened. She thinks I might judge her.

"*Te necesito,*" she whispers in her native tongue.

I understand Spanish. I'm just not very fluent.

"Come here," I drawl, keeping my voice calm and steady.

Her head jolts, then she walks toward me, not meeting my eye. Once she's in front of me, her back hits the tailgate. I lift her chin and peer into her doe eyes.

"Flower, you did nothing wrong, you hear me?"

Her chin trembles, then she nods.

"I wandered off. I wasn't trying to get with him. He caught me by surprise when I was looking at some beautiful art." She swallows. "He came up behind me and said he'd show me a rare painting in a room. Then, when I followed, he locked the door and..." She stops and tries to turn away.

"It's okay, baby. We don't have to talk about it. I will repeat myself. You did nothing wrong. It's all him. If anyone ever lays a hand on you or hurts you, they will deal with me. I'll be the villain you need me to be." It's true. I've always been protective of Rosa, even more so now that she's all I think about… dream of.

Tears form in the corner of her eye. "Thank you for defending me. I appreciate it. Not just for tonight, but for the past years. For always being there for me." Her voice is thick with emotion. Her tender gaze is like a gentle stroke against my cheek.

I brush the tears that roll down her face. "Rosaline, I'll always be here for you." I clear my throat. "Let's not get all mushy. You don't want to see a grown man cry."

A smile parts her lips.

My hand grips her waist at each side, lifting her to sit on the truck. Her skirt rides up before I let go. I let my hands slide down to her warm, silky, bare thighs—just a small stroke of my fingertips. Heat runs throughout my body, pumping hot warmth into my heart. A feeling I cannot entertain for a variety of reasons. It doesn't help that she cat-crawls on all fours to the back of the truck, ass up, skirt riding up with each movement, giving me another glorious view.

Fuck.

"What happened?" she asks.

I guess I cursed it out loud. Exhaling a loud, exaggerated breath, I answer, "Nothing."

I run my fingers through my messy hair and stare at the water, the calm night, and listen to the sound of the soothing waves.

"Come here," she calls out. "Come look at the stars with me."

I rearrange my extremely hard dick straining against my jeans. Damnit, this is not the time to get fucking hard when she was assaulted and is emotional. When I turn to face her, she's leaning her head on the rear back window, ankles crossed, gazing up at the stars. A memory comes to mind.

Rosa leans her head on the bed of my truck, as we do our weekly stargazing. She studies the constellations she's mastered, finding some of them easily with the telescope I gifted her, but tonight, she's spotting them with the naked eye. I'm impressed with how much she knows for a ten-year-old. Tonight, I had plans to go partying—graduation parties. I wanted to celebrate my accomplishment of completing thirteen years of schooling. I'm surprised my mom showed up, although she had an emotionless expression and clearly would have preferred to be anywhere but there.

When Flower mentioned she planned a graduation celebration for me, I didn't have the heart to tell her no. So, I canceled with the guys—now I'm having rich, hot chocolate. I'm sure Rosa made it with two packages for one cup because I feel the sludge of chocolate slither down my throat. She topped it with marshmallows, which I'm sure are stale. Dominic, Liam, and Mark joined us briefly before they split to watch TV inside.

A smile curves my lips. Rosa looks cute in her pigtails, chocolate mustache, hands laced together on her tummy, and looking up at the sky.

"Lay down," she orders. Bossy. She pats the pillow next to her—the pillow she laid for us all.

"Alright, kid." I do as she says and look up at the stars.

She sighs, relaxed. "I always wonder how many secrets the stars have or how many wishes go unanswered. So many people wish on falling stars. Millions of people wish upon that same star. I'm guessing less than half of those people get their wish," Rosa says, turning her head to look at me. Her nose crinkles, then she sits up, reaching for her hot chocolate. Rosa's small hands wrap around the disposable cup.

"I used to wish my mom would come get me. Then I stopped wishing for that. Because what if she came back and took me away, and I'd never see my tía Andrea, Liam, Dominic, Mark, and you again? She would take me to Mexico. I sure am glad the stars didn't grant me that wish, and I hope they never do."

My heart shatters for a little girl to wish for her mother. Maybe it's because I know how it feels to wish for a parent to want you.

"You started wishing for your tía to be your mother?"

Her eyes widened as she set the cup down. "Shhh, you're going to ruin my wish. No one is supposed to know your wish," she whispers so low.

I tug on her pigtail and say, "No one will take you away from Andrea. She's your mom; she raised you and loves you. She would never let that happen." I tickle her side to ease her worries.

She shakes in laughter, then finally settles herself on the pillow, tucking in a blanket. She smiles up at the sky. Just then, a shooting star rockets across the sky. She closes her eyes to make her wish. So, do I. I wish for so many things. I wish I would find the right person someday so I won't be the lonely prince from my story. I wish that I'll be a great father and not like the father who left me. I wish my brothers grow to be great men, and I wish that Rosa's wishes and dreams come true.

My memories fade when Rosa calls my name. "Are you going to come sit, or are you just going to stand there like a lost animal?"

I chuckle at her jabs.

I hop onto the bed of the truck and take a seat beside her, my shoulder gently brushing against hers. Rosa's head tilts to the side. Her gaze glitters over mine. Her smile reaches her eyes. My heart kicks up at her beautiful smile.

"It's so peaceful. Beautiful. You come here a lot?" One of her brows lifts.

"I found it while riding my bike when I was sixteen."

"Oh," she says and looks up at the sky, a habit she's had for as long as I've known her. Stargazing.

Being friends with Rosa for so many years has its advantages. I can usually tell what she's thinking without her saying a word. She's wondering why I haven't brought her here and if I've brought girls here.

"I've never brought anyone here. I used it as a way to escape from… Well, you know the way my mom has always been, especially when I was younger."

Rosa reaches for my hand and squeezes it. "I know, and I understand you needed a breather. She put a lot on you. How has Rachel been acting lately?"

I lift a shoulder. "She's hardly home. There's nothing new about that. The only difference is that she's paying all the bills. She's planning on buying a bigger house and is making good money. At least that means that now I can save for my own place." My eyes drag down to her hand laced with mine—thumb caressing me in gentle strokes.

"Maybe she found herself a sugar daddy," Rosa snorts.

I let out a throaty laugh. I haven't met anyone she's seeing, but I'm sure she is. She tells my brothers she's working late, but I know she's not.

"I wouldn't be surprised," I drawl.

She lets go of my hand to pull her skirt down. We stay silent, taking in the calm ocean breeze. It's been a while since I've felt so content. Maybe it's because things are starting to look up, and I can finally have the money to move out and not pay the bills for my mom.

That's part of it, but something deep down tells me this feeling of contentment is because of Rosa. She's always been part of my life, but it's different now that I see her in a whole new way. Reese has been pushing me to just go for it. Why should I care about anyone else's opinions? The doubts in my mind tell me she's still too young, and I don't have my life together enough for her. Maybe someday I will, although it might be too late by then, and she'll move on.

11

SANTIAGO

"IT'S BEEN A LONG TIME," Rosa murmurs pensively. Her eyes gaze out into the horizon. She nervously twirls the edge of her lightweight red blouse, a habit she has whenever she's uneasy or self-conscious.

I wait for her to finish.

"It's been a long time since we've done any stargazing. I guess it got too immature for you, huh? I get it," Rosa rambles. Her words fly like she's speeding down a highway.

I can't deny it. We got older. Things changed. She was a kid and a good friend.

I would never spend time stargazing with a teenage girl. It wouldn't seem right. So I quit. But perhaps I overreacted. We'd been stargazing since she was seven. She would have night-mares or an anxiety attack. When she woke up crying or even screaming, I suggested we lie on the grass and gaze up at the stars. It ended up being something she loved to do.

Sitting here with her now is intimate since we both feel the pull. I'm unfamiliar with romance or relationships.

"Gazing at the stars is not at all immature." I take a deep breath. There's more to say. "I'm sorry I've been distant, but as we got older, things just changed. I had my shit, and you had friends and did teen stuff." Absentmindedly, the palm of my hand lands on her thigh. I can tell by the goosebumps on her knees she approves of me touching her silk-smooth legs. "I've missed you," I say earnestly.

Her head suddenly jerks back, as if surprised by my confession. "You missed me?" she asks, her eyebrows raised in disbelief.

"Of course, Rosa. We've always had a strong friendship. I was always around, even if I seemed distant."

She nods.

I can't seem to move my hand from her leg. She seems more at ease and less shaken up. I brush my hand up and down her leg. "How are you feeling?"

Those beautiful eyes drop to where my hand lays. "Better now that you're here with me. You've always made me feel safe." She shifts her body, facing me. She looks nervous but also determined. "I can still feel his hands all over me. I need to erase his touch." She shifts a little closer, and it looks like it's taking a lot of effort to look me in the eye. "You know... I've never been with anyone intimately." My eyes go wide, and the rest of me feels hot. "I need you. I need you to erase it all from my mind *and* my body. I want you to... be my first."

She closes her eyes and takes a slow, steady breath. Definitely not what I was expecting to hear. A wave of disbelief and shock washes over me. She wants me to be her first in every sense. She had already given me her first kiss, but now she's asking for more. My grip on her thigh tightens as I process her words.

"I thought you said you've been with other guys?" That's what she said to Mark.

She rolls her eyes. "How is that possible if you were the first guy I have kissed? I never kissed Ryan, and I'm not even into him." She chews on her lips and then adds, "I know you're seeing Monica and probably other girls. I know you prefer it that way since you don't want to be strapped down to only one. I…I just need it this once…and you can go back to ignoring me." She blushes, looking everywhere but at me.

I'm frozen. This isn't something small, and she knows damn well it isn't. Yes, it's no big deal with other women. But Rosa is not those… women, and she's not the type to fuck and leave. She's lost her mind if she thinks we could go back to "ignoring each other" as if nothing happened.

Crossing this line with Rosaline would change everything. If we were to take it further, and things didn't work out, it would ruin us. The friendship that we built as kids.

She's still in college and has a future. Her art could take her places. How would that work? I run my fingers through my hair, gripping them hard.

"If you don't want this. I'll leave you alone and never look your way again. If that's what you want," Rosa mumbles, folding her hands between her thighs. Awkwardness and embarrassment paint on her beautiful face. Of course, she feels awkward. I haven't answered her.

Fuck it. Fuck all my reservations.

I turn to her, cupping her cheeks. I try to infuse each word with lust, want, need, and love. "You don't understand, flower. Once I undress you, once my hands roam your silky bare skin, once I'm inside you, and I taste every part of you, you belong to me, Rosaline. This is not a one-night stand or just some casual hookup. You will utterly belong to me, just as I will belong to you. There's no going back, regret, or mistake," I say, my tone light, my thoughts dark.

Rosa's gaze roams over my expression, searching for something.

"Is that what you want, Rosa? Because once my tongue traces down your bare body into your pussy. It's fucking mine. I'm claiming you under the stars, baby, then when I take you back to my house, I'm claiming you there on my bed. Do you understand what this means? I'm never letting you go, Rosaline. *Fucking. Never. You're. Mine.*"

Her lips curve into a smile, and she fans herself. "*Cristo,* that's hot as hell. You're going to send me into cardiac arrest before anything even happens."

I chuckle and lift her off the bed of the truck, sitting her on my lap.

"Santiago, I'm too heavy for you to—"

"You're perfect, flower." I groan as her ass hits my engorged dick.

Rosa gazes up at me with adoration in her beautiful chocolate-colored eyes. "I want this." She points between her and me. "But you know what this also means. You'd be my boyfriend." Rosa turns from me bashfully.

I reach out and hold her cheeks in my palms, feeling the warmth of her skin against mine. I slowly trace my fingers down the curve of her neck, pulling her closer to me until our lips are almost touching. I can feel her unsteady breath mixing with my anticipation as our bodies draw closer together.

"Yes, I'll be your boyfriend, and you'll be my woman. I want you to know I haven't been with anyone since the day you kissed me at my house. I don't want any other woman. Only you."

Before she can even process what is happening, I press my lips against hers in a desperate kiss. She responds just as I hoped, with equal fervor and need. Our kiss is filled with passion and desperation, both of us seeking comfort and reassurance in each other's embrace. I have never felt as fulfilled and content in another woman's arms as I do with Rosa. It feels natural, as if she was always meant to be mine. She moans into my mouth. It's the sweetest, most pleasurable sound.

I pull away from her, giving her space to breathe before I drain the life out of her. Rosa's lips are red and puffy, evidence of our passionate kiss. Her warm arms wrap around my neck, holding on tight. My lips press on her delicate neck. I've been dying to kiss her shoulder where her red blouse hangs, which gives me access to skim my lips along her soft, natural, light skin. Tugging on her blouse, I ask, "May I?"

Rosa gives me a nod of approval, still trying to catch her breath. "You never have to ask to rip my clothes off, Santi. I've dreamed of this moment for so long." Her confession does something to me.

I've never had someone genuinely interested in who I am as a person. They only seem to want my body and nothing more. They disagree with my profession of choice and not having my life completely together because I prioritize taking care of my siblings. Then again, I've never given myself to anyone like I intend to with Rosa. I've never had a girlfriend, and I wouldn't have it another way, Rosa being my first and only.

"Good to know, babe," I smirk, slipping her blouse off.

Damn. Fucking perfect. My gaze scans her body like I'm studying a lottery ticket. Mmm, I just scored my grand prize. I hit the jackpot. She shivers as the pad of my thumb caresses the top of her breasts from one to the other. Reaching around, I unclasp her laced bra. With anticipation, I bite my lip.

A guttural sound erupts from my throat as I take in her breathtaking beauty. My gaze lingers on Rosa, who is now turning ten shades of crimson and hastily attempting to cover herself. I can sense her deep-rooted insecurities bubbling to the surface, but to me, she is nothing but beautiful. She's always been oblivious to her beauty. Although I didn't see her in an intimate way back then, she was a pretty girl.

"Don't hide from me, Rosa. You're gorgeous."

"You've been with prettier and more experienced women than me. I'm no comparison to them."

I hate how she sees herself. If only she could see what I see.

"Rosa," I mutter, my lips pressing on hers to quiet her. They continue their journey, trailing down her neck. "Stop fucking talking about yourself like that. You're mistaken, sweetheart. I've never been with anyone better. No one has captured my interest like the woman in front of me. You know me better than anyone, Rosa. When have you seen or heard me claim a girl as mine?" I brush a strand of hair covering her beautiful face. Her stare rolls over me, the same feverish flame in her eyes mirrors mine.

"Never," she moans as my thumb swipes her peaked nipple.

"Exactly, sweetheart. Now, I'd like to continue to show my girl just how much I want her body, how much I want to claim every part of her. Starting with these melons, my tongue is dying to taste."

Cupping her breasts that overflow in my hands, I bring one to my mouth, giving them both the attention they want. By the way Rosa tugs on my hair and grinds on me, I know she likes me sucking on her sensitive breasts. My erection painfully presses on the zipper. I'm so close to pulling it out. The need to relieve myself is maddening. It's too soon. Rosa's a virgin. I need to take my time with her and warm her up.

While my mouth is devouring her breasts, I unzip the side of her skirt. She stands, letting the skirt drop. She sits back down on me, straddling me and leaving her in just her thong. A feral groan drips from my lips as I gaze at her pussy, eating the material of her thong. That perfect landing strip makes my mouth water with the need to run my tongue up and down.

Running my hands between her inner thighs, I relish how slick and wet she is for me. I insert one finger, stretching her. She's so damn tight. "I like you wet for me. Having you soaked is a bonus." My voice comes out raw and overworked. I barely recognize it.

She purrs when I insert a second finger. I love seeing how flushed I'm making her, how I'm the only one who will ever get to see her this way. There's no way I'll ever let her go. Rosa has always been mine, even before I knew it.

She feels so damn good. Her eyes roll back in her head as I pump gently into her. *Oh, sweetheart, just wait until I'm plowing in you. She'll feel every part of me.*

"Lay down, Rosaline, and spread those beautiful legs for me."

She doesn't hesitate. Her new confidence oozes out of her.

Breathtaking.

My hand goes to my swollen dick over the thick material of the jeans. I give it a good squeeze, getting the blood flowing. Breathtaking sums up every word in the English dictionary. I could say beautiful, stunning, amazing, gorgeous, and so on. However, she is all those words. But breathtaking is every word wrapped in one. My chest heaves as my heart does jumping jacks in my ribcage. Shock and adrenaline course through my body like I have just been tossed into a freezing lake. But my body cannot move while my heart races in an erratic rhythm.

Maybe I'm being the king of pussies, but this is more than anything I've felt before. Her curves, breasts, and every inch of her are worth worshiping. Perfect. Sexy.

My fingers grasp the delicate lace of her underwear and rip it off in one swift motion, revealing her bare skin beneath. My breath catches at the sight of her, spread out before me, vulnerable and enticing.

12

ROSALINE

A SMALL, relaxed breeze wafts in the air, and the aroma of the salty ocean's roaring waters fills the night. After the chaotic and unpleasant experience I had at the party, I'm grateful that I reached out to Santiago. The way he stood up for me and showed his support is…well no words can describe what he did for me tonight. I can't even find the right word. I want him all over me. I want to be marked by Santiago.

I needed him, the man who had been a constant presence throughout my life. What I never expected was for him to claim me as his girlfriend. To want me in every way possible.

You will utterly belong to me, just as I will belong to you.

Santiago has never mentioned having a girlfriend, and when he confessed his preference for me, my heart fluttered. I've never seen him look at other women with hungry eyes as if he wants to devour them.

If lust wasn't overwhelming me, I'd laugh at just how ridiculous this night is going. This is all new to me, and I feel slightly uncomfortable stripped naked in front of him.

My body vibrates, and goosebumps spread over me like wildfire—an inferno scalding my insides when his lips meet my inner thighs. Plush, hot, gentle kisses work their way up to my sex. His sparkling eyes dance with eagerness. Santiago's thick fingers brush my clit. With a quick swipe of his lips, his husky voice rumbles between my legs.

"You want my tongue in your virgin pussy, Rosaline?" He inserts a finger. My body arches to his touch. "Hmm, baby, do you want me to eat the shit out of you?"

Cristo.

This side of Santiago is new to me, of course. I've never heard him dirty talk. He always watched how he spoke in front of me. His filthy words heat my insides. I love this side of Santiago, where he feels comfortable with me and with exploring this new thing between us.

"Yes, please," I beg.

I don't care if I sound desperate. I need him. Lifting my head up, I peer at him as his lips twitch upward. Wordlessly, he dives in. When his tongue fills me, I cry in pleasure. My hands tighten into a fist on the flimsy blanket.

Ignoring the metal floor panels etching my back, I buck my hips, getting more friction. His skilled hands grip my hips and pull me closer. The sensation of his hot breath on my skin sends shivers down my spine as his tongue dances inside me, swirling and teasing with every movement. His teeth graze against my sensitive flesh, sending electric pulses through my body. He knows just how to devour me, leaving me completely lost in pleasure. Two fingers hook, and then he thrusts, stretching me while his tongue sucks around my clit. Santiago moans in the hottest way, making my tummy tighten, and I can feel a strange sensation.

"Santiago," I mewl, my voice hoarse and dry.

Something in me explodes. Hard and fast. It radiates through my body like nothing I could ever even have imagined.

He licks me dry, leaving me in a state of wow. Like, holy shit, just imagine what else he can do.

His hooded stare has me squirming, his lips glistening with my juices in the moonlight. "Damn, Rosa, you taste so fucking good." He licks his lips. "I'm addicted now, baby. Expect me to be in between your legs every chance I get."

I prop myself up, peering at him fully clothed. I frown, displeased that I can't see what's underneath all that clothing. His brows jog up in question to my frown. I lift my hand, gesturing up and down his body. "You're fully clothed while I'm here, bared naked for you. Fewer clothes would be great, Santi."

He chuckles huskily, making me melt. His dimples indent boyishly.

He beckons with his finger. "Come undress me, sweetheart. I want your hands all over me."

I get on my knees and make my way toward him. He sucks in a sharp breath when my naked body stills in front of him, nipples brushing his shirt. His hands trace the curves of my body.

"You're so sexy, Rosa."

"Thank you," I say bashfully as I lift his shirt off his sculpted body and toss it with the rest of the clothes scattered in the truck's bed. We are both on our knees. Eagerly, my palms move gracefully on the dark, coarse hair, and I drop kisses all over his chest. I can feel him shudder with desire. I'm the one making him feel unleashed and uncontrolled. His grip tightens on my hips. My lips trail downward and stop when I get to the V line.

"Hot," I say, my tongue tracing each line. "Sexy." I look up at him through my lashes. My tongue runs down his navel to the button of his jeans. "Mine."

He grabs a fist full of my hair and thrusts his engorged erection into my face. "Yours," he croaks, his voice strained, his eyes dark. "I like this side of my Rosa. And I'll be the only one to see it," he drawls as I unbutton his jeans and unzip them.

I speak honestly. "It's because it's you." With any other guy, I'm sure they would have taken advantage of me and left. But with Santiago, everything is different.

"It's just me and you, babe."

I glide his jeans down to his thick thighs. My eyes widen at his massive erection in his boxers. His bulge is visible through his tight boxer briefs, leaving my imagination to wonder what lies beneath. I've never seen a penis up close, or at all.

"If you keep staring at my dick, it's only going to get harder, Rosaline. I'm trying to contain myself, flower, and be patient about burying myself in you and showing you just how mine you are."

Damn.

With a shaky hand, my thumbs hook to the elastic of his boxers, gliding them down, and his penis bobs out. I'm a tingling mess on every nerve, and my veins rocket with a thirst like an addict needing their fix. Santiago watches me as I reach for his hard, massive cock. I'm in need of exploring his body, intending to make him fall apart and satisfy him in ways no one has. The position we are in makes it hard for me to take him in my mouth. So, I stroke him up and down. Our eyes lock. He leans until our foreheads press together, and he groans.

"Feels good." Santiago's hot breath seeps into my pores.

He tugs at my swollen nipples when his lips capture mine. There is hunger in the way he lifts me. Our lips tangle, tongue thrashing. He lays me down. I can feel his erection poking at my entrance. When his lips trail down my breasts, he sucks, devouring each one. My nails dig into his back as he keeps worshiping my breasts. He stops and looks up at me—my body melts like butter at how he peers at me with love and adoration in those eyes.

"Rosa, I don't have condoms with me. Fuck, baby, I'm sorry."

"I'm on the pill. I started last month because of medical reasons." The drumming of my heart has me take an enormous breath to control myself because I have to ask him a question. "Are you clean? You have been with other women," I utter, trying not to look him in the eye.

He lifts my arms up, pinning me in place, and I'm forced to look right at him.

"I'm clean, sweetheart. I've never been without a condom. You're my home, Rosa. I've never felt okay without one until you."

I nod, and a tear rolls down my cheek, overwhelmed by emotions taking over. As we lay intertwined, his fingertips trace every curve of my body, worshipping each inch like a devoted follower.

I look into his eyes and see pure adoration reflected back at me. He kisses away the tears that have fallen from my cheeks, leaving only contentment in their place.

"Do you still want this?"

"Yes, I want you. I need you."

And with my simple plea, Santiago eases inside me. I suck in a breath. "That's it baby, take another breath." He takes it slow until he bumps against my resistance.

"I'm going to take you slow, baby. I'm going to make love to you. I've never made love to anyone. You're my first, sweetheart. I'm no gentleman, but I will be for you. But next time, I'm going to fuck you deep and raw."

Chills race down my spine. I never could have imagined experiencing this kind of intimacy. It's an unparalleled connection with the man I've loved and shared so much with for as long as I can remember. Our bodies and souls are now intertwined in this special bond we've created.

"I want it all with you, making love, fucking hard, fast, raw, and deep," I say with a hard, ragged breath as he slowly goes deeper.

When I gasp, his mouth covers mine with urgency, distracting me from the sting of pain. He's not even all the way in, but I can feel his thickness stretch through me in the most fulfilling way. His tongue ravishes mine while his hand kneads my breast. Santiago takes the opportunity to tease my nipple, intensifying his thrusts as he consumes my cries with a deep passion.

"That's my girl. You're doing good, baby. The pain is over."

His hips thrust in a circular motion as my insides pulse with the bundle of nerves as he eases in and out. The pain is relieved with pleasure. His callused, warm hands roam, feeling every crevice and slope of my body. Santiago pins my hands up, entwining our fingers.

My legs wrap around his waist. He moans my name.

"More, please. I'm close," I cry out.

He's gentle, but his thirst is deep, penetrating my whole body. I can feel it in my bones. God, and he said this was gentle and sweet sex. Just imagine when he fucks me hard and deep.

"I could get myself to go longer, but I don't want you to be sore and in pain—." He grunts and curses, his body shakes, and can feel him pulsing and enlarging inside me. "Come with me, sweetheart. Come all over my dick."

A piercing scream shatters the stillness of the night. I can feel the warmth of his release trickling down my leg, mixing with my own. We are panting heavily, our bodies slick with sweat and tangled in our embrace. His arms slide from our pinned position and wrap around me tightly.

He leans up a little to peer at me. "Are you okay?"

I peck a kiss on his cheek, then his nose.

"I'm good, great actually."

He smiles ever so slightly. Those dimples indent, and I lean to swirl my tongue in them. He chuckles and drops a kiss on my lips just before he pulls out. I gasp when the moonlight reflects on us, and I can see the ting of blood on his dick and on my legs trailing down.

"Relax, Rosa, it's blood. I fucking love that it's your blood on me, and no one will get to have you as I have." Possessiveness paints his tone.

He grabs a hand towel from his utility box hooked on the bed of his pickup truck. Gently, he cleans us up. "That will have to do for now. Let's get dressed. We'll stop and pick up something to eat on the way. Then we'll head home so you can clean up, and we can lie in my bed and watch whatever you want, even those rom-coms you love," he says, his voice drifting as he grabs my clothes, handing them to me.

He's still completely naked. I love how he puts me first, but then again, that's Santiago for you. He's always putting others before him. He's perfect.

"Sounds like a plan," I mumble, shoving my shirt on.

Once I'm dressed, I look up at the still night. It's a great, perfect night to make love under the moonlight. I can't believe it. I look up at the glittering stars above and silently express my gratitude for all the wishes I've made that have seemingly been answered by bringing this man to me. Something deep down tells me things are not going to be that easy for Santiago and me.

13

SANTIAGO

A TEXT FLASHES with Max's name. Attached is the video of me beating the shit out of James and him assaulting Rosa.

Max: *Took it down. You did a number on him. Fucker deserved it.*

Me: *Thanks, Max. I owe you.*

Max: *Nah, man, you were protecting your girl. Anytime.*

My girl. The thought of calling Rosa my girlfriend brings a smile to my face. Our intimate moment tonight, unlike anything I've ever experienced before, is truly spectacular. We drove back to the city, and I stopped at a burger place. In the drive-thru, I reached for Rosa, pulling her toward me. As of tonight, she became the air I breathe, oxygen into my lungs. I see the doubt in her beautiful eyes. But I'll prove it to her. She's the only woman I want. We still need to talk about our families. How are we going to tell them? I'll do anything she wants. If I have to go through fire to keep Rosa, I'll do it.

When we arrived at my house, we ate and then I ordered Rosa to take a shower to relax and soothe her soreness. It took everything in me not to join her. I knew I wouldn't be able to contain myself while she's completely naked, water lavishing her body. It would only make me want to pound her up against the wall. It's too soon.

The faucet turns off, and a minute later, Rosa steps out of the steamy bathroom, filling my room with steam. My gaze roams over her body. She's worn my clothes, along with my brothers', a dozen times before, but now it hits different. It turns me on seeing her step out in my T-shirt and shorts. I make a note to let her know she can't wear my brothers' clothes anymore. I only want to see her in mine. I'm not jealous. I'm just a selfish asshole who wants his girl in his clothes.

"Damn, baby, you look good in my clothes." I give her a kiss. "You're fogging the whole bedroom up," I tease, knowing she'll blush for me. "Your feet look like Pink Panther, all pink, almost red."

She swats me on the chest playfully. "You know I'm a sucker for hot showers." She looks at her reddened feet. "I guess I do look like Pink Panther. I never thought of it." She giggles, then her eyes widen. "Is anyone here?" she whispers, suddenly worried.

"No," I say, reaching for her hand and intertwining our fingers as I guide her to my bed.

She mentioned she told her aunt she's staying the night at Jasmine's before all this shit happened with the fuck-head. I pretty much made her stay with me tonight. "The guys are staying with Liam. You know your aunt. If they're drinking, she won't let them leave. And my mom? I don't think she's coming home tonight. She hardly does."

Lifting the covers, Rosa snuggles in. I follow behind her, cradling her in my arms. This is all new to both of us—being in a relationship. However, with Rosa, it feels right, like we've done this a million times. It's natural for us to react this way since we've always known each other inside and out. Especially now that she gave herself to me.

"She's probably with her sugar daddy," Rosa says.

I laugh and gently place my hands in front of her neck, bringing her to eye level. My lips crash on hers. She welcomes me with desperation, matching my own. She moans when I press harder, bruising her lips. Our tongues dance, teeth clashing. I want her to know that I don't regret it. I want her to see how much I want this. Us. Deepening the kiss, I push my erection into her belly. She breathes into my lungs and wraps her arms around my neck, pushing harder into our passionate kiss. I'm like a starved man eating her face off.

Breaking the kiss, we both pant, gasping for air. "You're a great kisser," she practically purrs.

"I've never kissed anyone like this, and I think you're an amazing kisser. I'm wondering how many guys you've kissed." I tease. My brows raise in question.

"Just one. He's just a skilled teacher." Her hand moves to my hard-on. She rubs it up and down over my boxers. "I didn't get a chance to pleasure you," she grumbles, looking like someone stole her favorite candy.

Cupping her cheeks, my tone low, I assure her. "Sweetheart, you please me by simply laying in my arms; you pleasured me by giving yourself to me tonight and giving me the best sex of my life. If you insist on giving me a — blow job, you can wake me up tomorrow with one." I wiggle my eyebrows at her.

"It was the best sex of your life?" She snorts, making it seem like I'm bullshitting her.

"It was, and I'm positive it will always be that way with you. Now go to sleep. It's past midnight."

She yawns and nods.

I turn off the bedside lamp and tuck her closer into my arms. Her head snuggles into the slope of my neck, and her arms rest around my shoulders. "Good night, beautiful.

Tomorrow, we will talk about what you want to do with the news of us as a couple. The ball is in your court. I'll let you decide."

"Good night, Santi. Thank you for everything," she mumbles, dozing off.

I'm pussy whipped by this woman already. But then again, I'm sure I've always been. It's just different now. I never thought I would find someone. The thought of a family, wife, and kids always crossed my mind. Falling in love and being loved. I always chose to put my brothers first. They needed me, and I couldn't let myself get distracted.

Now I understand why Dominic was so caught up in having a life with Mila. He was in love beyond words with her. He wanted marriage, kids, a family, something we never experienced in our childhood. It seems to be ingrained in our DNA, this longing for a sense of belonging and kinship.

I gingerly place a kiss on Rosa's temple and relish how gone I am for her. I can't imagine sleeping in an empty bed anymore. I'll need her with me always.

WHEN I WAKE, Rosa lays with her arms wrapped around my neck, legs looped over mine, and her shining black hair spread all over my pillow. Her lips are pouty as she exhales.

Fucking beautiful.

I've never been the type to worry about what women think of me. However, with Rosa, I can't help but wonder if she'll wake up regretting us.

Temptation yanks at me to drop between her legs and ravish her with my tongue to stir her awake. I want her to see what it would be like to have her wake up in my arms. It's foolish of me to want this with her so soon. Rosa is young and innocent.

Instead, I trace her luscious lips with my tongue. Within

seconds, her arms wrap around my neck, pulling me in deeper, then her tongue slips into my mouth.

I'm relieved she still wanted this—us. She makes me feel goddamn insane and out of control. I swallow her moans, and her body melts into mine. She wants me just as much as I want her. When her nipples harden against my bare chest, I lift her ass, grinding my erection on her. I can't stop.

A knock at the door makes Rosa stiffen and pull herself from me. I didn't hear my brothers walking in the front door.

"Santiago," Dominic calls out. We locked the door to the bedroom, so I continue to skim my lips on Rosa's neck.

"Yeah, what is it?" I lift her shirt to get another look at her melon-sized breasts. I would love them even if they were small because it's her. I adore her body. She's curvy and full-figured. Although she's self-conscious at times, I'll make sure she knows and feels how sexy she is. She tries to pull her shirt down, but I don't let her. My brothers won't come in.

I whisper in her ear, "Shh, baby," then suckle on her breasts.

"I'm going to look for furniture. Do you want to go with me?"

Swirling my tongue on her hard nipples, I answer Dominic, "I would, but I have to work today. We can go later."

Rosa arches, visibly desiring her breast in my mouth. I want to know what gets Rosa off, what she likes. I want to know her body inside and out.

"That's alright. I'll see if Mark wants to go. What the hell are you doing in there? You can't open the door?"

I move to her other breast, sucking hard, watching Rosa lose control, her mouth gaping open and containing her moans. My mouth skims down to her stomach.

"Jerking off," I chuckle, joking, tugging on her nipples as Rosa jogs her brows up.

"Jesus Christ, didn't need to know." I hear him leave, and his door closes from his old room.

"You look sexy, legs spread." My tongue vibrates in her pussy. "And taste incredible." I'm an unselfish person, but with Rosa, I'm going to be selfish and keep her for myself.

Nails dig into my scalp as her hips thrust like a powerhouse until she comes all over my face.

"Oh my God, that's amazing," she says, ears and cheeks red.

I lick my lips to taste every drop. I'm still having a hard time believing this woman is mine.

"You've been staring at the clock all day, bro," Reese grumbles, looking down at his clipboard. "You seem different." He peers back up and stares at me like a creep. "I would say you got laid, but you never look like this. You almost look like you're…glowing," he muses, tapping a pen on his chin.

"Fuck off," I retort. "Glowing? Isn't that what chicks do?"

He shrugs. "Hell, if I should, know. But something is up with you. Where did you take off to last night? You were hysterical when Rosa left."

I scoff at him. Hysterical is hardly accurate.

"I take it back, not hysterical. You looked furious and so fucking jealous." His brown eyes bulge, then he slams the clipboard on the hood of the Audi I'm working on. "No way, man. I don't fucking believe it. You did it?"

"Did what?" I reply, leaning against the car.

"You went to spy on Rosa, and then you hooked up, right?" He beams, proud of himself as if he solved a grand mystery.

"Me? Spy on her? I wouldn't do that." Would I?

"You didn't deny hooking up?" he says, nose up.

"We didn't hook up."

He stares at me, looking stupidly smug, and leans against the Audi.

"She's my girl. My girlfriend."

Reese starts grinning like an asshole and claps me on the shoulder.

"This stays between us until Rosa is ready to tell my brothers, Liam, and her aunt. We both wanted to wait so we could at least enjoy one another before shit hit the fan. If it does." We wanted to wait. I wanted that also. To have her all to myself, but at the same time, I didn't want to hide. Not anymore.

Reese shouts like a complete idiot. "I knew it, bro. About. Fucking. Time." He grins. "Girlfriend, huh? Never thought I'd see the day you would claim a woman as yours."

Grabbing a shop towel, I wipe off the layered grease smeared on the car I worked on. "I've never felt this way about anyone. I can't think straight," I admit. How can I suddenly feel like I can't breathe without her?

"It's no surprise there. You've been that girl's knight in shining armor since she was three. She's always wanted your full, undivided attention, and you gave it to her. Why do you think girls felt threatened by Rosa? You gave her more attention than any girl, and back then, she was only a kid you loved and cared for."

He is right about how girls always felt threatened, especially fucking Marissa. I never understood because she was young then.

He continues. "Do you remember how she always cried for a bedtime story? She would have Liam peddle her down the street in her My Little Pony nightgown." He throws his head back, laughing.

How can I forget those memories? It happened so many times because she wanted me to tell her a story. She's always taken a unique place in my heart. Only now, I've given her my whole damn heart for keeps.

14

SANTIAGO

"OUR FRIENDSHIP HAS ALWAYS BEEN SPECIAL." Glancing at the clock, I realize there are still thirty minutes until she meets me here. She's shopping with Jasmine and her aunt. I can't help but feel a sense of anticipation, like a child waiting to receive a new toy. I am eager to see her.

"It may sound cliché, but it's true. You and Rosa will be together." Reese casually shrugs, reaching for his clipboard.

"Never played you for a romantic," I tease. "In all seriousness, I understand what you mean. Never in all my years would I have thought I'd end up with Rosa. It's crazy how a simple kiss can change everything."

"I'm happy for you. I agree with you guys keeping it to yourselves before the shit storm begins. Liam's going to throw a fucking fit. He's protective of her," Reese says while staring at his phone ringing, then clipping the call off. I notice it's his girl, Kathy, calling. They've been on and off since high school.

"What's going on with you and Kathy?"

Reese shoves his fingers through his brown, wavy hair.

"I'm going to break it off with her tonight." His voice is gruff with disdain.

"Really? For good, or are you taking a break again?"

He snorts. He knows I don't believe him. It's been a cycle with them. She's not my favorite person. Kathy has always played games with him.

"For good. She's cheating on me." He laughs, shaking his head. "When I was going down on her, she had hickeys between her legs."

My eyes expand.

"Yeah, man, and when I asked who she was fucking, she played it off, saying she got a bruise by jumping a fence and then pretended to be offended."

"What a bitch."

"I'm sure it's the guy from her work. I've seen them staring at each other when I've gone to pick her up. The other night, she called me to let me know not to come get her. She said a friend was taking her home." He rakes his chin.

"Sounds like a great time to get out," I say.

"Get this, she got pissed because I didn't go back to eating her out. I told her to have the fucker do it, and he could have my sloppy seconds. She slapped me. I slammed the door and left. She's been calling me non-stop."

Deep down, I know he's hurting. He's always cared for her, and loved her. Reese avoids showing pain, just as I have.

"It sucks, man. You're better off without her. You gave it your all, and she shit on you. She's never appreciated what you've done for her."

He groans. "I know, bro. I'm tired of her games. I'm ready to let her go for good."

I nod while he's lost in thought. She's going to be trouble like always. She tries to reel him in, giving him some type of guilt trip.

My heart stops as the front door swings open.

Rosa's black hair flows like a river, long, silky, and smooth. Her tight denim jeans hug her perfect curves. The dark, royal blue tank top is snug on her breasts, with the hem of her shirt showing enough skin to make me want to tug it down so my gaze doesn't wander on her.

Damn, I'm a goner.

"Hi, Santi." She blushes, her voice low and reserved for me.

My shy Rosa is back. I admire how hard she's been trying to come out of her shell. It's difficult for her. Until last night, the only thing she's really confident in is her painting.

"Hi, Rosa." I shamelessly take in the beautiful sight in front of me.

A throat clearing reminds me it's not just us, and I'm glad it's a Saturday. It's just Reese and me.

"Hey, little Rosa." Reese runs to her, lifting her up as if she's his girl to twirl around. "Glad you came to see me. Looking mighty h—"

"Finish that, and I'll cut your balls off. Step away from my girl."

He chuckles, knowing I'd flip out on him. I've never given a rat's ass before with other women. But now that he knows my feelings for Rosa, he's busting my chops. He's also been protective of her.

Rosa's gaze flicks toward Reese, and I can tell she is nervous.

"He knows, sweetheart. He won't tell. In fact, he's all for it." I wink and tug on the belt loop of her jeans, pulling her closer to me. Brushing a stray curl away from her face, I take a deep breath and inhale her floral scent. She truly lives up to her nickname, as she smells like a beautiful rose. She molds into my arms. Damn, just these couple of hours away from her felt too long.

I'm in so much trouble. I'm falling for her too fast, too soon.

"Sweetheart." Reese snickers with a wolfish grin.

Rosa giggles into my chest. She, as much as Reese, knows I've called no one sweetheart or baby. They are both making fun of me, which has me grinning. I pinch her side, and she yelps.

"You're so going to get it, flower," I muse.

She peers up at me with those long eyelashes. "Oh, yeah? What do you have in mind, big guy?" Rosa offers me a warm, flirty smile.

I love that she's always been relaxed with me, sharing anything and everything with me. She's not like this with anyone. It makes my heart beat like a drum. To have this side of Rosa reserved just for me.

"Sorry to interrupt this,"—Reese points between us— "but I need to head out. Will you lock up?"

Leaning to peck a kiss on Rosa's cheek, I nod to Reese.

"Yeah, man, of course. Call me if you need anything." I raise a brow his way.

I'm positive Kathy has cheated on him before. He helps her pay for rent, but she doesn't want him to move in. Probably so she can go fuck around. I'm not fond of the bitch, but I'm here for him.

"Laters, Rosa. Call me if you're into a threesome," he jokes to rile me up.

"Fuck off," I shout after him while leaning on the car and pulling Rosa closer than she already is. My hands are resting on her round ass. I wouldn't share this woman with anyone. One night with Rosa shifted my entire life. All I see is her. It terrifies the shit out of me because she's young. We might be eight years apart. However, in eight years, a lot can happen. We mature. We grow. What if she gets bored with me? What if I'm just a fleeting infatuation for her, and it will fade once she's actually been with me?

Having a family was always something unattainable for me. I've wanted that—a wife, children, the whole package. But after time, reality set in. I'd never met a woman who sparked my interest, and it would have been a bad time to fall for a woman when I had to deal with my mother. Who would want a man who had to take care of their brothers and protect them from their own mom?

With Rosa, I see…a future. She makes me feel like I could settle down with her. Have the picket fence and all. But Rosa's young. Settling down is not in her cards yet. She needs to finish college, see the world, and make great art. I'll do everything in my power to give her what she deserves.

As Reese's footsteps fade down the hallway, I pull Rosa toward me. She melts into my arms, and her hands caress my face as our lips meet in a passionate kiss. Our bodies press together; the door slams shut, and we lose ourselves in each other's embrace.

The urge to lay her in the back of one of these cars is tempting. My heart bulges in my chest… I'm losing control, and I don't know how to stop it. What do I have to offer her? Nothing but my heart.

At my age, I should have my life put together like a puzzle, but I don't. Rosa needs more than I can offer her. At least right now.

15

ROSALINE

IF THIS IS ALL JUST a dream, then I never want to wake up. Everything feels perfect, and I could live in it forever. It's like living in an eternal night, but peaceful, with no darkness or fear. All my life, I've been searching for this feeling of contentment, and now, in this dream, I've finally found it.

It's not that my aunt hasn't given me everything, but she's also been living in gray since her husband passed. Since the first day my mom chose a man over me—locking me up in the closet, leaving me alone for hours—I've always felt as if I was never good enough. I know my mom's leaving triggered it. I never want to be someone's second choice again; I want to be their first.

Santiago's lips crash against mine with a primal intensity. His hands grip my body, strong and unyielding, tracing the curves of my back and squeezing my ass. The pressure of his touch sends electric shocks through my skin. Santiago's caress is in every move he makes as he devours me with an insatiable hunger.

My hands slide into his thick, dark brown hair, drawing him deeper. We pull apart, and his eyes gleam with lust.

"You make my fantasies come to life," I whisper into his chest. He lifts my chin to peer into my eyes.

"I'll always make your fantasies come to life, Rosaline. What lies deep in my thoughts...well, let's just say you make me want to do things I've never done before. You're the one I want to share all my fantasies with."

A shiver runs up my spine.

Cristo.

"I want to share mine with you as well. If you only knew what filters through my mind."

He smirks, and his dimples indent. "I never played you as a dirty girl, Rosaline. My innocent flower."

I roll my eyes playfully at him. "There's nothing innocent about me. I'm the dirtiest of dirty jokes and the queen of dirty thoughts."

He snorts. He actually fucking snorts. His head tilts back, and a loose laugh escapes his handsome face. I pinch his hard abs, and it only makes him laugh harder.

"Queen of dirty thoughts, huh?" he teases.

Folding my arms to my chest, I flutter my long lashes at him.

God, he must see me as Rosa the Saint.

Cabron.

While I might be inexperienced, I certainly don't have an innocent mind. My *tía* Sugar says I have the face of an angel. Pfft. If only. My mind is as dirty as a man's. Little do they know I've imagined Santiago in so many ways. Jasmine and I always have our minds in the gutter when we talk about guys, but for me, it was only Santiago who I wanted to think about.

"I've been corrupted." I toss the words while looking around the shop. It's been a while since I've been here. He leans against the car, amused.

"Oh, yeah." His lips turn up, watching me. He thinks I'm shitting him.

"Uh-huh." Stalking toward him, I lean into his chest. "Three years ago, I saw a man completely naked. I walked in on him."

"What the fuck, Rosa." His forehead creases. "A man or someone your age then?"

"Shhh," I quip, running my finger down his chest. "Definitely a man. I didn't see his penis, junk, dick, or whatever you want to call it."

My lips straighten in a line, trying to contain my laugh. He's jealous. It's in the way he's gripping my waist and his jaw is clenching. I've never seen this side of him. I like it, so I continue.

"He was coming out of the shower when I walked in on him. Only got a clear view of his bare, tight ass. A perfect one, too. I've thought of that ass many times—"

"Seriously, Rosaline," his hands cup my ass as he leans in, his lips trail my neck to my ear, "you think I want to hear my girlfriend talk about another man's ass? Another man's naked body?" His dark chocolate brown eyes peer into mine.

Getting on my tiptoes, I place a kiss on his stubbled jaw. I still can't believe this man is mine. I've dreamed of him ever since I knew what a crush was.

"Can I finish now?"

"No!" he bites out.

Ignoring his outburst, I continue. "His backside striking gold. I thought of all the ways he'd bend me over—"

"Rosa, enough! Who is it? Jasmine's brother?"

I cringe. Jasmine's older brother, Miguel, is like a big brother to me.

"Heck no, gross."

"Then who?"

"I'm talking about you, Santi. *Cristo*, if you let me finish, I would have gotten to that part."

His face freezes. The jealous intensity is gone.

"I didn't know you were showering. And well, my virgin eyes got quite the view—and the thoughts that powered through my mind. Mmmmm."

That sexy smirk is back.

"'Striking gold? Tight ass? Ways he'd bend me over?'" he says arrogantly. The tip of his tongue runs between his lips. A little cocky smirk appears on his face. He reaches for my arms, placing my hands on his ass. "Go ahead, baby, get a feel. I'll even flex for you. It's all yours."

My ears burn hot. Ignoring my skin going crimson, I give his tight butt a good squeeze. Just like I imagined it.

"Now I've given you another fantasy. Thanks for letting me into your imagination." His tone is husky and beaming like a light candlestick.

"Cocky much? Just seconds ago, you were about to explode on me."

He pecks at my lips.

"This is what you do to me, Rosa. You make me feel things I've never felt before... Jealousy is new for me. I don't want any other man to occupy your fantasies. I want to be the only one." His words spark a fire within me, especially when his eyes caress me.

"It's always been you."

He nods, then inhales my scent in the crock of my neck. "And my fantasies are all you. You smell so damn good."

I laugh. "Like what?"

He takes my hand, walking us to the back of the shop. "You smell like you, sweet and flowery." He stands in front of the restroom. "Let me wash my hands. Then we will head out."

My heart races in my chest while I admire him. His defined cheekbones and stubble on his beautiful olive complexion. His brown hair is combed back, and a few strands fall to the side, adding to his handsome appearance. He truly takes my breath away.

Santiago straps my helmet on like last time, but now it has a different meaning. I jump on the back, wrapping my arms around his waist. The reserved seat is mine. No one else has had that spot. Santiago's hand glides down my leg, gentle and caressing. I'm not sure where we are going. He said for a ride. Mainly to get away from those who know us. He respects my aunt and Liam, and he doesn't want them to fight with me. Just because they love him doesn't mean they will love us together. I'm a little worried they might make a big deal about it.

My fingertips glide over the defined muscles of his torso, feeling the heat through his thin cotton T-shirt when I run my hand down his hard length. He groans through the light breeze as we kick up speed. I continue to knead his pulsing cock. We leave the busy city streets behind and venture down quiet back roads, where a light breeze enhances the scent of the ocean. I hold on tighter as we pick up speed, leaning into his broad back as he deftly navigates the twists and turns. Every time we brake at a stop sign or at the lights, Santiago leans back and grabs onto my leg. His thumb moves in a circular motion.

We make it to a hidden spot on the beach. I jump off the bike, and Santiago unstraps the helmet. The waves crash up against the rocks. I'm glad he brought us to a place where it's only us. I want to get as much alone time as we can.

"Are you all right, sweetheart?" Santiago asks as he slips his helmet off and hooks it onto the handlebars.

Sweetheart.

I dissolve every time he says it.

"Perfect," I breathe out, grinning like a fool. I'm happy. He makes me happy. We stand watching the waves crash and inhaling the breeze. Santiago stands behind me, his arms wrapped around my waist.

"Good."

We both fall into a comfortable silence, taking in the ocean's peacefulness around us.

"What's going on in that head of yours?" his husky voice rasps as he nibbles on my earlobe.

Leaning my head on his chest, I look up at him. "You come here a lot?"

His dark brows arch inquisitively. "That's what you're thinking?"

He has a thing for finding hidden treasures.

"No, just wondered."

"I just drive past it a lot when I'm riding. Now what I want to know is if you're okay after what happened at the party?"

I stiffen in his hold. I'm not sure if James was going to rape me. I've never heard of girls complaining about him or fearing him. All the girls want him. James grabbing me without my consent was definitely terrifying.

I shrug a shoulder. "I'm fine, honestly. You made me feel better. Santiago, you've always made me feel safe. But that's not what I'm thinking about." I lock eyes with him and notice his features soften from the worried expression he had. He kisses my temple tenderly.

"I'll always keep you safe, Rosa. What's going on, baby? What's bothering you? Let me fix it." His tone holds a rough edge, and the weight of his words conveys seriousness.

I believe him without hesitation. I turn and wrap my arms around his neck. What I love about Santiago is that he wants to fix everything for those he loves and cares about. But who's going to fix his problems? He's carried the weight his mom burdened him with at such a young age.

"I'm thinking about what Liam and my t will say about us.

Honestly, I couldn't care less. What I'm worried about is, will you pull away?" My words drip with insecurity.

His lips brush mine, then suck on my bottom lip. "Rosa, when I said you're mine, I meant it. No one could keep me apart from you, flower. It might get ugly. Your *tia* might not approve of us. Liam, well… that one will be tough. Liam has always been protective of you, which I'm grateful for. We could be over-thinking it. Your *tia* loves me." He kisses my cheek, nose, then lips. "I'll be here until the day you decide you don't want me. Even then, I'm not sure I can keep away." He smirks.

Instead of a response, I crash my lips on his. Santiago parts his lips with eagerness, giving me exactly what I need.

He's wrong. I'll always want him. I gave him my heart and soul all those years ago when I first stepped foot on his doorstep. The first night he called me flower, little did I know he'd be the one I'd want forever with.

16

CHRIST, the way she kisses, you would think she's had more experience. Thankfully, I am the only one who has tasted her lips, and I've been her one and only. She may not be my first, but she's my first in all the ways that count: my first girlfriend and the first I've made love to. There will be many more firsts we will share.

We pull apart, both of us out of breath. "I'll always want you, Santiago," Rosa drawls, her voice breathless.

"I'm glad because I feel the same." My words are robust with honesty. A pillar couldn't keep me away from the woman standing before me. I walk toward a pile of rocks that looks like it's set up for a fire pit and grab one. "Have you ever skipped rocks before?"

She looks up as she slips her shoes and socks off. "No, can't say I have," she replies, joining me at the edge of the water.

Angling myself, I bend, then flick my wrist. The rock spins, bouncing into the water.

"That's so cool." She picks up a rock and inspects it. "Is this good? Or does it need to be a certain type…I mean, shape?"

"It needs to be flat and light." I reach for a good-sized rock and hand it to her. "You have to angle yourself like this." Standing behind her, I tilt her—bending her slightly. Rosa leans forward, ass up, aligning with my now growing erection. "Not forward, Rosa, to the side."

She wiggles her ass to the side.

Fuck.

"Then firmly wrap your index finger around the rock. Okay, now bend your wrist backward and take your swing, baby."

Without a second thought, she takes her swing, and the rock sinks into the water. "Arg, I'm trying again," she whines, collecting another rock. She tosses it, and it sinks once more. She huffs, then paces up and down, looking for a rock. She picks one up and then throws it aside, searching for the right one.

I lean on my bike, amused at how riled up she's getting over getting it right.

It took me years of practice to get it. My dad taught me at a young age, and when I finally got the hang of it, he was gone.

My eyes follow her like I'm in a trance. She tries again. I laugh when she screams. It's obvious it sunk.

Rosa throws her hands up, and her feet sink in the sand. "You think this is funny, huh? Mr. Big Shot is good at every-thing," Rosa taunts. "Of course, you're experienced in everything."

"I've had a lot of practice," I coax.

Her hands fall on her hips. My lips tip up into a smirk while her eyes taper, holding onto every ounce of control she has over me.

"Oh, I know. You showed me last night." She frowns. "Don't worry. I'll get better," she mumbles.

Now I'm confused.

"Are we still talking about skipping rocks? Because I was, but it sounds like you're talking about the great sex we had last night." I beckon with my finger. "C'mon here, Rosa."

She sways nearer. Pulling her to me, I lift her chin.

"I'm going to make one thing clear, sweetheart. Regarding us, it's not about practice or experience. The chemistry we have is beyond anything I've ever experienced. We're like gasoline and kerosene. We fucking lit the night. You're all I see, Rosaline Acosta," I say, hearing the truth in my words. There's a difference between wanting to get your dick wet and wanting to give pleasure to the woman you need.

Her chin trembles, and her eyes water. "You say the sweetest, hottest, most perfect things. You make me melt. You'll have to scoop me up to take me home."

With my thumb, I wipe a stray tear. "It's the truth," I whisper, nuzzling her neck with pepper kisses. "What I can't stop thinking about is what my queen of dirty thoughts has been thinking about. What kind of dirty things does she do to me?" It's even more beautiful when I have her blushing.

Her ears turn crimson. She giggles. "There are so many things where I'd blow you out of the water, and I'm definitely a better ride than Lucy."

My head tilts back into a full, throaty laugh.

She's too fucking adorable.

Lucy is the name I gave my Harley when I bought it two years ago.

"Prove it," I challenge.

Rosa always loves a moral challenge. "All right, I'll prove it here...right now."

A surge of excitement runs through me, as if I were about to conquer the highest peak.

Rosa steps back, placing her index finger on her lip, and stares at the water. Knowing Rosa this long has its advantages. She is unsure, an overthinker, and is likely giving herself a pep talk. I sit and wait and observe my girlfriend. I study every curve and contour of my girlfriend's body, admiring the way her perfect round ass fills out her tight jeans. The denim clings to her hips like a second skin, accentuating all the right places and making it impossible for me to look away. Those hips are a work of art. Fuck, and those hips are perfect for holding onto.

"Santiago?"

I blink as Rosa calls my name. She has the ability to leave me spellbound.

"Yes, baby?"

"Take a seat on your bike with your back toward the handlebars," she instructs.

I can't help but feel a surge of eagerness and desire, though I keep my lips pursed to hide my smile. I do as she says.

"Okay, now what?" I say as I lean into my bike, trying to relax. It's not like you can get comfortable on a bike, but whatever she's planning must be good if I'm being asked to sit the opposite way. When I lift my head to glance at Rosa, my heart goes crazy.

Ba-Boom. Ba-Boom.

My breathing picks up, then gets strangled by the amount of heavy breaths I'm taking. My dick is enlarging to its capacity in my jeans, hitting the zipper. A throttle groan withdraws from me.

Rosa sheds her shirt, followed by her bra. She tugs her jeans off, leaving her in a blue thong.

Beautiful. Sexy. Hot. Mine.

As she moves closer, her hips sway in a mesmerizing rhythm, and I am left speechless by the intensity of my desire for her. I could die a lucky man tonight. Wait, fuck that—no dying, then some other motherfucker would have her. My gaze follows her every move. Rosa straddles the bike, sliding toward me. Her fingers brush my stomach, causing goosebumps in their wake when she slips my shirt off. I'll let her do anything she wants. She's in control. My gaze is glued to her beautiful face and body. If this is just scratching the surface of her fantasies, then I'm in for a lifetime of heaven. Because this is a man's wet dream, getting fucked on his bike. She's so damn wet it bleeds into the seat, marking her territory.

My words are caught in the back of my throat. My hands are itching to touch her. When I reach for her, she shakes her head and unzips my jeans. She has me lift my ass to shrug them down as far as they'll go.

"Rosaline," I manage to say, my tone dripping in seduction. Reaching for her heavy, full breast, I brush her nipple with my thumb. Warm, elaborate strokes with her tongue coat my cock. She gags, and that only has me groaning in pleasure. "That's it, baby. You're doing so amazing," I praise. Wrapping her hair around my hand, I push her deep to the base. When I know I'm close, I lift her head. "Fuck, baby, that was so damn sexy. It's too good. I'm so close. I don't want to cum yet. You're fucking sexy." One hand goes to her soft, delicate neck, wrapping around it, and the other goes to her clit, inserting two fingers.

She moans when I begin to pump in her. I kiss her with a crazy amount of need. Her body, her taste, her heart, her soul summons me. Ripping her thong off, I lift her without breaking the kiss and have her straddle me. As our lips meet, the sound of contented sighs fills the air. Our bodies move in perfect sync, and waves of pleasure pulse through us with each embrace. Gripping onto her hips, I swirl her around. We melt into each other, lost in the ecstasy of our embrace.

Rosa moves her hips in a rhythmic circle, pressure building inside her. Fuck. She tightens, and my cock swells. I've never felt so damn intoxicated like I am now. We part from our kiss, and I can't help but admire her red, swollen lips and hooded eyes.

"Oh, Santi," Rosa cries when my mouth covers her breast. She arches her back, her hair hanging loose and swaying in the light breeze. The palm of my hand roams her delicate skin, then lands on her ass. She's a hell of a dream.

Should I be worried that someone might drive up and see my girl buck naked? Although I'd cover her from anyone seeing what's mine, I wouldn't mind them seeing how good my girl rides me. Then I'd stab them in the eye because no one walks away breathing when they lay eyes on the woman who's captured my soul like a fly caught in a web.

My tongue brushes her engorged nipples. She tastes so damn good. When she bounces on my cock, all thoughts are incoherent. My eyes want to roll back at how crazy she's making me. I'm losing it. Her walls clamp on my dick until it's squeezing the hell out of it. "Goddamn, sweetheart, you're making me crazy." I'm losing control. I want to flip us over and fuck her hard, rough, and raw on the ground. However, for now, I'm letting my little flower take control just this once. Maybe.

"Bounce on it, baby, like this." With my hand on her waist, I lift her up and down, watching as my cock goes in and out. Thank the fuck my bike is not some flimsy thing. She rides me hard. Rough. We're both close to losing it—our climax is so near. Before I can catch my words, they slip out. "Marry me, Rosa. Marry me, baby. Be my wife." My voice strangles with raw vulnerability.

Her beautiful glossy brown eyes meet mine. She rocks faster, and her arms wrap around the nape of my neck. She moans with each thrust. "Do you mean it?" she whispers, our mouths so close.

I kiss her hard. I might be losing my mind, but I know what I want.

Tearing from her swollen, soft lips, I respond, "I mean it, Rosaline, not because I'm induced with lust, and not because you're riding my dick like a damn queen. I love you, Rosaline Acosta. I'm so crazy fucking in love with you."

Her mouth crashes on mine, sucking the living daylights out

of me. Thank God she didn't freak out when I said the *L* word because I surprised myself. It's impulsive of me, but it feels right. One might think it's too soon to fall in love, but I've known and loved her all my life. It might have been in a different way, I knew the night Dominic told me she was going on dates that I'd fallen in love with her.

The intensity of her climax reaches its peak, and she cries out in ecstasy, her voice echoing against the crashing waves in front of us. "Yes, baby," she breathes between moans, "I'll marry you. I want this, too. I love you so much," she says, her words filled with pure love and desire.

As if on cue, our bodies unite in an ultimate release, like two halves finally coming together to create a whole. Our connection is electric, pulsing with passion and love. Just like the tide that ebbs and flows before us, we come crashing down from our euphoric high, savoring every moment as it washes over us.

There are no other words to put it. I'm a selfish asshole. I want to keep her because I'm terrified of losing her. Now, I finally see what's been in front of me my whole damn life. Only now, she's mine—the queen in my story. I want to make her my wife. It's impulsive of me, but fuck it. When have I ever taken something for myself?

It's crazy that I'm asking her to marry me while my dick is in her, but it's as romantic as it gets. It would be wild to ask a woman to marry you when you just asked her to be your girlfriend the night before, yet this is not any girl. This is my Rosa, the girl who always stood by my side, the girl I've always cared for. But now my love for her is different. It changed throughout these past weeks. I'm in love with her.

We're panting, entirely out of breath, still wrapped in each other's arms. Rosa leans back to peer at me. "What's the verdict? Am I a better ride than Lucy?" she pants, her breasts rising and falling.

Fuck me.

Those lips curve ever so slightly when I give her a wicked smile. Such innocent words with a wicked meaning behind them. "Hell yeah, baby. I've never come like a damn fountain." I look down to see us both dripping wet. My jeans soaked. "We made a mess of ourselves, didn't we?" She looks down, then blushes. I kiss her lips. "Let's get you cleaned up."

She wiggles off of me, and her legs wobble as she tries to stand. Rosa leaves me speechless. She's like a beautiful painting come to life. The ocean serves as her backdrop, its waves softly crashing onto the shore. The sunlight cascades down on her, reflecting toward the tranquil blue-green waters below.

17

ROSALINE

MY MIND IS in a complete lust haze, and my body feels like I jumped repeatedly on a trampoline. I'm still trying to process it all. This was erotic, wild—mind-blowing sex. I know I have nothing to go by other than last night, which was amazing. He was slow and gentle, and he made love to me with so much tenderness, but right now, we fucked like wild animals. I rode him like I was on a racetrack, hitting first place.

He asked me to marry him, to be his wife. His voice is husky, vulnerable, and his words linger in my head. Does he still want to marry me now that we are down from the crest of our orgasm? I answered him honestly. He's all I've ever dreamed of. Of course, I want to marry him. I know what I want.

Santiago hops off his bike, tucking himself back in his jeans. He's soaked around the crotch. I'm sure it's more my mess than his. "Hold on, babe," he says, opening the saddle bag and taking a clean shop towel out. He crouches down, cleaning between my legs. My face heats at how close he is to my private area. It took everything in me to strip down for him in public. It's not like there's anyone around, but it still took some major guts to do it. Jasmine always said to embrace it, and I did. The heat in his eyes gave me a boost of confidence that he liked what he saw.

He gets back up and collects my clothes. The sun rains down on his bare chest, highlighting his golden skin. Santiago is gorgeous, which is why many women fawn over him. He's built with his broad shoulders and muscular biceps—he's muscle all around.

I bite my lip, peering up at him. He towers over me as his gaze rolls up and down my naked body. "You're the most beautiful woman I've ever laid eyes on, Rosaline." He hands me my clothes. "Get dressed, sweetheart. Then we will talk about our plans."

Plans? Like marriage? I nod. My heart races out of my chest. "Okay."

Cristo.

Get a hold of yourself, Rosa, before your heart gives out. I haven't spoken to Jasmine. I texted her last night, letting her know Santiago picked me up. She's going to shit her pants when she finds out we went from being boyfriend and girlfriend to being engaged in less than two days. It's insta love.

Once I'm dressed, I walk toward Santiago. He's staring at the rolling waves and smoking a cigarette. Standing beside him, I look up at him. "You should stop smoking. It's bad for your health," I scold him like a child. That only makes him chuckle. He flicks the cigarette butt onto the sandy ground, then pivots his boots to snuff out the flame.

"Already being the protective soon-to-be wife. Huh?" He grins.

I reward him with a luminous smile mirroring his.

"After smoking since I was fifteen, I'm ready to quit. I have a new addiction...You."

Oh God. My heart.

Soon-to-be wife. Just the idea of being called his wife throbs at my insides. I'm tempted to throw myself into the rolling waves to cool down. "I'm glad to be of help to your health, old man," I tease.

He raises one dark brow in response. A smirk so evil bends his lips, and his eyes drop to the curve of my neck. I take a step back.

"Old man?" he muses, taking a step forward. "This old man, who is eight years older than you and not twenty years older, can catch his prey within seconds and eat his prey in one sitting until she trembles." Santiago's lips twitch into a cocky grin.

His wicked mouth sends a shiver down my spine. His eyes go back to my neck. My ticklish spot. A sharp, vibrating scream comes out, and I run. My feet struggle through the damp, mushy sand. A deep chuckle echoes behind me, taking me back to our childhood days when he would cheer me up with tickles whenever I was down. It's a reminder of how he always knew how to make me smile. He catches me in record time, both of us toppling over on the wet sand with him on top of me.

I squirm, shaking in laughter as he tickles my neck. "Stop," I choke with laughter, trying to catch my breath. "You're going to make me pee my pants." I wriggle.

He places a kiss on my nose and rolls over next to me with his elbow buried in the sand and his hand resting on his temple. "Told you I'd catch you in seconds."

"Only because it's hard to run in the sand."

He scoffs. "Only because I was the fastest in track and baseball."

I tilt my head back to take in the vibrant sky above, and then turn to meet his gaze. His intense stare makes me lose all sense of control, and I can't help but feel myself melting.

"High school was a long time ago… for you."

"So? I work out."

"Good point," I say.

He grins, and then his expression turns serious. "I love you, Rosaline. I've always loved you, but now I'm in love with you. You're all I think about." He wraps a strand of my hair on his finger. "These two days have been the best of my life. I know it's crazy as fuck, but I want to marry you. I feel like I've been with you a lifetime, just differently. Listen, if you want to elope this weekend or next, we can. If you want to wait until you graduate from college, we can, flower. All I know is I can't live without you." His voice is raw and worshipful.

Oh, lord.

Any woman would be lucky to have Santiago fall in love with them. Many have tried to capture his heart but failed. Santiago has never looked at a woman like he's looking at me. I would know since I've always been around. It thrills me to know I'm the one he's fallen in love with, who captured his heart, and who he wants to spend forever with.

My gaze lingers on his lips. "I love you, Santiago. I've always been in love with you from the very first time I understood what love meant. We shouldn't wait. I want us to get married this weekend. Santiago, I want to be your wife, the woman you come home to and wake up to."

He breathes out slowly as if he'd been hoping for my reaction to match his own.

He leans to kiss my lips. "I want that too, flower"—kiss — "to wake up to you every morning"—kiss — "to lie in bed with you every night"—kiss — "and for you to be my forever." Kiss. "Vegas, it is. This weekend, baby."

My smile grows. His dimples deepen with the vast grin he's wearing.

"I CAN'T BELIEVE this is happening. I've dreamed of being your maid of honor, and I can't be there. You know I'm happy for you. In fact, I'm so excited I might throw up on this table," Jasmine whines, with her elbows resting on the table, hands laced.

"Please don't," I say.

Jasmine got food poisoning at the party and could barely even check her messages. I have been sitting here for an hour, filling her in on everything that's happened.

"I know you want to be my maid of honor, and you will, but this weekend, it will be just Santiago and me. We plan on telling everyone once we are a married couple. In the meantime, Santiago is going to get things situated, getting us a place of our own. Then we will have a wedding for the family." I breathe out a mouthful.

Jasmine hugs the straw with her pouty lips, her long Dollar Tree faux lashes batting at me. She's a frugal shopper like me and gives zero fucks. "Fine, I guess I'll have to wait," she grumbles, setting her iced coffee down. "So, tell me, how is he in bed, you lucky bitch?"

I bite my lip, thinking about Santiago and how we spent Sunday in bed all day. Dominic has an apartment, and Mark is helping him build some furniture. We locked ourselves in his bedroom and ravished each other. He showed me how much he loves me.

Rachel came in and out of the house a few times. It's not like she acknowledges Santiago. The woman is plain evil. She's never taking care of her kids. She plays the part, especially around people. Around my *tia*, she acts like a doting mother.

"It's private. All I'm going to say is... amazing," I say, smirking while walking toward the packs of sugar. Jasmine follows behind.

"Aye, Rosa." She leans on the counter, fanning herself and then flicking a crumb around.

"What is it? I know something's up. You're staring at a crumb a little too long."

She sighs. "What about college, Rosa? Are you planning to go back?" She peers at me. "I'm not trying to rain on your parade, but maybe you should wait on getting married, figure out school and all that. You wanted to go to the school in Oregon." Jasmine's eyes soften.

I know she means well. We've talked about this throughout high school. Our plans were to move out of California and start a new adventure.

"I'm still planning on going to college. I'm not sure if I'll go back to Oregon. I haven't decided. Santiago wants me to go. He knows how much it meant for me to attend that art school." I'm getting flustered. "How are things with you and Tank?"

Jasmine had planned to attend the same college as Tank in New York. She was terrified to move out there, and she had fears he would change into a stuck-up jock. It would have been a big move, and she wasn't ready. So they decided to test their relationship long distance, and if it works out, she will move to attend college there, or wherever he goes, once he's drafted.

"Things are good, but some girls tagged him in a photo, and it bugs the shit out of me. They're taking photos with him. It's not the pictures though. It's how they're looking all dreamy-eyed at him that bugs me. I asked if he hung out with them, but he said no."

"Do you want to move out there?" I ask.

A pang in my chest guilts me. Maybe it's me she doesn't want to leave behind. If she wants to go, I'll stay here and finish up. After all, now I have a reason. Santiago is my reason.

"I don't know. I'm a little nervous. You know he has his full-ride football scholarship. I'm just worried I'll go out there, and he'll find someone better. He's always been the popular guy."

She stares off into space. Jasmine's lack of self-assurance surprises me. She has always been the one to smooth out my doubts and lift me with her unwavering confidence. I hug Jasmine. It's what she needs.

She squeezes me tight. "I'm scared to move so far and be alone—the what-ifs keep cycling in my head. He's going to go pro. We all know it. What if things change, and he wants some chick with more experience? You know the way those types of girls are. They look for a meal ticket. Girls like that will find ways to ruin relationships." Jasmine sniffs. "If things go south, I'll be all alone with a broken heart," she says, pulling away.

A broken laugh escapes her lips, revealing her emotions.

"I know it's scary. It's a big step moving in with Tank. I know he loves you, Jasmine, but if you don't trust him, you should tell him how you feel."

"I'm just warring with myself." She sighs. "I'll talk to him. And I do trust him. It's the bitches I don't trust." She laughs.

"You're beautiful, Jazzy. There's no competition. Tank looks at you like you're the most beautiful girl," I say while tossing my cup in the trash.

We walk to our vehicles with Jasmine's words digging into the back of my mind. Should we wait to get married?

ONCE I'M HOME, I sit and have a quick bite to eat. My *tia* left me a bean and cheese burrito wrapped in foil before she headed to bed.

My heart aches. I haven't seen Santiago since Sunday night. We both have been busy. I've been painting. I'm thinking of opening an Etsy shop, getting ready for my next year in school, and leaving for Vegas. Just to think, by the end of this weekend, I'll be his wife. Butterflies flutter in my belly. I know what I want, and being Santiago's wife is all I've ever wanted. The judgmental people will say I'm too young, but when you love someone more than anything else in this world, age becomes just a number. There's no better man than the man who's been my rock and who knows me better than anyone. It feels right.

After taking a shower and moisturizing, I change into my comfortable night shorts and tank top. As I towel dry my hair, I feel the urge to pick up a paintbrush and create something beautiful. Pulling out my paints and a fresh canvas, I close my eyes and see the painting I want to create.

My phone pings with a text message.

Santi: *Baby, open your window so I can come in.*

What the hell? Excitement radiates throughout my body. Opening the window, I find him climbing the tree by my window. He looks handsome in a black shirt and black jeans. A strand of his dark brown hair falls to his brows. He looks incredibly sexy, with a sharp jaw and rough stubble.

"I missed you, sweetheart," Santiago whispers, his lips brushing against mine. "Two days without you is too damn much." He holds my hand as he walks to the door and locks it, before pressing his lips into mine. Our kiss is heated and passionate, with a thousand bolts of electricity running up and down my body. My nipples brush along his chest. That rewards me with a groan. He swats my butt, pulling away.

"I missed you too. Did you just get out of work?" I ask.

He sits on the bed, pulling me down onto his lap.

"A while ago. I went home to shower first—then to see you. I didn't think you'd appreciate me getting your room full of oil."

"I wouldn't mind. I love all of you—what drives you, your passions, and your desires." I mean every word. I'll never look down on him just because of his profession. His eyes darken with lust.

"Rosa." A low groan escapes his lips as his tongue glides along my collarbone and then lingers behind my ear, tracing a path of desire.

"Hmm."

"Rosaline, I love you. Is it crazy to think the love of my life was under my nose all these years?" Santiago murmurs.

"Not crazy at all. I've felt the same way my whole life. I've been waiting for you to catch up," I whisper.

Santiago blows kisses along my neck, sliding the strap of my tank top down.

"I'm caught up, baby. I'm here"—kiss — "forever" — Kiss. "Now that I caught you, I'm never letting you go. You're all I need."

I throw my head to the side. The heat of his lips sends a pool of desire between my legs. When he stops and lifts my chin to peer at him, I groan, missing his lips. He laughs.

"Don't worry, I'll take care of you in a minute, but first, I have something to give you." He leans to the side, digging into his pocket.

I hadn't even noticed the bulge on the side. I gasp when he opens a small black box—a diamond ring… an engagement ring.

"I know I didn't propose in the most romantic way, kneeling for you—the traditional way. But in that moment, it all felt right. You bring out emotions in me that I never thought were possible." He turns from me, exhaling. Santiago is the type to bottle up his emotions. He clears his throat. "You drive me crazy, Rosa. You make me want to race to the altar, build you a house, and fill it with my babies." His brown eyes grow wider as he realizes what he just said about having children.

The thought of having children with Santiago one day has my insides bursting into flames. It excites me to the bone. Can you imagine little Santiagos running around? Oh God, I could melt into a puddle. Seeing the shock on his face, my excitement shoots through the roof. My heart races when I realize that we both want the same thing. He's probably worried that I'll panic or reject him, but I want it all—every bit of it.

The gut-wrenching emotion is back. It is all too good to be true. I've been left behind before. What if he leaves me at the altar… or what if someone intervenes?

18

SANTIAGO

FUCK, I'm moving too fast. I know it. I'm not an experienced man when it comes to relationships. Obviously.

Truth is, I want all those important parts of life with her. I want my kids to have the life I never had, with two parents who love them. I know Rosa would want the same after what her mother did to her. At least, I hope so. She had her aunt, but she's always felt that empty gap—a mother's love.

My eyes flicker to Rosa, who's staring blankly at the wall. Damnit, I broke her, scaring the shit out of her.

Why couldn't you take it slow, Santiago? Get to the altar first, then talk about having kids in the future.

"Flower, I didn't mean to spring it all on you. We can take it all a little at a time. I didn't mean to scare you—"

"It doesn't freak me out, Santiago. It excites me. My dream has always been to have a family someday. I'm glad we're on the same page." She beams like a glowworm.

I can't help but grin at Rosa. Her smile takes my breath away every damn time.

I slide the ring onto her finger, then press a kiss to her knuckles. The ring is stunning on her, even though it's not extravagant or flashy. However, it came from the heart. I sold one of my motorcycles to buy Rosa her engagement and wedding rings. Although I have a good amount of money saved up, I'll be using it for our apartment. My plans are to move out once Rosa and I announce it. I want Liam and her aunt to see I have a home for her. To her family, it might be illicit for us to be in love knowing my age or that I've known her since she was young, and I barely have my life together. But fuck, I love her.

"It's beautiful," she whispers to my lips.

"Rosa, who are you talking to?" her aunt Andrea asks, standing on the other side of the door.

Rosa stiffens on my lap. Rubbing her back, I soothe her and nod.

"No one, *Tia*, I'm watching TV and getting ready for bed."

"Okay, did you eat your burrito I left you?"

"Yes, *Tia*, thank you. *Muy bueno*," Rosa shouts while I lift her shirt up. My tongue moves circles around her hard nipples.

"You're welcome, sweetheart. Good night, *mija.*"

"Good night, *Tia.*"

We can hear Rosa's aunt head back downstairs to her bedroom. I continue my quest on Rosa's breasts. Her breath quickens with each lap of my tongue. I lay her on the bed, and, not so gently, I strip her bare.

Liam has his own place, so I know he won't be walking up the stairs.

Two hours left to Vegas. Rosa is using one of my jackets balled into a makeshift pillow, pressed on the passenger door window.

She's been asleep for the last hour. She's absolutely sexy. In a couple of hours, she'll be my wife. I hate hiding, although it's for the best so I can get our home in place. There is nothing that would make me happier than parading her around as the woman I love. At least this weekend, we can be all over each other without having to worry about who we will bump into. I can't help but feel a wave of pride wash over me as I think about Rosa being mine in every way. It's pure happiness and contentment that I can't quite put into words.

My memories trace back to when Rosa was nine, and I was seventeen. Her aunt Andrea asked me if I could watch her. Rosa was sick, but Andrea couldn't miss her shift at the diner and Liam was watching his grandmother in the hospital.

Rosa lies on my bed with a wet cloth over her forehead to help with her fever.

I just gave her Tylenol twenty minutes ago, so hopefully, she'll start to feel better. Rosa's lips curl upward, and her doe eyes are centered on the TV, watching My Little Pony.

"How are you feeling?"

"Good. Better." She crinkles her nose. "Tissue," she demands, her hand out and eyes not leaving her show.

"Okay, I'll get you a tissue. I won't scold you on manners since you're sick."

She frowns. "Sorry," Rosa whispers.

"It's okay. I was just joking. How about I make you some soup?"

She nods and tucks herself into a red, fluffy blanket. When I reenter the room ten minutes later, I am carrying a tray with her favorite soup: chicken and stars. Her face lights up as soon as she spots me.

"Soup fit for a queen," I announce, bowing playfully.

She laughs. Without hesitation, she takes the spoon and devours the soup, slurping loudly on the broth. I lie next to her, watching Animal Planet.

"How come you didn't go to school?" she asks, licking the rest of the soup on her lips.

"I stayed to watch you, kid. Let's hope the guys don't get sick, or I'll have to stay to watch them, too."

She nods and goes back to watching TV. I ruffle her hair.

"What are you watching?"

"I'm learning about gray wolves," she mumbles, taking another slurp of her soup. "Did you know gray wolves mate for life and are fiercely loyal to their pack? They don't cheat on their mates. They love them forever." Another slurp. "I wish humans mated for life, because then I would know who my daddy is, and my mom wouldn't have left. Your daddy would have stayed, and then maybe your mom would be nice. I wish people could be like the gray wolves." She slides the tray onto the end of the bed and sits up to turn to me. "Are you going to get married one day and be with her forever like a mate? Because you can't break her heart."

In this moment, my heart aches as I see the impact of her mother's absence and not knowing who her father is. It has me wondering if she will crave—when she's older—to be loved in a way she's never experienced. Will she want to be cherished and loved? I hope so. I hope when she's older, she finds the right man who will treat her right because this little girl watching me needs it and deserves it.

Maybe in some ways, Rosa and I are alike. We both crave to be loved, to be the first choice, but both our parents took the easy route and made us second.

"I'm not sure, but if I find the right girl, yeah, I'll marry her in a heartbeat, flower, and I'll never let her go." My gaze is downcast toward Rosa, who has the saddest puppy eyes. Her eyes water.

"Oh, are you okay? Are you feeling sick, or is something hurting you?"

"No...I'm just scared you'll forget me if you get married. I don't like the girls you hang out with."

I pull her into a hug.

"Aww, Rosa. Me and you are best friends. I could never forget you, *and honestly, I don't plan on getting married soon." Or ever. "You're my girl." I wink at her, and that puts a smile on her face. "How about you take a nap?"*

"Okay," she says, snuggling into the blanket.

A LOUD GROAN startles me from my memory. Rosa sits up and stretches, and her shirt rides up. I don't hide my intense stare roaming every sharp curve of hers. Rosa is a goddess. She might not see it, but I do, along with other men who always gawk at my oblivious fiancée.

"Babe, eyes on the road."

"It's your fault. You look so damn good, baby."

She huffs. So oblivious.

"I'm wearing jeans and a shirt, and I'm positive I have drool dried on my face." She laughs, wiping her face. "I was probably snoring. It's a major turnoff."

"There is nothing about you I find unappealing. In fact, everything about you ignites my passion." I pat the seat next to me. "Come here, I need you close."

She doesn't hesitate.

"You look handsome with those sunglasses. Don't let me get started on how the hem of your shirt hugs your biceps." Her fingernails rake my arm, causing goosebumps in her wake. "Those dimples are hot." She leans, her soft, plump lips brushing on my cheek. My arousal grows.

My hands grip the steering wheel, my gaze pinned on the road. Just a simple kiss ignites a fire in me. It's like she has the power to bring me to life. Every time she's around, I feel like I'm truly living.

"Rosa." My voice is gruff and pleading for her to stop before I pull over and pin her down, showing everyone how very much mine she is.

"Yes?" She breathes on my arm, making the hairs and my

dick stand up.

My body overheats like an old car. "Rosaline, you're making it hard not to pull over and fuck you."

Her gaze drops to my erection. "Oh."

"Yeah, 'oh,'" I quip.

Rosa's lush lips curve into a coy smile.

"Twenty-five more minutes. You can see the strip from here —" I gasp when she tugs on my zipper. "Rosa, what are you doing?"

"What does it look like?"

"What happened to my shy, innocent, quiet Rosa?" I drawl as she reaches around my boxers.

"Oh, she's still very much in there, but it's you. You're my home. When I'm with you, I can let loose. Remember, I'm the queen of dirty thoughts." She laughs as I aimlessly lift my ass so she can snug my pants down a little. My hands slide up on the steering wheel to make room for her.

"You can always be yourself with me, Rosa. I love your dirty mind."

The air feels like it's getting knocked out of me as she strokes and her mouth wraps around it. Thank God the highway is not bumper to bumper, only a couple of semis and vehicles passing me. My windows are tinted, that's a bonus. I've never had a blow job while driving.

With one hand on the steering wheel, I grip her ponytail. Her head bobs up and down. It takes a great amount of effort to stay focused while driving when I can hear her slurp. My mouth goes dry as I grunt my release while keeping my eyes on the road.

"Damn, Rosa."

She gives me a haughty smile, pleased with herself.

"You complete me in every way."

"I feel the same. I couldn't be happier. I'm glad it's me you fell for."

I turn into the hotel's garage parking lot. When I finally find parking, I turn to Rosa and press my lips on hers. Like usual, they part—as eager for my touch as I am hers. She'll always be my girl, the one I'll reach for, the one who really knows me—the one I'm destined to love.

Does she think the same?

19

ROSALINE

WE MOVE WITH URGENT HASTE, practically sprinting to our room as if our lives depend on it. Our bodies are aflame with desire. The intense heat generated between us could easily spark a blaze in the building. Every touch, every breath, fuels the fire that smolders between us. We stumble into the room and lock the door. He's turned me into an addict, craving everything Santiago.

He pins me to the wall, and his hot, soft lips melt on my collarbone. A tug on my jeans has me moan as his fingers caress my belly. Desperately, I remove his shirt and run my hands down his V-line to his waistband. He shivers at my touch. With that, my heart races, knowing I make him react this way. It's me he wants. *Forever.* Until death, do us part.

Santiago's mouth crashes on mine, teeth clashing as my fingers slide into his hair. His calloused hands slide up my thighs, squeezing as he lifts me, walking us to the bed.

"Strip for me, flower, then spread your legs," he commands.

I do as he says. Licking my lips, savoring his taste on my lips, I slip my shirt off, then unclasp my bra while staring into his lust-filled eyes. I'm left in my underwear, but before I can tug them off, Santiago does it for me. "So beautiful." His finger runs along my clit. "So wet for me, Rosa."

My body shakes as he thrusts in his finger.

"Look at me, baby." His voice is raw.

Biting my lip, I keep my eyes trained on his, watching as he kneels for me. Santiago is incredibly handsome. His tattoos make him look sexy and gruff at the same time.

His tongue swipes down while I try to compose myself and not let my eyes roll back. I cry his name as he nips, sucks, then thrusts. Every time, my orgasms hit a high peak.

He tugs his jeans off, along with his boxers, leaving him completely naked. His dick hangs heavy, dripping with pre-cum. He gives it a couple of strokes. I don't know why, but I find that hot as hell. He smirks, watching me bite my lip. He's sexy as fuck.

Santiago, his tall frame looming over me, devours my breasts. When he slides inside of me, my nails dig into the taut muscles and intricate tattoos that cover his back. Each thrust sends shivers down my spine, a mix of pleasure and pain. The sunlight from the hotel window dims, making his body glisten with the sheen of sweat.

"Harder," I scream, not caring who can hear us.

"Fuck, baby," he groans as he thrusts like a devil plowing into the gates of hell.

The weight of him on top of me is almost suffocating, but I can't get enough. Santiago kisses with so much emotion a stray tear slides down. His lips press on each tear, and I melt by how sweet and kind he is to me.

"I love you, Rosaline. God, I love you. Say, 'I'm yours, forever.' Let me hear, baby."

"I'm yours, Santiago. Forever. And you're mine."

"Yeah, baby. I'm yours. Now, come for me, sweetheart."

Our bodies shake, he groans his release, and we both fall from the highest mountain.

"Dammit. I'm starting to think you were sex crazy before being with me, and it's making me jealous." He rolls off me. "You've been fucking me like you have been filming in some porn movie."

I snort, very unladylike.

"Seriously, the way you fuck me, blow me, and the way you feel when I'm inside you is astonishing. My body, my heart, my soul will only ever crave you, baby. You marked—etched your name all over me."

"Good, because I feel the same way," I say, turning to my side, elbow propped on a pillow.

He replies with an arched brow. "You think I fuck like a porn star?" he asks and gives me one of those smiles.

I smack a pillow in his face. "That's not what I meant."

"So, you don't think so?" he pouts.

My body shakes with laughter. He's so ridiculous, and of course, I think he does. The man knows what he's doing.

Santiago rolls on top of me, nuzzling in the crook of my neck. "I'm teasing you. I know what you mean, and I'm glad we're on the same level." He pecks at my cheek. I can feel him go hard underneath me. "I'm so ready for another round, baby. The thing is, I want to wait until tonight when we're married. I want to make love to my wife."

My smile widens. I'm so giddy.

Wife. Ahh.

"I can't wait."

He chuckles. "Me neither, Rosa." Just then, there's a knock at the door. Santiago rolls off me, reaching for his boxers. "Fuck, baby, I forgot. I have a surprise for you." Santiago grabs my clothes, tossing them to me. "Get dressed." He walks to the door while I race to put my clothes on. "Hold on," he shouts.

My eyes widen when I see my best friend walk in with Reese. "Surprise!" she screams. I throw my arms around her, pulling her into a tight hug. "Santiago asked us to come." She beams.

Stepping back from Jasmine, I get on my tip toes and plant a kiss on Santiago's lips. "That's sweet of you,"

Reese scoffs, barging in. "Well, he had no choice. He needs his best man beside him. Of course, I only had to bring the maid of honor with me because Santiago said so." Reese signals toward Jasmine.

Jasmine stands with her hands on her hips. "I told you I could drive myself, but you insisted on us driving together. When I mentioned inviting my boyfriend along, you shut down the idea."

"Why would we want your boyfriend? He'll run his mouth about their marriage. The guy is an asshole," Reese retorts dryly.

"You're the asshole who wouldn't let me stop at the bank to get more cash. You rushed me out the door. Now I have to share a room with you because the hotel is booked." Jasmine flashes a weary grimace.

"Tough shit, kitten. Sharing a room is not all that bad. You act like we don't know each other. On top of that, it's got two queen beds. If you need money, I got you. You're overreacting."

My eyebrows jog up as I turn to look up at Santiago, whose lips twitch with the scene unfolding in front of us. Kitten?

She groans so loud I pinch my lips tight to hold my laugh. Reese smiles. He loves her reaction.

"I have a boyfriend. I can't be sharing rooms with you." Jasmine points at him sternly.

Reese slides his hands in his brown silky hair, his biceps flexing as he does it. There's no denying that Reese is an attractive guy, and Jasmine has had a crush on him since they were kids. However, she hasn't mentioned him in recent years, so I can't help but wonder if she's moved on from her childhood infatuation.

"Then go sleep elsewhere. There is a perfect bench outside. Sleep there." He goes to stand in front of her. "So, what is it? Do you want to sleep on a bench or in the same room, kitten? Fuck your boyfriend. Maybe you should ask him where he's been sleeping?"

"What's that supposed to mean?" Jasmine sneers, her arms hugging her waist. "And yes, I'll sleep in the same room. I have no choice."

"Nothing," Reese says, looking at Jasmine. "Just so you know, I sleep in the nude," Reese admits. "So, no taking peeks under the sheets." He grins at her and winks.

Jasmine's nose scrunches up in disgust. "I'm sure you can manage wearing clothes this weekend."

"Nah, sleeping with clothes makes me itchy. Besides, I like to air my balls out."

"Oh, my God, I'm not sleeping in a room full of ball sack stench." Jasmine makes a gagging noise.

That does it. The laugh I've been holding, I let it out.

"All right, we don't want to talk about your naked ass, especially in front of my girl," Santiago says to Reese, who is grinning at me.

Santiago grabs his bags, letting me know he's going to Reese's room to get dressed while Jasmine and I get dressed here. My eyes water, and my heart skips a beat when he says a limo will pick Jasmine and me up to take us to the chapel.

I know Santiago has been working his ass off all these years, helping Rachel with bills, and taking care of his brothers. I overheard him tell Reese he bought them school clothes. It's not that Rachel didn't have money. It's that she used the money meant for her kids for her pleasures. Now that he said Rachel is taking care of the bills, he's been saving money to move out, and I hate that he's using so much of it. I wouldn't mind a taxi picking us up or us riding together.

~

I LOOK at my reflection in the mirror and blink the tears back. A deep purple hue dusts my eyelids, courtesy of Jasmine's deft hand with a smoky eye shadow palette. My normally mundane appearance is transformed into something bold and striking. My dress is simple but beautiful, an off-the-shoulder white gown with a slit on the side and tight around my breasts, showing plenty of cleavage. Jasmine and I went dress shopping together. Santiago insisted on paying for my dress, explaining that it's the man's duty in his tradition to make purchases like this.

"You look gorgeous, my friend. I can't believe you're getting married to the man you dreamed of your whole life." She wipes a tear from the corner of her eye and laughs. "How many times did we lie in bed and talk about the guys we crushed over? I love you, Rosa, and I'm happy you're getting your fairytale."

My eyes sting as I forcefully hold back the tears that are threatening to fall.

"No, crying, Rosie Posie. Let's go get you married."

I nod, my heart swelling with emotion as I embrace my friend. Her long brown locks cascade down her shoulders, framing her glowing face. She radiates beauty in her navy-blue dress, and the fabric hugs her curves and highlights her feminine figure.

It's time to marry the man I've always loved. A part of me feels guilty going behind my *tia*'s back along with the rest of our family. But this is about our happiness. There's no way I'll let anyone keep me from him.

~

157

THE LIMO PARKS in front of a chapel on Las Vegas Boulevard. A stunning chapel awaits, adorned with intricate decorations that add to its beauty. As I step closer, a symphony of excitement erupts in my belly. The sun is setting on the horizon, red-yellow hues decorating the sky. Jasmine loops her arm in mine. Holding my gorgeous bouquet of white roses in one hand, I walk toward the chapel's front door. My breath hitches when I see my handsome, soon-to-be husband waiting. He stands tall and confident in his black slacks and crisp white button-up shirt. The fabric hugs his toned biceps, making them seem impossibly large.

His warm, chocolate-brown eyes glide over my body, lingering on each curve and angle, filled with a mixture of love, lust, and adoration. His gaze traces my skin like fingertips. The need to squeeze my thighs together is maddening. The line of my underwear was showing, so I just took them off. But now I feel even more exposed.

My heart races like a herd of wild horses. In this moment, time seems to stand still as we melt into each other's embrace.

He's hot as fuck.

Santiago steps toward me. "Rosaline." His voice is gruff and faint.

I love how he says my full name. Full of emotion.

"You're the most beautiful woman I've ever laid eyes on. So fucking stunning." He kisses my cheek, and I liquify at his touch. "And so goddamn sexy," he whispers in my ear. "Damn, your tits look mouthwatering, baby. I can't wait to undress you."

I chuckle, and my face burns. I turn from Santiago to see if Reese is paying us any attention, but he's not. He's gazing at Jasmine, who's obliviously watching all the other couples show-ing up.

"You look handsome. I want you to know I'd marry you with or without rings, babe, even with paper rings. Your love is all I want."

He swallows and says, "Ahh, fuck it," and smacks his lips on mine.

My arm clings to his shoulders as his mouth devours mine. His touch has me floating on the highest mountain. We pull apart when a throat clears behind us.

"We are ready for you," a tall brunette woman utters with a smile.

"We'll be right there," Santiago replies.

The woman nods and walks back into the chapel.

"Sorry, baby, didn't mean to maul you. I was trying to wait until we are married, but you look too pretty and perfect not to."

"I don't mind at all," I say coyly, stroking his soft, smooth cheek.

He looks so young, freshly shaven. He holds my hand as we walk to the altar. Jasmine and Reese follow behind.

My stomach churns with a mixture of emotions: excitement and fear. Maybe the fear comes from my family not knowing.

20

SANTIAGO

ROSA'S warm hands shake in mine as a tear rolls down her cheek. "Baby, are you okay? We can turn back." It would break my heart if she wanted to, but I'd rather it be when she's fully ready.

"God, no. Santi, I'm so happy. I've envisioned this moment in my head so many times. I'm ready to be Mrs. Delgado."

Fuck yeah. Just the thought makes me hard.

The priest stands waiting, and he is not pleased that we have kept him waiting. The ceremony starts.

"In the name of God, I, Santiago Delgado, take you, Rosaline Acosta, to be my wife, to have and to hold from this day forward, for better or for worse, for richer or for poorer, in sickness and in health, to love and to cherish, until parted by death. I love you, Rosa, with all my heart. I'll always work on being a better man for you."

I slip the ring on.

A tear slides down her beautiful face. She's so sexy, so damn stunning, like the goddess she is.

"In the name of God, I, Rosaline Acosta, take you, Santiago Delgado, to be my husband, to have and to hold from this day forward, for better or for worse, for richer or for poorer, in sickness and in health, to love and to cherish, until parted by death. I love you too, Santiago. I've loved you all my life."

As I swallow hard, my throat tightens, and a lump forms. Warm tears sting behind my eyes, as if daring me to release them. I press my hand against my chest, trying to contain the staggering emotions that threaten to consume me.

It's as though there's a weight in my chest that's making it hard to breathe, and I'm struggling to keep it all together. Rosa slips the ring on my finger. With a wide smile her gentle hands squeeze mine.

Oh, Rosa, you're the diamond I've been waiting for, the queen to the lonely king.

"I now pronounce you husband and wife. You may now kiss the bride," the priest announces.

I grab *my* wife by the waist and kiss her like there's no tomorrow. Reese and Jasmine cheer from behind.

I've made some impulsive decisions in the past, but nothing quite compares to eloping with Rosa, my childhood friend and now wife. She's always been the one person who truly sees me for who I am.

"I love the shit out of you, Rosa Delgado... my wife." I wink. Fuck, I love the sound of that. She kisses me repeatedly. All I can think of is taking her back to the hotel, where I can rip the dress off, spread her on the bed, feast on her, and fuck in more ways than one.

"I love you too. God, you make me happy. *Cristo.* I don't know what to do with myself. I'm the happiest I've ever been," Rosa whispers, brushing her lips on mine.

"Hey, congratulations, you guys," Jasmine pulls us both into a hug, tears running down her cheek.

Reese slaps me on the back. "Congratulations, man, you deserve it. You deserve to have an incredible woman by your side. You do a lot for everyone. It's time you did something for yourself. Getting your happiness."

Genuine praise from my best friend means a lot. We've all grown up together, and I'm glad I married my best friend. Our two best friends are here.

Once things settle at home, I want to hold a wedding for Rosa with our family.

"Thanks, man. I appreciate you coming. It means a lot to us," I say to Reese.

Grabbing my wife's hand, we walk out of the chapel into the Limo. Jasmine and Reese will meet us at a restaurant to celebrate before I take my wife to the hotel.

WHILE THE LIMO idles in traffic, I lift Rosa and set her on my lap. The slit in her gown works to my advantage. The palms of my hands glide up and down her legs. Fuck, her skin is so soft and silky. I love how heated her body feels against mine. Her nipples pebble through the white satin dress. It hangs low, giving perfect access to her shapely full tits. My hands move slowly up to her round hips. When my gaze peers to Rosa, I ask, "No underwear?" My eyebrows curve.

"No, they were in the way," Rosa states, licking her lips. Her breathing picks up as I insert a finger. She's so wet. Always wet for me. My girl is always ready for me. With another finger, my wife throws her head back, mouth parted. I cover it with a kiss and pump harder as she moans my name. I've learned to be attuned to Rosa's needs and her body. She clamps around my fingers. With that, I pump into her pussy harder, giving her what she needs to come all over my fingers. Our mouths bruise in the flame of our kiss. She's so fucking tight around my finger I hit the spot that makes her come all over. Her arms wrap around my neck, anchoring me down.

"You're gorgeous coming all over my finger, wife. Lick, baby." She does. Her warm, sexy mouth takes my fingers, licking and sucking them clean. Damn. My aroused cock pulses painfully, rubbing in my slacks.

"Good girl," I praise. Dying for a taste of her pussy, I take her lips in my mouth, sucking, slipping my tongue into her mouth to get a taste of her.

She tastes like a dream, and it has me wanting to do unholy things to my wife.

TEN BEERS and two shots of whiskey, and I'm feeling slightly intoxicated but there is no comparison to the lust I'm intoxicated with. After hours of celebrating with our friends, we retired for the night. I lean against the door of the hotel room and watch Rosa remove her dress. It falls to the ground in a waterfall of silk that resembles a delicate rose petal. Next, she reaches up to her head and carefully pulls out a butterfly pin. Her long curls cascade down around her shoulders.

Gorgeous.

She stands naked in only the necklace I gifted her and looks like a sculpted statue. Words can't describe how beautiful Rosa is. Her slender waist stresses her curvy hips. I adore her flawless figure. Where she sees imperfections, I see a stunningly beautiful woman crafted into a masterpiece.

After kicking off my shoes, I unzip my pants, and they fall to the ground. My cock has been waiting to bust out to claim Rosa as my wife. Not keeping my eyes off her, I slip my boxers off. My dick feels so damn heavy. My wife saunters toward me—

hips swaying. She grabs a fist full of my shirt and rips it off, buttons flying all over the place.

"So impatient," I groan as she kneels and embarks on kissing the tip. My head falls back on the wooden door. My hips reel up with the thrust of her mouth, and when she grabs my ass, wildfire spreads throughout my body. Her tongue strokes all the right places, every pulsing vein. "Look at me, husband. You taste so good, and I'm going to swallow every drop of you."

Holy shit

She fucks me hard and fast. A fountain of liquid streams into her mouth, and she eagerly drinks it all. With a gentle hand, I help her up and support her shaky legs, picking her up and carrying her to the bed.

"Santiago, I need you," she purrs, her hand slipping between her legs. Rosa spreads her legs wider, showing me her pink pussy wet and ready for me.

Fuck

"Play with yourself, Rosa. Let me see you play with what's mine."

She moans my name.

"Insert a finger, baby," I instruct.

She complies with no hesitation. I kneel at the end of the bed, my tongue darting between her thighs. I nibble and leave my mark, relishing her pleasure.

I'm hypnotized by how her body responds to my touch, and how she pleasures herself. Her mouth gapes open, her nipples erect, full, and ready for me to play with. When I remove her finger, she whimpers. With one hand on her breast, I roll a thumb over her nipple. I insert a finger while my tongue licks her folds.

As she tightens her thighs around my head, I quicken the speed of my tongue. Just as I sense she is about to climax, I withdraw from her.

Sliding into her slowly, we both moan. Her muscles stretch

to accommodate me. The intimacy is so strong between us as we connect. The desire I hold in my heart for my wife is something I never thought I'd feel.

She's my wife—mine to fuck, mine to please, and mine to love.

She makes me want to act all fucking cheesy and shit. I want to make her sing my name, to possess her soul. It's a wicked thought, but it only applies to *my wife*, the only woman I would let in my heart.

The urge to make love to her, to ruin her from her wanting anyone, is maddening. Call me possessive. Fuck it. She's always been mine, and I'll ensure it always stays that way. The ring on her finger says it all.

With each thrust, the weight of my balls against her flesh reminds me of how good she feels, adding to the pleasure, and I'm losing control. I watch her arch her back, taking all of me in. "Don't cum yet, sweetheart," I command, pulling out and flipping her onto her hands and knees. The sight of her flushed face and tangled hair only makes me want her more.

"Santi—"

I don't give my girl time to complain about pulling out before I slam into her from behind. Rosa has the best tight ass I've ever seen.

"Yes, harder." Her voice shakes as I slap her ass.

I dive in balls deep while reaching for her breasts.

"I need to—"

"Not yet, flower."

The explosive sensation is there, and we both feel it. I need to spill into her, but not yet. I wanted to take her from behind to get a clear view of her glorious ass before flipping back. I clench my jaw and grind my teeth together, feeling the tension building in my body. I start to move my hips in a slow circular motion, sending jolts of electricity pulsing through my every vein. My body is on fire, fueled by an endless source of energy, like the Energizer bunny.

"Damn, baby."

When I flip her over on her back, tiny beads of perspiration cover her body and glisten off her light skin, making her look goddamn remarkable. My mouth swoops to take her lips. We kiss hard, then soft, then hard again. I look into her eyes, plowing into her. "Rosaline Delgado, you're fucking mine, my wife, my goddamn world."

Thrust. I grit my teeth and fight back a moan. Staring at her feverish eyes, her nails dig into my back like razor-sharp knives. Her legs wrap tighter around my thighs. When Rosa clenches on my cock, my body roars.

"Come for me, baby, come all over your husband's cock." I pound home, burst into her, and fill her with my seed. If my wife were older, we would have a serious talk about tossing her birth control pills.

She screams my name, and the sounds she makes—

Fuck.

We come together in shuddering waves. It's like coming off the highest peak of a mountain. We come hard, fast, and long. I've never come so long. It's like my cock is drained. I lean my head on my wife's forehead, both of us catching our breaths.

I want to be the only man who ever hears my wife's screams of pleasure, the only man to fill her needs—the man who hears the moans that come out of her lips.

She's my queen. I'll be her protector, the one who puts her needs over mine, even if it breaks me in the end. *Even if it shatters me to pieces.*

21

ROSALINE

"ROSALINE, ARE YOU READY, *HIJA MIA?*" my aunt yells from the living room.

Liam and my *abuelita* are also waiting downstairs. Today, I'm doing an art presentation to showcase the school I attend. It's a college fair at one of the high schools. There are also a couple of other schools having guest speakers. I straighten out my navy blue dress, glancing at my reflection in the mirror. In some ways, I feel different. I wish I could say I feel older and wiser, but that's not the case. My heart is lighter and giddy, consumed by an overwhelming sense of wholeness. I am completely and utterly in love with my husband. My soulmate. The thought makes me squeal with joy.

It's been four weeks since we eloped, and I couldn't be happier. I long to proclaim to the world that he belongs to me and wear his ring. Each night, I retrieve it from my drawer and slip it onto my finger before falling asleep, only to return it to its hiding place in the morning. We meet every night. We go for a ride on his motorcycle, or he sneaks into my room, or I go over to his. Each night, he makes love to me to show me how much I mean to him.

Santiago and I discussed that next week, once things settle down, we plan to let everyone know we are a happily married couple. Regardless of what they think, we are married and moving in together. Well, as soon as Santiago gets a place.

"Rosa, hurry up."

"I'm coming, *Tía*." Grabbing my purse, I rush downstairs. I'm greeted by my protective brother-like cousin, who has a grin on his handsome face.

"I'm so proud of you, little Rosita. Man, where has the time gone, huh?" Liam wraps me in a hug. "Remember when we were kids, and we always fucked around and sneaked off to The Ring?" He chuckles. "Now you're a college student."

Yup, I remember sneaking off to the racing ring where Santiago was with chicks. I smile at the thought of my evilness when I would run to Santiago, and he would always walk away from those girls to hang with me.

"Good old times," I murmur.

"Rosita *qué bonita*," my *abuelita* says with her warm, beaming smile. Her soft, aged hands cup my cheek. "You've grown into a beautiful woman, Rosa. You have come a long way. This is your mama." She points to my aunt. "I'm your, *Abuelita*, and that young, handsome man"—she points to Liam— "is your brother. Your *tía* might not have been the one to bring you into this world, but she raised you and loved you like her own." She taps my nose with a kiss. "Remember, Rosaline. In order to grow as a woman and person, you have to emerge from the shadows. They will always be your anchor."

I swallow the knots in my throat.

Abuelita is the type of woman who can see right through you.

By shadows, she means the pain I carry in the pit of my heart. The childhood pain that left me numb. I've grown accustomed to letting my family, Santiago, and the Delgado brothers lift, shelter, defend, and protect me. They tucked me under their wings, letting me stand in their shadows so others wouldn't notice me because of my insecurities. Being alone is better than chancing rejection, and it is why I've never had many friends. I keep my circle small for that reason. I know I'm loved. I know I'm right where I belong. To this day, I can still smell the musky, dark closet where I'd sit for hours. When thunderstorms hit, it takes me right back to that place.

Wrapping my arms around my *abuelita*, I inhale her warm, comforting scent.

"*Gracias, Abuelita*. I know I'm right where I belong. I would not have it any other way. You are my family, and I know I need to work on myself more, and I will. I love you all."

I appreciate her giving me a boost of confidence. We huddle into a group hug before we head out.

They always remind me I have them, and that I'm not alone.

MY BREATHING PICKS UP. My legs shake like a baby fawn. I don't know how many times I've cleaned my sweaty hands on my dress. You can do this, Rosaline. Crowds of people swarm around, and my anxiety floods me like a river. Panic attacks like this happen to me at times around extensive crowds.

I try to distract myself by thinking about the night we got married when we had the best sex of my life. The memory of his tongue flicking and vibrating against my skin sends a sudden electric jolt through me.

Oh, for God's sake. Now I'm aching and horny as fuck.

They call my name, and I walk to the podium.

My freaked-out eyeballs search for my husband. When I spot him, my heart flutters. He nods, reassuring me. Santiago stands tall, his broad shoulders stretching the fabric of his crisp black collar shirt. As he grins, dimples appear on his cheeks, accented by a perfectly stubbled beard. He runs a hand through his styled hair. He's a fresh breath of air. When I mentioned I volunteered to deliver a speech he offered to come listen.

As I speak, the words effortlessly flow from my mouth. I grip the notecard that I meticulously prepared for my speech about what the art school has to offer and why it's one of the top schools.

When I look up at the crowd, I spot Marissa. I haven't seen her since the day Santiago kicked her out. She's squatting next to him, talking to him. Her hand falls on his knee. A surge of green jealousy powers through me. I hate the bitch. Her cousin is graduating as well. That must be why she's here.

She's beautiful…older, mature. Something inside me pulls on my heartstrings like an out-of-tune guitar, drawing out my uncertainties. Would Santiago be better off with a woman his age? Mature? Maybe if I weren't such a chicken and told my aunt, things could be different. I might be worried for nothing. They adore Santiago. I know my insecurities are taking over like they always do. Also, Santiago wants to show them he has a home for us before telling them.

I choke on my words then clear my throat, trying to regain myself. Santiago peers up and removes her hand. He tells her something, and she gets up and leaves. It seems she's still in love with him. Only a bitch would pull a move like that—talk to him to get his attention while I'm doing a speech.

Everyone claps as I smile into the crowd and walk off the podium back to my seat. I appreciate my family coming to hear me. Santiago walks up to Liam, followed by Mark. It's sweet of them to support me, knowing how bad my anxiety can get, although I'm working on it. Santiago gazes at me. Something is weighing down on me, call it a sixth sense.

"Hey, baby, I'm proud of you," Santiago whispers in my ear, his hot breath tickling my neck. His lips brush my temple, and I shiver.

If only I could thaw in his arms right now and let the bitch Marissa see he's mine. "Thank you," I murmur, mustering a Colgate smile.

"Let's all head back to the house, and I'll make something to eat," my aunt Andrea bellows over the crowd's loud noise.

"Come on, you're coming with me." Santiago tips his head at me.

Giving him a nod, I follow.

Ten minutes into the drive, and I've been quiet the entire time. My mood went sour real quick.

Santiago sighs. "Are you going to tell me what's on your mind, Rosa? You've been pretty quiet for someone who should be bouncing off the walls."

"Seriously, you have to ask?" I snap, irritated. Immediately, I feel guilty. I'm acting childish. He did nothing wrong.

He turns toward me, his hand reaching out to take mine in a gentle grasp. He gives it a reassuring squeeze. "I have a suspicion about what might be bothering you," he says. "But I didn't want to bring it up in case I was wrong."

Staring at our entwined hands, I let out a frustrated breath. "What did she want?"

"Baby, I'm married to you—"

Jealousy claws at my insides like a bad toothache. His lips twitch slightly at the corners. "What did she want?" I repeat.

"Nothing important."

She probably asked him to fuck her. I wouldn't be surprised.

"Santiago." I close my eyes and pray for some patience because I'm struggling to control my anger. Why won't he just spit it out? "You think this is funny?"

"No, of course not. It's just you look cute jealous."

My tongue clucks in the resemblance of a serpent ready to strike. Jealous. Of course, I'm heating up with jealousy.

"Let's say you were never my first, and I've been around the block."

He frowns.

"All this time, you saw me grinding on guys, making out with them—especially the same dude constantly attached to me, like a pestering flea. Then we get married, and he comes around. How would it make you feel?"

He pulls into an empty parking lot and shuts the truck off. "I would be fucking jealous, Rosa." He slides his hands through his sexy hair. "And I haven't been around the fucking block."

I shrug and look out the window. "Answer me."

"She wanted to know if I wanted to hang out with her."

"You mean fuck her."

"Dammit, Rosa. I didn't pay attention to what she said because I was listening to your speech. I mentioned I'm taken for life. She will find out soon who I'm with." He adjusts the steering wheel, then glides me toward him, lifting me on his lap. "I'm sorry. I know you had to see a lot of shit I've done. But there's nothing I can do about that. I can't say I should have saved myself for the one because I never thought I'd find her. Now I have, and I'll make it up to her." His voice drips with raw emotion.

He'll make it up to me.

My heart soars in a cloud of lust. He couldn't have said more perfect words. He kisses me passionately, and I melt into his arms. "I'm sorry I acted crazy."

He chuckles.

"No, not crazy, baby. You had reasons." He pecks my lips again. "A couple of more days, and then we don't have to hide. Regardless of how your aunt and Liam act, you're mine."

A relieved sigh leaves my lungs.

Just then, my phone rings. I frown at my phone. The caller ID says unknown number.

"Hello?"

"Rosaline," a female voice answers.

My body stiffens, and my heart beats uncontrollably. Santiago grips onto my waist, seeing my discomfort. My heart recalls the familiar voice, but I won't give her the satisfaction. Instead of calling her by name, I ask.

"Who's this?"

"Rosaline, it's me, your *mamá*."

Seventeen years later, she calls out of the blue as if she has the right to call and claim her name as *mamá*. She lost that privilege the day she walked out on me. Santiago's jaw clenches at hearing her voice.

A malicious, angry laugh escapes my lips. "No, Tina. You're not my mom. My mom is Andrea. She's the one who was there for me all these years. She's the one who raised me as her child even after losing her husband." Angry tears run down my cheek as my fist grips Santiago's shirt. "She loves me. Unlike you," my voice cracks.

"Rosaline. Your *tía* didn't tell you, did she? I called and asked her to let me speak to you several times. I wanted to go get you."

The weight on my chest makes it hard to breathe. Santiago holds me tight. She tried calling me. I waited for her phone calls all these years.

"Andrea didn't let me speak with you."

I shake my head. "I'm glad she didn't let me speak with you. Because a mother doesn't lock their child in the closet for a man. A mother doesn't leave her child to start a family with another man and leave her firstborn as if she was nothing."

"Rosaline...." She lets out a breath. "Congratulations," she says, then the line goes dead.

She thinks I graduated this year, which shows she doesn't

know my age. She wouldn't know that because she knows nothing about me.

Tears stream down my face, ugly and unstoppable. My husband embraces me tightly, just as he has done for years, even on those stormy nights when the memories come rushing back to haunt me.

22

SANTIAGO

LEANING INTO THE RECLINER CHAIR, I go over today's work orders. The shop has been relatively busy lately. Reese's dad has been recruiting customers from a shop closing a few streets down.

"Hello," I say, multitasking by holding the phone on my shoulder and shuffling papers around.

"Hello, Mr. Delgado. This is Charleston Town Homes calling to let you know you're approved. All we need is for you to come in and sign along with a deposit and the first month's rent."

"Sounds great, thank you. I'll drop in this afternoon."

Fuck, yeah.

Finally, I have been waiting forever. It's been two weeks since Mark's graduation. As soon as I sign the lease, I'll furnish it and surprise Rosa. Once I get that done, I'll talk to Liam and Andrea. See how it goes. I know Liam will be livid. There's no doubt about that. Although I understand he's protective, he should be relieved it's me and not some asshole who knows shit about her and won't treat her right.

My heart jackhammers in my chest at the thought of Rosa and me living together as husband and wife. These last weeks have been fucking hard without having her by my side. We see each other every day, yet it's not enough. I want to taste the air she breathes and to wake up beside her every morning. The thought of coming home to her, inhaling the sweet scent of her perfume mixed with the warmth of her embrace, ignites a fierce desire within me. The sight of her tousled hair every morning is everything a man could want.

"Hey, bro," Reese says, ushering himself into the doorway with a devil's grin smeared across his face. Damian follows him. "Look what the cat dragged in."

"Long time no see, asshole." I grin, calling out Damian on his disappearing act.

"Been busy," he clarifies.

"Doing?" I ask.

"Getting pussy whipped," Reese interjects, laughing.

Damian shrugs with a smile. "I like her pussy. So why fucking not?"

Damn. I know that feeling, and I don't give a shit.

"I asked my girl to marry me. We've been planning it," Damian announces.

"Congratulations, man." I stand and pat his back.

"Whoa. This is out of hand, guys. Too many of you are getting married," Reese utters, waving his hands in the air. "While you're trying to melt your chick's world with proposals and planning, Santiago did it all in a weekend."

"What! With whom?" Damian shouts. "You married Monica?"

"No!" I shout defensively, scrunching my nose. "You haven't been around or called. I married Rosa."

His eyes go as big as a slow loris. "Rosaline. Little Rosa? Your little Rosa?" His hands go to his chin. "Huh."

If he's going to criticize me, his ass will be handed to him.

"Didn't I tell you she changed? I guess you took the bait. That girl has always looked at you like the brightest star in her universe. It doesn't surprise me. You've always cared for her." He grins. "Congratulations. When can I see the new Mrs. Delgado?"

Reese snickers. "So, when are you getting your place?"

"Probably today. Once I get it furnished, I'll move Rosa in. She can decorate any way she wants."

Reese nods, leaning on the wall.

"Where's your girl now?" Damian asks.

"She's doing something with Jasmine." When she returns to Portland, it will be hard, but we will make it work. I can move with her once I get Dominic and Mark situated. Dominic might own a restaurant and have his place, but he's struggling. Now, I know his pain. If Rosa disappeared from my life, I'd be the same.

The guys continue their conversation while I wrap shit up around here so I can get to the apartment complexes. Then I'm picking Rosa up and taking her to dinner. Maybe dinner on the pier. A nice romantic dinner.

Holy shit. Who am I? Romantic?

If my brothers and Liam saw me, they would flip. How often did I mess with Dominic when he and Mila were all lovey-dovey? Carrying my keys, I go to the truck and notice a large for-sale sign posted on the building that used to be a thriving shop. An idea comes to mind.

MY EYES DEVOUR my wife as she fiddles with her fish tacos. She squeezes lime and adds garnish. The white dress she's wearing highlights her gorgeous figure. The glistening lights from the night reflect on her flawless skin. She's wearing her wedding ring. My chest swells with pride. Despite her physical closeness, she feels distant, so I pull her chair closer to mine. The warmth of her body radiates next to me and fills the space between us with a comforting presence.

"Santiago," she mumbles, dragging her plate with her. We're seated in front of the water with heaters surrounding us. A string of lights wraps around the outside sitting patio.

"Have I told you how hot you are?"

She licks her lips. I grab a napkin, wiping her chin.

"You did. Thank you." Her smile glows like a damn lighthouse. "Never would have played you as such a romantic." Amusement glints in her eyes. "I love it." She leans into my side, and her flower scent does something to me. Then her soft lips skim my cheek so fucking slow. A shiver runs down to my dick. All I can think of is slipping my finger under her dress. She leaves a kiss on my cheek. The place is buzzing with people. It doesn't seem like it's going to clear out soon. *Later*, I say to myself, rearranging my dick.

"I'll be a hopeless romantic for you, Rosa. I'm not very good at it, but I'll try for you. You know anything I do or will ever do will be in your best interest." I'll always put her first. That's how I'm wired. Rosa, along with my brothers and Liam, have always been my top priority.

"I love you, Santiago. So much. I can't wait for us to start our life together." The tips of her nails trace the ink on my arms.

The lease is ready on the townhouse. Tomorrow, I'm ordering furniture. Then, this week, I'm talking to Liam privately. I'll let my brothers know when that's sorted, whether or not they agree.

My hand slips up her dress, her bare legs warm and soft. Rosa takes a bite of her cheesecake just as I slip my fingers higher. She's so wet.

Dripping.

She moans, swallowing her dessert.

"Take another bite, baby," I order, and my wife obliges beautifully. Pumping harder, I can feel her walls tighten on my fingers. One of her hands clenched the table, and the other her fork.

The dickhead Ryan, the one Rosa was going to date, is sitting across the way from us. He has been watching my wife, his eyes traveling all over her body. Although he's on a date with Marissa, he keeps staring at her. I find it odd they're dating. Marissa's sister could have introduced them she's Ryan's age. The wanna-be jock knows I'm fingering my wife. He's not looking away.

"Another bite, sweetheart. How close?"

"So close," she purrs, swirling her tongue on the frosting. I'm fucking possessive of Rosa, and I don't give two fucks who knows it. I will make it known she is mine, and I'm hers. Inserting another finger, her head tilts back, and she takes another bite. People will think it's a damn world-winning cheesecake. With one deep thrust, she comes hard. She makes a mess just how I like it. I kiss her possessively. Then I turn to the dipshit and lick my fingers like I just had a prime steak. I smirk, tossing cash on the table.

"I'll clean you up in the truck. I want you to walk out like that, Rosa."

She doesn't ask. She grabs her purse, and we walk out. Her eyes widen as we pass Ryan. I thought she knew he was here. I guess not.

I grip her tight hot ass, guiding us out to the truck. She stops walking. Her beautiful eyes turn into a madwoman—a grimace of disbelief. "Did you finger me just because he was there or for her?"

I slip my hand into my jeans pocket without meeting my wife's eye.

"Yes and no."

"Elaborate."

I let out a breath. "Rosa, I'm stupidly, ridiculously, and wholeheartedly in love with my wife. I'm a jealous, possessive man with you. These are all new feelings for me. Men are not allowed to objectify and ogle your body as if it belongs to them. This wedding ring on my finger justifies you're mine—the same finger you just came on. And as for Marissa, who gives a fuck about her? I sure don't. Now she knows who I belong to."

"So you're okay with him or another man seeing me? Knowing how I look when I moan and come." Her eyebrows jog up.

When she puts it that way, no, I don't want other men seeing how she comes. It's for my eyes only. But the imbecile needed to see she would never be his.

"No, I'm not okay with it, but he thought we were hanging out just like always. Wanna-be-jock didn't know we were together. Also, I wanted to feel you, baby."

Her arms fold to her chest, making them bounce. "I'm sure now he's going to spread the word. It's not like I went all ballistic when Marissa was resting her hand on your leg or when she asked to fuck you," she whispers, averting her gaze from mine.

"No one stopped you from going ballistic and making it known, Rosa. I understand you were on the podium doing your presentation, but things could have been different if we had told everyone. You could have told Marissa something or put your hot lips on me for her to see. I'm not saying you needed to go ballistic, but I sure won't let any man come near you. That's just me, baby. Let's go back to my house. No one is home."

She sighs and laces our hands together. "I want to make it known, Santi. I'm tired of hiding."

"Then let's make it known."

~

As THE TRUCK rolls up to Rosa's house, my heart beats wildly. I waited until Rosa went to Jasmine's house to talk to Liam. I didn't need her here when things got unhinged. There will be fists thrown, I know that. It makes it so much worse that I didn't just date her. I went off and married her.

Maybe I should smack him on the back and say, "Hey, brother-in-law," or "Hey, cousin." Will I get a "welcome to the family?" Officially, we've been like family all our lives.

I don't knock. We never do. Liam sits on the blue couch, tinkering with a carburetor-rebuild kit. He looks up and grins.

"Hey, bro, how's my favorite shithead doing?" Liam smirks.

I scrub a hand down my face. "Favorite? Did I get bumped up from Dominic?"

"You're ramped up to *numero uno.* Dominic has been busy getting his new place set up. He's busy with his restaurant. He never talks about the woman we shouldn't speak of, but I know he thinks of her daily. The restaurant is all for her. Deep down, I know he wishes she'd come back or that if he opens a restaurant, it will draw her back in. It's unhealthy for him to still hold on after all this time. The asshole needs to get laid." He chuckles.

I've been so caught up with Rosa that I neglected to pay attention to my brother. Recovering from cancer takes time and years to heal. On top of that, he had to deal with Mila's disappearance. Liam is right. It's unhealthy.

"I'll talk to him." Taking a seat in the recliner, I point to Liam's activity. "What are you up to?"

"Practicing on how to rebuild a carburetor. So, when I work on my dad's old truck, I get it right. It helps me get my mind off shit. I need to tow my dad's truck to my place."

Fuck, I slide my hands in my hair, thinking about how to start the conversation.

"Can you do me a favor? Can you get me a paintbrush from Rosa's room? So I can dust off the nooks and crannies," he asks.

"Sure." I stand and head up the stairs to Rosa's bedroom.

Immediately, when I walk in, I inhale her scent. Her bed is made with her pink bunnies placed in between two pillows. Opening a container, I find painted canvases—so many of them. My smile stretches. Rosa was indeed obsessed with me all these years. There are so many painted canvases of us together, and some of just me throughout the years. She's an incredible artist, no doubt about that. Lifting one of the canvases, I stare at the painting of Rosa and me on our wedding night. My heart swells to three times its size. She is stunning. The smiles on our faces reflect the intense love between us.

All those years of drawing with her and coloring have paid off. I laugh to myself. Her paintings need to be in an art gallery.

She's brilliant.

A stack of letters on her desk grabs my attention. My hands slick with sweat, I go through each one. Withdrawal letters. When I asked her when fall classes started, she said in August and as much as she would miss me, she was excited to hurry her ass up and finish. The school Rosa attends in Portland is one of the best art programs, Bachelor of Fine Arts in Painting and Drawing. She had a full-ride scholarship, and it's been her dream school. She promised me she wouldn't drop out to attend here.

She lied to me. She hid it.

A knot forms in my throat. I said I'd always put her first. However, to her, it won't seem that way.

Your dreams are my dreams, flower.

With a heavy heart, I put the letter back and walk out of Rosa's room.

23

Rosaline

Jasmine: *Can we meet tonight at your place, mine, or somewhere else? I want to talk to you about something.*

I wonder what she wants to talk about. Whatever it is, it doesn't sound good. That has me worried.

Me: *Sure, of course. Is everything okay?*

Jasmine: *I don't know. I'll tell you everything.*

Me: *K. I'll text around eight.*

My nerves are a jumbling mess, worrying about what Jasmine has to say and talking to my aunt about my so-called mother calling me. I set the phone on my bed and head downstairs. My sweet, beautiful aunt sits on the sofa, and next to her is a tin of cookies. I sit beside her and open the tin to eat a savory sweet cookie before I give my aunt the news. A girl could use a dose of sugar.

My shoulders deflate, along with the hope of a cookie. In the tin is my *tía's* sewing stuff, from buttons to needles. You name it, and it's in there, but no cookies. I shake my head, and my *tía* laughs with a pretty, bright smile.

"You're cruel." My hand drops to my knees, fiddling with my fingers. "My mo… uh, Tina called the day of the art presentation speech I had." She places the needle and thread back in the tin. "She said she tried calling me, but you wouldn't let her speak to me."

She tucks a lock of hair behind her ear. "I'm sorry, Rosa. I never told you, but I had my reasons."

"Why didn't you let me speak with her?" I'm curious why, when all I ever did was wonder if she wanted me. Maybe she did. No, no, she didn't. She chose him.

"Because you're mine, Rosa. My baby, my daughter. She left you without a care in the world. How could she do that? Abuse you, neglect you, abandon you. She might be my sister, but you will always come first. I would never allow her to hurt you, to manipulate you. She's married to that man and has three kids with him, honey. I would never let them take you from me. Why? So she can treat you differently because you're not his?" Tears stream down her cheek. "I love you, Rosa, so much. You brought a light into my darkness. I know it's wrong for me to say, but I'm grateful you're here with me… that she left you to be my daughter. I hope you can forgive me, honey."

I wipe my tears and then *Tía's* with the back of my hand. "I'm not upset, *Tía*. I could never be upset with you. As a kid, I wouldn't have understood, but now I do. I always wondered why I wasn't good enough for her to keep. The love you've given me is the love I need from a mother. It was the rejection Tina inflicted that stung."

This is why I've had so little confidence in myself. Being thrown away like a rag doll makes you second-guess yourself.

"I know, sweetheart. What she did and how she did it is a pain that will always sting. Until one day you have little ones of your own. That's when your heart will heal because it will fill with so much love. You will look into your child's eyes and love them more than anything in this world, and you will say, 'I will not be like her. I will put them first.'" Her warm hands cup my cheek.

I melt into her motherly embrace.

"I love you, *mija*."

"I love you too, *Tía*," Now would be an excellent time to tell my *tía* I'm married. "Listen, *Tía*, I need to tell you something—"

Just then, her phone rings. "Give me a second, honey. It's *Abuelita*." I nod.

After only a few words, *Tía* rushes for her keys. "Your *abuelita* fell. I'll be back in a bit. Nothing serious."

I stand to get my shoes to go with her, but she's already out the door. Instead, I head back to my room to wrap the gift I made for Santiago. It took a lot of willpower to make the portrait I made for him. I know he will love it. Excitement courses through me.

THE AIR FEELS stale walking into Santiago's house. It always feels that way when Rachel is around. Rachel is a beautiful woman, but her personality makes her appear vile.

"Hello, Rosa." Her lips pinch into a fake smile.

Santiago emerges from the kitchen. My heart cracks at the sight of him.

"Hi, Rachel."

"I'm heading out tonight. Remember what we talked about, Santiago," Rachael says sharply.

Santiago ignores her as she slams the screen door and gets in her car.

Once Rachel is gone, I go to Santiago. He looks exhausted,

with dark circles around his eyes. I texted him last night, but he didn't reply.

"Rosaline." His tone is husky and soft. His eyes reach mine. With the palm of my hand, I cup his cheeks, and the stubble pokes into my palms.

"Are you okay? You're not getting sick, are you?"

He steps back.

"Feels like I have the worst kind of sickness. But I'm not sick." His disarrayed look appears as if he's been continuously running his hands through his hair. "Let's go to my room," he drawls.

I grab the wrapped painting and carry it with me.

He slams the door behind us. My stomach churns. Something doesn't feel right. He's not acting right. A couple of boxes sit on the bed.

Santiago leans his forehead on mine. "Rosaline, kiss me, baby." His words are strangled. Just the sound of his voice pains me.

Our lips meet in a slow, fiery embrace. Every touch sends tingles down my spine, igniting a fire that spreads throughout every inch of my body. It's like our souls entwined in this kiss, sending tiny tendrils of passion to every inch of my being. The type of kiss you feel to the bone—one to always remember. We kiss and kiss for what feels like long minutes.

Two steps back, three steps back. He leans on a faded scratched-up dresser.

"What's going on, Santiago? You look like you haven't slept." I sit on the bed and peek into the boxes.

He's packing.

He casts a glance over his shoulder while standing by the window. His body slumps, and then Santiago shoves his hands into his black jeans. The gray tank top shows all his muscles and a peek of the top of his gorgeous wolf inked on his back.

His head is cast down when he says, "I'm going to be gone

for three days. I'm going to LA to talk business with a guy about a shop."

His head is still down.

"Oh, okay. Is that what has you in a sour mood?"

He blows out his cheeks. "Fuck," he shouts.

I jump off the bed, startled by his outburst.

He yanks his hair in frustration. "Rosa, I fucked up."

Nausea rips down to the pit of my stomach. Did he cheat on me?

"We should have waited."

WAIT! WHAT! "What the hell are you talking about?" I shout frantically.

"We should have waited to get married."

"You regret marrying me, Santiago?"

He turns to look up at me from staring at the wall for too long. Worry lines crease his forehead.

"No, Rosa, of course not. I don't regret it. I just think we should have waited. You're still young. It's my fault I was moving too fast. You have so much life to experience and too much to learn."

I move at rocket speed to get close to him. "Where is all this coming from? We both wanted this. We didn't move too fast."

My fucking heart is lurching out of my chest.

"I'm fucking close to twenty-eight years old, Rosa. Instead of getting my shit together, getting a place, first, providing a home. I did the opposite. I rushed it. We hid from everyone, for fuck's sake. You have so much going on, and you're in college. I'm still fucking here, living at home, a married man with no damn money. It's irresponsible of me. I don't regret it, but I regret rushing it."

My fingers jab at his hard chest.

"It's the same fucking thing. You regret marrying me. You can't half-ass the regret, Santiago."

He grabs my hand. He plants a hard kiss on my knuckles and then turns from me.

"You're young, too young, Rosa. I'm being selfish with you." A slight tremor of anger taints his voice.

"I'm so tired of everyone telling me I'm too young for this and that. Everyone makes decisions for me. How about what I want?" I want to scream. "You regret it now because I'm too young. I'm a kid, right? That's what you've always called me. 'Hey, kid.' I'm too young for you... not experienced enough. Fuck you." Anger suffuses me, making my voice rise. "What do you want, Santiago? I know you well enough to know you're not just starting an argument for no reason."

Santiago grabs my waist, pulling me to him. The warmth of his body fills with tension. His breathing... heavy. "It has nothing to do with not being experienced. I love you, Rosaline. I feel like I should have been more mature and done things in your best interest. We should have waited until we both got our shit together, mainly me." His thumb caresses my lips, and his hooded eyes are filled with regret.

I see it. Every part of me feels it.

"Go back to Oregon, flower. I know you hid the applications for the new enrollment packet. This college has been your dream...we should take a break. We both need to get our shit together. I'm not good for you, Rosaline. Not yet, at least. I'll only be holding you back." He swallows the sludge of his words.

Violent, ugly tears stream down my cheek. "Don't tell me what I want. I know what I want, and what I want is you. If I want to ruin my scholarship to be here, then I will. I don't care if I go to a school that has a crummy art program. I'd ruin myself for you. That's why I didn't tell you. I knew you would react like this. I was waiting until I spoke to the school in Oregon to let them know to drop my full ride. I already enrolled here. All I had left was to pick my classes."

"Exactly. I'm not letting you ruin yourself for me. You have so much in your life to look forward to."

With every word he says, my heart cracks slowly, shattering into glass. I clench his shirt tightly in my fist, a mixture of anger and pain coursing through me, refusing to let him go, holding on for dear life, for us.

"Then come with me to Oregon," I plead. I'm losing him. I know Santiago. I know his heart. He might love me, but he regrets marrying me.

"I can't," he says gruffly.

"You can't, or you won't?"

He doesn't answer me. He stays silent, looking out the damn window, giving me his back.

I know his answer without him even having to say it. He wants me to go without even trying to work things out between us. It's easier for him to push me away. He thinks he's not good enough, but I know he is more than enough for me. It's the money or his brothers or some other thing. He uses every excuse he can to avoid facing our problems.

"Both. It's best if we take a break, Rosaline. It was a mistake."

He may as well have cut my veins open with a knife. I can feel the blood pouring out of me. Pain oozing out.

"A mistake. I'm a mistake?" Grabbing his shoulder, I spin him around with hulk force. His hands move to brush my tears, but I slap them away. "Don't fucking touch me."

He flinches. "No, Rosa, not you. You're not a mistake. What I meant is it was a mistake to rush into marriage. We should have waited until you were done with school—the school you've always wanted to attend, not these shitty ones."

"Well, it's too fucking late because we're married, you asshole, because we both wanted it. I don't regret us, and I don't regret falling deeper in love with you, but it's too late now. The damage is done. You regret it."

"No, Rosaline." He shoves his hand in his hair, yanking on it.

"I don't regret you. I fucking love you. It's just…best if you move back to Oregon to go to school. It's the school you've worked hard for. We need a break to sort things in our heads. I want you to go clear-headed. I want you to follow your dream. We both have been in a lust fucking haze. We need time apart, that's it. We'll figure things out in time."

I nod, stepping away from him. Every part of my body feels numb. I don't know how my legs are moving. I'm not going to beg him to want me, us. "You want a break. I'll give you a permanent break. *It's all or nothing for me.*" I point at him. "You did this. You killed us. I can't get over the word 'regret' because I could never utter those words to you. I never thought that the one man who meant everything to me would be the one man to toss me away."

His eyes close, and for a second, pain is written all over them, but not the same pain that matches mine. Mine is tenfold more.

"Rosaline." His voice is raw with emotion.

Reaching for the doorknob, I turn to give him one last glance. "You're just like Tina. You pushed me away. Second choice again." I don't give him time to say anything. I slam the door behind me. I hurry to my Jeep, leaving a trail of shattered fragments from my heart in my wake. I quickly climb into the driver's seat.

The front door slams open. "Rosaline," Santiago roars.

As I speed off into the darkness, I'm left with only a shell of my former self. Trust issues have caused me to keep my inner circle small. Fear of rejection has always held me back from getting close to anyone. Santiago was the only person I let in. And this pain is a million times worse than the night Tina left me.

Grabbing my phone from my purse, I send Jasmine a quick text.

Me: *I'm on my way to your house.*

Then I jump on the highway.

Tears flood my face. I'm crying so much it's hard to see the road. I called the colleges here to enroll and went to orientation. I didn't care if it was shitty or if I lost my scholarship. I love Santiago, and I chose him. It's just a school. I would have been fine attending the university here and obtaining an art degree here.

Now, all I want to do is leave. If I stay, the pain will be too much for me to bear. Maybe Santiago is not the marrying type of man.

24

ROSALINE

THE SOUND of gravel crunches under the weight of my Jeep and rattles in my ears as I drive up to Jasmine's house. Jasmine sits on the white wooden steps of her house. Her chihuahua Luna comes running toward me as I hop out of the Jeep. When Jasmine's head snaps up, I notice she's wiping tears.

"Rosa, what happened?" She hears me sniffle.

I extend my arms for a hug. It is obvious we both need it.

"Oh, Rosa, we are both a mess. You go first. What happened?"

So, I do.

"You know he loves you, right?"

I give her a half-ass shrug. "Not enough. He asked for a break. Who does that weeks after we get married? Only a person who regrets it."

My head spins. I can't even think straight. I'm emotionally drained and confused. "He wants me to move to Oregon," I murmur.

She went with me to enroll at the university here, and she planned to go with Tank to New York.

"Then maybe we should. Maybe we need to get the fuck out of here," Jasmine says, her chin trembling.

"Your turn. What happened?"

She wipes a tear and then looks up at the twinkling stars. It makes me wonder if Santiago is looking up at the same star.

"I broke up with Tank."

My eyes widen. She loves Tank, so this comes as a shock to me. That's not what I expected her to say.

"I cheated on him."

A gasp leaves my lips. I didn't see that coming.

"What?"

She cries into her hands.

I kneel next to her, soothing her back. "Tell me what happened. How did you cheat on him? Was it an accident? Like you got drunk or something?"

"It was on your wedding night." She sobs.

Oh, fuck.

"I slept with Reese. Not once, but twice. At that moment, it all felt right, but after, I felt like shit."

Now I'm really in shock. I know she's always had a crush on him, but I didn't think...well, hell, I don't know what to think. Reese was flirting with her.

"Here I was, worried that Tank would break up to be with other girls and then convince me to leave with him. I opened up to him about my concerns, and he reassured me I was over-thinking things. He even told me he wanted to marry me some-day. Then I cheat on him. I'm the worst kind of person. I didn't have the guts to tell him why I wanted to break up."

Cristo, what a night.

I sit in the armchair next to her. Jasmine leans her head on me. "I understand you feel horrible for cheating on Tank. I know cheating has always been a deal breaker for you, but the girls in those pictures appeared too close to him. We still don't know if there was anything to that. Maybe I'm wrong, but you've had doubts about this relationship for a while. That's why you didn't leave with him last year."

"I called the University of Oregon Art Institute to let them know I'll be back, and they still have dorms." She sniffles. "They asked if I had a roommate who wanted to room with me."

There's no way I can stay. Santiago will always be a part of Liam's life, which means I'll be forced to see him. I can't bear to see him.

If he wants me to leave, then that's what I'll do. Things will never be the same between us again. I'll be damned if I'm second to anyone. I am certain that I won't find a love like ours elsewhere.

~

SANTIAGO

MY LEATHER-CLAD body leans into the sharp curve as my motorcycle roars off the highway and onto the familiar streets that lead to my house. The wind whips through my hair, and the powerful engine rumbles beneath me. For the past three days, all I can think about is Rosa. It was painful being in LA, knowing I needed to get back to speak with her. I had an appointment about a shop and I also needed the days to clear my head.

Every word I said to Rosa stung like salt to a wound. I don't regret her at all, not even us getting married, but I don't want her to regret not going to the college she's always dreamed of going to. That is something I couldn't live with. It hurt like hell to push her to leave, but I know Rosa. She'll stay and not be happy at the art school here. That's the last thing I want. I haven't spoken to her, so I'm not sure what plans she has now.

She's so fucking wrong. I'm not like her mom. I chose her dream, her happiness over mine. I could easily keep her here with me, knowing she has that scholarship. Rosa, my beautiful wife, has always hidden in everyone's shadow.

She's stubborn.

She needs to spread her wings and fly. To rise from the ashes. I don't need a break, but I knew that would be the only way to push her to go. She has a full ride. She's been working so hard for all these years. I can't let her transfer here and lose it all, especially her scholarship. I won't be the reason why she holds back from attending the school she loves. My Rosa needs to grow and experience life.

I can't go with her. I don't have the money since I just got us a place. Hell, I don't have money to completely furnish it or enough for food. I need her to know that I don't regret her and another reason I said I regretted getting married early is I'm not financially stable. After draining my account for the apartment, I have zero to my name.

Yes, I knew she was going back when we first discussed it, but I told her we would figure out a long-distance relationship. Not for her to toss that dream away.

And I can't leave my brothers. They are grown men, but I don't trust my mom. Plus, Mark still lives at home. Leaving my brothers would be like leaving my children behind, and Dominic is going through a hard time.

I want Rosa to have college experiences, and we can see each other long distance. Once things get better, I can move out there with her. I need to explain all this to her. It might seem like I'm choosing my brothers, but I'm not. I'm choosing her dream.

I'll take a shower and head to her house and explain to her.

Unlocking the front door, I walk straight to my bedroom. My footsteps pound on the floor, eager to get to Rosa. Peeling my shirt off, I notice a manila envelope on my desk addressed with my name. The blood slowly drains out of my heart and shatters into pieces. She said I killed us. No, she drowned us.

I said, let's take a break for her best interest, not because I didn't want her. She thought I regretted her. That's absolutely not true.

She left a note.

SANTIAGO,

I'm on my way back to Oregon, and it will be a while before I return. You hurt me. You pushed me away. I never expected you to regret us. I don't want to see you or hear from you. You're just like my mom. You wanted a break, so you got it.

Love you always,

Rosaline

A loud roar vibrates from my chest.

25

SANTIAGO

TWO MONTHS later

I'VE KEPT myself busy these months without her, trying to think how it all went down, how I fucked up. I had rushed to her aunt's, but she was gone and then I tried calling her, but it went to voicemail. I've waited for her phone calls, but I know it's me who should call my wife. I texted her but got no reply. Maybe she changed her number.

I park at what was supposed to be our apartment and sigh, turning off the ignition. Those words in her note crushed me. *"You're just like my mom."* You were never second, Rosa. Ever since I was a kid, I've always carried so many responsibilities at such a young age. I'm the one who kept it all together. What if I move with Rosa, and shit goes down here?

I know my wife is my top priority, but I also want her to

learn to be independent. That's why I felt a long-distance relationship would be good for a while. How am I supposed to have a wife if I can't support her properly? Also, I need to get my finances together. Then I could move out there, or if she wanted to wait, she could finish school before moving back here. Either-or, I need her.

MY MIND HAS BEEN SUCH A JUGGLING mess, I've forgotten to check the mail. I'm waiting for some paperwork from the bank. Fishing out my keys from my pocket, I unlock the box, finding it as full as I expected it to be. Noticing a larger envelope among the others, I pull that one out first.

It's from Rosa. My heart ricochets against my ribcage. Jogging to my apartment, I rush to unlock it, and tear the envelope open.

My blood drains. She did this. She broke us without giving us a chance to talk it over. She broke every piece of us, with the divorce paper in my hand and a note attached to it.

SANTIAGO,

THIS IS *the only way for me to move on from us. In the end, you did this to us. You gave me no choice.*

LOVE YOU ALWAYS,

ROSALINE.

· · ·

My heart drops to my stomach. All I want to do is roar her name so she can hear the anger and pain in my voice from where she's at.

PART TWO

"I will be your everything. Your light when you're lost in darkness, your anchor when you are adrift in a sea of chaos, and the villain fighting for you. I'll gather the broken pieces of our love and rebuild until we are whole." –Santiago.

<u>Reader, before you proceed:</u>

Part two is in present time, following the timeline of the end of *Recklessly You*

26

Present

Santiago

Around two years later

After stopping at my regular coffee place, I make a left turn to my shop. As soon as I lay eyes on the sign that reads Delgado's Automotive, a wave of pride wells up inside my chest. I've worked my ass off to have my own shop. Business has been so good that Reese's dad retired when he started losing customers.

He wasn't mad. He was proud. Reese wasn't interested in taking over, so he just closed down and is now my assistant manager; I figured I'd bump the fucker up.

The smell of grease in the shop never gets old. I smell like a grease monkey all the damn time. It reminds me of who I am and how far I've come.

"Hey, boss," Antonio greets me behind the front counter.

I give him a nod and head to my office.

I meticulously review all the work orders we currently have. There is so much work that I need to hire more mechanics.

"Knock, knock."

I look up from the stack of paperwork. Dominic stands in the doorway. Sometimes pride hits at the weirdest moments. My fucking baby brother is the proud owner of two restaurants. He's overcome so many obstacles and become a good man.

"My wife wanted to drop off lunch for you, so I decided to join her," he says nonchalantly.

I lean back in the chair, hands behind my head, with a grin on my face. My brother is a jealous man when it comes to his wife. "Where is she?"

He tosses his head back, pointing to the shop where all the guys are working. We can hear Mila talking to Reese and giggling.

"You're a jealous shit," I tease.

Dominic laughs.

"Ah, there she is, my favorite sister-in-law," I tease, grinning, leaping out of my chair to greet her with a hug. My nephew is strapped to her chest like a baby koala.

"I'm your only sister-in-law, you big dork," Mila sasses.

I place a kiss on her forehead and kiss Luca, who is, I think, three months old. Dressed in a blue beanie, little mittens, and a cute faux leather jacket I gave him, he looks stylish. But he smells of sour milk. He's adorable and has the signature Delgado dimples. Luca looks so much like his older brother, Dante, who is now six. Dominic discovered he had a son with Mila when they found their way back to each other.

My sister-in-law is such a fierce woman. She's been through hell, but she's still standing. Guilt always consumes me, knowing I ignored her phone calls all these years and lied to my brother. Rather than harboring any resentment toward me, she greets me warmly with a sisterly smile on her face. She's so great, and she has the family over to Sunday dinners at their house.

I gesture for her to sit in my seat behind the desk, and she leans back, patting Luca's butt. He coos, sucking the life out of his mitten. Dominic leans up against the wall. His gaze stays pinned on his wife with love and devotion. Shame hits tenfold when I think of how I suggested him to date another woman, sleep with other women, and even agreed with Rachel when she pressured him to take another woman into marriage when Mila was absent. I had no business meddling in his life. It always tugs at my chest, seeing them and others so in love.

"We have new items on the menu, added by me." Mila smiles, pointing at herself. "I brought you a chimichanga filled with chicken and green *chile*. It's topped with a yummy salsa. I had to teach Mario how to cook some of my recipes."

"Thank you, I appreciate it. I'm sure it's good. Everything you cook is amazing."

She waves her hand in the air. "Not as amazing as my husband's cooking. He's the real chef." She winks at Dominic.

She's right. Dominic's cooking is on point. He can create the most amazing dishes.

"We came to see how everything went with the bank. Liam, so kindly informed us you had a tantrum the day you helped us move to the new studio."

My eyebrows ride up in amusement. A tantrum? What a snitch. They all think I've been pissed because of what has been going on with the bank. Which is true, but that's not the only reason my blood is pumping hot.

A lot has happened throughout the years. Rachel co-signed the loan I applied for to get my shop. The bank has been giving me shit about it. Turns out they can't do anything.

"Tantrum? Seriously, he's ridiculous. While Mark and I were waiting for him outside in the freezing cold, Liam, Mr. Lover Boy, was inside, grinding his dick on Sophie."

Mila throws her head back into laughter, scaring poor Luca. Dominic snorts. Sophie is Mila's best friend. The one guy we thought would never settle down is anchored by Sophie, and he doesn't give two shits about it.

"Everything went better than expected. The people at the bank were just being assholes. They didn't know what the hell was going on. I took my attorney to the meeting with me. Since Rachel is merely the co-signer, there's nothing they can do about it. It's a loan that I'm paying for. They asked if Rachel contributed to the down payment. She didn't. They have no proof. The attorney set them straight, thank God." I let out a long breath of relief.

"That's awesome, brother; glad you took care of that shit. The last thing we need is to deal with the aftermath of Rachel's fucked up shit." Dominic's face twists into a sneer.

I can't blame him. Rachel was the one who tried to destroy both his and Mila's lives.

"It's over, Dominic. She's out of our lives." It's like a breath of fresh air. We both sigh.

As soon as the front door clicks shut behind my brother and his wife, I eagerly peel back the plastic wrap covering the Styrofoam tray. The mouthwatering aroma of melted cheese, spicy meat, and crisp fried tortilla fills the room, making my stomach growl in anticipation.

Tomorrow is New Year's Eve, and I've grown to dislike holidays. Everyone around me is married or has someone they love in their life. For the past two years, I've learned to live with the hollowness in my chest. Dominic is happily married, and Liam plans on asking Sophie to marry him. They all think I'm incapable of falling in love or I don't want to fall in love. What they don't know is I was in love, but she shattered my heart and replaced it with a dark, hollow shadow.

∾

THE WALLS of Rocko's Bar shake with the infectious energy of laughter, cheers, and drunk exclamations. Patrons sit at wooden tables or lean against the worn bar. Their movements are exaggerated by alcohol as they clink glasses. The walls vibrate with the energy of the crowd. I pull out a chair and wave down Will, the owner and good friend of ours.

"Hey, Santiago. How's it going? The usual?"

I nod and look through the crowd. We've been regulars for years. We would always meet here after work. Now, times have changed. The guys all have someone to come home to. Will slides a beer my way and Reese and Damian slide onto the stools beside me.

"What's up?" Reese drawls, running his hands through his bushy beard. He acts like I didn't just see him fifteen minutes ago. "What are your plans for tomorrow? For New Year's Eve? Wanna hit the club with us?" He points to Damian.

"I'm not into clubs. You know that." I'll be thirty in a month, and clubbing is not for me. I'm too old for that shit. Maybe if I had a partner to go with, it would be more appealing to me.

"It's not for us either, but we're just going to drink and watch. You never know what you will find." He snorts, taking a swig of his foamed beer. Reese is still single, and Damian is now divorced.

Janet, the bartender, saunters toward us, her hips swaying in movement. "Can I get you guys some appetizers?" She smiles with those red-stained lips.

"You know that would be great. I can go for some nachos with extra jalapeños. How about you guys?" Reese utters with a stupid, amused grin on his face, watching Janet as her eyes eat me up like a hungry hyena.

"I'll have some wings," I tell Janet.

She nods and runs her fingers on mine. Janet has been trying to hook up with me since she started working here two years ago. She's pretty and kind, but she's not my type of pretty. I move my hand and grab my beer. She frowns and walks off.

"You should just hit that up already," Reese mouths into his glass.

I roll my eyes at him. "You know why I don't."

I would never.

"I don't fucking get it. You know what you have to do. Just do it, and then fuck Janet. One night is all you need."

"Mind your own damn business, Reese." Damian gives him a grim, scolding look.

"Hey, I'm trying to help him. He'd feel better if he did."

"Well, that's not helping. It's called sticking your nose where it doesn't belong," Damian fires back.

They act like I'm not sitting here, listening to them fight about me. It's a good thing the food arrives on time. We dig into our appetizers and wash them down with salty, cold beer.

Changing the subject, I ask, "Did you schedule the interviews for tomorrow?"

Reese swallows his food, wipes his mouth with a napkin, and then nods. "Two mechanics. Great references and strong work ethics. Not to mention, their experience is fantastic. I set the interviews up for the morning."

"That's good to hear. Hopefully, it works out because we're swamped."

The conversations flow, and more drinks are passed around. Damian goes over his private investigator business, which he started a year ago, and then he speaks of his divorce. Just the sound of those words sends a knife to my chest, taking me back to that night when I opened that envelope.

"I thought the guys were coming," Damian murmurs.

"Liam has been buried in Sophie's pussy ever since she moved back with him. He's been MIA, and Dominic is busy. He's a family man. He has two kids, and he helps Mila. Mark is probably at home." Mark moved in with me when all the shit happened with Rachel. Mark has been quiet. It's not like it was his fault. He did nothing wrong.

Grabbing my black leather jacket from behind the stool, I slip it on, getting ready to leave. Reese clears his throat really fucking loud, no doubt wanting to get my attention about something important he's about to say. He's always been like that.

"She's here. She's back. I ran into her at the grocery store. She's moving into her new place today or tomorrow." His eyes go wide, and he presses his lips together.

"You'd think you would have told me this earlier."

"Didn't know how to tell you." He shrugs.

My blood runs cold, and my lungs collapse. I'm not sure if I should be happy Rosaline is moving back, or if I should be pissed at having her around, especially if she's with another man.

27

ROSALINE

I GROAN INTO THE HOT, steamy *atole* my *tía* prepared for me. It's been so long since I've been back. Well, I've been back twice—once for New Year's last year and again for Mila's and Dominic's wedding. Those are the only times I've been here in two years and a couple of months. I worked myself to the bone with school and work. I doubled my classes just so I could keep my mind busy and finish faster. Watching my *tía* spread butter on my toast makes me sad, knowing I missed so much in the last few years.

The pain seeps into my bones. So much has happened since Mila returned. Rachel committed her crimes, and then Liam got shot. I wasn't here for any of them. The guilt eats at me. Would things have been different if I had stayed? I would not have let Rachel manipulate Dominic. He would have never gotten engaged to a psycho because I would have knocked some sense into him. However, that is over with. What matters is that Mila and Dominic are married and have two beautiful kids.

I'm not sure if I'm happy to be back. The encounters I had with Santiago the last time I was here were not good. I've grown and changed since I left. The pain I've carried has given me strength. I've become a master at hiding it, burying it, and forcing a smile on my face.

"Rosa, are you okay?"

I give my *tía* a warm smile. "Yes, perfectly fine, *Tía*. Thank you for the *atole*. It hit the spot on this cold day."

She doesn't look convinced. "How's Ivan?"

I feel my body flinch at his name. The story behind Ivan is a long one. Jasmine and I lived in the dorms for some time until she got kicked out, so we moved to an apartment. We met a girl from school named Alley, and we all became good friends. She had a close friend, Ivan, who was her boyfriend's friend. She's known him for a while. He was always around, hanging out. Within those years, he asked me out, but I kept refusing. My heart and soul, have only wanted one man. I wasn't ready to move on. For the last two years, he hung out with us. I viewed Ivan as an okay friend.

One night, I was on a phone call with Liam, and he mentioned that Santiago picks up one-night stands. My heart broke. I suspected this. But having it confirmed is another thing. My family never found out that Santiago and I, for a short time, were husband and wife.

Picturing him with other women killed me. I became sick with nausea. A couple of weeks before last New Year's, Ivan asked me out again. He came along with me to visit my family, and he had dinner with us. It was the first time we'd been together without Jasmine and Alley. Jasmine suggested I give it a try but to tell him we should take it slow. The pain and the depression became unhealthy for me. So, I talked with Ivan. I didn't mention my reasons for taking it slow, but just that we needed to take it slow, like snail slow. He agreed.

"We're not together anymore, *Tía*. It didn't work out," I mumble, taking a mouthful of toast.

"Oh, honey. I'm sorry."

I shake my head at her. "It's okay, *Tía*. It was nothing serious." Because it wasn't. It's over and done with and will never happen again.

She frowns at the bruise on my cheek like she has in the last hour. It's fading into an angry yellow-looking bruise.

"Some Vicks will help," she suggests.

I laugh, and she groans. "*Tía*, I'm fine. As I said, I tripped when packing; I'll be fine. I'm headed to the apartment—or townhouse. The moving trucks should be here. I need to scope out the place. It better be nice. Liam will be strangled if it's not. I can't believe I agreed to let him pick for me."

Liam suggested I let him pick. He supposedly did a walk-through and made sure it was a safe area and mold-free.

AFTER STOPPING at my new job as an art teacher at a private art school, I map the address to the townhouse apartment division on my phone. My plans and dreams still lie in opening my own art studio and getting a master's in art—one thing at a time. At least now I'm more stable and mature, even at twenty-two, I'd like to say I am. Parking my new Audi, I wave down the movers who look lost. Selling on Etsy has bumped my income.

A tall, skinny guy with sandy blond hair stands with a clipboard in hand. His intense gaze drags slowly up and down. Feeling uncomfortable, I take my coat from my arm and swing it on.

"Rosaline?" he says, rolling the *R*.

"Yes, that's me," I say, zipping up my coat to cover my breasts.

Cristo, what a perv.

"Where would you like your stuff?"

I pinch the bridge on my nose. "Preferably in the apartment."

He chuckles like he's at a comedy show. "You're a firecracker." He winks, walking toward the moving truck.

Oh, for fuck's sake.

The area is clean and quiet. Everyone around seems to mind their own business. As I unlock the door and enter the apartment, the bright, modern space welcomes me. The living room is bathed in natural light, thanks to tall windows that stretch from floor to ceiling.

The modern kitchen has sleek, stainless-steel appliances. A vast island catches my eye, surrounded by polished countertops. I climb the stairs to explore the two bedrooms, each with its own unique charm. Overall, it's a beautiful home that feels like a peaceful sanctuary. I love it. Liam did good.

The movers walk in with my bedroom set, and I direct them to the bedroom I want it in. I also need to let them know to be extra careful with my art supplies and canvases.

While they're setting up my bedroom set, I unpack my dishes. I wipe them and place them in the cupboard, and like always, my mind wanders to Santiago. Through the years, I've wondered what he's doing. Has he stopped thinking of me? When I'd stare at the stars, was he looking at the same star I was? Does he still love me?

When I last saw him, he didn't seem happy to see me. I was nothing more than someone he regretted. He always seems angry, but he did this. He pushed me away. *I* miss him. All of him. Our marriage was not the only thing we lost; it was just a small part of something much bigger.

My therapist suggested I speak to him to help me move on. I don't see how that would help. There were times in those years when I wished he would knock on my door, but it never came.

I recall the one New Year's I came down to visit. I had not intended to invite Ivan, but he invited himself. Anyway, I thought maybe it would make Santiago jealous. But no, we argued. He called me a slut, and without thinking, I slapped him. He gasped, but just before I left, he said, "Good luck with your pencil pusher." The second time I saw him was at Mila's wedding. Ivan had been there as well. Santiago asked me to dance. I shouldn't say asked. He gripped my waist and dragged me to the dance floor. Then he swayed me around the dance floor, fingers digging into my waist. I felt the electric shock between us. I don't think he felt anything. We were angry-dancing like we were in a boxing match. During those times, I wanted to ask him the question that had been at the tip of my tongue, but he never gave a shit and would just insult me.

I couldn't believe Santiago would treat me like that. He had never acted this way before. But it confirmed that I was nothing more than the too-young girl he regretted marrying once the honeymoon phase ended.

My phone rings, and my smile grows when I glimpse at the picture.

"Hello?"

"Hey, how's everything going? I've been worried about you. We miss you already," Jasmine says in a soft tone.

My best friend and I have been through so much in the last few years, and we've held each other up.

"I'm doing well so far." I sigh. "I just started unpacking. My apartment is pleasant, in a quiet area, and has a security system —that's a bonus. The moving truck is currently unloading. I miss you guys, too. It won't be the same without you here."

My heart warms when I hear the little guy in the background holler at Auntie Rosa.

"I'm so relieved, Rosa. I'm happy you're not alone and with your family. When do you start work?"

Fuck, I run outside when the guys start manhandling my art.

"Hey, can you please be gentle with the canvases?" I shout to the men. "Sorry, I'm talking to the movers," I tell Jasmine. "I start next week. I figured I'd get situated first. Also, I spoke to a woman who owns an art gallery. I showed her my portfolio. She loves them and wants to display them."

She squeals.

"Aye, Rosa, that's amazing. You're such an amazing artist. There's no doubt someone will buy your work. I'm so happy for you."

"Thank you, so how's business going? How's my guy doing?"

She chuckles when her son Philip yells, "Can I talk to her, Mama?"

"I've been selling a lot of sculptures and my famous coffee mugs in my Etsy shop. We're talking like you've been gone for months. It's only been two days." We both laugh. "Philip wants to talk to you." She passes the phone. I can hear his heavy breathing. He's two going on three soon in a couple of months. Hint: the reason she got kicked out is that she was pregnant.

"Hewow."

"Hello, sweetheart. How are you doing? I miss you."

"Tia Rosa. I pwy… Chubwy. He is licking me."

A giggle escapes my lips when I hear his dog, Chubby, lick him, and he giggles.

"I miss Chubby."

"You talk to Chubwy?"

"No, he can't talk on a phone, silly."

"K. I bisit you. Mama said soon."

"Yes, baby, soon we will see each other again. I miss you like crazy."

"See you, tia." I stop pacing outside when I smell cigarette smoke. It's a familiar scent.

"I'll let you go, baby. I'll call you tomorrow. Kisses. I love you, sweetheart."

The line clicks. I hold the phone to my chest and take a deep breath. I can feel him behind me. What the hell is he doing here?

It's not like he would come to help unpack. Slowly, I turn around.

My heart gasps even though my mouth is frozen shut. He's even more handsome as he ages. His olive skin reflects in the light, giving it that shine. He's definitely more muscular. His muscles bulge through the long sleeves he's wearing. His jaw is tightly clenched, and there is no warmth in those eyes that have always looked at me with tenderness. It hurts. Like always, I put my mask back on and build those walls.

"What are you doing here?" he spits.

My eyes go into slits, and my pain turns into anger. I gesture with my hands to the moving truck. "I live here, you idiot. What are you doing here?"

He laughs, and it's not a this-is-so-funny or a happy-go-lucky laugh. It's a sarcastic, evil one. It's like karma just stabbed me in the back.

"I live here." He points to the door that happens to be next door to mine.

What the fuck, Liam? Idiota.

Just fucking great. Now I have to live next to the man I'm in love with—my ex-husband. Watch him walk in every day and see him bring women home.

"Fuck," he shouts.

I try to take a nice deep breath to calm myself, like my therapist taught me. Finally, I turn all the way to face him, taking some steps toward him. "I didn't know you lived here. Liam picked the place for me. Don't worry. I'll stay out of your way."

His intense gaze stays pinned on me, and he takes another puff of his cigarette. I thought he stopped smoking.

"Good." The word is short and spiteful, like he wants me to stay away. He doesn't want to see me.

My lips set in a grim line. "Good. The less I see you, the better, asshole. Who knew you could be so malicious and hateful? It would have been better if my mom had carried me along with her with her sorry life and abusive tendencies rather than meeting you."

He stiffens, and my body shakes with rage. It's a lie. I'd die a million times to have what we had throughout our years, but I'm too fired up.

I know my words sting because I feel it, too. His hands fist up as he takes a step toward me. He's closer than I want him to be. The familiar scent of smoke and grease lingers around me. His eyes soften from his hard, dark, angry ones when he sees the bruise on my cheek.

"Rosa, what is that bruise from? Who hurt you?"

He's about to touch it, but I flinch, stepping back. He's startled by my reaction.

I cover my cheek with the palm of my hand. "N-nothing. I tripped and fell," I say, then run back to my apartment and slam the door. I lean against the door and sob, and pray he believes it. Santiago was the only one who could see through me—before he laid us to rest.

28

SANTIAGO

WALKING INTO MY OFFICE, I slam the door. I went home for lunch, and Rosa was there, of all places. She has to be my next-door neighbor. Now I have to witness her with her boyfriend, the pencil pusher fuckhead. He looks like a damn prick. My jaw clenches, recalling listening to her phone call with the asshole. *"I'll let you go, baby. I'll call you tomorrow. Kisses. I love you, sweetheart."* Her voice dripped with honey, all sweet and shit. She never talked to me like that. And she's in love with someone else. It hurts like a sledgehammer to the heart.

Shoving my hands in my hair, I can't stop replaying how she flinched when I reached to touch her cheek. I did it absent-mindedly. What pains me is how she thought I'd hurt her. She's scared I'll hurt her? Does she really not know me at all? It's best we both keep our distance.

There's a knock at my door. I look at the clock. One of the guys I have to interview rescheduled for this afternoon. It must be him.

"Come in," I drawl. My mind is in a haze. Rosa did a number on me. I glance up. My gaze is trained on a blond, busty woman waltzing in with tight blue jeans and a low-cut shirt showing her tits. She sits on the chair in front of me. I clear my throat at the pretty woman in front of me. "Can I help you?"

She laughs. "Yes, I'm here for the interview. I'm Billy. Nice to meet you." She extends her hand.

Reese failed to mention that Billy is a woman. Her laughing makes her breasts bounce. I look away. She might have great tits, however, I can't help but think of Rosa because no one compares to her. Looking at any other woman always makes me feel like I'm being disrespectful to her.

I proceeded with interviewing her. She has a lot of experience—color me surprised. I've never come across a woman who knows more than some guys I've hired. She says her dad taught her at a young age. The only problem I have if I hire her is the guys will be distracted. I can't have that, although they will need to learn to keep their shit together.

She crosses her legs and leans in the seat. "I can see you're swamped with work. I get shit done. You won't have a problem with me, and I'm good with my hands." She smiles.

My lips twitch into a half smile.

"You have a lot of experience, Billy. I think you'd be great. It's just that—"

"The problem is the guys, right? You think I'd be a distraction?" It seems like she's had these types of problems before.

"Hey, I know it's not your fault, but yeah, that's what it is," I admit.

She sighs and twirls her hair around. "I assure you, I'm not interested in dating anyone in this shop. I'm not into dick," she says flatly.

I can't help but laugh. She reminds me of Liam's girlfriend, Sophie, who has that spunky personality.

Once my new employee leaves, I walk into the main shop,

searching for Reese. He's under a truck. "Did you know Billy is a woman?"

He slides out, his stomach shaking in laughter.

"No way, really?"

I guess he didn't know. "Yes, and I hired her. She has skills. I couldn't very well not hire her because she's a woman. That would make me a sexist."

"Is she hot?"

I shrug.

"God, you're a blind man."

"She made it clear she's not into dick."

He snorts. "My cock can make any woman straight," Reese says with confidence. "Did you decide about the club tonight?"

"Nah, I'm heading home. I'm going to grab some beers. I'll spend the New Year's at home or see what Dominic is up to." I give him a bro hug. "Guess who my new neighbor is?" His brows arch at my sharp tone. "Rosa," I say dryly as I step out the door.

"No shit!" he shouts. Reese and Damian are the only two who know what Rosa's betrayal has done to me. I never expected her to end things like how she did. Yes, I pressured her to leave only so she could pursue a career she dreamt of. I never saw her as a mistake. I thought she would at least call me. It wasn't until I saw her with that guy when she came to visit that I felt she had forgotten us. I had hoped to speak with her, but she wasn't alone. The betrayal of her with another man pains me.

I THROW my keys on the table. They slide off, and I grumble in annoyance. I pick them up and glance at Mark, spread out on the couch, reading a book.

"Are you going out tonight?" I ask, sitting on the other couch and turning the TV on.

He looks up from his book. "Guess who I just saw?"

Oh, hell, I forgot Mark and Rosa are good friends.

"I don't know." I play dumb.

"Rosa is our new neighbor. Liam thought it would be great if she lived close to us. I agree. Andrea is making food at Rosa's, so I'm going over there in a bit."

Dull pain claws at my chest. It's going to explode all over again. I don't know why I do this to myself. Her boyfriend will be there. My hands shake with the thought of him touching what rightfully belongs to me.

"Are you coming?"

"No!"

"What the hell's your problem with Rosa? I noticed when she was here for the wedding, you acted like an ass. You and Rosa have always been tight. What happened?" Mark sits up and throws his hands up, giving me a look as if he knows something is going on.

"There's nothing to talk about."

"Bullshit. You're in love with her."

My head jolts. It's not a question—it's a statement. He figured it out.

"I don't want to talk about it." My voice is gruff. I'm not in the mood to go over the past with him. It only brings up memories I've worked my ass off to bury.

"Don't act like an asshole with her. Learn from the shit Dominic did. Talk to her. Whatever is going on, I know she cares for you. If it's because of Ivan, I guarantee if you tell her how you feel, she'll choose you because that girl has always loved you." He shakes his head once. "You're an idiot. I love Rosa like a sister, Santiago. Don't fuck with her. If you're going to play with her heart, then leave her alone."

I respect Mark for sticking up for her.

He stands up from the couch, clearly not pleased with me. But shit, how am I supposed to stay calm and collected when she has a man? Then I have to hear Liam say things like Rosa's boyfriend is nice, and he's a cool guy. He treats Rosa good. It makes me feel like I'm not good enough for her.

And maybe I'm not.

I sigh. "Thanks. I mean it. What are you reading?"

The cover has a man and a woman tangled together. I never thought Mark read romance.

He lifts the book up. "Romance, baby. I was watching the kids for Mila and grabbed one of her books. She has a buttload of books, by the way. But it was the first in a series and now I couldn't put it down. She let me borrow it." He laughs. "Damn, you need to read romance. Liam calls it a guide to fuck a woman right."

I can't help but snort a laugh. Liam is reading romance. *Oh, Jesus.*

He continues, "It's good. Like you would have never thought there were hot scenes." He smacks the book. "Good stuff." He laughs so hard he's holding himself up on the wall. "Your face. You look horrified."

"Kinda, ya. Are you, Mila, Sophie, and Liam in a romance book club?"

He taps his chin. "That's a great idea. I should bring it up to the girls."

"For fuck's sake, Mark!" I grunt a laugh.

"I'm joking. I'm going shower and get ready."

Right, he's going next door. He runs upstairs while thinking about what he said. I don't know if she loves me.

But what she said earlier… It was as if a thousand weights caved in my chest. She would rather have suffered with Tina than have ever met me. We both hurt each other, but I'm not the one who filed for divorce and then found someone else as if we had been nothing.

~

ROSALINE

IT'S BEEN a week and a half since I moved into my apartment and since New Year's. My aunt made some *posole* and *menudo*. Mark came to hang out, including Dominic, Mila, and the kids. Dominic kept asking if Santiago was coming. I didn't expect him to come. I'm sure he had his own plans.

Today's my first day at work, and so far, I love it. I started the class by teaching them how to blend colors. The basics. It's an adult class. I do have some private lessons that I teach as well.

"Ms. Acosta?" One of my students waves me over.

I walk over to him, and he gives me a boyish smile. He's tall, probably about two years older than me.

"What do you think?" He points to his painting.

Once we went over the basics, I instructed them to paint a tree with the colors I had taught them how to blend.

"Looks good. Honestly." It does. It's easier than you think to go wrong with a tree. I've seen it.

"Are you lying to me? If it looks like something a toddler made, I won't get my feelings hurt."

My smile widens. His smile is contagious.

"I would never, Samuel." I shake my head and laugh. "Your leaves are on point. It looks beautiful."

He eyes me, unsure if I'm being real about it. "Thank you. I checked out your social media page. You're incredible. Your paintings belong in an art gallery going for millions."

My cheeks and ears grow hot.

"That's why I feel my work looks like a toddler painted it compared to your work," he admits.

The last thing I want is for my students to feel self-conscious. "We all start somewhere. I've been painting since I was four." I smile at the memories. "And I have a degree, so don't compare yourself to me. You're doing great." I give him a pat on the back and make my rounds around the class.

The day went better than I thought. I had no anxiety speaking to the class. I've worked on that with my therapist. I'd like to say I'm proud of myself for not chickening out.

My phone buzzes on my desk. The blood drains from me when I see who it's from.

Unknown: *Call me!!! Now!*

Me: *Fuck off. Stop calling me.*

I know it's Ivan. Who else would it be? I hate him. Shoving the phone in my purse, I sigh, letting out a heavy breath.

"Hey, Rosa, how was your first day?" Grace, another instructor, asks.

"I loved it, I had so much fun."

"That's wonderful." She soft cheers for me. Her ass-length hair waves all the way down her back. "Listen, I wanted to ask you if you'd like to join me for a drink. My husband is working late tonight. I figured we could wind down and get to know one another." She gives me a cheerful smile.

Grace is a couple of years older than me. The times I've spoken to her, she seems nice. As much as I would rather go home to my empty apartment and cuddle under a blanket and binge-watch something on Netflix, I do need to clear my head. A drink might do the trick.

"Sure, that would be great."

She clasped her hands in a cute way. "Okay, how about we meet at Rocko's? Do you know where that is?"

My heart thumps. That's the guy's spot. I pray Santiago is not there. "Yes, sure. I'll meet you there."

"Let me get my coat."

I nod and finish packing my bag.

Fifteen minutes later, I'm standing in front of Rocko's, waiting for Grace, when Liam and Sophie walk out.

"Rosita, what are you doing here?"

I roll my eyes at Liam. He's so overprotective.

"I came to have a drink with a friend. Hi, Sophie." I hug her.

She's so beautiful. Her blue eyes shine like the ocean. I met her at Dominic and Mila's wedding. She's such an amazing person. I love her for Liam. My eyes go to the sparkly ring on her finger, and I gasp excitedly.

"Oh my god, you're engaged."

Liam smiles from ear to ear and nods.

I jump and hug Liam and Sophie. "Congratulations." I'm so happy for them.

"Thank you, Rosa." Sophie's eyes water, and she snuggles into Liam's side. They make a perfect couple.

"How do you like your place?" Liam asks.

"I love it. Thank you. It's nice and quiet."

"Good. I'm glad. I figured if you lived next to Santiago and Mark, it would be nice. It would be safer"

If only he knew the man he calls best friend and big brother, who is my ex-husband and the man I'm in love with. He wouldn't have moved me in next door to him.

I pinch my lips together. Sophie's head tilts, and she stares at me. Maybe I gave away too much the last time we were at the beach. "Yeah. It's wonderful to have them around." I muster a smile, and Liam laughs.

"I don't know what's going on between you two. You didn't visit much, and when you did, all you two did was argue." He gives me a displeased look.

Liam was upset that I ghosted him. I didn't want to know about Santiago's love life.

"I know he acts like an overprotective brother."

Brother!

The word makes me barf. Liam is the definition of blind. He's so oblivious even Sophie snorts. I swear it took him months to open his eyes and see he was in love with her.

Grace steps out of her car, and thank the heavens for that.

"Santiago is in there," Sophie mouths at me. She definitely knows something.

I nod a quick thank you. I brace myself for what I'm walking into.

29

ROSALINE

THE SECOND I open the wooden doors, my heart wants to jump out of my chest. I spot him sitting on a stool with Reese, a couple of other guys, and a woman sitting next to Santiago.

Grace and I sit at a round table, not too close to them. I can't help but wonder if he's dating her or if she's just a hook-up. This is exactly why I didn't want to move back here, but I couldn't stay in Oregon either. My gaze involuntarily keeps sliding toward him.

The server approaches our table with a small notepad and pen in hand. I smile and ask for a mojito while Grace confidently requests a pomegranate martini with extra lime. The server scribbles down our orders before walking away with a nod.

The woman lays a hand on his shoulder. She tells him something, and he laughs. A full-blown, beautiful laugh. Santiago's happy, from the looks of it. He owns his own shop now, and I couldn't be prouder of him. He's not struggling the way he used to.

"Is everything okay?" Grace asks in a soft, concerned tone.

I'm horrible company. My mind is on Santiago and what he's doing. I should turn my chair so I'm not facing them. My gaze goes back to Grace. Something about her gives me a warm feeling. I can trust her. I've never been big on sharing anything personal, but the need to get this off my chest is suffocating me. Only Jasmine knows.

"The guy in the black leather biker jacket is my ex-husband."

Her eyes bulge into golf balls.

"I've known him my whole life. We got married when I was twenty. Things went sour quickly. He said he regretted us rushing into marriage. He wanted me to move to Portland for college and said that it would be best if we took a break. At first, I was angry, but when I thought about it, I figured he wanted me to follow my dreams. Then, a girl he hooked up with on and off in his teens to early twenties approached me at the airport. We happened to run into each other. I was flying down to surprise him two months after I left.

"Damn. That's crazy," Grace says, glancing over her shoulder at Santiago. "I'm guessing this little run-in wasn't a happy one."

"Not so much. See, before me, he was with a woman named Monica. The airport girl showed me pictures of him and Monica. She was at his work." I take a deep breath and try so damn hard not to cry. Grace pats my hand. "Um…she was pregnant in the photos, and Santiago had his hand on her belly with a smile on his face. She said it was his."

"Oh, my," Grace breathes.

"I never planned on divorcing him until I saw those photos. Then it all clicked: he wanted a break and to move me away because Monica was pregnant. I rented a car at the airport. I was heading to his house when I saw a woman jogging. It was—

Monica. She was pregnant. I didn't believe Marissa, but it was true. I saw it with my own eyes."

"Did you kick his ass?" Grace asks.

"No. No one knew I came down, and I went back to Portland that same day. I'm not sure if he ever told his brothers he has a kid. Because no one has spoken about it or mentioned it. I just know I can't be with a man who got another woman pregnant, even if it was before we were together."

Her warm hands lace with mine. "I'm so sorry, Rosa. Believe me when I tell you. I won't gossip about this. I'm here for you. I'm heartbroken."

I peer toward Santiago. The woman leans closer, her breasts touching his chest, and she whispers something. He winks at her, and she laughs. Jealousy and anger pool in my belly at the thought of him taking her home to his bed.

To this day, I can't get the image of those photos out of my head. He has a child with Monica. He might not be with her, but he has a child with another woman.

"Let's go, hun. I can't bear to look at him myself." She half laughs.

Just then, the server arrives with the drinks. I move my purse to make room for the drinks, and the strap catches the waitress's hand, spilling both drinks. Santiago turns around. The surprise on his face makes me angry. My eyes harden, mixed with pain and fury, or even loathing. I don't blink. His eyes soften. Maybe, just maybe, he can feel the pain in me.

Standing, I grab my coat. Grace follows. Once we're outside, I place a hand on Grace's shoulder. "I'm sorry, Grace. I didn't mean to be such a killjoy. Rain check? Maybe somewhere else next time?"

"Don't worry about it. We will definitely get together again."

Santiago steps out of the bar, searching for me.

Grace mouths, "I'll see you tomorrow."

I nod and spin on my heels toward my car.

"Rosaline," Santiago calls out.

I keep walking. What do we have left to talk about? The past had me run away.

"Flower!"

My body goes still. His pet name for me.

With a heavy heart, I veer to face him, and it kills me. He nervously rakes his hand in his sexy hair. Then he laughs. "I don't know why in the hell I'm telling you this. Not like you give a shit, but nothing happened with the girl in there."

Adrenaline runs through my veins, hot and ready.

"Then you shouldn't have told me if you don't give a shit. You seemed pretty cozy with her, but that's just you, a fucking slut. Yeah, you heard me. You called me one when the real slut is you—sleeping your way around."

His jaw clenches. He steps closer, ready to spit his venom.

We went from shine to rust.

"Me? You're the one with a fucking boyfriend. You're the one in love with another man."

I don't correct him. I don't have a boyfriend, and Ivan was never one to me. We labeled it as that, but I never touched him or let him touch me as if we were lovers. He felt more like a good friend than anything else in the beginning.

Santiago is staring at me as if he wants to kiss me or strangle me. I'd take the latter. His lips on me would just piss me off. It's clear he's jealous by the way his nostrils flare.

"Go back inside with your bitch. Her legs are probably spread open for you. Then you can pass her to Reese. Since you guys like to slut around the same circle." I know I'm being a bitch, but I'm not going to let him walk all over me. I might be in pain from the grief he caused, but I've grown and healed from the torment my mom caused. I'm not that scared little girl anymore. Except for the storms, those still trigger me. Maybe someday those will fade.

I'm pissed at Reese about how he left Jasmine after sleeping with her, knowing she had a boyfriend. I don't have the energy for him. I'm dealing with too much other shit. My nose scrunches with disgust. His hand goes to the pockets of his jacket. "Rosa."

When I pivot, he grabs my arm. "I'm not going to—" Santiago stops when I flinch and jerk to get away. He lets go. Ignoring my reaction, I shrug at his words. He can do what he pleases, just as he has been doing, and now he has a child as a result.

Getting in my car, I blast the first song that comes on: *"This Is Me Trying"* by Taylor Swift. It's quite fitting. My wheels squeak out of the parking lot. I glimpse Santiago in the rearview mirror. Standing...staring.

As I drive back home, a shooting star rockets so close I can see the bright light.

I don't wish for Santiago like I used to. We can't ever happen. I wish for the hole in my heart to heal. I'm physically and mentally tired of the pain. I just want to be happy. In a couple of months, I'll head to London to get my master's. Then maybe there I can heal and be cheerful.

I'm relieved Santiago and I haven't bumped into each other in the two days since the bar. Maybe he's keeping his distance like he wanted. It's Sunday, and Mila called this morning to invite me for dinner. I wanted to ask who's going over, but by the way it sounded, it would just be me. When she said, *Come over for dinner, and fill us in on how it is in Portland.*

Opening the cupboard, I search for ingredients to make chocolate chip cookies. My *tía* always taught me never to go empty-handed when invited to someone's house. Dante will love chocolate chip cookies. I take out my ceramic mixing bowls and measuring cups. Then I get all the ingredients, and the only thing I can't find is sugar. How could I not have sugar? I grab my car keys. I'll just run to the store. Closing my front door, I see Mark coming out of his house.

"Hey, babe." He winks like he always does. "Or should I say 'hey, neighbor'?" He snorts.

"You haven't changed. You're still a dork."

Mark is just as handsome as his brother. The only thing missing are the dimples, and his skin is a tad lighter.

"Where are you heading off to?" he murmurs while texting someone.

"I was heading to get sugar. Now that I think of it, do you have some?"

"Yeah, it's in the cabinet. The apartment is the same setup as yours. There's no one home. Help yourself." He opens the door, grins mischievously, and walks away like his ass is on fire.

I stay stiff in front of the wide-open door. Maybe I should just go to the store, but he said no one's home. I peek in, my eyes roving the whole area like a ninja ready to strike. My heart begins to go thump, thump. Tiptoeing in, I go straight to the kitchen. I glance behind me then search the cupboards until I find a jar filled with sugar. There's no doubt my blood pressure skyrocketed while searching for a Ziploc bag to fill with sugar. I feel like I'm breaking in. And Santiago is going to jump out from behind me. It's quiet. Once I fill the bag up, I walk into the living room. It's clean and smells like him.

I should rush out the front door, but, of course, my curiosity gets the better of me. Nosy Rosa has to walk up the stairs. I'll take a peek at his bedroom. I want to inhale his scent and maybe steal a hoodie or T-shirt.

Cristo, Rosa.

He's going to come in and catch you, I say to myself. This would be a good time to curse my Aunt Andrea and *Abuelita* for their nosiness that rubbed off on me.

When I reach the bedrooms, I must look like a hound dog

sniffing out its prey. The primary bedroom is Santiago's. I can smell his manly scent mixed with his cologne. He has a king-sized bed. It looks like a semi new bedroom set not used. The painting on the wall catches my attention. This portrait was for sale in my Etsy shop.

He bought it?

The painting is of the cliffside where he took me the night I gave him my virginity. The stars reflected off the ocean—a memory of us. I can't believe he bought it. He must have used a different name when he bought it. My heart swells, knowing some part of him still cares about us, although it's too late.

I tiptoe to his closet. Not going to lie to myself. I'm checking for women's clothes. It's a walk-in closet. My heart slams on my ribcage when I see the painting I gifted him the night he shattered us. He has it hanging in the closet. I gifted him a nude painting of me. Oh, God. I reach up to take it back, but hesitate.

I hear a *thunk*, and I look over my shoulder in panic. Nothing. Did I just imagine it?

On his nightstand, he has a lamp and a phone charging. He probably forgot his phone. I need to hurry before he gets back. Yet I open the drawer from the nightstand. No condoms. A junk drawer. And photos of us.

I jump up when I hear a moan coming from the bathroom. How did I not hear the shower going?

"Oh, baby." He groans then. "Fuck, that's it, baby."

My heart sinks to my stomach. He's in there with a woman. He grunts loudly. She must be on her fucking knees. I'm so close to barging in and dragging her out and then punching him. His moans and groans are supposed to be mine. A tear skates down my cheek.

"Yes, that's it."

I don't know why I'm torturing myself by listening to him get sucked off.

"That's it, sweetheart. Good girl. Harder."

My legs shake, and I stagger toward the door.

"Oh, baby, I'm coming. Rosaline, that's it."

I freeze, and my hand goes to my mouth.

"Rosa, my flower, so damn beautiful," he grunts.

The shower turns off, and I know I should leave but my legs have taken root to the floor and my brain is overflowing with questions. He jerked off, thinking of me? Excitement flutters in me, yet it shouldn't. I won't be with a man that got another woman pregnant. Even if he didn't cheat on me, it's still bad. And I love him, but he "regrets us getting married too soon" and betrayed me.

The hurt and betrayal uproots my feet, and I turn to leave when the door swings open. Not wanting to look like I'm running away, I spin around like an idiot. Surprise makes my eyebrows jump. Santiago stands in front of me naked. One hundred percent naked. I can't look away.

His body is different. He stares at me in surprise, eyes wide, tongue curled on the top of his lip. My eyes won't obey the order to look away. My heart is beating like it's going to explode. He's more muscular and has more tattoos, including one on his chest. I can't see what it is because my eyes are going wild. He's wearing a necklace, and his wedding band is on the necklace. I'm shocked he still has it.

My eyes drop to his dick. Oh, my god. Does this thing grow as you get older? Because it looks larger. My eyes open even wider. A piercing? He has a piercing! He's hard as a rock. My arousal is making me so damn wet. He's handsome and godlike. I feel like a woman who just stepped out of prison and hasn't seen a naked man in ages.

Hot. Desperate. Aroused.

My gaze goes back to his dick then rolls back to his beautiful face. He's watching me—he's dripping from the shower. Sexy. Hot. "You got a piercing," I mumble. *Shut up, Rosa.*

Oh, lord, take me. I'm about to die in so many ways. Closing my eyes, I take a deep breath. When I open my eyes. I swear he's smirking.

I start walking backward. "I...I came for sugar... Yeah, I came for sugar. Mark let me in." Another step back. I wave the bag at him. The things I want to do to him. Stop it! You don't want anything from him! Another step back. "Cookies. I need sugar for cookies. I...I—"

My calves collide with his bed frame, and I flop on his damn bed. *Great, Rosa, the wrong way.* I jump up and run out, not stopping until I reach my apartment. Shutting the door behind me, I rest my hand to my chest. My breathing is constricting, and my lungs can't get enough oxygen. *Damnit, Mark.* He set me up.

I slide down to the floor, and my head tips back against the door. My mind is still there, seeing him in all his glory. One night, while we were in bed, I mentioned how some girls at school were talking about a guy they slept with who had a piercing. They said it was crazy pleasurable for women. Then he said Damian has one, and yes, that it takes sex to the next level for women, according to what Damian said to Santiago. The thought of him getting a piercing just to please women disgusts me.

My eyes burn with unshed tears. It's been two and a half years, and the pain is still raw. How do you move on and stop loving someone you've loved your whole life? I don't understand how people fall out of love. Our love always felt like it was destined by the stars. The stars seemed to align and guide us toward each other, their twinkling lights mirroring the sparkle in our eyes.

Maybe that's why I'm so drawn to the art of star-searching the sky, hoping to catch a glimpse of a shooting star or a constellation that reminds me of him. And maybe that's also why I'm drawn to the mysterious allure of wolves, creatures that seem to roam freely under the same stars. He has a wolf tattooed on his back. Now, it seems our love was not what we thought. Maybe it was doomed from the start.

30

ROSALINE

ONCE I RECOVER from my state of shock and pain, I go back to finishing my batch of cookies. So now, here I am, standing in front of Dominic and Mila's beautiful home. It's gorgeous. It's their dream home with the beach right in their backyard.

"Rosita Bonita, you came. I'm so happy you're here, honey," Mila says in a welcoming, sweet voice. She looks me up and down with her beautiful green eyes. "Rosa, you have turned into such a beautiful woman." She shuts the door behind me. Mila is the kindest person. "Dom, Rosa is here. Dante, come say hi to your auntie."

I stiffen. *Auntie.* I'm not with Santiago. Does she know something?

"I hope it's okay if the kids call you auntie. We're all family. Sorry, I figured it would be okay."

I clear my throat when I notice Santiago standing in the foyer. He's just watching like a predator.

"Oh, yes, that's fine, of course." I smile, handing her the container of freshly baked chocolate chip cookies.

"Thank you, they look yummy." She grabs my hand, guiding me to her enormous kitchen, passing Santiago. She eyes Santiago.

It feels like everyone knows something, and I'm in the dark. Dominic envelopes me in a hug, placing a kiss on my forehead. Dante comes running to hug me. He looks just like his father.

"Hi, Auntie Rosa."

I kneel to hug him. Mark emerges from the room with Luca. The smile on Mark's face is priceless. I'm in awe of seeing him hold his nephew.

"Hi, sweetie. How are you doing?" I ask Dante.

"I'm good. Guess what? I have a swear jar. Uncle Mark said it was a good idea, but Uncle Santiago said it was a bad idea. I think it's because he says lots of bad words. And Dad said it's a bad idea because he's going to go broke."

He's adorable.

"Thank you for letting me know ahead of time."

He nods. "You're welcome."

Mila laughs.

Liam and Sophie walk in. If I had known everyone would be here, I would have canceled. I've known them my whole life. They were once my family, yet with how it all went down with Santiago, I feel like I'm intruding. This is his family. I shouldn't be here. This is why I need to leave soon. I can't live in the same space as him. The hairs on the back of my neck tell me his gaze is on me.

"Dinner is ready. Let's eat. We have Sunday dinner every week, Rosa. I want you here," Dominic says. My stomach fills with stones, and sweat trickles down my neck.

Sophie hugs me, taking her seat next to my cousin. Mark hands the baby to Santiago, and they all sit. An empty chair is next to Santiago.

Sophie jumps up and whispers with a hand on the side of her mouth, "You want to switch spots?"

I know Santiago heard her, and I love her for it. It makes me want to laugh. I'm sure everyone can feel the tension because things are not the same as when we were younger. They don't know about the hooking up or eloping that caused us to become distant. Lesson learned: don't marry your best friend.

I shake my head at her. "It's okay," I mouth. I would get more attention if I did, and questions would be asked.

Santiago looks sexy holding a baby. I'm sweating profusely and can't help thinking if he held Monica's baby as sweetly and I think of ours. I think I'm going to be sick.

Mila made barbecue chicken, steamed vegetables, and baked potatoes. Everything smells delicious. The dishes are placed in the center of the long table. Santiago's legs spread, brushing on my bare legs. I want him to move it. His touch is like an addiction. All I can think about is him naked. He's not acting like a dick. Maybe because everyone is here.

I'm confused about the piercing. He has our wedding band as a necklace, but a ring on his dick to please women.

I lift my plate to serve myself. A drumstick rolls off my plate. "Fuck," I mumble.

"Auntie Rosa, come on. Get your purse. No cursing. Pass it over, honeybun." Dante snickers.

We all laugh. I pass him a dollar.

"She's not your honeybun," Santiago murmurs teasingly, and elbows Dante next to him. Santiago reaches to serve himself with Luca in his arms. Luca is busy sucking on his hand.

"Here, let me help you," I offer, taking the serving spoon from his hold.

His thumb brushes my fingers. He nods and swallows, sitting back down.

I give him a heaping serving of everything. Sophie and Mila are watching. I'm sure Sophie told her something. Dominic and

Liam are eating like cavemen, so damn oblivious. Mark is smirking.

Him too. *God.*

Luca tilts his head back and smiles at me. I smile at him. He looks like Dante and Dominic. I lean over and kiss his forehead and then remember who has the baby in his arms. Santiago looks at me with an expression I can't decipher. Maybe with love.

We are strangers. We have both changed so much over the years, and we no longer know each other. He doesn't know my struggles and experiences, and I don't know what he has been through, either. Two years might not seem like a lot, but your whole life can change in the blink of an eye. *Mine did.*

We eat, and everyone chats about what's been happening in the last weeks. Liam has stories for us since he's a detective now. Luca spits up on my leg. Mila quickly takes Luca, and Santiago grabs a napkin, then bends down to clean up the mess. He holds onto my leg with one hand and wipes away the milk with the other. His arm travels up to my thigh, and I can feel the sparks of electricity between us, like a dazzling fireworks display. After he finishes, he sits back in his seat.

"How's Ivan doing?" Liam asks. "When is he moving in?"

The name makes my stomach sour and travels up my esophagus. Fuck, Liam has to ask.

Santiago stiffens and his knuckles go white, gripping his fork. His jaw clenches. I can hear the grinding of his teeth. He's jealous and angry. Or maybe not.

Sophie stuffs a spoonful of mashed potatoes in Liam's mouth. "Have a bite, baby. Aren't they good? Special recipe: extra butter."

Liam nods.

Bless her soul. Liam looks like a chipmunk.

"No, he's not moving in." I stand, taking my plate with me. I don't give anyone a chance to ask more. I don't want to talk about it with them. Instead, I wash my plate and tidy up the kitchen.

As I enter the living room, Santiago is gone. I inhale deeply, filling my lungs after the intense conversation.

Sophie comes over to me. "I don't know what's going on between you and Santiago. All I know is I can feel it. I know you two have a history. Anyone who grows up as friends will have one. I'm here for you if you need someone to talk to. Mila, too. She suspects something. Maybe we can have some girl time and talk about these Neanderthals." She laughs.

"Thank you. I'd like that." I could really use a girls' day.

Thanking Dominic and Mila, I make my way back home. My phone rings on the screen of my car. Ivan's name comes up. I hit decline just like I have for the past weeks.

ANOTHER WEEK HAS PASSED, and I haven't seen Santiago. Just Mark coming and going. I do smell the strong scent of cigarettes, and that's how I know he's in the front or the small backyard. He stormed out on Sunday dinner like his ass was on fire when Liam mentioned Ivan. I don't get why he gets jealous when he sent me away while his pregnant old hookup had his baby.

It's Friday, thank God. I serve myself a glass of wine and make my way upstairs. Unfortunately, I need more than wine to relax. I've been sexually frustrated. It's been two years and a couple of months since I've had sex. Seeing Santiago triggered it more than anything, especially the day I saw him come out of the shower. I slip my leggings off, then my shirt and bra. I turn on the vibrator that's been keeping me company. I know it's unhealthy for me to keep fantasizing about him. This is the only way I can get myself off.

I spread my legs and then touch myself. I moan, thinking of

Santiago's hands all over me and then his mouth. My moans get louder when I insert the vibrator. He's inside me, thrusting deeper. Harder. "Yes, please." I'm picturing his lips on my neck. "Harder," I say to myself, pushing in. Memories remind me of how he felt all those times. The vibrator penetrates more profoundly, making me orgasm, hitting all the right spots. "I'm coming." I moan.

I sigh in relief. It's not the same as having him, but it's much needed.

After a few minutes of catching my breath, I take a shower. Once I'm out, I put on my pajama shorts with a matching button shirt. Then dry my hair. When I'm not painting, I find solace in reading as another way to relax and pass the time. My phone buzzes as I pour another glass of wine.

Sophie: *Hey, chica, how's it going? Mila and I wanted to know if you wanted to have a girls' night tomorrow. We can have drinks somewhere, anywhere.*

Mila: *Hey you, Rosita Bonita. Yes, we need drinks. And I need a break from motherhood. A small break because I love my guys.*

Me: *Sure, that would be great. We could do my place, the bar, the club, or whatever.*

Mila: *The club sounds good, but unfortunately, my husband would probably...not probably throw me over his shoulder.*

I throw my head up and laugh. She's right. He is jealous.

Sophie: *Same. You know Liam. God, ladies, we are with a bunch of brutes.*

Me: *My place it is. We can order takeout. Have some drinks.*

I grab my book, wine glass, and a blanket to sit in the backyard to read.

Mila: *Sounds good.*

Sophie: *I'll bring snacks. Hey, let's watch Dirty Dancing.*

Mila: *God, Sophie, I'm sick of that movie. I've watched it a million times with you, and even Liam is sick of it.*

Sophie: *What did you just say? How can you be tired of it? And how do you know Liam is sick of it? Did he tell you? I'm going to ask him when he gets home from work.*

Mila: *Yes, ask him. But he won't tell you the truth. Ha.*

I snort into my glass. You gotta love them.

Sophie: *Fine. I'll think of something. See you tomorrow.*

Me: *See you tomorrow.*

Mila: *Yes, tomorrow.*

CozYING up on the wicker bench, I open my book. Tonight, I'm reading a romance novel. If only life were like a book. A gentle breeze brushes against my cheeks, sending a slight shiver through my body. Despite it being January and still cold, I had grown accustomed to the chilly weather from living in Portland.

I smile into my book when the male hero whispers sweet but hot and dirty words to the heroine. I swoon and melt all at once.

Santiago's door swings open, and he stomps out like a man who's ready for war. After a few seconds of huffing and puffing, he lights a cigarette. He doesn't seem to notice me. If he does, he doesn't make it known.

Following his lead, I disregard his existence and carry on with my reading.

31

SANTIAGO

MY THOUGHTS ARE SPIRALING out of control, consumed by Rosa. She's everywhere in my mind, and even at my brother's house. In my damn room while I'm dripping wet naked. It's laughable. And she's my next-door neighbor. Not two or three houses down. Her door is right next to mine. We share the same walls. And now I have to hear her moan while the asshole fucks what's not his.

Her beautiful body belongs to me. Those moans are supposed to be mine. She makes me insane. All I think about and wonder… is whether she's looking at him how she looked at me the other day when she snooped into my room. Those eyes caressed my body, making me grow harder. Every hair on my scalp stood to attention. Every skin cell tingled. Every neuron fired. It took every bit of self-control not to toss her on the bed and do things I dreamed of.

"Fuck," I shout, running down the stairs.

Mark jumps off the couch. "Where are you going?"

"To rip the mother fucker off of her!"

"Who?"

"Rosa! Who the fuck else?"

"Jesus. Santiago, what don't I know? This isn't just protective shit." He points to the couch. "Sit. Cool down, and let's talk."

I started from the beginning, and it all spills out.

Mark blows a hot stream of air. "Damn, that's some heavy shit. But I get it now." He peers up at me from his glass. "She still loves you."

I give him a half-assed shrug. It feels good to talk to someone other than Reese. "If she does, she has a funny way of showing it. She didn't give us a chance. She ignored my calls and texts. I fucking tried. And she loves another man. He has her, not me. You've seen that clown."

Having her this close isn't just frying my circuits. It's unhinging me. I need this woman like I need air. I've said this a million times. No one has ever made me feel this way. Why is he better than me? So, many times, I wanted to tell her, and the thing is, I tried, but she seemed happy when I would see her. The last thing I wanted was to ruin her happiness.

"Why are you afraid to talk to her? I get that you're pissed off, but you won't know unless you talk it over with her. She might want you back," Mark says with confidence.

"I've been living in hell without her, and now that she's this close, I guess I'm afraid of rejection. I won't know how to handle it."

His phone pings, and he stands. "You won't know unless you try, bro. You know, I'm happy it's her you're in love with. I won't tell the guys until you're ready, but yeah, you and Rosa will work it out. I know you will. You guys have always had a special connection. I'm heading to the club. The guys are waiting outside." He pats me on the back, and I give him the "be careful talk."

Leaning on the iron fence in the backyard, I balance a

cigarette in between my lips. I give the "I Love Vegas" lighter a shake and light my cigarette. The flower scent always clings to me. It lingers everywhere she's at. Rosa sits on a wicker bench reading. I know she knows I'm outside. She hates the smell of cigarettes. I don't see the pencil pusher she's with. He must have left.

I glance up at the stars because they always remind me of *us*. "Did you know that Perseus, when he died, became a constellation? And Andromeda was also taken to the sky to shine next to him?" I don't know why I'm asking her.

It's a love story. As the porch light illuminates her stunning face, she looks up at me. She's changed since the last time we were together. She's older, more put together and mature, stronger, and she's grown. More than anything, I hate myself for missing out on seeing her bloom. She's a fantastic artist. I'm proud of the woman she's become.

"Yes, I do. Why?" She looks up at the sky.

I know she doesn't want me near, but I walk through her opened gate and toward her. She watches me with a curious eye.

"It's a great love story. They were written in the stars."

Her lips curl into a smile. "So, I've heard," she whispers.

Blowing out the smoke, I shove my hands in my pocket to keep myself from wanting to touch her to make her moan. The calmness I was feeling is out the door and replaced with anger.

"Where's the pencil-pusher pussy?" Blood rushes to my face, hot and ready to find him inside and bust his shit-eating grin for taking the woman I'd take a life for.

"Who are you talking about?" she snaps.

She defends him. It pisses me off more. "The asshole you were fucking." I throw my hands up.

"I think I would know if someone was in my house." She waves one hand up toward the door. "Why do you care about what I do? You're the one sleeping with every person you come across," she shouts.

A dark laugh throttles from me. "It means everything to me, *wife.*"

"I'm not your wife." Her eyes throw daggers.

"Funny because our marriage certificate says otherwise. I never signed the divorce papers." I take a step closer. "And I never will, wife."

"What the hell do you mean, you never signed them?" she roars.

"It means my fucking wife has been having an affair."

She stands. Seething with anger.

She shoves her finger in my chest. "You don't know shit about me. You lost that privilege the day you fucked up. As for you, I've heard from Liam you flirt and take women home. So, don't come at me with that."

"Liam doesn't know shit. I've never taken women home. He assumes only because he thinks I'm single. And so does Dominic. They don't know shit. I had to play the fucking part. Because then they'd ask why I wasn't with anyone, why I wasn't chasing tail. I had to fake being a damn flirt when they were around. When I told them I wasn't up for being with women, they could hardly believe it. I hated every part of it because I wanted you. How long do you think I could keep a lie by telling them I wasn't interested? You've been gone for close to three years. I had to play the part for years because my lovely wife didn't want anyone to know, and she took off on me before I had the chance to speak with her. When the guys never questioned me about us, I knew you never wanted our truth to be revealed. Then you send divorce papers."

Her eyes widen with disbelief as she studies me. In an attempt to prove my words, I grab her hand and run it over my erect dick. "It hasn't been touched by another woman. It's been you since the day we've been together, unlike my lovely, unfaithful wife."

She shoves her hand away, creating space. She's shocked. "We're still married?" she asks faintly.

"Yeah, wife."

She shakes her head. "I didn't cheat on you, Santiago." She fiddles with her thumb.

"Do you not know what cheating is? You've been with him for a year, Rosa. How easily you fucking signed the papers. You fucking left me."

Darkness crosses her eyes, and she clucks her tongue. "You pushed me away. You regretted getting married. You told me to leave. You wanted a break." She shoves me back. It's a long overdue fight. "You wanted this. I asked you to come with me. You denied me. Don't give me your sorry excuses."

Her chin trembles.

"I did all this for us, for you. I pushed you because you had dreams, Rosa. I didn't want you to regret it. I wanted you to grow, to spread your wings. You were never second. *I chose you*. It may not have seemed like it, but I thought I was doing the best for you. It wasn't to control you. I could have easily kept you here with me, but I knew, deep down, you wanted that. I didn't want you to regret it later and blame us for getting married so soon."

She paces up and down the small box-size yard.

"Flower?"

"No, no, don't call me that. You lost that privilege, too. We can't be friends or anything else anymore. We can never go back from this," she croaks.

My heart explodes with pain. I know I'm to blame. I pushed it, and I didn't handle it right.

"I went to Portland a couple of times."

Her head jolts up.

"My intention, Rosa, was to fix things. I went weeks later and saw you with Jasmine and friends. You were laughing, and you looked happy. So I left. I figured that's what you wanted."

My body, like a magnet, moves toward her. "Living without you was hard. I went back again. I saw that fucker Ivan talking to you. It didn't look like you were with him, but I was jealous and hurt. I left. You seemed better off without me. Then Liam tells me you're dating him. It killed me, baby. I was doing all this for you to have a career. I didn't want a break. I should never have said that. I wanted you to get settled in Portland, and then we would work on a long-distance relationship. I went to LA when I told you. Remember, I was going to be gone for three days?"

She nods.

"It was so I could try to get the shop I bought. I was doing it for us, so I could provide for us. I barely had enough money. Not enough to feed my wife after all the expenses I made. Rosa, that day I came back from LA, I planned to tell you everything, but you'd gone back to Oregon early and you didn't want to see or hear from me. You fucking broke me. I came to see you a few times, but each time, you were with friends. When I received the divorce papers, I went up to look for you to find out what the hell was going on, and I saw you with him. Then, you added to the pain by being with someone else. He had his hands around your waist. Touching you, placing kisses on your cheek. I had to shove it down to let my wife be happy because I couldn't let her go, and I didn't sign those papers. I wanted to keep her for me." My voice is raw and overworked with emotion. Tears roll down her cheeks. Gently, I wipe them with my thumb.

"I never slept with him," she whispers.

I huff. "Seriously? I just heard another man fuck my wife. Do you not realize your bedroom wall is shared with mine?"

She gasps and covers her mouth, and her cheeks go redder. "No one was with me. I...I was—"

"Fucking yourself," I say.

She nods, looking at her toes.

I want to laugh now. Not at her, but at me, because I feel so damn relieved. "So you never slept with him?" I find it hard to believe. "Aren't you together?" Not that I want to talk about him.

"I've already told you I never slept with or kissed anyone else. I ended things with him. I only pursued a relationship because I thought you were being unfaithful, and we were friends. I was trying to find ways to move on. As you can see, I couldn't."

My heart leaps with relief. Thank goodness.

"You haven't been with anyone since me?" I have to ask again.

She sighs. "No."

"You love him, though, don't you?" My voice sounds muffled. *Please don't be in love with him.*

She frowns. "No, of course not."

"I heard you tell him you love him."

Her eyes narrow. "How so?"

A breeze feathers past us, causing her hair to get in her face. Absentmindedly, I tuck it behind her ear. Our gazes meet. She's gorgeous. Those lips are so luscious I want to bite into them.

"On the phone when I was standing at the door when you were moving in."

Her brows arch. "Oh, it was Philip and Jasmine I was talking to."

"Who is Philip?" I growl.

She rolls her eyes. "He's Jasmine's son," she whispers.

I'm shocked. "Jasmine has a son?"

She nods and steps back. Suddenly, I want her warmth to return.

"If you two weren't together, then why would he come around? Why did you let him touch you?" Jealousy boils my blood. He might not have had her, but he was around.

"Like I said, I thought you were with others. That was the main reason, or I wouldn't have never accepted."

"What does this mean for us?" I ask, desperate for anything. I don't mind sleeping on the floor if it means sleeping in the same space as her.

"Nothing. You broke us. I've been through so much these last few years. You regretted us getting married. Those were the last words I heard from you. You pushed me away. I never cared about money, all I wanted was you. You shattered me. While you were entertaining another, I was grieving the loss of my baby. I had a miscarriage. I lost my baby because of the stress you caused."

My entire body goes numb. Guilt and regret crashes over me like a tidal wave. She was carrying our child.

"Rosaline…" My mouth goes dry. "You were pregnant?" Heavy tears spill over and roll down my cheeks.

She leans and places a kiss on my tears, and I don't deserve it. "I love you, Santiago. I can't lie to you and pretend I don't. Part of me will always love you. But I had to mourn the loss of you and my child. I don't know how to come back from that."

She walks inside, closing the door behind her. My wife, the love of my life, I broke her. Broke us. The pain is bone-deep. I pushed her away in a moment of self-pity, but the consequences are too heavy to bear. The night I went looking for her and saw her smiling and laughing. She was faking it, breaking inside. If only I would've talked to her. She needed me. I left her to deal with the pain on her own. How could I have been so reckless and careless? I am torn between wanting to run back to her and begging for forgiveness and running away from the consequences of my impulsive actions.

My gaze goes up to the night sky. I pray to God, the stars, to anyone who will hear me to grant me a chance with her to mend our broken hearts. I don't deserve her love, but she deserves to be loved. To be shown she is loved. I'll be that man for her—the man she needs. She'll always be my priority. I fucked up but never because I didn't love her. Everything is about her...for her. I bettered my life to provide for her. The shop is for her. For our future.

She lost our child. She lost the light in her heart. I'll love her for both of us and show her the way back to us. I vow to remind her of the fire that still burns within her heart. I'll reignite the spark that has once glowed brightly. I'll do whatever it takes to show her that the light in her heart is still burning strong. Our child is in our hearts. I'm in her heart.

3 2

Rosaline

My eyes go heavy as I mix my coffee. All night, I tossed and turned, knowing Santiago is on the other side of the wall after the partial confessions we shared last night. I'm not sure how to feel that we're still married. A part of me is relieved. I don't know if that's the right thing to be. He still loves me enough not to sign those papers. However, there's a part of me that's angry at him for stringing me along when he has a child with someone else, and I lost mine. I avoided asking him about the baby to avoid the heartbreak.

My initial plan was to confront him about the pictures of him having a child with her, but circumstances shifted. When we moved to Portland, after settling into my dorm room, I was a mess. Confused about what I should do. I missed him, but he wanted a break, which made me feel second. Then, weeks later, nausea hit like a tornado. I bought a pregnancy test from a pharmacy, and it was positive. I was over the moon to have a baby with my husband. I planned a surprise trip. I was going to fly down there and give him the surprise of a lifetime. The memory makes my heart drop.

Rolling my luggage to my rental car, I hear my name. It's Marissa and her sister. She's pushing a luggage cart.

"Rosa, hey. How's it going?" She beams, but her smile is not friendly—it's fake.

"I'm good. How about you?" I ask.

She tosses her hair up, and her sister has the same malicious smile as Marissa. "Good, we are off on a girls' trip. Are you here to congratulate Santiago?"

My brows lift. How would she know I'm pregnant?

"Congratulate him about what?"

She giggles. "Oh, about his and Monica's baby."

I can feel the color in my face drain. She must see it because she smirks. "That's not true." I defend us, Santiago.

She shakes her head. "I thought you were close." Then she looks at her sister. It clicks. Marissa was Ryan's date at the restaurant that night. She saw us kissing. She pulls up her phone, scrolls through it, and then hands it to me.

I'm sick to my stomach, and my heart drops to the ground. Santiago touches Monica's belly and smiles wide. Another photo of her smiling at him like she lit up his world. The phone shakes in my hand. With a broken heart, I pass the phone to her, mustering a smile.

"See, told ya. He'll never be yours." Her brows rise.

I rush out the door, not sparing her a glance. I hate how she affects me. I rub my flat belly. Maybe Marissa did some kind of Photoshop, and maybe Monica's not pregnant. I'll ask Santiago. When I get close to his mom's neighborhood of his, I see Monica jogging. As I get closer, my heart shatters, and the car idles. Monica is pregnant with a small belly. She stops and takes a sip of water, rubbing her pregnant belly. I do the math. She could be four months pregnant. Tears fill my vision. I turn back to the airport.

. . .

253

No one knew I had gone down to visit. When I got back to Portland, I went to the doctor, and they did all types of blood work. They confirmed that I was nine weeks pregnant. It made me angry to think that if I were to call him and share the news of our baby, it wouldn't have the same meaning for us anymore. He already had his first baby on the way. He was clearly excited about it. Yet, I couldn't keep it from him. Even if I wanted to, he would find out I had a child from Liam. I picked up the phone so many times. I rehearsed how I planned to ask him about the child he had with Monica and then tell him about ours. I was a mess that week. I could hardly sleep. I was so stressed. And then I miscarried.

I stir my cold coffee right before I pop it into the microwave —my phone buzzes with an unfamiliar number with a Portland area code. "Hello."

"Rosa, why aren't you picking up!?"

I freeze, hearing the familiar angry voice. My eyes close, and I steady my breathing. I've been through so much, and I don't need this man's shit.

"Ivan, stop calling me. I've explained to you several times that I don't have feelings for you. I told you we wouldn't work for the past months when I tried breaking it off. You keep insisting, but after what you did, I want nothing to do with you." I hang up and block the number.

When I met Ivan, he was a nice guy. We were friends for a long time. He asked me out a couple of times. I said no. I wasn't interested at all. Then, when Liam said Santiago was hooking up again, Ivan asked me out to dinner. I agreed, but in those months, trying to date him felt wrong for me. I never once shared my personal life with him. There was no chemistry. The most I felt for him was as a good friend, nothing more. Sure, he would hug me and kiss my cheek, but that felt like a best friend hugging you. I kept breaking it off with him, but he wouldn't give up. He was friendly and sweet… until he wasn't. He showed his true colors.

From the beginning, Ivan was very persistent. The first week, when I told him I'd give it a chance, it felt wrong, so the following week, I ended it. When I went down to visit my aunt for New Year's, he invited himself, telling everyone we were a couple. I left it and I didn't correct him because I was pissed and hurt.

When we returned to Portland, I reiterated to him we were definitely *not* a couple. He ignored it and hung around. When I went down for Mila's wedding, he offered to come with me, just in case something happened while driving alone. I agreed that maybe he was right.

We had a good time as friends. We went to the beach, he kept trying to lift me up, and I splashed water on him playfully doing my best to keep him away. We went to a club with Liam and Sophie, and it was fun, and we danced. He held my hand, not intimately, just guiding me to the dance floor. He kept trying to kiss me. I told him no and that we were not dating. He kept persisting. He wouldn't accept the rejection. I was tired of his shit. It was too much. He kept coming around, and I kept pushing him away. He didn't get the hint.

The first time I noticed something off about him was about five months before I came home. He knocked on the door late at night. His eyes were bloodshot.

"Rosa, I want to take you to dinner," he said.

I stepped outside and shut the door behind me. I didn't want him to make a scene. Philip was sick, and Jasmine hadn't slept a wink. Ivan had his hands in his shredded jeans pockets. He's attractive and has some bulk to him, but nothing compared to Santiago's.

"Ivan, you don't seem well. Your eyes are red. I think you should go," I said.

"I'm fine. It's just allergies. I want to take you to dinner. I know you've been avoiding me."

No shit, I wanted to say. "I think you need to leave."

"I *need* you, baby."

I hated when he called me baby. It made me want to vomit. I wasn't his.

He sighed, leaning up against the door. "You're overdoing it. I'm inviting you to dinner." His voice rose.

I nodded. "Okay, I'll meet you there." I agreed to get it over with so he would not cause problems.

He shook his head. "I'm here already, Rosa. Let's go to the Thai place."

When we arrived at the restaurant, his mood did a one-eighty. He dragged my chair next to him. "Don't you think we should take our relationship to another level?"

"We," I said, pointing to him and me, "are not in a relationship. We really never have been and never will be."

He leaned in, put a hand on my thigh, and squeezed. I shook his hand off like it was a parasite. What guy wouldn't get the hint, you know? But this, it felt like he was trying to be intimate with me by touching my thigh.

"Don't be a bitch, Rosa. I've been patient long enough."

I turned to look him in the eye. He had powder under his nose when he sniffed. His eyes were wild. "I feel like I'm being pretty patient with you right now."

"Don't you think it's time you sucked my dick?" He licked his lips, then reached to cup my breast, but I smacked him before he could touch me. His laugh made my skin crawl.

"Are you on drugs?"

He shrugged.

"Look, I'm leaving. Do me a favor and leave me the fuck alone. Don't show up at my place."

He grabbed my arm. "You're staying. We will have dinner,

then I'll show you what you've been missing," he whispered in my ear.

Blood drained and left me pale as a ghost. He was on something, and I knew he would force himself on me. I stood and told him I was going to the restroom. I ran out the door, called an Uber, and went home.

Things escalated from there.

The microwave dings, announcing the coffee is ready, and at the same time, my doorbell rings. No one is at the door but a brown paper bag with a sticky note. Picking it up, I read the note.

Good morning, my beautiful wife. I love you—your husband.

I peek my head out as he's walking to his truck. Shutting the door, I open the bag up. Pan dulce. My favorite. He knows how much I love sweet bread. My smile grows as I bite into the concha. He made my shitty morning so much better. Who can resist a concha?

I SPENT the rest of my morning and afternoon cleaning and tidying the house for girls' night. Juggling the snacks and liquor bags, I pull my keys from my coat pocket.

"Rosa, let me help you." Mark rushes to my side, taking the bags. He smells of citrus and is freshly showered.

"Thank you. I saw you this morning coming home at the crack of dawn. Where were you, mister?" I turn to arch a brow at him while twisting the knob.

He tosses his head back in laughter. "Sheesh. You've taken your over-protection to the next level, my dear sister-in-law." He shuts the door behind him, placing the bags on the round, wooden, colorful table.

My mouth falls open.

He smiles and closes my open mouth with two fingers.

"How long have you known?"

"Yesterday before I went out."

"Oh," I mumble, fidgeting with my fingers.

"You know what I think?"

"No. What do you think?"

"I'm glad it's you, that he's in love with. I know you crushed over my brother as kids. You would stare at him all dreamy and shit for hours." He laughs. "In our teens, I noticed even more when you became jealous. Girls always crushed over my big brother. He's the badass, tattooed biker. I'm a believer that love is written in the stars. Maybe you'll find your way back to each other. I know you have a boyfriend—"

"I don't have a boyfriend. He never was. Did Santiago mention we talked last night?"

He shakes his head. "No, how did that go?"

I sigh, pulling out a chair. Resting my elbows on the table, I answer him the best way I can without saying much. "No, we're not. Santiago and I won't be getting back together."

His brows draw together in a deep frown. I want to ask if he knows anything about the child Monica had. Although, I have a feeling Santiago has been hiding it from more than just me. I haven't seen a child at his house since I moved here. Or maybe something happened.

He leans on the island, ankles crossed. "That's too bad. He loves you. I haven't seen Santiago with anyone since you've been gone, Rosa. I thought it was strange that he wasn't fucking around, but I understand now."

When Santiago admitted he hadn't been with anyone else, I was surprised. "I know he still loves me." I stand and unload the bags. "Would you like something to drink?"

"Nah, I better go. I have work. It's good to have you back. I'm proud of you."

"Thank you, and I'm happy to be back."

"So, when is your art exhibit show? I'd love to go."

"It's on Wednesday night."

Mark struts toward me, wrapping me in a hug.

"Mark, I've been meaning to ask. How have you been with, you know...um, with everything that happened with Rachel?"

He gives a faint laugh. "It's been a year, and I'm still in shock she would do something like this. Honestly, I'm glad she's gone. She was toxic. If it weren't for Santiago, I don't know what our life would be like."

I give him a tight squeeze, then hear Liam's loud, husky voice.

We step outside to find Liam helping the girls with trays and bags. Mark waves at Liam and the girls and takes off. Just as Santiago steps out of the house, I see him from the corner of my eye and smell the faint scent of a cigarette.

Liam extends his arms and shouts, "Rosita." He still treats me like a child.

I roll my eyes at him and snuggle into his warm embrace.

"Don't drink too much," he says.

I step back to give him the stink eye.

"Don't let her drink too much," he tells Sophie.

They exchange a look. She's looking at him like she's going to slice his balls. He sighs and looks at me.

"Fuck off, Liam. I'm not a child."

I hear a snort from the side of me. I turn slightly, peering from the corner of my eye. Santiago's lips lift into a smile.

"What happened to you? Portland turned you feral," Liam teases.

Sophie cuts in, "Shoo, detective. I'll call you when we are ready for you to pick two drunk women up."

I cover my mouth with a laugh. "I like her." I point to Sophie, peering up at Liam, "She has you by the fucking balls. You needed that."

Mila giggles, and Sophie has a proud smile on her beautiful face.

Liam huffs, his lips turn into a small smirk. "I'm out of here." He turns to Santiago, who is still standing there—watching. "If they get all girls gone wild in there, and male strippers show up, call me." Liam half-jokes. He stays silent, thinking, and his jaw tightens.

Santiago mirrors the same expression. I can see him from the corner of my eye. Now I'm starting to wonder how thin my walls are. Will he be able to hear us? He heard me the other night.

"Oh my gosh, that's a great idea," Sophie taunts Liam.

Mila shakes her head laughing. "You're really asking for it, Sophie?"

"I love the punishment." Sophie winks at Liam.

He walks back to his car.

Oh, God. I don't want to think of my cousin that way.

"We should just go to the strip club," I joke as we walk into my townhouse. I'm only saying it for Santiago's ears. I look back at him to make sure he heard me. He tosses his cigarette on the gravel and grinds it with his boot.

"I'd find you and toss you over my shoulder, baby. Then I'd strip for you. You want a show, I'll give it to you. But only for an audience of one." He turns on his heels and slams the door, leaving my mouth dry. Visions of him naked dance in my head. *Cristo*, that's hot.

I close the door behind me with my mind in a haze. Sophie and Mila's mouths gape open in surprise. My lips go glued together in a straight line. And here it comes.

"Holy guacamole, hot!" Sophie shouts, fanning herself. "Big bro Delgado has it going on. 'I'd find you and toss you over my shoulder, baby. Then I'd strip for you. You want a show, I'll give it to you. But for an audience of one,'" Sophie tries mimicking Santiago's husky voice.

Mila looks up at me. "Wow, I've never seen Santiago like

this. He's been painting the wrong picture for us. It has me wondering so much. You need to fill us in."

I nod. I need someone to talk to. Mila knew me as a teen, and she's always been nothing but pleasant to me. I trust them.

"Are you ready for a roller coaster of a story?" I can't help but give them a slight, sorrowful grin. It's a story of love and heartache.

"I'm ready. But first, let's get the appetizers going and drinks flowing and order takeout," Mila says, opening the appetizers she made from their restaurant—a cheese sampler with meats, another tray of bite-sized flautas.

Sophie pops open a bottle of *Rosé* of *Cabernet Franc*, a local wine from one winery here in San Diego. It tastes like home. I turn on some music, so my nosy neighbor won't have his big ears plastered to the wall. Mila orders some Chinese, while I take out some throw blankets and pillows. Once we're settled, I start.

I omit certain details because they are meant only for me and Santiago. I don't say anything about Monica because that's a conversation I need to have with Santiago. Maybe later, when I'm brave enough to ask Santiago about her and his child. I just tell them something happened, I can't say at this moment, and they nod.

Mila and Sophie sniffle when I tell them about the baby I lost. "I'm so sorry, Rosa. You went through so much alone. I mean, I know you had Jasmine. Well, you had each other."

We did. Jasmine found out she was pregnant days after me. She was twelve weeks pregnant. She wasn't sure who the father was, and it broke her. Jasmine is not the type to sleep around. That's just not how she is. On top of that, she felt heartbroken. When she started showing, knowing I lost my baby, she felt guilty and sorry. And when Philip was born, we couldn't help but think they would have been born days apart. I've never resented her.

"We did. Our relationship had its ups and downs, but we've always stuck together."

Mila smiles and peers at Sophie. They share a bond too, a similar one to Jasmine and me. Sophie was Mila's rock when she went through hard times.

"I can't believe you're married. How does it feel... well, how did it feel being married to an older man?" Sophie mumbles into her wine class. I pick up a flautas and dip it in sour cream.

"I was on cloud nine. To snag the man I've always wanted. It was special. He was everything then." My memories take me back to the beginning. I stand and walk to the kitchen to refill my glass. A lonely tear runs down. Mila pats my back, and I turn to face her.

"Rosaline, I know you're hurting, honey. I've been there. We are family. Maybe not blood, but we are family. Dominic and Mark love you like a sister. But you and Santiago share something so special. He fell in love with the beautiful girl who loved him from the beginning, loved all of him. You see, honey, all those other girls from his past didn't love him. They liked the idea of him. Santiago is a beautiful, wonderful man, inside and out. He's made mistakes with me, and I forgive him. He loves his brothers like they are his sons."

More tears flow like a river.

"Before you left, how were things with Dominic?" she asks, swallowing hard.

Dominic was working hard to move into his apartment and open a restaurant in hopes of Mila coming back. Dominic was in an unhealthy place.

"He was in a dark place, Mila. He couldn't function without you."

Her eyes water.

"Santiago thinks with his heart. From what I heard him say, he loves you and is possessive of you. And I'm not sure what else happened or if part of why he didn't follow you had to do with Dominic and Mark. But you two are the only ones who know it all. It's your story. Maybe you both need to clear the air and talk."

We hug, and it's nice. She does it so motherly.

"Come on, sister-in-law, let's dig into the food and watch a rom-com. Thank God Sophie didn't bring *Dirty Dancing*."

"I heard that," Sophie shouts.

I think of Mila's advice for us to clear the air and talk. We need to, but it hurts. I am certain that I love him, yet in my heart, it feels as though the light switch is flipped off. The warmth I used to feel when looking at him is idle, leaving my heart feeling heavy and uncertain. I'm torn.

33

ROSALINE

AFTER DROPPING three of my paintings at the exhibit for tonight's show, I go to work to teach two private lessons. Today is a short day. Then, I book an appointment for a spa and facial. When I ask for a facial and spa, the woman at the counter sweetly advises me they have a three-for-one special. I don't bother to ask what the third is because I assume it's something like a pedicure. No, it's a Brazilian wax where I flop my legs open like a frog and let them tear me apart. Front to back. Now I'm sitting in my car with my ass on fire and a swollen, red vagina. I'm stopping at the dollar store to pick up some aloe vera ointment. With all this traffic, the drive to the store will take about fifteen minutes.

I sigh because as much as I want to not think of him and keep my mind busy, something always reminds me of him. How can you forget someone you've known your whole life? You can't. He doesn't make it easy, especially now that he's not acting like an asshole. He's still my husband and his morning drop-offs add to it. Sunday morning, he left a red velvet cupcake and an iced coffee with a note saying:

Good morning, wife, I've missed you so much. I love you. Love, your husband.

Monday was a croissant with bacon and eggs and an iced coffee a note.

Good morning, my beautiful wife. I'm sorry for hurting you. I never intended to, Just know that you mean everything to me. You're the one thing that matters to me. I love you. Love, your husband.

Tuesday and this morning were the same breakfast and coffee on my doorstep. We have not run into each other or spoken since that night.

After what feels like an eternity, the traffic finally moves. I navigate off the highway with a left turn.

Fuck. My whole area hurts. How do women get this done religiously? It's painful. I do it at home, but nothing like this. I feel...hairless. When I see the dollar store sign, I exhale with relief. I need aloe, coconut oil, and ice packs.

I park and check my phone as I get out of the car. Jasmine sent me pics of Philip with spaghetti all over his face. I open the door with a smile and the sound of a familiar voice makes my body go cold. My heart sinks into my stomach and blood drains into my feet. I turn slowly to see where that voice is coming from, and what's left of my heart splinters in pieces.

Monica is holding a small boy's hand and talking to him. I can only see the side of the child. He has olive-toned skin and a dimple on his cheek. Everything in me wants to crumble. My legs shake. She has a son with a man that's supposed to be mine. I'll never have that. Never.

Monica looks up and gives me an uncomfortable, unsure wave. Frantically, I sprint back to my car, digging in my purse, searching for my keys. Slamming the car door shut, I peel out of the parking lot. I'm driving so fast, with tears flooding down my cheeks. The proof is there. Although I didn't see the boy's face, I saw the side of him. The skin, the dimple—he looks like Santiago.

The sound of something hitting the frame makes my stomach drop. I quickly pull over to the shoulder and get out, heart racing. I wipe my tears and inspect the damage. Two large nails protrude from the left tires. Fuck. The air is whistling out. I get back into the car, searching for my phone. And it's off… The battery is dead. Damnit, I planned on charging it after I left the dollar store. It was at four percent when I looked at Phillip's pictures.

Why today of all days?

With my eyes swollen and my vagina on fire, I hitchhike down the street. I probably look like a lunatic walking like I have a rash on my vagina and ass. Never doing this again. It's not like anyone is going to see if I'm groomed or not. The wind whips my hair flying around my face.

I freeze when I see the sign for Delgado's Automotive. Why is the universe out to get me? Annoyed, nervous, uncomfortable, I stand on the road, debating if I should keep walking. I don't want to see him, but I need a phone to call a tow truck, and my ass can't take any more friction.

Santiago

"Okay, crank it," Billy shouts from under the car of the old Nissan.

I give it another crank, and it dies.

She slides out. Her jumper is a little loose on her. She cleans her hands with a rag. "Thanks. I appreciate your help. I think I know what's causing it."

"What made you want to be a mechanic?" I ask.

"Are you asking because I'm a woman?" She fists her hand on her hips playfully.

I shake my head. "Yes, and no. Most women don't enjoy getting dirty." My Rosa does, though, with paint.

"My dad. He taught me. He would always say never to depend on anyone. I ended up enjoying it. Also, because it reminds me of him. He passed two years ago."

"Sorry to hear that," I say wholeheartedly.

She smiles and nods and gets back to her task.

I walk out of the shop for a smoke. My gaze drifts to a woman on the side of the road. She's just standing there. Why is she just standing there? Where in the fuck is her car? I look around. I don't see it. I jog toward her, and her puffy eyes go frantic. My heart rips from my chest. She's been crying.

"Baby, are you okay? Where's your car?"

She looks anywhere but at me, and that kills me. I want her to look at me.

"I got a flat tire, and my phone died. I just need to use a phone to call a tow truck. Please let me use yours." Her voice is distant and rough, with no warmth in it.

"Rosa," I say, my voice low, "look at me, baby."

She doesn't.

"Okay, let's walk inside the shop. My phone is in my office."

She nods and follows.

My brows furrow when I notice her walking a little bowlegged.

Billy pops out from under the car. The way Rosa goes still, her gaze boring into Billy's, tells me she remembers her from the bar. My stunning wife is giving Billy eyes like she can pierce a hole in her.

"Billy," I say. "Can you do me a favor? Her car died nearby. Get a tow truck to drop it off here, please."

Billy nods and walks up to Rosa.

Rosa looks up at me, throwing daggers. I know she's thinking, 'how could you have her speak to me when you flirted?' I can just hear her. Rosa is still watching her, then glares at Billy with anger and jealousy. My wife being jealous has my ego bursting.

"Can I get your name?" Billy asks with a clipboard in hand.

I say nothing. Despite the fact that my gorgeous girl hates my guts, I can't look away. She doesn't need a work order. She's my wife. What's mine is hers. Rosa's lips straighten in a line. She eyes Billy, studying her.

"Rosa Acosta."

"It's Rosa Delgado," I correct my wife and take a deep breath of her flowery scent.

She turns to me as our eyes meet.

"Billy, meet my wife," I say, looking at Rosa.

Billy drops the clipboard and extends her hand. "Nice to meet you, Mrs. Delgado. I'm sorry. He should have introduced you when you walked in, and I would have shaken your hand." She smiles at Rosa.

"Nice to meet you," Rosa says with less enthusiasm.

"Wow, you're stunning, Rosa. You're absolutely beautiful." Billy stares at her—all the way up and down—way too long for my liking.

"Stop ogling my wife. She's not your type."

Rosa's lips turn up.

Billy giggles, and my girl tells her where her car is.

I beckon, gesturing with my head for her to follow me to my office. Opening the drawer from my desk, I grab my keys. Rosa peers into my office. When I bought the place, I decorated it with different automotive related picture frames I got at a thrift store.

"You did good. I'm proud of you," she whispers so low.

My heart does this crazy thing. Her approval means everything to me because I did it for *her*, for *us*, for *our* future.

A rock forms in my throat as I swallow and nod at her in

thanks. She leans on my desk, palms holding her up. I look down at her legs spread apart. "Rosa, are you okay? Are you hurt?"

"I'm peachy. Had an incident. Girl stuff." She stands with her hands to the side.

"Oh, okay. Um…I can give you a ride home. I'll have the guys take it to the tire shop for you and have them drop it off at the house."

"Thank you." She pivots away, still not looking at me.

It makes me want to pin her on the desk. To tell her so many things.

Ten minutes into the drive, she stares out the window without a word. California traffic is a nightmare right now. I'm grateful for it. Traffic is not moving—car accident ahead. We are stuck. She fiddles with the hem of her blouse. I've known Rosa all my life. When she's nervous or something is bothering her, she fidgets.

"Rosa, what's wrong? I know something is going on." She shakes her head and stares out the window. "I know we have a lot to talk about. It hurts me to see you like this. It kills me to see us like this. I've missed you, and my heart aches so damn much we lost our child, a piece of us—"

"Fuck you. Fuck you! You don't get to talk about our child!"

"What? Why? What's wrong?"

"Were you ever going to tell me? Huh? Did you plan on keeping it a secret forever? I saw the pictures." She breaks into sobs. "I hate you!" she screams.

I try to reach for her.

"Don't touch me. Are you seeing her too?"

My brows skyrocket. "Rosa, calm down. Baby. I'm lost. I don't know what you're talking about."

She turns to me with swollen red eyes, flushed cheeks, and pain in her heart. I see it, I feel it.

"I saw Monica with your *son*." Her gaze turns molten. "Do

you see them? Do you play the good dad?" She spits every word out.

With traffic still at a standstill, I put the truck in park, unclip my seatbelt, and slide toward her.

"My love, I don't know what you're talking about, baby." I try to cup her chin so I can make her look at me, but she flicks my hand away. "Explain it to me because I do *not* have a son with Monica. Thank God. Who told you this?" Anger strikes like a whip. Someone lied to her to hurt her.

She sniffs and finally looks at me with pain in her eyes. "I...I saw the pictures of you smiling with her and touching her belly, and I saw her when I came down."

I close my eyes and throw my head back.

"Sweetheart, Monica is married to her son's father."

She shakes her head stubbornly. "Don't lie to me. I did the math. I saw the photos. You looked happy. And the child has your skin and dimples."

"He's *not* my son, Rosaline."

Her nose goes up in the air. "Are you sure she just didn't tell you that you have a son?"

I unbuckle her then drag her onto my lap. She sucks in a painful breath when I set her down. I stare at her bottom, wondering what the fuck happened. She wiggles, trying to get off me, and that only makes me damn hard. It's been two and a half years since I've held her, touched her.

"Baby, listen to me. I don't enjoy talking to you about shit like this because it's fucked up. You're my wife, Rosaline. I don't relish talking about another woman to you. Yes, I know Monica was around for a while. You know everything about that, but what you don't know is I had more of a friendship with Monica than anything else, and no, nothing like ours. It doesn't compare. I never told her anything like when I talk to you. You've always assumed she was always with me, but she's

Reese's cousin. A lot of those times she was hanging out with him."

Her eyelashes have wet tear beads hanging on them. Brushing them off, I continue. "You act like we were constantly fucking. I apologize for talking about this to you. I respect you as my wife, my lady. You need to understand she and I didn't have chemistry, nor were we attracted to each other in a way where I couldn't take my hands off her. It was a fucking man thing, wanting to get off. That's all it was with her. And I *always* used protection. I know it's not mine because I hadn't slept with her in a long ass time. Way before you surprised me with a kiss."

I give her ass a squeeze.

"From that day, I never slept with anyone, Rosa. That was weeks or months before we got together. Yeah, she was flirty at your birthday party. I know she wanted to sleep with me, but not for the reasons you think. She was using me and the other guys to take the edge off. She had been in love with someone else for a long time. The day at your party, she noticed me staring at you, all jealous and shit. Monica encouraged me to be with you."

Her brows knit together. "She did?"

"Yes, she did. That's why she left. That day, in that photo you saw, she went to the shop to see Reese. She told me she was pregnant and that our love—mine and yours—and our history encouraged her to go find the man she'd been in love with. They slept together and had a baby. Yes, I smiled because I was congratulating her. You think I would be all smiles if it were mine? Fuck, I would've had a heart attack because the only woman I want to have my kids with is you." My hands grip her waist, holding her in place.

"He has dimples," she mumbles.

I laugh. "Rosa, many people have dimples. His father has dimples."

"You met him?"

"I have at Reese's family barbecue."

She sighs like she's releasing years of pent-up weight on her chest. I hate that she's been carrying this for years. Cupping her cheeks, I peer into her eyes. "Now, who in the hell told you this lie, flower? Is that the reason for the divorce papers?"

She nods. Fuck.

"Marissa and her sister," she spits out.

Fucking bitch. My body trembles with rage.

"Fuck." I shove my hand in my hair and pull on it. "Why didn't you tell me the day of?"

"Because you pushed me away, Santiago. You said you regretted us getting married. You broke my heart telling me to leave. I came back when I found out I was pregnant to surprise you. I ran into Marissa at the airport. She showed me the photos on her phone. How was I supposed to feel? Then, I was going to confront you, but I saw Monica close to your mom's house. She was clearly pregnant. It all finally made sense, you regretting marrying me and wanting me to leave so I wouldn't find out."

Rosa's head sinks onto my chest, and the tears come like a waterfall.

"It killed me to file for divorce. I did it after I saw Monica when I returned to Portland. I couldn't bear to see you have a child with someone else. I wanted to call and ask if the child was yours, and to tell you about being pregnant. But I thought, how is he going to react? He already has a child on the way—"

"It's my fault, Rosa. I pushed you away. And not because I didn't want to be with you or because I regretted marrying you. I wanted you to have your dream career. And I couldn't move with you to Portland. I had money issues at the time, not enough money to take care of my wife, and I was too prideful to just say that. Then I needed to know my brothers were in a good place before I left with you. I should have been honest and told you all of this to begin with. Maybe if I had, you would have come to me about Marissa. Maybe the stress wouldn't have caused you to lose our baby. I'm so sorry."

She lifts her head. Her eyes look indescribably sad. Absent-mindedly, I rub her empty belly.

"You would have been a good dad."

Fuck that word. *Dad.* Makes my heart expand and flutter.

"I still want to be, sweetheart. I want a baby with you—lots of them. I'm near thirty, Rosa. I want kids." I kiss her cheek and bathe in her scent.

Our eyes stay locked with one another. Two damn years we've missed together, all because of mistakes we've made. Bitch Marissa, she caused it all. She's always been obsessed with me.

"I should've done so many things differently."

She slides off of me, and I hate it. I know she's still worlds away from me.

"It was stupid and naive of me to believe Marissa. She was just trying to sleep with you again, wasn't she?"

I nod because she was. She knew Rosa was gone. "She came looking for me at work twice, and I told her to fuck off. She's always hated you since you were a kid. She is the type to feel jealousy with anyone. It was my fault for keeping her around when I didn't give a shit about her."

One sexy brow arches.

"You did keep her around for too long. I get it though. She was your first, and you were hers, probably. Of course, she was obsessed with you." She blows out a breath and then closes her eyes.

I fucking hate she had to see me with Marissa and Monica, but a lot of it has to do with our age difference.

"I'm sorry. If I could go back in time I would." I sigh. "I never had feelings for her or any other woman. I know why. Because I'm meant for you. It was always supposed to be us."

She smears her tears with the back of her hand and tries to hold back any new ones.

"After all this truth, baby, where does it leave us?" I ask her again. I'll always wait for her.

She peers at me with those beautiful eyes and fiddles with the hem of her blouse. "I...I...don't know. These past two years has been a lot. Believe me, I'm relieved you don't have a child out there," she murmurs, her voice soft. "I need time, Santiago. We have been through so much. We missed out on each other's lives. You don't know what I've been through—my schooling, where I worked, what I've done, who my friends are. Nothing. Just like I missed out on your accomplishments. Maybe we can take it slow."

Her eyes water, and I hate to see her cry. All I want to do is hold her in my arms and make everything better.

"I apologize for everything with Rachel. I wasn't there for you when it happened. I wanted to be. But I just couldn't reach out."

I wish she would have, but I didn't contact her either. I understand now.

"The loss of these last two years of your life—our life—gut me. But I'm here now. I'm not going anywhere. You come to me when you're ready for us. No matter how many breakfasts and love letters it takes."

She blushes hot pink.

"We can take our time and talk about everything that's happened."

She nods. "I like that."

Thank the fuck. It gives me some type of hope for us.

Traffic moves after the hour delay. I notice she keeps shifting in her seat. "Are you going to tell me why you keep moving around like your ass is on fire?"

She tosses her hands in the air. "Because it is."

I can't help it. I snort a laugh. She chews on her bottom lip. I know Rosa so well. That chewing on the lip can mean a couple of things. One is being turned on, and I know that's not the case at this moment. So it's that she's thinking of whatever is going on.

"Fine, I'll tell you. Don't laugh. I made an appointment for a spa and facial. The woman said they have a three-for-one-special. I should've asked what the third thing was. It was a Brazilian wax. I've never had one before. And it stings like a mother," she scuffs angrily.

"What's a Brazilian wax?"

"It's when they wax you like a hairless cat"—she points to her pussy—" all the way to your butthole. Zero. Nada. No hair." She wiggles some more.

I can't hold it in. I laugh so fucking hard.

She grimaces at me, her eyes narrowing and her lips pursing tightly together. But then she breaks into a laugh. She actually laughs, and the sight of it takes my breath away. My wife is a dream. Her jet black hair sways, and her lips are full and inviting. Those curves I just want to grip on. She's perfect.

"Okay, not funny." She groans, trying to stop herself from laughing. "I was on my way to buy aloe vera and ice packs because all this happened." She points down to her crotch. "It's red...pretty irritated. The ripping of the wax hurt like hell. She put moisturizer on it, but I'm sure I'll need more for later because it seeped into my clothes." She shudders.

"Can I see?" My lips tip up into a smirk while her eyes taper in.

"Absolutely not." She peers at me, but I don't miss how her gaze wanders up and down my body.

I lick my lips, thinking of her pussy. I'll keep trying to win her back and when I do, she'll see I'm not like those who left her.

34

ROSALINE

A DAY at the spa is supposed to be a calming and rejuvenating experience. Instead, it has been chaos. Despite the relief of finding out that Monica's son is not Santiago's, I can't help but feel foolish for jumping to conclusions. In my defense, Marissa made it believable. And between my fight with Santiago and those pictures, I was not in my right mind. At some point I need to let it go.

We have lost time and years, but we never lost the love we have for one another. As much as I love him and want to jump in his arms, it's too soon. I'm not there yet. We still have so much to talk about and settle, kind of similar to starting over. Then, there's Ivan looming over my head. Fucking Ivan. He won't stop calling me. In my defense, again, I knew him for a year and a half. We were just friends, hanging out in our circle of friends. He was different, or that's what I thought. Maybe he could be someone I could trust. So, after the third time of him asking me out, I said yes. There was never any chemistry whatsoever, but he was a nice guy and one date wasn't going to end the world. I tried to let him down easy after that, but he would say, "Come on, don't give up yet." I wouldn't call it a relationship, but he did. He'd been nice about it. Then, one day, he snapped.

"Baby, I grabbed a bunch of shit." Santiago hands me the bags and jumps into the truck. "There's your favorite ice cream in the bag. Maybe that will cheer you up from the horrible day you had. I found aloe vera. They had two different kinds, so I grabbed them both and coconut oil and aftershave."

I missed him calling me baby, sweetheart, and flower.

I peer into the bags and smile. "You remembered cookies and cream and the side of Oreos."

He laughs. "Of course. You always crumble them in. I remember buying this for you when you had chicken pox, and you've been doing it since."

I hide my smile. He remembers—not just what I like, but why I like it. I remember that day. My aunt couldn't miss work and usually asked Rachel to help, but it was always Santiago who did. Now that I think about it, I'm sure my aunt knew it was Santiago watching me all those times. She trusted him. I guess it was a mother's instinct. Santiago went on his dirt bike to the grocery store and returned with Calamine lotion, cookies and cream ice cream, and Oreos. It became my favorite.

"You think I'd forget, flower?" He works up a cocky grin, his chin up. He's handsome.

"I would never," I tease, and it almost feels like I'm flirting. *Not yet, Rosa. Take it slow,* I reminded myself. *You've been through a lot.* But it feels good to converse with him again. His eyes darken, and I swallow. I'm the mouse teasing a lion.

"Why men's aftershave?"

"The aftershave is for down there, baby. It might help."

My eyes widen. *What the heck?*

He snorts at my reaction. "It helps with the irritation and

leaves it smooth as butter." He licks those fine lips. Smooth as butter.

"Huh," I say. Men. It will probably sting with the alcohol in it. He starts the truck, and we drive back home.

MY PURSE IS like a treasure chest. I'm digging in there, searching for my keys. Then I remembered I left them at the shop so they could tow my car. "Fuck," I shout.

Santiago is already twisting the key in the knob to his door.

"My keys are at the shop. I don't have my house key. I'll have to call management."

"Rosa, I can't let you go back to your own place when you're unwell. Come to our home."

He acts like I have the flu when all I have is an irritated, swollen, and red private area. He doesn't give me time to respond. With a gentle yet firm grip, he leads me into the house. He puts the ice cream in the freezer, grabs my hand, and leads me upstairs. I stay quiet, processing what I'm doing.

"You can use my room to put the ointment on. You don't want to be in the living room in case Mark walks in."

He is right. I forgot about Mark, and I don't want him to see me shove my hands down my pants and apply it. Same for Santiago.

"Okay, thanks." My eyes wander around the room and look at whatever I want. I jut my chin. "My painting?"

His ears go hot, and it's cute. Santiago never gets shy. He scratches the back of his head and sets the bag on the bed.

"Yeah, although we weren't speaking, and I was pissed at you —you know because I thought you were with him, I still loved you, and that outweighs everything else. Our home needed a piece of you. The week before it all went to shit, I rented this place for us. Even after that, I followed you on your social media for your art. You're talented. And your paintings make me feel close to you."

My heart warms up like a fuzzy sock. Then melts.

"That's sweet." I can tell he's uncomfortable—I shouldn't say uncomfortable. He puts his heart out for me to see, making his face grow hot. I give him a confession of mine. "Every night, I wear my wedding ring to bed. It's the only way I felt close to you." It's an accurate statement.

He fills the space between us. My pulse surges. With significant effort, I try not to flinch when the palm of his hand strokes my cheek.

"Mine is close to my heart all the damn time." He pulls the neck of his shirt open to reveal the chain around his neck. "I love you so fucking much it hurts, Rosa."

The love, want, need, and longing is visible in his eyes. A tear runs down my cheek. He catches it with a simple kiss.

"Now, how about you lie down so I can help you with the ointment?"

"Absolutely not."

"Why not? It's not like I haven't seen it." He shrugs. "I mean, unless you want me to lick it better. My saliva is liquid gold to your pussy."

Cristo.

It's tempting, really tempting, but we finally started talking today, clearing the air between us without throwing proverbial punches. He smirks, shoving his hands in his jeans.

"Most definitely not. I know what your tongue can do, and that will only lead to other things, and we agreed to take it… slow, remember? I'm not ready."

He deflates.

It hurts to disappoint him. I toss my purse on a chair next to his desk.

"Okay…well, I'll get out of your way. If there are areas you can't reach, let me know. I'll be a complete gentleman." He smiles a little.

"Okay, thank you."

He nods, closing the door. I exhale and peel my pants and underwear to my ankles. Twisting the tops off the tubes, I apply below the waist, then try to work my way farther down. Instantly, I'm relieved. The moisturizer she used helped a little, but I have sensitive skin. The cool aloe is soothing. It's still angrily swollen. The lady most definitely didn't have much experience. I groan, trying to reach farther around, but my gut won't let me. Fuck!

Knock. "Are you okay, Rosa? I heard you yell."

I had not realized I yelled. Dammit, I need to hit the gym, maybe yoga.

"I'm fine. Just trying." I breathe out, strangling my airways every time I try to breathe. The door flies open, and my legs shut like the door behind him. Can things get more humiliating than this?

"You're a stubborn ass. Let me help you."

I shake my head.

But he ignores me and grabs the tube. "Open up."

"No way."

He spanks my thigh.

"Rosaline," he says gruffly, and his tone has me obliging.

I flop my legs open like a frog. He bites his bottom lip and takes a deep breath. "Fuck, baby. It's inflamed. That woman did a shit job—there's a couple of spots where it bled but nothing major."

My face boils when he gently rubs the cream. Slowly. It takes every bit of me not to moan. He takes his time going over every nook and cranny. Concentrating. You know, when you're in high school and they have you dissect a frog, and you're concentrating on finding the organs? This is what it looks like.

"Does it hurt when I touch it?" He swallows, then inhales and closes his eyes, almost like he's controlling himself.

I nod, but he can't see me. He's applying the cream. Swallowing. "No, it feels better, the cream is soothing it." *Your touch is.* That is really what I should say.

Then, he blows to allow the cream to seep into the skin. A light, cool breeze feathers my flesh. It makes me flustered and dizzy.

"The aloe's soaked in, so now I'm going to coat it with aftershave. It's lotion. It doesn't sting. It will help with the irritation." He adds the aftershave lotion, and it's cool to the skin. "All done, baby." He gets my undies and jeans from my ankles and jogs them up.

"Well, that's not embarrassing and awkward." I blow out and sit up.

He returns from the bathroom, wiping his hands with a towel. He peers at me with those eyes I love.

"Not awkward at all. Not for me, at least. You're my wife." He shrugs. "Weird shit is always going to happen in marriages. You've always had a knack for some crazy shit happening to you."

I laugh because he's so right. "Yeah, shit always happens to me."

"Let me tell you some crazy stuff about married people." He scratches his chin. "You know I never knock. I'm starting to think I should, though. I walked into Dominic's house. He was sucking on Mila's tit. She was crying, then he spit into a bowl. I spin around, mortified. Seconds later Dominic runs to the sink to rinse his mouth. It turns out Mila's breast, nipple, whatever, swelled and she was in pain from breastfeeding. She had a clogged nipple. She went to the doctor, and nothing worked, so she asked Dominic to unclog it for her."

"That must've been traumatizing for you and Dominic." I'm glad he told me. It slightly lessens the embarrassment.

His tongue swipes at his lips. "It was." He laughs. "Do you want to lie here or on the sofa? I'll make us something to eat."

"Sofa." I stand, and my heart hammers against my chest. Santiago extends his hand, and I spot a new tattoo peeking out from his sleeve. I take the offered hand, and my fingertips tingle. It's an exhilarating sensation to know he still wants me after the impulsive mistakes we've made. His huge hands hold onto mine as if I might slip away. His arms flex in my hold. Santiago's sleeve rides up. I spot a couple of tattoos on his arm. He has more new ink than I thought.

"New tattoos?" I point out. We stand at the foot of the stairs.

"Yeah." He lifts his sleeve up, showing me the stars and moon above a cliff. His skin has an imprint with my painting, the one in his room. His smile lifts. "It's where I go to think or just to get away. Then it became our place. The night you gave yourself to me. The night I played for keeps. So, when I saw your painting. I had to have it. There's no fucking way I'd want anyone to have something that represents us. If you're my moon, I'll always be the wolf howling to you."

Twirling a strand of hair with my finger, I reply, "So, you used a different name to buy it?"

He touches his tongue to his top lip, then smirks. "Yeah, I didn't want you to know I bought it. I was worried you would cancel the order."

I shrug. "Probably would have."

His eyes flicker over my body and idle on my lips. Without thinking, I lick my lips. He wants to kiss me. I know it's stupid of me not to kiss my husband. But, I just can't, not yet at least… too soon. I just found out the truth today. I told him we should take it slow. Kissing will lead to us in bed, and we still have things to sort out. I have checked off two important things we needed to talk about, what's left is Ivan.

"What other tattoos do you have?" His body deflates from my rejection.

He shows me his other arm, a rose on his forearm. Then he slips his shirt off, showing every bit of muscle he's accumulated throughout the years. "And this one." He points to the one on his chest, on his heart. My name, Rosaline, and at the bottom of my name reads, *my wife, my life.* Thinking back to when he stepped out of the shower, I hadn't noticed any of these. I was so focused on his pierced dick. I can feel my face grow hot.

Have you ever experienced the sensation of floating on the serene surface of the ocean? The warm sun beats down on your skin as seagull's cry out overhead. Each time a gentle wave lifts you up, your heart flutters with excitement. That's how I feel, like my heart is soaring and drifting like a light feather.

Filled with desire, I take two steps closer, leaving no space between us. My breath seeps into his skin, then I trace each letter with my finger, leaving goosebumps in my wake. I love the way I make him feel.

I gently place my lips on his warm skin, tracing the inked patterns with my own. Stepping back, I meet his gaze. He looks down at me with a mixture of wonder and devotion.

"I love it."

"Yeah—"

There's something powerful about a man choosing to ink your name onto his skin permanently. It represents his complete loyalty and love for you. The way he's looking at me, all triumphant and happy.

"I have a new tattoo."

His brow lifts. He thinks I'm pulling his leg. I was a wuss back in the day. But when you're grieving you welcome the pain, surrender to it—to numb the pain in your heart.

"You think I'm messing with you?"

He leans with the palm of his hand on the wall. Looking all sexy, shirtless, and shit.

"I'm not, husband," I blurt, not meaning to. *For fuck's sake, Rosa.* Facepalm right to the head. He likes it. His face is a firework show, dimples popped in, cute and all. The aroused ache between my legs doubles. As it is, I'm already wet. Tonight, I'll have to relieve myself. My face must be on fire.

"Show me, wife."

Oh, heavens. His jeans hang low, showing his v-line. Straightening up, I compose myself into a woman who's not affected by him and who is not sweating like she ran a marathon. This is what he does to me.

"It's in a private area." I peel my eyes off him, glancing around the house, rocking on my heels.

"Did you forget that I just saw you with your legs spread open seconds ago?"

How could I forget?

"That's different…it wasn't for pleasure or sexual." I square my shoulders. "That was for medical purposes."

His head pulls back, and he smiles, amused.

"Then I should examine your tattoo for medical reasons. Where is it at?"

"I have two." I lift my fingers up.

He whistles. "Damn, you left for two years and came back all tatted gangster and shit."

I snort a laugh.

"I missed that laugh," he whispers—his smile sags along with mine.

I missed everything about him.

I clear my throat. "There is one on my breast and the other on my back," I utter.

"Fine, you don't need to show me. I'll wait until I get you naked." He flicks his tongue on the roof of his mouth. His gaze rolls over my body shamelessly. "I'll work on lunch," he says and walks out with a wink.

My entire face feels like I'm hovering over a steaming bowl, leaving me with a flushed, feverish sheen. This is worse than the spa. I need my car back so I can get my keys to my house. This is too much too soon.

35

SANTIAGO

HOW BAD WOULD it be for me to say I have a spare key to her house and fail to mention it to her so she could stay at my house? Really, it's our home.

I mean, come on, her legs spread on my bed? It's the cherry on top. It took everything in me not to roll out my tongue.

An hour later, Reese called to say her car is ready. Mark announced the other night that she has an art exhibit show tonight. My initial plans were to show up, but now that she is at my house, I told Reese to have the guys do an oil change, change the spark plugs, change the air filter, and give it a detail— anything to give me more time with her.

She's been dialing management to open the door for her. Her exhibit is creeping closer, and she needs to get ready. I offered to take her shopping for all new stuff, but she refused. So, I finally whip out the spare Liam gave me. He said in case of an emergency.

My beautiful wife stares at me with those eyes I could drown in. "All this time, you had a key?"

"It slipped my mind."

"Oh, it just slipped your mind that Liam gave you a spare key," she growls.

"It did," I lie.

"So, when will my car be ready? I need it. It shouldn't take this long to get tires."

No, it doesn't, but she doesn't need to know that. I'll do anything to spend more time with her.

"Another hour or so. It needed an oil change. So I told them to do it."

She glowers at me, her lips pursed. "It didn't need an oil change. The sticker on the windshield says so because I just got it done before I moved here."

"Your safety is important to me." I shrug it off.

"Do you think Reese can drop it off at the art show?"

"Why there?"

"Because I'm taking an Uber, and that way, I can drive back."

She's shit out of luck because I'm taking her. Arms crossed to her chest, she peers at me, leaning on the kitchen island.

"Billy's dropping it off here later."

The face she's making. It's like I said. Satan's ripping through the gates of hell.

"Billy, huh? The one where you were all 'last name Delgado. This is my wife'?" she says in a husky voice, mimicking mine. "The same Billy you were all snuggled with at the bar? The same Billy who was whispering in your ear while you were laughing like a little schoolgirl?"

A vibrating laugh stirs from my chest. It's the wrong move to make. Clearly, she's not laughing, and she's pissed. She grabs the key from the counter and sprints out the front door. Fuck.

"Flower, wait," I call after her while she's shoving the key into the knob. "Baby, what's going on?"

She unlocks the door and turns to peer at me. "I have no interest in a man who plays games. After everything I've been through with you and life, in general, I'm not doing this dance with you. If you're into Billy, then do me a favor and sign the papers, and fuck you for that. And if you did it to make me jealous to spite me, double fuck you."

I pull her through the doorway and slam her against the wall, my fingers dig into her waist.

She flinches, but I pay no mind. My hand gently covers her neck, my thumb lightly strokes her soft skin, and her pulse races. Her breathing becomes heavy and uneven under my touch. "I'm into my wife. You're all I want. You're all I see—"

She looks me straight in the eye. "Then fucking act like it."

"Billy's gay."

"I don't give a flying fuck what she is. You knew we were still married. But from where I was sitting, it looked flirtatious—intimate even. And I'm not the only one who thought so. My co-worker who was with me that night thought the same. Gay or not, she shouldn't have been that close to you, whispering to you and touching you. And you allowed it." She spits out every word. "I expect the man who signed a marriage certificate with me to show me some damn respect."

"Like when you paraded around with your asshole boyfriend? Having him hold you at the beach when you were in a fucking bikini? And you laughing, having a good ol' time?" I should have kept my mouth shut.

She pushes me away hard.

"Hey, asshole, in case you forgot, we were supposedly divorced. The only reason was because I thought we were divorced, and the main reason was that I thought you had a child with another woman. And according to Liam, you were always flirting with women and taking them home."

Anger burns deep inside me.

"Bullshit, I never took a woman home. I fucking told you, Rosa."

"And I fucking told you that Ivan wasn't my boyfriend, but you don't seem to believe me either. You said you made it look like you were single in front of the guys... to the point you would flirt with women. It became so natural to you that you didn't notice you were doing it. It shows it's become your norm." A disgusted glower contorts her mouth.

She's not wrong. It became a norm to pretend. How dumb can I be not to notice Billy sitting too close, although I'm not into her, and she's not into me.

"I never flirted with men nor him, my so-called boyfriend. Never. He was only ever one of the girls." I noticed she seethes when she speaks of him. "And you don't know shit about the years I've been gone."

She keeps reminding me of that. Not much has changed in my life, but supposedly hers has.

"I didn't flirt to hook up, Rosa. Just innocently to get the guys off my ass. I couldn't tell them I was married to a woman who hated me."

"I don't give a shit. It was more important to you to let the guys see you were chasing ass than to respect me. If you didn't sign those papers, then you shouldn't have gone out flirting. If I'm all you want and see. Then. Fucking. Act. Like. It." She looks at me up and down. "Therefore, I'm not jumping in bed with you at the snap of a finger. Who would want a man who is too busy proving to the guys he's chasing ass when the only ass he should have been chasing was his wife's? You want me, then prove it—like you should have done at any point over the last few years."

Fuck. I don't have anything to say.

"Two years I waited for you to knock on my door. Two years! And it never came." Rosa walks to the foot of the stairs.

"I'm going to get dressed. Close the door on your way out." With that, she stomps up the stairs.

Never expected my wife to so thoroughly rip me a new one. She's absolutely right. Respecting Rosa has always been a top priority for me. I made a mistake by portraying myself as a single man so my brothers and Liam wouldn't grill me. In the end, who gave a fuck if they did? What kind of role model was I being, having them believe I was flirting with women? I am their older brother, their protector. I raised them and should have set a better example for them.

Most definitely, I regret disrespecting her by flirting with other women. I would never cheat on her. I love her too much, and I lost myself when Rosa left. I'd go to the cliff and dream of her. I lost track of my family and myself. Dominic and Liam are the ones setting the example now. The day Liam fell for Sophie, he didn't look at one girl, not even a glance. Dominic? His fuck up is my fault, but now that he has his girl back, he devotes all of himself to her and his kids. With Mark living with me, he's different. I want to say he has a good head on his shoulder.

I messed up. She witnessed it with Billy, but in all truth, I didn't see it as flirting because I wasn't… She got too close to me. I didn't register it in my head. I know she didn't intend to, but I noticed Rosa glancing at me with pain in her eyes. That's why I followed her out. Rosa's right. It became a norm for me.

When Rosa first left, I masked the pain and worked on bettering myself for her. I kept my distance from women when we went out for drinks. Until the guys noticed. They started grilling me. So I pretended. Guilt consumed me, ripping me to shreds when I flirted with a woman who wasn't my wife. It did every time. I never touched or said anything sexual to them. It was more like small talk than anything. I fucked up big time.

I should have knocked on her door the times I went to Portland. We would have fixed all this mess Marissa made, and I'd have been there for her when she lost our baby. With a sigh, I run my fingers through my hair in frustration. Just when I thought we were moving forward, we take two steps back, but I'm determined to fix our relationship and bring back the spark that will help her realize she's the *only one* I see now and always.

Once I shower, I pump on two sprays of Tom Ford Tuscan Leather cologne. It was fucking pricey, yet I didn't give two shits. When I knew Rosa was back, I bought it. I smother a dollop of gel between my palms before running my fingers through my hair, carefully shaping it into the perfect messy style she loves. I'm leaving one piece slightly longer than the rest, knowing it will make her wild. She always loved tucking the long strand back, and I can't say I didn't enjoy her so close and touching me. She always turns me on. Once I'm dressed for Rosa's art exhibit, I head back to her house. She tossed the key on the table, so I took it with me on my way out.

I'm waiting. I know she's up there still. I can hear her rustling through the drawers. I don't know how she'll react to me being here. Just in case, I dressed to the nines. I need to bring out the charm for her. Maybe hex her into wanting me as bad as I want her.

As I lean on the sofa, with my legs spread, I pick off some lint from my black slacks, paired with a Royal-blue button-up shirt with short sleeves. My head jolts up when I hear the clicking of heels coming down the stairs.

Holy fuck.

Her dress is a shimmering silver, the halter straps high-lighting her toned arms. The V-neck plunges down to showcase her full, perfect tits. I straighten up to watch her from the shadows like a lurking villain, unnoticed by her, as she moves around the room. Her long black hair reaches her ass. I bite my lip when she bends to pick up a paper that fell to the floor. That ass is so damn sexy. She's stunning. All I can think of is bending her on the table. With the thought, I groan. She flinches, and half a scream fizzles out when she looks at me. "Santiago, you scared the shit out of me." She places a hand on her chest. "What are you doing here?"

I stand and traipse toward her. "Picking you up, sweetheart. We're going to the exhibit. I'm your ride."

Her eyes cast a glance over my body in approval. I strive for it. She's everything to me. Without her, I'm nothing.

"Thank you for your time today, but I don't want to take up any more of it. I've already called an Uber to pick me up," she says, avoiding eye contact as her gaze returns to her portfolio.

It strikes a match in my heart. No amount of distance can make me draw a veil over her body or erase the memory of how to read her body. The distance has only made me desire her more than anything. She's still upset with me. That much is obvious.

"Rosaline, you're my wife. Your time is mine. Your dreams are my dreams. You bleed, I bleed, you hurt, I hurt."

She turns to me, taking my breath away. Those maroon lips are calling my name.

"Fuck, you're gorgeous. You look incredible." My gaze goes back to her round ass although I can only see a fraction. "You know how much I love your ass."

Her ears go red. "You don't look bad yourself." Her gaze caresses my body just how I like them, too. "Uber should be pulling up."

"Cancel."

"Santiago."

"Cancel, Rosaline, or I will walk out and tell them to leave. I'm going with you. I'm supporting you."

She pivots to her portfolio.

Her scent is like a drug luring me in. I lean into her, my front on her ass, letting her feel how hard she makes me. I bury my nose in the crook of her neck. She doesn't push me away. It's been so long since I've been this close to her. Years of jerking off to her name on my lips and envisioning Rosa all over me. With a tight embrace, my hands rest on her waist as I press myself against her. Starting at the base of her shoulder, I plant kisses along her skin, moving up to her neck. I can sense her desire, matching my own intense longing. She tilts her head more to the side. Damn, I missed her. That flower scent drives me crazy.

"I'm sorry, baby. I never meant to hurt you. I'll always do anything to protect you. I never cheated on you and never looked at any woman with desire. You're my type, my kind of beautiful. I'm in love with you and only you."

"You never stopped? Even when you hated me?"

I kiss and suck behind her ear a little harder than intended, leaving a mark. "I've never hated you. Loving you is like a never-ending hunger, a need to devour every piece of you. You are my lifeblood, and without you, I'm nothing."

"Even when you called me a slut?" She stiffens.

My head rests on her shoulder. I'm not denying it. I called her that out of anger, and it slipped out of my mouth before I could catch it. My heart shattered when I walked into her aunt's house last year. She was standing with a guy. He had his fucking hand on her waist. It took everything in me not to rip him off of her. But with her aunts, uncles, and Liam there, what could I do? Nothing. I waved her outside so we could talk, but I was so pissed, all I did was call her a slut.

She slapped me and walked off.

I exhale with remorse. "I'm sorry. I never meant it, baby. I was just so damn jealous I was going out of my mind."

"I figured, but it still hurt. I'm sorry I slapped you." She sighs when I plant another kiss.

"I deserved it."

"Still, but that's not us."

It's not. She runs her fingers down my forearm to my hands.

Her touch is a zap of electricity washing away all our lost years and reawakening my body with her caresses. She stops at the golden band on my finger. "You're wearing your wedding ring?" she whispers.

I spin her around and cup her cheeks.

"I'm done with this shit, Rosa. I don't want to hide my love for you. Didn't from the beginning. You know I went to your aunt's house to tell Liam about us. He had texted me he was there. That's when I saw your college enrollment for here."

Her tears flicker off her eyelashes.

"You will always be first, Rosa. You're my top priority. This ring is me showing you—and everyone else—you're all I want. I don't find other women attractive because you're all I see, even when I was being stupid trying to keep the guys from finding out. I never touched or dirty talked to them. So many times, I wanted to tell the guys about us because I hated pretending, but I didn't know what you wanted. And you thought we signed the divorce papers and sent them off, so yeah, baby, I'm done. I couldn't function without you. I want to hold you in my arms in front of our family." I kiss her cheeks and forehead everywhere but her mouth. I know she's not all in with us yet.

"The night in the backyard when you said you don't know how to come back from this, does it change anything now that you know Marissa lied?"

Silence.

"I'm sorry you had to go through losing our baby on your own. I wish you would have told your aunt if not me. Rosa, I will be your everything. Your light when you're lost in darkness, your anchor when you are adrift in a sea of chaos, and the villain fighting for you. I'll gather the broken pieces of our love and rebuild until we are whole."

Tears run down her cheeks. Rosa snakes her arms around my neck, and our foreheads touch.

"I'm so tired of being lonely, Santiago. I had Jasmine, but I still feel so empty without you. You complete me. I want everything you said. But there's this part of me that's terrified you'll just push me away again." Her eyes are glossy, tired, pained.

Pushing her away to go to college ended up all wrong. She might've earned a degree, but it ended up tainting her experience, mostly because of Marissa's bullshit lies. If I ever see that bitch again, I'll rip her a new one, since I can't beat her the fuck up.

"Rosa, I pushed you away, not because I didn't want you. It was to put you and your needs first. It just all went wrong. I'm not going to lie to you. I'll never push you away intentionally if it's putting you first, but never without going over it with you. That's where I went wrong last time. We'll take it slow like you wanted. You set the pace, okay? And I'll continue showing you— you're my everything."

Her lips softly graze mine, and a gentle warmth spreads through me like an electric blanket on a cold night. Time stands still, and the world fades. Her breath, warm and sweet, mingles with mine, leaving me breathless and longing for more, but I wait for her. Grabbing a handful of her ass, I push into her. I have the worst case of blue balls. Two years of pent-up frustration. "Feel that, baby, that's how much I want you."

She pants on my lips. A car honks, startling her.

"Oh, I forgot to cancel Uber."

Fucking Uber cockblocker.

I grab her sweater from the sofa, walk out, and wrap it around her shoulder. I'll tell the guy to fuck off and take my wife to her exhibit.

We are taking baby steps.

Better than nothing.

36

ROSALINE

WE DRIVE in silence to the exhibit with my legs crossed, keeping my arousal in check. Santiago parks in front of the exhibit and jogs over to my side to open the door. We walk in with his hand on my waist.

The place is swimming with people. The spacious room overflows with an array of sculptures, each one unique in its design and execution. My gaze goes to the marvelous paintings on the wall. My mouth gaps at the beauty in them. I'm always drawn to the story behind them. There's always a story behind my work. In the haze of the crowd, I find a group of people gazing up at one of my paintings.

"Rosaline, you're here." Cassy Sanders, the gallery owner, walks toward me with a kind smile.

Wrapping her in a tight hug. I say, "Hey, Cassy, thank you for having me."

She waves her hand at me. "Honey, you're outstanding. You create exceptional work. Just look at the people. We have many interested." Cassey gazes up at Santiago and gives him a wide smile. "And who is this handsome man?" the fifty-year-old woman asks.

"Santiago Delgado. Rosaline's husband. Nice to meet you, Cassy." He extends his hand, and she takes it.

"Welcome, Santiago. Your wife is a remarkable woman. You're a lucky man."

He nods. "Yes, very lucky." His chocolate eyes gaze at me with pride.

Cassy gushes and clasps her hands together. "Come, you two, let's go chat with the interested buyers." Cassy's shoulder-length blonde hair bobs as she walks.

"I'd like to introduce you to Rosaline Delgado. She's the creator of this outstanding creative work." Cassy, along with the group, looks at me and smiles. Some of them wave. "Rosaline, please do us the honor to tell about your technique, style, and a little story behind your artistic work."

As I take a deep breath, I consciously release the grip of anxiety that has tightened within me. Immersing myself in my work, I find solace and freedom to express my passion for creating. It's a space where I can openly talk about what I love and unleash my creativity without any constraints. Santiago rubs my back, helping my body to relax.

"Hey, you, Rosie Posie. How are you doing?"

My best friend's voice always brings a smile. "I'm good, better than good. I'm getting there slowly but surely. How's my little boy doing?"

"He's good. He is playing with Miguel's kids. I'm in town. I came to visit Mom."

I squeal. I've been here for a month now, and I miss them.

"I'm happy for you, Rosa. Fuck, I still can't believe he never signed the divorce papers, and you have been married this whole time. It never clicked in our heads to check if he submitted them. That's love, baby girl. I can't say it isn't. No man would refuse to sign and be celibate for almost three years and not be madly in love. On another note, I can't believe the nerve of that bitch to lie about Monica's son. Fucking Marissa. We should jump her, Rosa, like a sneak attack, the cunning bitch. What do you say? I'll leave Philip with Mom. We can be the Chingona squad. I'll pin her sister down while you get Marissa in a John Cena headlock, then flip her on the ground and go to town on the punches."

I laugh, disrupting my class. I make my way to my office and shut the door behind me. "You have this all planned out, huh?" The bad-ass women's squad is what she wants to call it.

"Hell yeah, when you texted me everything that happened, I was pissed. So, tell me, how's that hunk of a husband of yours? How are things going now that you guys squared things off?"

Blowing out a big breath, I sit back in my office chair. It's been four days since I found out about Marissa lying. Four days since I yelled at him about him flirting with women to keep the guys from talking, and four days since he went to the exhibit with me.

He was the sweetest, most perfect gentleman at the exhibit. His hands were always at the small of my back. As I chatted with interested patrons about my paintings, I could tell he was proud to see me showcase my art. His chest puffed out with pride. He stood beside me, nodding approvingly or offering a quick anecdote about my creative process. When I'd introduce him as my husband, he would smile at me and wink, earning him a giggle. When I'm in my comfort zone talking about art, my anxiety brushes off.

"Okay, I guess. I told him I wanted to take things slow. He's trying to make us work, to fix our shattered pieces—"

"Look, I understand it's only been a couple of days since you two have been sorting things out. But, hell, if he's not the father of that kid, then fuck, you should be all over him. Have you even kissed him yet?"

Oh, how I want to kiss him. I see him daily, and his morning notes and breakfast don't disappoint. We had Sunday dinner at Dominic's. He wore his wedding ring. The guys were so oblivious they didn't notice. He comes over after work and eats dinner with me. We share stolen glances throughout the night. He helps me clean up, even though I tell him not to. I know he's tired from a long workday. Then we sit on the sofa and watch Netflix. He sits on one side of the couch, and I sit on the other. I know he wants me to cuddle with him and sleep in the same bed.

"No, I haven't. I want to. I'm having a hard time, Jazzy. I want him so bad. He's still the same person I left behind, but I am not the girl I used to be. But now that I'm back, I'm unsure how to be with him again. The chemistry's there. I feel it all the way to my toes—"

"Rosa," she interrupts me like always. "You just need to fuck him. Then, it will all fall into place like dominos."

"That's your solution? I mean, that piercing is tempting." And I still haven't asked why he has it. I could never find the right time. However, discussing his dick will only arouse me more.

"What piercing?"

"One on his penis."

"He told you about it?"

"No, I saw it."

She gasps. "You said you haven't—"

"I asked Mark for sugar, and he said to walk in and get it, that no one was home. Only he lied. I decided to be nosy and wandered off to Santiago's room, I heard him jerking off in the shower saying my name, and then saw him when he came out."

"Good lord, Rosa, that's hot. So, what are you waiting for? …

Did you tell him everything yet? If not, is this the reason you're holding back?"

I gulp so loud she can hear it on the other end.

She sighs. "He needs to know the reason you moved back."

Glancing at my class through my office window, I make sure they're still on the task I gave them.

"There's no way I'm getting him involved in my screw-up. I fucked up by letting Ivan in my life. I know him. He'll do something, and it will be my fault if something happens to him. What will he think of me?"

How will Santiago look at me? Ivan, who we all thought was a sweet, innocent guy, turns out he's anything but that. A fucking psycho.

"Rosa, listen to me. It's not your fault. Not at all. He was in our circle hanging out, portraying himself as a good guy. We'd all hung out with him for half the year before you started going out with him, and when you did, he still seemed pretty nice, until he wasn't. But Rosa, you saw him only as a friend, with no romantic chemistry. Your heart has always belonged to Santiago. If you don't want to tell Santiago, then let Liam know. I'll tell Santiago if you need me to."

Telling Liam will only fuel the fire since he's a detective. I know my cousin. He's protective, and he'll go over and beyond. I'm hoping if I just ignore Ivan, he'll leave me alone.

"Jasmine, it is my fault I listened to my dumbass cousin, and I thought he had a kid. It drove me to do it. When, in fact, I didn't want to, I forced myself—"

"Honey, you were only trying to move on with your life and we were younger. We both have grown. Ivan was just a rotten egg with issues. Please take care of yourself. How many times did you attempt to end things with him? Although there was nothing to end in reality. There was no closeness or attraction. You only saw him as a platonic friend, Rosa. He's fixated on you to the point where he won't let you go, and now he's constantly calling you. He's dangerous, and you know it."

I lean in my chair and stare at the ceiling, rubbing my face and letting out a groan.

"I need to take care of this on my own without telling the guys first. If things escalate, then I'll tell them. I'll be fine. Don't worry about me. Come over to the house before you leave. Listen, I need to go. The class is wrapping up."

A knock at the door has me spinning in my chair as I put the phone on my desk. A man from a local flower shop stands at the door holding a large bouquet of beautiful flowers. Standing to open the door, the man reads his clipboard.

"Rosaline?" he asks.

"Yes, I'm Rosaline."

He simply nods, shoves the flowers at me, and walks off. He doesn't give me a chance to ask if I need to sign. I inhale the fresh aroma of the mix of hydrangeas, roses, orchids, and craspedia, arranged in a gold metal container. A note is attached to it. I smile while reading it. *Always thinking of you.* It's not signed, but I just know it's from Santiago.

I make my way back to the class to check in on everyone. Once I help those who need it, I sit and paint on my own canvas. It's been a long time since I've painted freely other than for school. My inspiration has always been Santiago, and now I have him back in my life. My wrist strokes are deliberate, yet graceful, across the canvas. With each brush sweep, the trail of radiant colors manifests, weaving together in a mesmerizing dance. The sounds around me fade, and my hand moves like a soft breeze of the wind, guiding me to where my thoughts are in the moment. Each stroke breathes life into the once-blank canvas, creating a hue of a whispering symphony that passionately brings my thoughts to life.

I smile as I touch it up. The thing about art is when you see a painting, it captivates you. You want to know the story behind it. What was the artist feeling when they created it? It leaves you with racing thoughts and a wild imagination. What will people think when they view my painting of a girl kneeling next to a large gray wolf? He howls at the moon. The stars twinkle brightly. Will they know the great gray wolf represents the man I've always loved? The man I'm destined to be with. The gray wolf embodies loyalty, fearlessness, protectiveness, and intelligence. Its strong values of family and friendship are evident in its actions. I wonder if anyone will sense the deep connection between the girl kneeling before the great, massive wolf who saved her as a child and imprinted on her soul without him even realizing it. Maybe they will notice the girl tamed the wolf, and perhaps they will observe how he's mending their shattered pieces, with every piece shining a light back into her heart. Everywhere he strays, I'll follow.

One of the intriguing aspects of art is that we often do not know the whole story behind it until the artist shares their perspective. Love has the power to turn into endless stories and fairy tales. For me, my story will always be about the girl and her wolf.

"Hey, sweetheart, how's your day been going?"

Is it cheesy that my smile grows at the sound of his voice on my phone? It's like a soft melody. I unlock the door to my car and shove my purse in the passenger seat.

"Not so bad. It went by pretty quick. How about yours?"

When Santiago attended the exhibit with me, I sold three of my paintings for close to five thousand each. He congratulated me with pride in his eyes and would continuously kiss my cheek. The click-clack of a socket wrench bounces off the receiver.

"That's good. At least one of us is. Listen baby, I have to

work late. I need to get a lot of these cars out of my hair. We're swamped."

"Oh."

He must hear the disappointment in my voice. I've become accustomed to him having dinner with me like an actual couple.

"I know. I'm sorry, baby. I'll make it up to you. Can I take you to dinner tomorrow night?"

Tilting my head back, my dopey smile returns.

"I'd love to… So, is it a date?" My heart races as I ask, unsure why I'm even asking since we've never really gone on a traditional date before. A small laugh vibrates from the receiver. I bite my lip without thinking. A part of me wants to let out a small moan. Cristo, *Rosa*. I swear Jasmine is a mixture of Dear Abby and Dr. Phil. You talk to her, and she will knock some sense into you. Now, all I can think about is climbing him like a tree.

"It is if you want it to be because I'd love to take you on a date, wife."

"Yeah?"

He's letting me set the pace. Honestly, it makes me nervous to make the first moves. He's always been handsy with me.

"Yeah," he breathes out.

"My aunt wants me to join her for dinner tonight. I'll stop by her place." My aunt invited me over for dinner. I figured it would be the perfect time for Santiago to go with me so we could tell my aunt about us. But maybe it's better if I do it myself.

"Go to your aunt's so you're not alone. I'm not sure what time I'll be home, but you know where to find me if you need me." He says it like he's coming to my house, but it's his. My wall is next to his.

"Oh, and thank you for the flowers. They're, beautiful."

"What flowers, Rosaline? Who's sending you flowers?" he says gruffly.

It wasn't him. My stomach drops with a twist.

"The note had no name. I assumed they were from you. It must be my aunt who sent them," I say, while chills run down my spine. It must be Ivan who sent them. How would he know where I work?

"Hmm no man better be sending you flowers. I would fuck him up. Let's hope they're from your family, Rosaline." His voice drips dangerously low.

"I'm positive they are from my aunt."

"Better be, sweetheart."

We both disconnect, and I start the engine and set off to my aunt's house. I wish the flowers were from my aunt if not Santiago. The message on the note says otherwise. It scares the shit out of me. He knows where I work.

THE METAL SCREEN door squeaks as I open the side door of my aunt's house leading to her kitchen. My *abuelita* and *tía* sit at the table, drinking a glass bottle of soda. "*Hola, hola,*" I shout.

They both look up from their deep conversation. My aunt stands and immediately wraps me in her loving arms. I missed her warm hugs. *Abuelita* stands, her knees crackling as she walks toward me.

"*Abuelita*, sit. I'll walk to you."

She waves her hand at me to hush me. "Rosa, *hija*, I'm so happy you're back."

My *tía* kisses my cheek and steps back. My *abuelita's* arms hold me in a grip. She's strong for an eighty-year-old woman.

"*Abuelita*, have you been working out?" I tease, squeezing her biceps.

Her lips curve into a smile. "The only workout I do is lifting my cup of coffee and my concha." That makes two of us. "I thought you were bringing a guest," *Abuelita* says as she sits back down.

My aunt pulls out plates from the cupboard. She looks cute in a sunflower dress when it's still so damn cold.

"He had to work late, took a rain check."

My aunt raises a brow then turns to her casserole. "He?"

I nod. "Yes, Santiago had a lot of work. His shop is doing good."

My aunt and *Abuelita's* smiles grow the size of Texas. They've always loved Santiago, although once they find out he's my husband, we'll see what turn that will take.

"He's such a hard worker and a good man. He loves those brothers like they were his own kids. I'm still in shock about Rachel...I let you and Liam go to that monster's home. Those poor boys—I love them like my own. I wish I had brought them to live here." My aunt shakes her head, serving a plate of enchiladas. "Santiago has a strong head on his shoulder these last years when you were gone. He was working so hard to build his shop... something about him changed."

My insides dance. "What do you mean?"

My aunt sets the warm plates on the table with red enchiladas, rice, and beans. She looks up at me. "Like he had a purpose."

A brow rides up, and I say, "Oh."

Abuelita studies me like she does when she reads her gossip novella magazines. Her aged hands cover mine. She gives me a sad smile.

"I'm sorry, Rosaline," she says in our native tongue. "I know you've always crushed on him."

Was I that obvious?

"Now, I haven't seen him with anyone, but I'm positive he's in love." She pats my hand.

My aunt looks like she pities me.

"Oh, wow, what makes you think he's in love?" I ask, feeding into it. My aunt and *Abuelita* are the two gossip queens.

"It's written all over his face. When a man is in love, he has a purpose. She became the motivation he needed to better himself."

Abuelita peers at me sympathetically, like I'm a glass doll, ready to shatter. *Tía* Andrea sits next to me, rubbing my back. *Oh god, these women are about to find out in a bit that I'm that woman.*

"Rosaline, I'm sorry, honey, I wanted to tell you, but didn't know how. I went to Liam's a couple of months ago, and Santiago was there. I asked about his love life in private not in front of the guys, and he replied that he was in a long-distance relationship with a girl he had his heart set on. Santiago's face lit up as he spoke about her, like he was lost in a dream. He described her as the most beautiful woman and admitted that he was deeply in love with her. He also said that the shop and everything he does is for her. To be a better man for her because she deserves the world."

My heart swells. Santiago is already exceptional. He just doesn't realize it yet.

"Santiago is building a home for her out in the country. By some canyons, he claimed."

I'm an emotional eater, so I take a spoonful of enchiladas and stuff them in my mouth. Then a spoonful of rice. My eyes fill with tears. He is building me a house? Santiago has been working on a home when we haven't spoken in years. Did he have hopes I'd come back? He must have. What will he think when he finds out I never intended to move back? The only reason was that Ivan was stalking me. Waterworks cloud my vision. I can barely swallow my food. Aunt Andrea is panicking, and *Abuelita* is about to have a heart attack.

"Rosaline, I'm sorry, but I didn't know you had such potent

feelings for him. You've always been attached to him," *Tia,* mummers and her eyes soften.

I finally swallow and cry harder. I don't deserve him. He deserves someone better.

"He's my husband," I whisper, sobbing.

Abuelita hands me her handkerchief from her purse. Her eyes are wide as can be. When I peer up at my aunt, she has her hand on her heart.

"What do you mean, Rosa? Who are you married to?"

"The love of my life. Santiago, of course."

They both gasp, but I don't gaze at them. I stare down at my laced hands. "Let me start from the beginning. It's a long story. Please let me talk without interruptions because I love him, and I want both of your support."

"Okay," they both whisper.

So, I start from the beginning. I don't mention why I moved back or details about Ivan. Just the same that I revealed to Santiago. That I tried dating Ivan to piss Santiago off and that I tried to move on because I thought he was.

"Rosaline, honey, you should have called me. I would have been there for you. I would have hunted Santiago down, and we could have fixed this mess." My *tia* holds my hands softly and places a kiss on them. "That bitch, Marissa. I've always disliked her."

"Are you upset I married him?"

She shakes her head in a swift arc. "To be honest, Rosaline, there's no better man than Santiago for you. He knows better than any man could, and I know he'd always take care of you. You and him" —she chuckles—" were meant to be. How life unfolds itself. I remember you crying for him when you were only six or so. He would drop everything and everyone, even those hood rats. Any time you needed him, he was there. You developed a special bond. I'm just glad he fell in love with you when you were of age. Love makes you stupid and crazy, so you two went off to get married. I'd go back in time to marry Manny again."

Abuelita sighs. "He's a sexy man, Rosa."

I snort, not that I disagree. I'm just relieved to get this off my chest. I want Santiago and me to start over with a clean slate. That means I need to tell him what I've been withholding.

"You're his purpose. You are and will always be first with him."

"Liam doesn't know yet. Can you please not tell him until Santiago talks with him? I'm not sure how he'll react."

Tía peers at me with her warm eyes. "It's not my love story, honey. It's yours to tell. Liam might be a little shaken up, but he'll get over it. He's found love. He'll understand. Santiago is older, but that's not a big deal. I can count on him to take care of you. Those boys are nothing like their parents. There is good in them. Like I said, you'll always be first in his eyes."

37

ROSALINE

MY AUNT SAID, "He's a good man, Rosa. He let you spread your wings at the cost of the pain in his heart." She's right. He is.

Fishing for my keys in my huge Gucci bag, I glance up when I hear Santiago's door open. I notice Santiago's truck is not in his parking spot. He's probably still at work. A woman in a short, skimpy skirt walks out. Her gaze roams over my body with her big eyes. Drunk as fuck. She walks off like her ass is on fire. Seconds later, Mark walks out and locks the door.

"What the hell was that?"

Mark jumps, startled. "Fuck, Rosa."

"Where did you get her? Off the corner?"

He rolls his eyes. "I met her at a club."

"So, you're dating her?"

"No, Miss Nosy."

"Okay, you just fucked her?"

Mark pinches the bridge of his nose. "I tried, sister-in-law, but I couldn't."

"Oh." I look up at him. "Sorry to hear that."

He snorts a laugh. "There's nothing wrong with my dick. I just don't want some random girl. I thought I did, but when I brought her here. I changed my mind." He shrugs. "See you, Rosa."

I wave at him and walk into my home.

Stomping up the stairs, I'm feeling all kinds of things. I'm needy, aching, and tired, for one. A storm is brewing outside, which means my anxiety spikes. Taking a warm shower always helps.

The storms in Portland were bad. We had a neighbor who had a Great Dane. When the storms hit, lightning struck, and thunder roared. She would put an anxiety jacket on her dog, Poppy. It helped relax her. I was envious. I wanted one. When those nights happened, I would climb into bed with Philip and Jasmine.

When I moved from California, my anxiety was worse than it ever has been. Okay, I know why it was worse. Despite many therapy sessions, I couldn't shake off the memories of being locked in a dark closet, surrounded by the deafening sound of thunder. As a child, every second felt like an eternity.

When I step out of the warm, steamy shower, my bathroom looks like a sauna. Once I dry my hair and slip on one of Santiago's shirts I've had for the past years, I crawl into bed, pulling out my vibrator from the nightstand and my wedding ring.

Fat droplets of rain splatter against the window, blurring my view of the dark, stormy sky. The rumble of distant thunder sends a shiver down my spine, as I know the storm is quickly approaching. Lightning flickers in the distance, illuminating the pouring rain.

My hand slides slowly between my legs. At least my vagina is back to normal. The wax technician was right when she said once you go hairless, you won't go back. My skin is soft as butter. I moan as my finger brush my clit. As always, my thoughts go to Santiago. I miss the way his body felt on mine, how our skin electrified when our bodies joined.

Powering up the vibrator, I cry with pleasure.

"Fuck." I hear Santiago shout from the other side of the wall.

Shit, I didn't think he was home yet.

Management needs to do something about these paper-thin walls. I need this. I can't stop.

His head or fist bumps the wall. "Moan my name, Rosaline." He almost sounds breathless.

When my orgasm rolls in waves, I cry his name out.

Catching my breath, I roll off the bed to clean myself up. The sound of his voice causes my body to move in a hypnotic rhythm, like a snake swaying to a charmer's tune. I don't hear him anymore. A part of me wants to rush to his place and lie in bed with him, but I don't. The rain drums against the window; it would almost be soothing if it wasn't thundering.

A roar of thunder jolts me up from a deep sleep. The booming clap shakes the walls, and my heart races. I inhale and exhale to calm myself. I try to think of things to distract my mind from sinking into a dark place. My body is curled into a fetal position. A strike of lightning spawns another boom of thunder. The storm is on top of us, and lightning brightens up the room. With the beating of my heart and heavy breathing, I don't hear the front door open.

Footsteps up the stairs thump louder and louder as they reach the entry of my bedroom, and a dark shadow looms in the doorway. I'm terrified. What if Ivan's found me? My body relaxes when I see who it is.

Santiago steps into the doorway, his dark brown hair glistening with droplets of water from the rain outside. He comes into my room, quickly removes his shoes and drenched shirt, and then joins me in bed. With gentle strength, he lifts me onto his warm chest, our bodies fitting perfectly together like puzzle pieces.

"I'm here, Rosaline. You're okay." He rubs my back, and his spicy masculine scent soothes me.

"You remembered?" I ask, my voice muffles in his chest.

"When you love someone more than you love yourself, you never forget their fears." He kisses the top of my head. "I'd never forget anything about you."

I know he wouldn't—he's here like he's always has been. He traces the wedding ring on my finger.

"I told you; I wear it every night." There's a quietness that slices the air, only the sound of the storm. I kiss his chest; the touch feels good to my lips. "I love you, Santiago…goodnight."

Santiago runs his fingers through my hair. It's crazy how a person can be your remedy. Santiago is mine. We're that for each other. I snuggle into his chest, hearing the thumping of his heart.

"I love you too, my little flower." He sighs in contentment. "You're the light I look forward to every morning. For two and a half years, I've been in complete darkness."

Pain bleeds into every corner of my being.

I know what he means because I've been in complete darkness as well.

"Come back to me, wife," he whispers.

I tap my ring finger on his shoulder and look up at him. "It's not coming off in the morning." A loud clap of thunder hits. I claw myself into his chest. "I'm here…I'm back."

"With me?"

"Yes."

The most beautiful thing happens. He smiles so big it reaches his eyes and makes my heart ache at how handsome he is. Imagine yourself at the top of the highest mountain. You can feel a gentle light breeze brushing your skin, bringing a sense of solace after the chaos. This is happiness. This is what his smile holds. The same emotion radiates from his smile, reflecting my own.

"Good. It's where you belong."

I nod, laying my head back on his chest. His thumb caresses my cheek.

"Rest, sweetheart. I'm not going anywhere."

"Good night, Santi," I mumble. Although I drift to sleep, I can hear his joy in his voice. "Good night, flower."

WHEN I WAKE UP, I feel a pang of disappointment when I notice my bed is cold where he had been lying. However, it has been the most restful night in a long time. After a quick shower and getting dressed for work, I head downstairs, where I find a note that reads:

Good morning, beautiful. Sorry I left before you woke. I had to be at work early, and I didn't want to wake you up. I'll pick you up for our date tonight.

Next to it is a tall glass of iced coffee with a splash of cream and flavored white chocolate. This man is spoiling me to the point that I'll want this every day.

I head to work with a pep in my step. Today, I have only two classes to teach. I plan to spend the next half of my day painting at home. I would like to get my Etsy shop back up and running. Also, I spoke with an artist in London who owns an art gallery. She's heard of my work and offered to show my work in her gallery.

My plan to get my master's degree in London stands, but only if Santiago goes with me. That's something I need to talk to him about. Enrollment starts soon.

After a short day, I am back at home painting. Just before I got home, Santiago called to see what I was up to. I told him about the gallery showcase. He gave me an amazing speech about how great I was.

I dip my brush into a hue of brightness. I'm creating a spring portrait today. My thoughts are to do all seasons. Winter is my favorite. You get to wear sweaters and cardigans. What I love most about winter is the holidays spent with family.

My phone rings. I drop the brush and wipe my hands before answering.

"Hello, Mila."

"Hey, honey. Sorry to bother you, Santiago said you would be busy painting. But I wanted to ask you for a favor if you get a chance."

"Sure, what is it?"

She sounds breathless, like she's running around.

"Dominic and I are in a rut with the two restaurants and the expanded studio. I have to wrap up a couple of photo shoots before helping at the diner. We dropped the kids off with Santiago at the house. If you get a chance, can you check up on him? He looked excited, then I handed him Luca, and he looked freaked out." She laughs. "His three-month-old nephew is intimidating."

I laugh. I'm sure he is freaking out. "Sure, I'm next door. I'll head over."

"Thank you so much. I'm afraid he'll get overwhelmed."

I hang up the line and head downstairs, where the faint cries greet me. When I'm painting, I crank up the radio, so I haven't heard anything. I laugh to myself, and I can just imagine the stressed look on his face.

KNOCK, knock. Santiago opens the door with a wailing baby in his arms. I don't know what it is, but whenever I see him hold Luca, it does something to me. His disheveled hair looks incredibly sexy, like he's been yanking on it. His jeans have a grease stain, reflecting that he's always been such a hard worker. Santiago has always given a gorgeous, rugged, bad-boy vibe, and I've always loved that about him. He's rough around the edges, yet he's sweet as honey.

His shoulders sag with relief. "Rosa, thank the fuck you're here. I don't know what to do. He won't stop crying—"

I hush him with a kiss on the lips, then take Luca from his hold. That relaxes him, and he follows behind me. "Did you try feeding him?"

Dante jumps off the sofa, eyes wide.

"Yes, but he didn't want it."

"Did I just see you kiss Uncle Santiago on the lips?" Dante points out. "And Uncle, I heard you say the f-word again—more money in the swear jar."

Santiago takes his wallet out and gives him a twenty-dollar bill.

"Here, you little hustler, is my advancement for the day... Your Auntie Rosa is my wife."

I walk to the fridge to retrieve a bottle, while bouncing Luca on his bottom, and put it in the microwave. He miraculously stops crying.

"You need to say hi to your aunt before you start pointing fingers. Remember your manners."

He's going to be a brilliant father someday. I pop the bottle out of the microwave and test it on my wrist. I've had plenty of practice with Philip.

I walk into the living room when Dante runs to hug me. "Sorry, Auntie Rosa, umm, hi."

I laugh and squeeze him from one side, Luca on the other.

"Hi! Baby, are you helping your uncle?"

He nods. "How come I didn't go to the wedding?" Dante asks both of us, walking into the living room where Santiago sits, leaning back on the black leather sofa.

He bites his lip all hot and shit. How is it possible this man is mine? My whole body ignites. It burns through my veins, leaving my throat parched. Santiago pats the seat next to him.

"We didn't get married here?" I answer.

"When we have another wedding, you can be in it," Santiago tells Dante. He just nods and goes back to playing Xbox.

My heart kicks up when his hot breath licks at my skin.

"You holding a baby turns me on. Fucking sexy." Santiago places a soft kiss on Luca's head. "I see you stop fussing when your aunt shows up, huh?" He runs a finger caressing his soft cheek as Luca suckles on his bottle.

It's getting hot in here. Sweat gathers at the nape of my neck. He intoxicates me as an explosion of chemistry runs through my veins.

He peers at me, then lowers his head. "Do you…wonder who he or she would have looked like?" He glances at me. "From the moment you told me, I couldn't stop wondering. Guilt eats at me. I'm sorry. I know it's—"

With a sharp slice left, then right, I shake my head. Using my chin to hold the bottle, I lift Santiago's head up. "When I was little, my aunt taught me that hate is an evil word. She said we can dislike people but never hate them. I never hated you. There were days I was angry at you. I blamed you because I was jealous, hurt—that I lost my child, and well, you know, I thought you had a child with someone else. I went to therapy for a year. It helped me grieve, just not heal, not until I moved back. For the past weeks, you've collected me, piece by piece. You shined the light back on me and helped me realize that God has his reasons. This is the solace that holds me together."

He nods, and his Adam's apple moves up and down.

I add, "I don't want you to feel guilty because it's not your fault. We can heal together." I gaze down at Luca, who's falling asleep. I wipe his mouth and then burp him. "Maybe we can… you know, once we…sort shit out and start living like a married couple, we can have a family of our own."

Santiago's brows arch, and that earns me a cheeky laugh. "Yeah?"

I shrug. "Yeah. We are both in a good financial place. I have a career, and so do you. You own your shop."

"I agree. You've given me something to look forward to." His tone is dark, and dangerous lust fills his eyes.

Suddenly, my face and ears feel hot and flushed. It feels like we just met for the first time. My nerves and arousal has me sucking on my bottom lip.

"Stop it," I drawl, turning from him.

A husky laugh vibrates from his chest. "I can't help it. You're stunning, Rosa. You've gotten so beautiful and matured into an ambitious woman."

Eager to change the subject and draw attention away from me, I say, "Thank you...umm, so I told my aunt and *Abuelita* about us."

He runs his hands through his brown hair. "So, how did she react? She didn't start shit with you, did she?"

"Uncle Santiago, I heard you," Dante says without breaking eye contact with the TV.

"I paid you already."

"Fine."

"No." I shrug. "What can she do? I'm a grown woman. She said I should have told her when I left, at least when I was pregnant. She would have been there for me, maybe knocking some sense into us. She's happy. She believes it was bound to happen."

"What do you think?"

He's fishing for an answer. "I agree, always have." I hand him Luca to clean the spit-up on my shirt. "She loves you; she and *Abuelita* both do. They're glad it's you."

"Thank the fuck. There was no way I'd let you go, regardless of what they said. Did you ask her about the flowers?"

I hoped he had forgotten since I tossed them in the trash as soon as I knew they weren't from him. "Y-yes it was her," I lie, and guilt pains me. I know I need to tell him about Ivan. He smiles, relieved.

Santiago goes upstairs to change Luca's diaper while I walk into the kitchen to make Dante a sandwich. When I hear Santiago scream my name at the top of his lungs, I rush frantically up the carpeted stairs.

I run into the bedroom, my mouth gaping open. Oh, my gosh. My eyes have transformed to the size of golf balls. "R-Rosa, fuck. Help me!"

They are both covered in shit. Who would think a baby would shit so much? It came up from the top of his diaper to the bottom? Rushing over, I grab a towel to wrap Luca in temporarily. Santiago is gagging with tar-looking shit all over his shirt and hands. "It's all over me!"

"Let's get you both in the shower." I lay Luca on the bed, placing pillows all around him and run to the bathroom, twisting the faucet on. Santiago follows behind me. He looks horrified. "Shirt off," I instruct he lifts his hands up. Slowly, I take it off, trying my best not to get it on his face. *Oh, fuck.* "Jeez, who would think baby shit would smell so bad? I mean, the little guy doesn't even eat solids yet."

Santiago groans, holding his breath.

I snort. "Breathe before you pass out. Kick your boots off," I bark. Then I unbuckle his jeans, sliding his boxers down with them.

"Thanks—" He wretches. Hands in the air, he turns. I try to ignore that he is naked, and I just undressed him. The keyword is tried. I didn't succeed. Although he's covered in baby poop and reeks, I can't help but gawk at him. I stare at his broad shoulders, a testament to his strength—defined muscle rippled beneath smooth skin. I roam his body freely, moving down to his ass as he steps into the shower. Toned. Tight. I can't help but remember how my nails dug into them as he pushed in.

"Rosaline." His voice is raw and deep from me staring at him, and my gaze drops to his pierced cock.

Startled, I jump up when I hear Luca cry. Shit. "I'll be back with Luca," I shout, running out of the bathroom. Grabbing the diaper bag, I take out a container of wipes and a travel-size bottle of baby shampoo. Luca kicks and screams.

"It's okay, honey. I'm going to get you cleaned up," I coo.

He stops fussing and kicks his tiny legs. I don't know what it is, but I love smelling baby feet. Once he's cleaned, I grab a towel and head back to the bathroom with Luca. As Santiago continues to wash himself in the shower, I pull open the door. My breath catches as I see him, completely wet, dripping, and hot.

Cristo, why do I have to have a baby in my arms?

He eyes me, and I do the same.

"Here," I say, lungs deflating, handing Luca to him.

Santiago's eyebrows bounce up. "What am I supposed to do with him?"

"Wash him... Hold him, and I'll wash him?" I say to his cock. I shake my head. "I mean, you hold him, and I'll wash him."

"Baby, eyes up here, and I'm holding the baby."

Slowly and unwillingly, my eyes travel up, meeting his gorgeous face.

"What if he slips out of my hands?"

"He won't. Just let the water spray on his back."

He nods and takes Luca. Grabbing a washcloth, I lean in from the outside of the shower and squirt shampoo on it before washing Luca. If I weren't so flustered, I'd be laughing at how funny this entire scene is.

Gingerly, I wash his belly down onto his legs. Luca's a wonderful baby. He rarely cries, and the rest of the time, he just sucks on his fist, cooing in pure happiness. He looks so much like Dominic and Santiago, of course, his big brother, Dante.

Without thinking, I keep casting glances at Santiago. His eyes never stray. The tip of his tongue runs between his lips, and then he smirks. "We can add this to our awkward list of things that happen to us. If it were our child, it would be different. I'm in the shower with my nephew, who you could have washed in the sink or something."

My eyes close… He's right. This man fried my brain cells the second I stripped him.

"Wife, if this is your way of wanting to see me naked, then fine."

Rolling my eyes, I step back to get a towel.

The pulsing need between my legs accelerates. Without a care in the world, I examine every part of my husband's body. "You're my husband. I can stare if I want, and I don't need to make an excuse for it."

"Is that right, wife?"

I nod, then wrap Luca in a towel, taking him from Santiago's arms. My hands seem to have a mind of their own these days. I stroke his chest with a finger, slowly, all the way down. Goosebumps spread like wildfire all over him. I'm drowning with desire. He sucks a breath in when I glance at his piercing.

The overwhelming heat between us rages like wildfire, igniting every nerve and craving in my body. Deep down, I am also consumed by a fiery anger, a seething frustration for depriving myself of the intoxicating touch of his sculpted body all these years.

He runs his fingers through his wet hair. "Sweetheart, you're making me lose control. It's been way too long since I felt your touch."

The longing for his touch is like a physical ache, taunting and torturing me as I resist the urge to reach out and claim him as mine. The power he has over me is just as overwhelming as the force I have over him. Our chemistry is so strong. Tonight, everything changes. I'll show my husband he's mine and every fantasy I've imagined.

"When did you get it and why?" I ask, pointing at his piercing. I know now it's not for other women, but I want to hear it. He leans one hand on the wet tile, all hot and sexy. *Seriously. Ugh.*

He does it again and licks his wet lips. "For you. To pleasure you."

My heart flutters, soaring high into the clouds. He did this for me—to please me. What type of man would go through pain to please the woman they loved? Santiago is a selfless man with a heart of gold, always putting others before himself. The act of sacrificing and enduring pain for my pleasure, speaks louder than words.

"I got it two days before I found your college applications. I went to get it. My plans were to tell Liam and your aunt we were married, then bring you to our new home and pleasure you—show just how much you mean to me."

I want to melt and cry all at the same time. I glance at Luca, who's sucking on his fist, happily relaxed. Tipping one foot in the shower, I want to yank Santiago by his shirt, but he's obviously not wearing one, and I can't exactly pull him by his chest hairs. With my free hand, I wrap my hand around his neck and pull him toward me. His eyebrows go skyward. I want to show him how much his actions mean to me, how he's everything, and more to me. Pressing my lips onto his, I slide my tongue, tracing his mouth. He opens, and I devour his taste. It's short but sweet. The longing we have for one another has spiraled us out of control. He breathes like I robbed air from his lungs.

"I like it," I confess.

He turns the shower off and glances at me.

"Will you tonight?" I take a step back, feeling dizzy with love.

"Always. Every piece of you will be caressed." He says with so much love.

Oh hell.

"Call my brother and tell him to pick his kids up," he jokes.

I shake my head at him and laugh. Before I walk out to dress Luca, I say, "Don't even think about relieving yourself. I'll take care of it." I don't let him answer. I slam the door shut, taking a long breath.

38

SANTIAGO

WRAPPING A TOWEL AROUND MY WAIST, I step out of the bathroom hard as stone. Rosa has already gone downstairs with Luca. I'm not sure when things shifted between us. I've been working my ass off to get her to see that I'll always reach for her. Maybe it was after her exhibit or the night of the storm. Whatever it was, I'm glad I have her back where she belongs—with me.

I slip into a pair of comfortable gray sweatpants and throw on a T-shirt. My erection, which seems to have a mind of its own, won't subside. Of course, it won't. I can't stop thinking of all the dirty things I want to do to her.

My wife will be at my mercy tonight, and for the next couple of days, because there's no way I'm letting her out of my sight. I can't wait to shred every piece of clothing off of her, then bury my face in between her legs. Back before we lost one another, I was always gently making love to Rosa, but all that pent-up tension has me planning on going buck wild with her. Never in my crazy fucked-up life would I have ever thought of getting a piercing on my dick. My beautiful wife had mentioned how the girls at school gossiped about how they fucked some guys at school with pierced dicks. And how they bragged to her how good it felt, how well it pleasured them. Those bitches did it to mess with Rosa. They all knew she was self-conscious and had a tight circle. Just how Marissa knew and used it against her to fuck with her. What those tramps would never know is that Rosa married a man much older than her who would do anything for her. Her birth mother did a number on her, but now she's grown. I see it in the way she holds herself up.

She never encouraged me to get a piercing. However, she had that face, a curious one. All I've ever wanted was for her to have an adventure and experience life. If getting my dick pierced for her to have that, then so be it. It will be worth the pain I endured when I hear her moan as I push into her tonight.

"Baby?" Rosa calls out.

Jesus, that does something to me.

"I'm coming."

"Okay, do you want a sandwich? I just made one for Dante."

She's going to be a great mother someday.

"No, sweetheart. Don't we have a date tonight?" I shout, jogging down the stairs.

Right here, right now, I get a glimpse of my brother's life: a wife and kids. Dante sits crisscrossed on the floor, holding a controller in one hand and a sandwich in the other hand. Rosa rocks Luca in his car seat carrier thing-y, and he's already asleep. I don't blame my brother for not hanging out with us anymore at Rocko's. He has a beautiful family to come home to.

I ruffle Dante's hair as I pass him. He cocks his head at me and smiles, giving me a flashback of Dominic when he was young. His dimples suck in.

"Auntie Rosa said my baby brother pooped on you." He makes a gagging sound.

"Your brother shits like a man," I half joke.

He nods, and I laugh.

"He's pooped on my dad, too. My dad said I poop like a man because I'm in the bathroom for a long time reading."

Rosa snorts.

"Then I agree with him," I answer Dante.

The front door swings open, and Dominic walks in. *Thank the fuck.* Don't get me wrong, I love my nephews, but my blue balls need some serious attention.

I watch with a grin as Dante drops his remote and runs into his dad's arms. "Hey, bud, did you have fun hanging out with your uncle and Auntie Rosa?"

Dante pokes at his nose, then nods. "Yeah, I had fun."

In pure awe, I watch as my little brother gives his son a kiss on the cheek. He's dressed like a successful business owner in his pressed slacks and button-up shirt.

"I behaved, Dad."

"Good, son. How did your little brother do?"

Dante's lips twitch. "Luca did it again. He pooped on Uncle Santiago, and guess what, Dad? Uncle gave me twenty dollars for the swear jar. He had to pay ahead."

"Your Uncle is a potty mouth," Dominic jokes, tickling Dante and then setting him down. "Hey, Rosa, thank you for coming over and helping this dork."

Rosa stands to hug Dominic and waves her hand. "Oh, don't worry about that. It was fun."

"Fun but stressful." He laughs, lifting the baby carrier up to kiss Luca, who's sound asleep.

I lean back into the sofa, hands on my lap. Dominic glances at my ring finger, where my wedding rings sit. His brows rise.

"What's that, bro? Why do you have a ring on that finger?"

"Oh, Dad, it's because they're married, silly, and he and Aunt Rosa didn't invite us."

That little rat, I planned on telling my brother, but I've been busy, and so has he. Dominic's eyes bulge. He looks at Rosa and then at me. My smile grows like a burning fire while Rosa's lips go into a straight line. He peers at Rosa's ring on her finger.

"Fuck…shit…when? I mean, it's not surprising, really. You two have always been close."

"The summer she came down for her twentieth birthday."

"Oh, when she came down her first summer off college. And turned twenty?"

I shake my head, and his brows furrow, and he runs his hand through his hair. I know what he's thinking. "Yes, two years ago." I stand up.

"Let me get this straight: You two have been married for two fucking years? How did that happen? How did we not know? And wait a minute, she went back to school and has barely been home since then, and when she was, the two of you barely even said two words to one another! And I know you had women while she was gone, and she had a boyfriend. How can you be married?" Dominic's eyes narrow as he takes in both our faces, his lips twisting into a disapproving grimace.

"I'll explain it to you." I wave him over to follow me into the kitchen. I start from the beginning until now. "I never slept with any other woman. I just flirted to make it seem that way so you wouldn't question me. And Rosa didn't really date that fucker. She was mainly doing it because Liam told her I was with women."

"When did you start to have feelings for her, Santiago? You're older than her—"

I roll my eyes at him.

"No, shit, I'm older than her. It started after she kissed me unexpectedly when she came to visit. It didn't happen suddenly. It took weeks to admit the chemistry between us after that amazing kiss."

Dominic nods his approval. "So, why didn't you tell me? Does Mark know?"

"He figured something was up weeks ago, and I told him everything."

"And how about Liam?"

"I haven't had a chance to speak with him. He locks himself in the house with Sophie."

The air between us turns stale. I know what he's thinking, how I gave him shit about moving on to forget the love of his life while I stayed married to mine. He leans up against the kitchen window.

"How could you have been such a hypocrite? You were in love—you knew how it felt. While Rosa was gone, you fucked with my head like Rachel did. You encouraged me to move on. Your words were, 'You need to move on. It's unhealthy for you.' Maybe you were right. It was unhealthy for me. However, it wasn't your call; it was mine. The only reason I listened to you both was because I was fucked in the head. I'm not making excuses for my actions. What I'm saying is, how could you push me when *you* never signed those papers because you loved her too much to go through with it? Did you know I had to get drunk in order to sleep with them? Now, that was unhealthy. That's called not being ready."

He turns from the window to look at me. I hate myself even more for what I convinced him to do. I am a hypocrite. He carries guilt. Although Mila has forgiven him, it's there, and it's partially my fault for allowing myself to listen to the conniving bitch, Rachel. "I'm sorry. I never intended to hurt you or mess with your life. I thought I was helping you. It hurt to see you so lost. I never thought Mila would return. And I'm sorry for not telling you she called all those years. I should have listened to your feelings and helped you find her. I knew where Rosa was, and if she'd disappeared from my life, I would have been torn apart."

He sighs, walking toward me. He puts a hand over my shoulder. "It's all good, man. I know you never intended to. It's me who needs to let go of the guilt—Mila has, and I'll never know what I did to deserve Mila. What I do know is I'll live my life worshiping the ground she walks on."

I nod in understanding because I will do the same for Rosa. He points his chin up where Rosa is sitting with Dante. "Congratulations, brother. I'm happy you found love." He laughs, shaking his head. "I'm so fucking happy it's her. I've always known she had feelings for you, probably before she even realized it at a young age. She even got jealous when she was so small because chicks would talk to you. Rosa would pull you away from them. She would always find an excuse if it weren't a story."

"Thank you. I appreciate you not freaking out about this. It's Rosa who allowed me to love her. I never thought I'd find love," I admit earnestly.

Dominic frowns. "Why would I get weird about it?" His hands go up in the air. "Is it because it's Rosa and we've known her since she was little, or is it because of the age difference? I couldn't give two shits about that. What matters to me is that you're happy, and she's happy. I will admit it will take some time to get used to."

I grip his shoulder. "Good, little bro. Either way, she's mine."

"I can't believe you never signed the divorce papers." He shrugs. "I guess that's the Delgado way… Like nah, you want a divorce? It ain't happening. You're fucking mine."

I laugh. "Yeah, I guess so, huh?"

"I'm sorry about the baby you both lost. How are things between you two now?" Dominic leans on the kitchen island, ankles crossed.

I follow and lean my back against the island.

"Been working my ass off to win her back… She brings the cheesy romantic out of me."

Dominic smiles. He knows what I'm talking about.

"We talked a little earlier today. She mentioned she's ready to make things work. She wants to start a family, not now, but soon. I want that. I want what you have," I admit.

Dominic glances at the kids. Then turns to me. "Before I got my girl back, I hated the lonely feeling of coming home to an empty apartment. I used to envision coming home to Mila. Now I come home to the dream: my son runs up to greet me every time, and my wife stands there waiting for me. It's a feeling I never want to end. I can't wait until you have kids. You better get started. Your clock is ticking." He laughs.

I playfully punch him on the arm. "You little shit."

"Well, I guess I better get going."

We both walk into the living room. Rosa peers up at us both, concerned.

Dominic walks toward her. "I would say welcome to the family, but you've always been part of us, Rosie. But now you're officially my sister."

Rosa lets out a breath she must have been holding, then stands to hug my brother. "Thank you, Dom. I guess Mila is good at keeping a secret."

Dominic's brows go skyward, and Rosa smiles at him.

"Oh, my wife has a lot to explain then. It's time to go, Dante. We need to pick up your mom at the diner."

Dante groans. "Can I spend the night with Uncle?"

Ah, fuck. I love my nephews, but tonight, I want to spread my wife on my bed. Dante watches me, and of course, my beautiful wife has to give me the worst case of blue balls.

"Sure, your uncle would love to."

I shoot her a disapproving look. She just shrugs.

Dominic gets it and throws his head back, laughing. "Just wait until you guys have kids. You'll have the worst case of blue balls. Kids are always cock blocking you." He lifts the car seat Luca is strapped in. "Isn't that right, buddy? You cry at the worst times."

Luca pouts in his sleep.

"Ahh, I'm sorry. You're worth my blue balls."

"Dad, so can I?" Dante asks.

"No, not tonight. How about we call Uncle Mark and have him come over for a sleepover at the house?" I'll have to buy him a beer for that.

"Yeah, Uncle Mark is good at passing the Spider-Man game."

Dominic winks at us, making his way out, with Dante running out just after he hugs us both.

THE SECOND THE door clicks shut, I twist the double lock, then spin to my wife and pin her up against the wall. My lips skim along her neck. Tonight I want to take my time with her. Exploring Rosa's body has always been my favorite, capturing her moans, screams, and cries. Finding what makes her crumble at my touch. An hour of not touching her feels like days. Days of not touching her felt like years, and two and a half years felt like centuries of not having her by my side. She wraps her legs around my waist, grinding on my erection. My tongue runs along her collarbone as nails dig into my hair.

When I make my way to her perfectly shaped lips, she parts them, and our mouths crash with an untamed hunger. My heart is beating so fucking wildly. I move us from the pinned wall to the kitchen island, sitting her on the top. Ripping her leggings and underwear off, I lick, starting from her ankle, making my way up. She moans and squirms. She's so damn wet for me, so damn soaked.

"Spread your legs, wife."

She obeys, and her back arches when my mouth meets her smooth pussy. The longing I've had for so long melts into her delicate folds. With force, I thrust my tongue, earning her cries of pleasure.

Fuck, I missed her.

I lift her, taking her to our bedroom. Frantically, she strips me down and then sheds her shirt and bra. My throat flexes with a hard swallow. She has on her phoenix necklace, the one I gifted her at her birthday party, but that's not what catches my attention. It's the tattoo on her left breast, a small heart with an S in it. My fingers trace it, and she exhales.

"Rosa," I say, tone gruff, "turn around, baby." Another tattoo of a phoenix. "It's beautiful. You look so sexy with a tattoo, baby. I like them...both."

"Good...now...I've been dying to taste you since I caught you naked."

I smirk at the memory. "Oh, I remember, wife... You never told me why you came up here."

She licks her wet lips. I trace her body with my eyes. Her breasts are much fuller than before. I don't mind what size she is. I love her for who she is. She's stunning. I grip her curved hips.

"Tell me?"

She closes her eyes when I peck a kiss on her lips. "I wanted to see if you've had women up here. If there were clothes or any of their belongings here." She swallows and searches my eyes.

"What did you find, sweetheart?" My thumb swipes her soft cheek. How wrong she was to think I'd want anyone else. She ruined me from the beginning. She's all I'll ever want.

"Nothing...just my paintings and the one I gifted you."

The portrait she gifted me the day I lost her—a naked portrait of my sexy wife.

"You'll never find anything like that, Rosa. You hear me, baby? I'll only want you."

"I hear you."

"Good... Now, what were you saying, baby? You were dying to taste what?"

She licks her lips again, then kneels. Her tongue glides over my shaft along the deep piercing toward the base. When her nails dig into my ass and deep thrust my cock in her mouth, I'm about to lose it. Wrapping a hand around her silk black hair, I thrust harder into her. Fuck. I pull out when I'm close to coming.

Laying her on the bed, I dip two fingers in her and kiss her stupidly. My heart picks up its tempo with each stroke of her tongue. I've never been the type of man to think that people are destined for one another, or that the stars are aligned for them. But after all those stargazing nights with my girl, I'm a believer now. I'm holding the most gorgeous woman I've known all my life, the one I've always loved. I know her worth. It's more than the richest man could afford. A treasure I'll never take for granted.

39

ROSALINE

BEING AWAY from him for so long was like being in a drought, or starving. But I didn't know just how bad it was until this moment. Santiago has always been the good in my life. His kisses are fire, his touch is an erupting volcano scorching my entire body, satisfying my hunger and quenching my thirst. My moans fill the room as I arch to his fingers thrusting in me. His mouth moves to my breasts, sucking the tender nipple. My husband dominates my body with ease. He scrutinizes me as if he can't believe I'm here with him.

"I missed you." He licks between my breasts up and down the valley of them. "I never want to be without you again."

"I don't either. I need you." I cry in pleasure when he bites on my breast.

"What do you need, wife?"

"You, always you."

"And I'll always be here by your side, sweetheart. I'll always reach for you." Another nibble on my breasts. "But what do you need now, wife?" His fingers curve into the right spot.

"I need you inside me." I cradle his face in my hands. "Show me I'm all you see… Show me how much you've missed me, and I'll show you every fantasy I thought of in your absence."

"Fuck," he says. "Show me what goes on in that dirty mind of yours?" His hands slip out of me, then he licks his fingers. "How about we find out how good this piercing makes us feel? How well it pleasures my wife."

My wife. How I love when he calls me that.

I take a deep breath and try to relax my muscles as I feel the tip of him enter me. It's been a while for both of us. It's almost like I'm a born-again virgin, and he must be feeling the same way. He went through the most extended dry spell in his life. As he pushes in farther, I can't help but tense up from the sensation. The barbell feels fantastic inside me, even though it's not all the way in yet. My body responds by instinctively tightening around him.

My husband groans. "You good, baby?"

I nod. "Yeah, real good."

He laughs. Once he's in, he thrusts faster. His hips move at record speed like a racehorse getting to the finish line. Have you ever been high, like high as a fucking kite, and gotten a massage? I can't say I have, but this is how I'd imagine it. I'm intoxicated by his scent, his touch, and how he feels. The barbell inside me feels like a deep tissue massage, hitting all the right places as his cock moves in sync with my hips. It's almost too much to handle. But I can't look away from Santiago's intense gaze, which never leaves mine. His eyes tell me, "You're all I see." Pleasure courses like a river flooding me, drowning me in a sinking ship we're both on.

"Santiago," I cry, "it feels so good."

Another moan mixes with cries as he thrusts faster, harder. The barbell sensation sends waves of pleasure through my body, his shaft hitting every spot just right. Groans and grunts leave my husband's lips. My nails dig into his shoulders, and his hands go to the headboard.

"I need to...are you—"

"Come for me, wife. Mmm, that's it, baby." Thrust. "That's my good wife." His husky, overworked tone has me combusting.

All the broken pieces of myself have now been made whole again. My husband put me back together like always. My entire body shudders, head tilting back in soundless ecstasy. He moves hard and fast, jackhammering toward a desperate climax. Stars rocket my vision. His mouth clamps on mine as we both cry in pleasure. The chemistry sparks fly in every direction, reminding us who we belong to. He's mine, and I'm his.

"Mine," he rasps. "Don't ever fucking leave me, Rosaline."

"I won't.... don't ever push me away." Still on top of me—inside me.

"Rosaline, I won't—"

I buck my hips, and he moans. Still hard as a rock.

"You know, my love for you is selfish. I'll never let you go... It took everything in me not to rip that mother fucker apart for being so close to you, baby. I don't share, Rosa, but I had to remind myself I needed to let you fly. I just hoped you'd fly back to me. I will always put you first over everything; that's what loving you does to me."

I hate that he saw me with Ivan, and I hate with a passion how it hurt him.

I kiss the end of his nose, running my fingers down his brown, beautiful, soft hair. "I love you, Santiago. Everything about you. You're all I've seen from the day I laid eyes on you."

"I missed you. I don't mean just sex, but I missed your voice, the sound of your laugh, and those beautiful, brown, sparkling eyes. How you scrunch your nose when you don't like something, your touch, your smile, your gorgeous face, your heart, and your tits."

I swat him when he laughs, then wrap my arms around his neck. "I missed you too…so much."

He tries to slide off of me, but I hold him in place. I want to look at him in the eye when I ask. "Are you building a house?"

He tilts his head and bites his lip. "Yeah, sweetheart. I'm building us a house. It's close to being done." His tone drifts, unsure of how I'm going to respond.

"But…. what if I didn't come back?"

His throat flexes with another hard swallow. "I was waiting for you to finish school. Even though I was hurt and angry, I knew I had to tell you how much I loved you. I was waiting for the house to be up and ready and the right time to go back to Oregon again. I would have gone to get you. That was the plan. To get you to fall in love with me all over again. Like I said, you're mine, Rosa. I never signed because you belong to me alone."

Oh, I love him. He makes me swoon.

"I stumbled on a gorgeous plot of land for sale, just outside the city. It's surrounded by a river and sits close to a cliff, not the same one as ours by the ocean, but nice. The best part is you can see the stars clearly from there, and it's quiet for you to paint."

I wrap my legs around his waist and flip us over. His eyes widen, and he laughs as I straddle him. "You're wrong, husband. I don't need to fall back in love with you because I never stopped loving you. You're only making me fall in love harder." As I move my hips in a fluid, circular motion, his eyes fill with desire. "Will you show me the house? You always think of me when I least deserve it."

He tucks my hair in the back of my ear. "You deserve the world, Rosaline. I'll show you the house once it's done."

I keep moving. A moan slips from my lips, and I'll say the piercing adds more pleasure. He tweaks my nipples as my eyes roll back.

"The house would be nice for our kids." I envision kids playing and laughing in the home he built for us. He grips my waist, rocking us both.

"I'm going to put one in you real soon, wife."

EVERYTHING ABOUT BEING BACK in his arms feels right. For the last three days, I've spent my time at his place. Although he says it's our place, I'm not there yet. We wake up having sex and go to bed having sex. It's like we're two Energizer bunnies. It's a new us. We hadn't gotten to that point of exploring our relationship and marriage before our relationship went to shit.

But now I cherish the mornings, waking up by his side, watching his chest rise and fall, and the soft snores. I can't help but admire his chiseled physique as I let my eyes roam over his naked body. He stirs from his sleep and catches me staring at him. To be fair, he is doing the same to me. His gaze travels down my naked body.

In the past, I used to be embarrassed to be naked in front of him, but the way he looks at me and worships me makes me feel desired. My wide hips, round ass, not flat stomach. He doesn't mind it. His hands are always touching me.

I make us breakfast, his favorite eggs and chorizo, and fix him a cup of coffee. We talk about what's happened in the last couple of years. We shower together, then go to work. After work, I go home, and although he gave me a key to his place, I go back to mine until he gets out. I make us dinner. Mark joins us for dinner, and then we head upstairs to cuddle on the bed, which leads to sex. So yeah, that's how our days have been going. It's the weekend, and I couldn't be happier. Santiago is working half a day while I clean up my place, and then he promised a date since we missed the one we had planned.

My phone rings just as I spray the kitchen table with disinfectant. I toss the cleaning rag down and pick up my phone. It's an unknown number. I answer it.

"Hello?"

"Rosaline," a familiar voice says.

My heavy breathing picks up, and anger boils in my blood like a steaming pot. "What do you want, Ivan? Stop calling me," I shout.

"You! I want you back, and how about a thank you for the flowers?"

"We were never together, Ivan. I can't even count the number of times I told you this. But you kept pushing for something that would not and will never work. I don't have feelings for you."

He grunts, "I've been patient, Rosaline. You know what I want. What I need is to feel your body against mine. You never even kissed me." His voice sounds off, angry, and unhinged like the night he hit me.

"As I said, I don't have feelings for you. I only ever saw you as a friend. But we are not friends anymore, not after you laid your hands on me."

"Are you seeing him, that same guy you danced with at the wedding, the one who always kept his eyes on you?"

My hands tremble as I quickly scan my surroundings, suddenly feeling vulnerable and insecure in my home. *He's here. He's been watching.*

"He's my husband, Ivan. If you don't stop calling me, I will file charges. You know who Liam is—"

"Husband?" A dark laugh erupts.

Chills run up my body.

"He won't be for long, Rosaline!"

A boulder-sized knot twists in my gut.

"You know why? Because we are going to be good together." A ragged breath statics over the line. "I'm sorry, Rosa, for hitting you."

"Stop calling me." I end the call and take a seat, letting out a deep breath as I rest my elbows on the table and breathe in deeply. "God, what a mess," I say to no one.

THE DAY *after the restaurant incident in Portland, Ivan bought me a single rose, apologizing. His eyes weren't red, but he took a pill that he pulled out of a Ziploc. I asked him to leave, and he went mad. Then again, he showed up at school. Ivan didn't attend the same school. He was just friends with one girl we hung out with. I heard a knock at the door, and I assumed it was Jasmine. Without hesitation, I opened the door, but shouldn't have. Jasmine had a key, so it couldn't have been her.*

It was Ivan. He tried to kiss me. Shocked and disgusted, I pushed him away. He backhanded me so hard that it made me feel dizzy and sent a shockwave through my body. He heard Jasmine's car, and he ran off without a word.

That's when I became paranoid. Who wouldn't? I had a month to graduate. Jasmine and I had decided not to move home. But when this happened, my plans changed. If he kept harassing me, it would be better if I went back home.

When we graduated, we had a celebration at a restaurant nearby. My family all came for it. Two weeks later, he showed up. I was getting groceries. I hadn't noticed him standing by my car. He followed me inside. I tried closing the door on him, but he was stronger and pushed me onto the floor. He grabbed me by my arm.

"I heard you were leaving," he had shouted.

I ignored him and yelled at him to leave. My pulse was hysterical as he stood in front of me, high on something: coke, probably. Ivan's jaw clenched, and his eyes were wild. He grabbed my hair and yanked it, pulling some out.

"Why don't you want me, Rosa? I've been patient enough."

As I struggled against his grip, his hand came down on my cheek with a stinging slap. My mind flashed back to the terror of hiding in a dark closet as a child, but this was far worse. The fear pulsed through me as I wondered what he might do next if this would be my last moment alive. As I struggled against his grip, his hand came down on my cheek with another stinging slap. A neighbor next door heard my screams and pulled him off me. That night, Jasmine and I packed. She moved to a new apartment, and I moved back home.

I CLOSE my eyes and try to calm down. When the doorbell rings, I jump. On my tiptoes, I check into the peephole to see who it is. I sigh when I see Santiago waiting.

"Hi, sweetheart." His voice is a soft lullaby. He frowns, shutting the door behind him. "Are you okay? You look a little pale." He puts his hand on my forehead. "You don't have a fever." He's so cute.

"I'm okay. I was just cleaning. Umm…"

He kisses my lips. I want to tell him—I need to tell him—but I don't want to ruin our date he's been working so hard for over Ivan.

"After dinner, can we talk about something?" I know he will protect me. Now I know Ivan is around here. I didn't think he would come to California.

"Of course. Are you still up for tonight?"

I nod and bring his lips to mine. I need to taste him and inhale his scent. His lips move in sync with mine. He's so godly handsome, even with his hair a little disheveled from work. He doesn't smell like a cigarette. I think he quit again. His masculine scent makes my arousal go haywire.

I want to forget that phone call and that Ivan might still be here—for now. I want to obliterate that I moved to Oregon, that my husband pushed me to go for my own good. If I had never gone, I wouldn't have met the monster who won't leave me the hell alone. I wish I'd never run into Marissa. I wish my husband would have come knocking on my door. I want it to be all in the past, but it can't happen until I get rid of Ivan.

Right this second and every second of our lives, I want to get lost in my amazing husband. A need so fierce always bubbles in me to have his hot olive skin against mine and to feel the skin-to-skin contact. He's my safe haven, but he's so much to me: my other half, my best friend with a heart so pure.

His plump, soft lips captivate me. We stumble backward and collapse onto the sofa together. Our kisses are desperate, wild, and mind-blowing. Straddling him, I grind my hips. He's so damn hard. His beard stubble abrades my chin as I moan into his wet mouth. "Fuck, Rosaline, if this is the after-work welcome home greeting I get, then I've been missing out," he says gruffly as he eyes me, unzipping his jeans.

"I need you." My voice is hoarse. I struggle to shim his pants and boxers down.

"Are you okay?"

"Yep," I say, squeezing his cock. It oozes with pre-cum.

His head tips back when I wrap my lips around his dick. My tongue traces down every line of his velvet shaft.

"Let me come in your mouth, Rosa," he grunts.

My head bops up and down as his hips move, thrusting in me. He explodes in my mouth, and I swallow every drop. Eyes droopy, he smirks.

"That was good, wife."

40

SANTIAGO

I EASE into the Delgado Steak House restaurant parking lot. Dominic's high-quality fine dining restaurant. My plans were to take my wife on a date where my family would not be present, as we already meet for Sunday dinner. But my big mouth had to mention it to Dominic, and now he has planned a private room for us. Jumping out of my truck, I jog around the front to open the door for Rosa. She looks hot in a red V-neck dress, her black hair in a bun, and wearing the diamond earrings I gifted her after the wild sex we had this afternoon.

My wife's lips are stained red, her doe eyes sparkling in the night sky. "Have I mentioned how beautiful you look tonight?"

She blushes and nods. "You have, thank you."

Taking her hand in mine, I guide her in. The place is always buzzing. The flow of laughter and music from the jukebox fills the space. My hand is on the small of her back, and I walk us to the back room Dominic has reserved for parties and private matters.

As I step into the room, my jaw drops in surprise. I wasn't expecting to walk into a transformed dining room into a romantic oasis fit for royalty. Red rose petals adorn every surface, creating a fragrant path that leads to the candle-lit table in the center. Soft music plays in the background. Then I hear a fucking violin. I look around, expecting to find a person playing, but it's a Bluetooth speaker.

Never have I ever stepped foot into a cheesy, romantic atmosphere. When my wife gasps and throws her hands on her chest, it looks like she's about to cry. I've come to realize my wife has completely domesticated me. The whole married thing. She throws herself on me, kissing me and then pinching my cheeks. "You're so cute, Santiago," she purrs like I'm her pet rabbit. "I love this. How romantic you are."

I kiss her mouth, then pull a chair out for her. "You're welcome, sweetheart. Anything for you." I take the credit. From the corner of my eye, Dominic stands with Mila.

Dominic snorts, and my sister-in-law gushes.

A server takes our order, and it's nice to have this moment with her—just us out in the open together.

Moments later, our dinner arrives. I watch Rosa, memorize how she slices into her steak, chews, and then takes a sip of sangria. With a gentle pull, I grab the leg of her chair and scoot it toward me. She gasps, holding onto the table. Her face goes pale. Like earlier in the afternoon, she was as white as a sheet when she opened the door. I'm unsure what she has to talk to me about, but it has me worried.

"What's going on, baby?"

Her fingers drum on the table. "Nothing, I'm fine. Just thought I was going to slip off the chair."

"Your face went pale, like it was earlier."

She takes another nip of her drink. I mimic her with my beer.

"Umm, there's something I need to tell you."

I wipe my face with a cloth napkin.

"Umm, well, I went to Mexico City."

My eyebrows go into a straight line. "Okay, so this is why you went pale?" It doesn't add up, but okay.

"I went to see Tina."

Oh. Fuck.

A painful laugh vibrates from her chest. I grab her hand and squeeze. I'm not sure what possessed her to go after the way her birth mother treated her. Knowing Rosa as I do, she wanted closure or even hoped to develop a relationship with her. I absorb the pain rolling off of her—her pain will always be mine.

"What did she do to you? Tell me, and I'll go down there and give her a piece of my mind." I'd beat the living shit out of Tina's husband with gusto.

"She did what she's good at…pushing me away."

My wife's strength has always been a defining characteristic, and over the years, it has only made her an incredible woman. Rosa squares her shoulders and lifts her chin.

"When? And most importantly, why, baby? Why go see her? Don't tell me you went alone."

She sighs, running a finger along my knuckles. "Five months after I had the miscarriage, I asked Auntie Sugar for her address. I wanted to know why she did what she did, Santiago, because I would never leave our child. Never. I would love her or him as if my life depended on it, like they were my oxygen. I wanted her to look me in the eye and tell me why she left me. I went alone. No one knew. I needed to do this alone." She shakes her head. "You know what she said and did when she saw me?"

I lift her and sit her on my lap. "What did she say?"

"At first, she didn't recognize me when I knocked on her door. Our hug was stiff and awkward, like how you would hug a stranger—and not your daughter. She apologized for the pain she caused me before leaving and explained that she had to make a difficult decision. Her husband had given her an ultimatum: choose between him and me. He would leave her, of course, and she also said she couldn't live without him. No man could love her like him.'"

I kiss her lips over and over.

"'Difficult,' she said. How difficult is it to choose a man who didn't accept that you had a daughter? Sounded like a simple decision to me."

"Rosaline Delgado, you're an amazing woman inside and out. You might say she tossed you like trash, but what she left behind was a treasure so pure I know your worth; I know what I'm holding, sweetheart. Someday, you'll become an incredible mother because you know your worth. You're the least unselfish person I know. I can't wait until we have a child of our own, Rosa."

Tears spring in her eyes. I kiss each salty tear.

"Don't cry, baby. I'm sorry she hurt you. I wish you hadn't gone alone."

"I'm not crying because of her. I left her house free, without shedding a tear. I'm crying because of the beautiful words you said to me."

"It's all true, Rosaline. Let's finish eating and not waste a breath talking about that woman."

She smiles, then scoots back into her chair. We go back to eating our dinner.

THROUGHOUT DINNER, it's impossible to keep my hands off of her. My hands keep running up and down her bare legs.

Walking out of the restaurant, I see Ivan. I don't think Rosa saw him. She doesn't react. As soon as we reach my truck, I pin her against the passenger door in the empty parking lot. My hands cover her neck, I tip her head back, and kiss her possessively. Whatever that fucker wants, he needs to know she is mine. She said she never laid a hand on him. I believe her. I trust her. Once we get home, I'll ask her why she thinks he was there at my brother's restaurant, waiting. I assume for her. Parking the truck on the curb, I hold out my hand for Rosa to take as we walk back to the house.

"I had a great time. Thank you," Rosa says in a honey-dripping tone.

I laugh. She's delusional if she thinks I'm taking her next door to her house especially if that fucker is around here. I think it's time she moves into our house with me. I want all her belongings in our place.

"Night's not over. You're staying with me at our place." I swat her round peach ass. My wife has a smokin' body.

"Ah, finally, the man I've been waiting for," a deep, and unwelcome voice calls from behind.

The smell of his cigar lingers in the air, and my body stiffens. I remember that smell even though I haven't smelled it in over twenty years. You've got to be fucking kidding me. Wrapping my arms around Rosa, I hold onto her possessively. I don't look back, not until I get my wife inside. Fishing for my keys in my pocket, I unlock the door. Rosa turns to face the man standing looming in the shadows. She glances at me and then at him. Yeah, she sees the resemblance.

"Can't say I've been waiting for you." My tone seethes with venom. I glance at Rosa. "Baby, go inside. I'll be there in a bit."

She nods and closes the door.

When I was eight years old, he walked out, leaving us behind. Dominic and I stood watching him pack up, while Rachel cradled Mark in her arms. Rachel didn't look at him or cry. She didn't chase after him. He took one glance at us before he slammed the door of his car and drove off. I stood confused and lost. Deep down, I knew he wouldn't come back, and that's when I also knew I had to be my brothers' protector. I had to take his place.

Twenty-two years later, Victor Delgado stands on my doorstep. Now, I know how my wife felt standing in front of an absent parent. He hasn't aged much besides his salt-and-pepper hair.

"Santiago...son. I know I have no right to show up like this and have no right to ask if you could give me thirty minutes of your time." His voice is gruff but pleading.

My eyes stay centered on a streetlight in deliberation. Should I give him my time when he never gave us his? A part of me wants to say fuck him and go inside with my wife, but there's that small part that wants to know what he wants after all these years.

My stare stays trained on Victor, my head held high as I spit out, "You're right, Victor. You don't have the right to come here. You made it clear the day you left without a backward glance." My words are sharp and accusing, and my heart beats faster with each one.

Victor's expression drops, and his eyebrows furrow. It would be almost pathetic if he showed any signs of sympathy toward us now after leaving without a second thought on that day.

"I'll give you fifteen minutes." Only because Mark is at work.

He nods. "Thank you, Santiago."

Opening the door, Rosa sits on the sofa, watching a show on Netflix. Her eyes widen when she sees him behind me. She stands.

"Sweetheart, this is the sperm donor, Victor. Victor, this is my wife, Rosaline."

Rosa's lips twitch at my asshole-ness. My wife doesn't bestow him a smile, although Victor does.

"Nice to finally meet you, Victor." She extends her hand for him to take.

"It's a pleasure to meet you, Rosaline."

I gesture toward the recliner and say, "Take a seat."

Victor moves to the chair next to us. He's dressed in a black riding vest, just as I remember him. He has a beard now, whereas back then, he had no facial hair. In the pit of my memory, I remember women always glancing at him, but he never paid them attention. I'll be surprised if he didn't run off with another woman, and I have step-siblings. Fuck, he probably has another family.

"I'll go upstairs to give you two privacy," Rosa says.

I reach for her hand, sitting her next to me.

Victor sighs, peering at me—studying me. "I'm so damn sorry, Santiago. I saw the news about what Rachel did. I'm sorry. I can't say how sorry I am for leaving you three with that monster. I didn't think she'd go that far. I really didn't, Santiago." He laces his hands together.

My head tips to the side in confusion. Did he know she was capable of craziness? And he left us with her?

"What the hell do you mean you didn't think she'd go as far as to murder? Why don't you start from the beginning? Tell me why. Why did you leave your kids and never come back? Not even to visit?"

He runs his fingers through his salt-pepper hair.

"I loved your mother so much, but once Dominic was born, she changed. She became distant, cold, and unhinged. I lost her when she attended college. I supported her by taking care of you kids while she went to school. Then she started hanging out with a couple. She would take Dominic with her to study because they had a daughter his age. You would sometimes go, but you always wanted to stay with me.

"Rachel never invited me to go with her. I asked her if she wanted to invite them over so I could meet them. I thought that would make her happy." He laughs "But no, she wanted me far away from her *friends*. In her journal, she confessed her love for her 'friend's' husband.

"It wasn't until I saw the news story that I learned the identities of these people when everything came to light, and it was all laid out on the table that the friend was actually Dominic's wife's mother."

Rosa's eyes widen. She wasn't here when it all happened. When we found out what Rachel had done to Mila's family. I hadn't had the chance to fill her in on a lot, mainly because I didn't want to talk about it, and my focus was on my winning my wife back.

He continues, "Then, months in...she seemed like she was trying to make things work. She finished school. She stopped hanging out with the couple. Little did I know, she had blood on her hands the whole damn time. I didn't see past her fakery. Who would have known my wife was playing me? Then Mark came along. I was ecstatic." He clears his throat as it bobs.

"The day Mark was born...I found out he was not my son. Not because she told me. It was because he didn't look like me, and you and Dominic look so much like me. When I asked her, she admitted to the affair. She wouldn't tell me with whom. When I left, she didn't give a shit."

I groan and stand up, then pace the room. *Fuck.* I never wondered why Mark looked more like our mother, but now, come to think of it, he only has her eyes. He doesn't look like her. His skin is lighter. He has no dimples.

"So, is that why you left? If that's the reason, I get it. But I don't get how you could forget about your kids."

He shakes his head, his eyes hooded. Rosa stands and goes to pour him a glass of water.

"Thank you, honey," he tells Rosa. "Santiago, not a day went by that I didn't think of you boys. I wanted to take you and Dominic with me, but I know you guys would ask about Mark. I couldn't split you three up, and I gave Rachel whatever money I had left for you boys. I had no money or place to stay for months. I slept in my car. When I finally made ends meet, I rented an apartment and sent your mother money for you boys for the past years until you were thirteen—"

To contain my anger, I go to sit back with my wife. She's the only one who can calm me down. When I asked Rachel if my father had ever contacted her through all those years, she said no. "Why did you stop sending money? We could have used your fucking help."

His eyebrows knit, and he leans back. "Rachel asked me to stop, and she wouldn't let me see you guys. I think she didn't want you boys to know Mark was not my son."

"So, that's it, huh? You just gave up?" I bellow.

Rosa squeezes my hand.

"While you were out doing who knows what, I was taking your place. Rachel was absent the whole damn time. You know who took my brothers to the doctor? I did. Do you know who prepared their meals? I did. I washed their clothes, gave them medicine, listened to their struggles, and gave them advice. I helped with bills. Took care of my sick brother. Did you even know your son had cancer and that he could have died?"

His face goes pale, and a tear slides down his cheek.

"I...I didn't know, Santiago. Fuck. Fuck. When was this?"

"When he was seventeen, he was diagnosed. You know what the saddest part is? I had to lie to my brothers. I made them believe Rachel was mother of the fucking year. Everything I did for them, I had them thinking Rachel did it, so they didn't feel neglected by another parent." I'm disgusted by both of them. It was so easy for him to brush us off without even trying. "Do you have another family out there? Is that why you didn't fight to check up on us?"

"No, Santiago, I don't have another family. I never remarried. I can't fix the past. I made a shit ton of mistakes. But I tried to see you boys. I would drive by. I would see you working on your motorcycle, Dominic, Mark, and your friends playing, and I would see you as well, always with Santiago." He points at Rosa with a soft smile. "It brings peace to my heart. You two had each other.

"I went and ate at Dominic's restaurant. He doesn't know who I am, don't worry, but I got a glimpse of the fine young man you made him, Santiago. His family is beautiful. And Mark, I've run into him a couple of times when I was getting the courage to come see you boys. I'm proud of you, Santiago. You're a good man. You took on the responsibility of both parents. I apologize for that burden. If you three allow me, I would like to have a fresh start. Perhaps I can have a conversation with Dominic and Mark." His voice is soft and understanding. "I would like to ask Dominic for forgiveness for what Rachel put him and his girl through. If I had been around, a lot of this would not have happened. I can't say that about what Rachel did to her parents, but I could've been there when Dominic was sick."

I've always been observant, good at watching my surroundings. Now I'm thinking that so-called skill was shit because I missed that he was looming around, watching us. Allowing him into our lives is not something I want. I don't know this man. I don't need him to disrupt our lives. How am I supposed to tell Mark if I let Victor in? What I want to know is, who is Mark's father.

"Do you know who Mark's father is?"

Victor takes a sip of his water, then dips his head once and places the glass on the coffee table.

"I didn't know until today when I went to see Rachel. Never have I felt so much hate for a person. I had to give the bitch a piece of my mind. I cussed her out for treating you boys this way and what she did to Dominic. She told me what she did to Dominic and his wife. I was sick to my stomach. It took a great force for her to tell me who she had an affair with. Who Mark's father is." He laughs. It is not a "haha" laugh, but an "I can't believe this" kind of laugh. That has my nerves clutching at my stomach, dipping. With my hands on my wife's waist, I brace myself for what Rachel did. It doesn't sound good. Rachel is an unhinged woman.

"I remember she flew to New York for a job. At least that's what she said to me back then when you two were small. Now, she put it all together for me. She seduced a man, she drugged him by slipping something in his drink to have sex with her. This man doesn't know who she is or would never remember it, obviously. She was so obsessed with Mila's father she slept with his brother."

The blood drains out of me. I turn to Rosa, whose face has turned pale.

Mila's Uncle Roger is Mark's father, making him her cousin.

"Don't tell Mark about this. I've loved him since before he was born. I want to be his father, and I didn't leave because he was not mine. I left because she cheated on me."

41

ROSALINE

THE LAST TWO days have been a shitstorm. Did I ever think I'd meet Santiago's dad? Hell no. The second I turned to see the man standing behind us, I knew. Santiago looks so much like his father it's crazy. The man is very good-looking.

I'm not excusing his absence from his kids, but it's clear he wanted to be part of their lives. I don't think he knew how to anymore, if Rachel was fighting him on it, and he didn't know Rachel was not being a mother to them. He thought he was doing good by leaving them with her. He didn't know Rachel wasn't being a mother, but if he had known, he would have taken her to court.

Santiago shook his head at his father and said, "It was meant to be. I would have never had my girl all these years."

It broke and warmed my heart that he would go through it all again to have our friendship crafted into a beautiful love story. Santiago doesn't know how or if he should tell Dominic.

And Mark? Fuck, we knew Rachel was sick, but this is disgusting and scary.

"Rosaline?" my student, Samuel, calls out. Lately, he's been flirting, winking at me, or calling me beautiful. I ignore his flirtatiousness.

"Yes, what can I help you with?" I stand next to him, peering at his canvas. They say art is beautiful no matter what you create, but God almighty, this is not. It looks like a pile of shit. Today's lesson was to create a painting of the ocean. I had turned on calming music to get our minds and hearts into the zone to create a masterpiece. It helps relax the mind. I asked them to paint what they saw in the ocean, imagining themselves there. "Oh… that's great…um, are these rocks?"

"Yes." He breathes in like he's inhaling me.

Ignoring him, I take the paintbrush from his hold.

"You see, this is how we move a brush." I move the brush in strokes, but he's not paying attention. His hands move to my waist.

I start to sidestep just as he says, "Go on a date with me—"

"Remove your hands from my wife before I break them."

I jump, startled by the roar. My husband stands like the angry god he is, eyes dark with rage. Samuel jumps from his seat. While Santiago is a biker bad boy, Samuel is a preppy guy.

"Hey, birthday boy," I say as I walk toward Santiago, getting on my tiptoes and kissing his cheek, trying my best to soothe him. I have a full class, and he's already made a scene. My husband is not looking at me. His dark eyes are pinned on Samuel. "Santiago, let's go to my office." Taking his hand, I pull him toward my office. Shutting the door behind me, I turn to my jealous, raging man. Before I can let words out, he kisses me hard, passionate, and possessive.

"You let him touch you, Rosaline."

I roll my eyes at him.

"I didn't have time to rip his hands off when you came in all caveman. They were only there a second."

His hands cover my neck.

"No one gets to touch you but me. You wear my ring. You. Are. Mine…. Did you flirt with this man for him to think he can ask you out and have his hands on you?"

Jealousy is visible through his clenched jaw.

"Don't be ridiculous. He's, my student. I would never flirt with another man." Assuring him, I press kisses all over his handsome face.

He sighs.

"I know I'm sorry. My mind is not in the right head space after everything that happened. I trust you. It's him I don't trust," he says as he stares at my paintings. "I'm sorry I made a scene. It made me crazy."

I shrug. I would do the same. "How about I close up class, and we can go have lunch?"

Our plans are to have lunch and celebrate Santiago's thirtieth birthday today, and then he has to go back to work while I go home and make him a cake. He wants to spend the rest of the night together at home.

"Sure, I'll wait here."

WE SIT at a small Mexican restaurant halfway through our meal. We've talked about everything and anything, including his co-worker Billy, whom I've come to like. I know, I know, I was jealous at the time. But she's sweet and kind. Guess who's the jealous one now? Yep, Santiago—he says she flirts with me.

I've been wanting to address the elephant in the room. He hasn't spoken about his father. I don't know what he's thinking. Taking a sip of iced tea, I peer up at him. "Have you spoken to your father?"

He shakes his index finger, then continues eating a spoonful of rice.

"What are you thinking about all this?"

He sets his fork down and then wipes his mouth. I wait patiently with both brows arched.

"Honestly, I don't know what the fuck to think of it. He left, but just because he sent money for a couple of years doesn't justify his actions in getting a chance. Neither does driving by the house without stopping to see his kids." He tosses his napkin on the plate. "You know I spent years wondering if he'd ever come back. Dominic would ask about him. How fucked is it that Mark is not his son? Rachel was vicious, and we lived with a killer, a maniac."

When will our lives heal from the pain we have gone through? It seems like every time I think things are going to be okay, we get hit with a brick of news. Santiago, Dominic, and Mark want to move on from the pain Rachel has caused.

Lacing my hands over his, I lean into him and say, "Trust me, when you hear what I'm about to say, it's not me defending his actions."

He cocks his head.

"Listen, he looked like he had years of regret. You once told me he was a kind man when you were a kid. For him to accept Mark as his own is a start. I'm not saying I think you should give him a free pass. He should earn it. But let him try." The way I see it, Victor wants to try, but for Santiago, it's difficult to let him in. He's always been the head of the household for his brothers, their protectors.

His eyes flash as he crosses his arms. "I don't trust him."

"Just take it slow. There is no rush. But first, you need to speak with your brothers." Taking the last bite of my burrito, I add, "I haven't seen Mark." He hasn't been at the house. I think it's because of me that he's giving us privacy.

"I've called him. He finally answered. He said he's been staying with a friend."

After Santiago drops me off at my workplace, I head straight home to prepare for his birthday celebration. He mentioned getting off work around five, so I plan to have everything ready by then. In the meantime, I'll bake his cake to surprise him.

∾

ONCE I FINISH BAKING the black forest cake for Santiago and clean up the scattered flour on the counter, I make my way upstairs to take a shower. The water flows down my chest in cascading beads as I run my hands through my hair. The warm water calms the sinking gut feeling I've had all day.

Since I was young, I've always been one of those who could predict something was coming. Call it a sixth sense. I called Jasmine to ask her how she was doing to check if maybe my sour stomach feeling was about her. Jasmine and Philip are good—still in town.

Turning the faucet off, I wrap myself in a warm towel. I'll be wearing the red lace bra and panties set he likes so much. This is part of his gift. I figured, what the hell? I bought it to end the night because once he sees the shovel-head motorcycle I bought him, he's going to flip. A slamming door startles me. I finish getting dressed and run downstairs. I wasn't expecting Santiago yet.

"Santiago, you're home early—"

"What are you doing, Ivan…h-how did you get in?"

His smile is downright venomous.

"You've been ignoring me, Rosa. All I wanted was to see you." His eyes are bloodshot red. He's on something.

Ivan looks like the possessed demon I saw that night. His eyes dilate as he stares at me. I've watched a lot of Dateline stalker shows, and this makes me feel like he's one of them, a delusional, psychotic man. Did I miss the red flags of befriending this man because I was so fucked in the head?

I finally find my voice.

"You need to leave, Ivan. I have already told you so many times: we are not a couple and never have been. We were friends before, and now I just want you out of my life. I'm married—my husband is on his way. And you know Liam. He's in law enforcement, and he knows." I lie.

He doesn't flinch at my words, his brown, shaggy hair flops to the side. "You're a fucking bitch, Rosa. You're lying. You're not married, or you would have mentioned it," he sneers, and his breath reeks of alcohol. I don't need to explain shit to him.

My knuckles turn white as they cling to the edge of the granite countertop, and my legs wobble with fear. I try to steady myself, but it feels like the ground is moving beneath me. Ivan takes a step forward while I take a step back. His eyes eat up the ring on my hand. His breathing picks up, and I heave. Sweat trickles down my neck, and my heart palpitates as I reach for my phone. Before my shaking hands can get a hold of it, Ivan grabs it, tossing it onto the other side of the room.

"Get the fuck out of my house," I scream. I take a step back.

"The doors are locked, babe." He laughs. "It's just you and me." He sniffs, probably the powder lingering in his nose. "How about I show you how bad I want you?"

"Have you been doing drugs this whole time, Ivan? We can get you help." That was the wrong thing to ask.

Ivan throws a glass cup against the wall. I cower low as the shards of glass scatter.

"Fuck you, Rosa. You've always been Little Miss Perfect. Too damn naïve, but so fucking beautiful." He crowds me to the wall. In a panic, I pound on the shared wall of Santiago's apartment. I know Santiago isn't home, but Mark could be.

His tongue licks up my cheek. My hands tug on his shirt,

pushing him back while my head shakes to get him off of me. "Get away," I cry. "Move," I scream.

All he does is laugh, his lips so close that I knee him in the balls. When he jerks in pain, I run toward the door. With every beat of my heart, I pray Santiago gets here—someone—anyone. Ivan grabs my shirt and yanks me back then slaps me hard. I feel the hot sting on my cheek. My sobs choke on the back of my throat. No words come out.

"Fucking bitch," he roars. His hand goes up in the air. I cover my face, but the hit never comes. A loud thump hits the wall.

42

SANTIAGO

MY HEART FUCKING bulges like it's going to explode, surging with fear and fury. As I tear away the bastard who hit my girl. If it weren't for Jasmine, who visited me at work and revealed what my wife had been keeping from me, I would have remained unaware. I wouldn't have left work early to come home and ask my wife why she didn't tell me she had been in danger. Although I didn't expect him to be here right now, I knew he was in the area since I saw him a couple of nights ago.

Ivan flies to the other side of the room. I glance at my wife. Tears run down her cheek, and a red-purple mark is on her face. My heart breaks; a knife right to the chest. I'd do anything for her. I'd crawl through fire and shards of glass to get to my wife. She's my reason, *my* purpose, *my* person. I will eliminate anyone who lays a hand on her.

With each step, my heavy boots thud against the tile floor. My fists clench and unclench at my sides, and I can feel the heat radiating off my body as I approach him. He cowers and no longer looks like the attempted tough guy who had his hand on her just moments ago. His groan echoes in the empty living room as he collides with the coffee table while trying to scramble away from me. But I'm not finished with him yet. My anger simmers dangerously close to boiling over, and I haven't even laid a finger on him.

"You like hitting women?" With a strong grip, I tear his shirt with ease. Ivan cowers in fear as I tower over him, my muscular frame making him seem insignificant. I drive my fist into his jaw, then his stomach, then his nose. Blow after blow lands as I unleash my anger on him. "If you ever come close to my wife again, I'll fucking kill you and bury you myself. If you ever think about calling her, I'll find you and rip your tongue out."

Ivan groans in pain, blood spraying out of his nose. He wipes it with the back of his hand, he stutters. "F…fuck you." He holds his stomach, trying to get up. "She's nothing but a whore anyway, man. She's worthless—"

I grab him by the neck and round my fist in his face. "Disrespect my wife again, and I'll kill you on the spot. No one speaks to her that way." My knuckles turn white as I tighten around his neck, my anger roaring. When I walked in, she was on the floor and his hand was in the air. I felt like I was dying inside. I was so hurt and pissed at her when she first moved here, I didn't press about the mark on her face, and I didn't ask why she flinched.

Another punch, and Ivan gasps for air, but my hand presses harder.

"Santiago," Rosa calls out in a sob. Hearing the tremble in her voice only fuels the fire. My wife's voice fades. All I can hear is my fist hitting his jaw. I drop him, and he gasps for air, not giving him a second. I land another blow to his gut over and over until someone pulls me off him.

"You're going to kill him, Santiago. He's not worth living behind bars," a gruff voice echoes at my side.

I step back, and Victor stands next to me, hands on my shoulder, keeping me at bay.

"Attend to your wife, son. Go check on her. I'll get the dickhead out of here."

I nod, adrenaline buzzing throughout my body.

Victor lifts him off his feet, and I turn to my wife, shaking, on the floor. Slowly, I kneel, she throws her arms around me.

"I—I'm sorry. I'm sorry."

"Shh, baby." I gently kiss away the tears and the redness on her cheek, then comfortingly rub her back. "Are you hurt anywhere else? Did he do anything else to you?"

She shakes her head.

"I'm here, sweetheart."

She clings to me like I'm her life support. "I'm sorry, Santiago, I didn't want to burden you with the mess I got myself into. I thought I could handle it."

Caressing her hair, I drawl, "You did nothing wrong, Rosa. Remember—your pain is my pain. I'm always here for you. Jasmine told me everything."

"Fuck," Victor yells when a loud crash hits the floor.

Immediately, I stand with Rosa in hand.

Victor rubs his head. "Motherfucker, he threw a pan at me and ran."

I want to run after him, but instead, I call Liam. I don't want to leave her alone.

While we wait for Liam, Rosa sits on my lap on the sofa. Victor helps her with an ice pack. I am still not sure why he's here, but now is not the time. "Rosa, you should have told me… I'm the one who's sorry. I should have done so many things differently, baby. You and Jasmine had to deal with all this shit alone."

She sniffs. "I was so scared. That's why I moved back. I didn't think he would follow."

She came down twice from school, and he was with her.

Something about him threw me off, but I thought it was me being jealous. I recalled he was the one telling Liam they were together, and that they planned on moving in together.

"Are you mad?"

With a finger, I lift her chin. "Rosa, no, of course not. Like I said, you did nothing wrong. The guy is a fucking psycho. He didn't get the hint from the beginning. He's the one with issues, and you're moving in with me. I don't want you here alone at all, at least until he's caught." She's staying with me, anyway. It only makes it permanent.

Rosa's face sags. I can see the torment in her eyes. Nothing upsets me more than seeing the pain in her beautiful eyes, the fear she's been carrying. I failed to protect her.

"You should have talked to Liam about this, Rosa," I chide her, but then I realize I shouldn't make her feel guilty about it.

She grabs my hand and blots a napkin on my bleeding, scraped knuckles.

"When I moved back, I thought about telling him. But I hoped Ivan would leave me alone. With everything going on between us, I put it on the back burner. I was too scatter-brained." She sighs. "You guys have always looked out for me. I didn't want to be naïve Rosa anymore, and most of all, I didn't want to show weakness. I couldn't do things alone and live far away from my family. I've been so tired of being scared all my life. That's why I went to see Tina: to move on and grow."

Tucking a strand of hair behind her ear, I say, "You have always been strong, Rosa, even more so now, but this is different. There's nothing to be ashamed about. He's dangerous. He hid it well. Sometimes, we need some help, especially in these situations. He hurt you, baby, multiple times."

"I wanted to tell you so many times, but I stalled."

She buries herself in the crook of my neck and sobs.

"The cops are here," Victor shouts from the front door. He's been keeping guard.

"Rosa," Liam utters, running toward us. Rosa lifts her head. "Are you okay? Fuck…tell me what happened." His gray eyes storm, observing Rosa's swollen cheek. A police officer stands near him while the others start a search for Ivan.

Rosa starts from the beginning of how she met Ivan and continues until now. I hate that he practically forced himself to be part of her life when she was going through a lot. She didn't realize or ignored that he could be a danger to her. But in truth, who would know? You see people on social media talking about crazies they date on dating sites. You never know.

"You should have done a fucking background check on him, Detective. Aren't you the one who told me how great he was?" I sneer at Liam. I know it's unfair for me to say that, but I'm furious right now. Every part of me wants to go find him for what he did.

I haven't given a shit about telling Liam about Rosa and me. He's scrutinizing me for how my hands are wrapped around his cousin.

"And who are you to her?" the officer asks, jotting down all the information in his notebook.

My eyes don't drift from Liam. "Her husband. I'm her husband."

Liam's eyebrows shoot up like rockets, and his jaw clenches. "I need to speak to you outside, please." Liam's voice is gruff.

A strong breeze hits me as we step outside, lights flashing around the neighborhood.

"What the fuck do you mean you're her husband?" he whisper-shouts, hands shoved in his black slacks.

I shrug. "Like I said, I'm her husband."

"Yeah, I heard that…but when did this all happen?"

"Now is not the fucking time for you to go all police mode. Use that damn energy to find the asshole who hit her," I say dryly. "I married her after her twentieth birthday party. The summer after her first year of college. I had never been interested in Rosa in that way before then. I know the wheels in your head are turning, but it was never like that. I'm not some pervert. She kissed me that summer, and from then, things changed. We went a little crazy and got married. The rest we can talk about later. I need to check on Rosa. And we need to find that son of a bitch. I won't sleep until he's found."

He's still standing, mouth gaping open.

Liam grabs my shoulder. "We will talk about this later. You didn't cheat on her, did you?"

"No, of course not." Turning from him, I walk back inside. Victor talks to an officer, giving the make of Ivan's car.

I grab a water bottle from the fridge and hand it to Rosa. She's standing, leaning against the wall in a haze. "Come here, baby." My hand extends for her to take. She does. She lays her head on my chest. I jolt when I hear a door slam, and even the officers jump up.

Dominic comes in, eyes wild. "What the hell is going on?"

I dig my fingers into my hair, pulling at the roots in frustration as I try to understand everything. Rosa peels herself from me. I gesture for him to follow me as I head toward a quieter corner to explain everything in detail.

He groans, peering at Rosa. "Is she okay?" He draws in a long breath.

"She will be... How did you know something happened?" Surveying his posture, his hands are fists into a ball at his side.

"I didn't. Is it true he's back?"

I quirk a brow. My lips form an O. Victor. "Yes."

"Fuck," he semi-shouts. "That's why I'm here. Mark...came to the restaurant. He said he was leaving. I tried talking to him. He was rambling. Then he said he overheard Da...Victor talking to you." He throws his head back, pinching the bridge of his nose. "Tell me my wife and Mark are NOT related. Tell me he heard it wrong and that we share the same father." He grips the counter. "Mark's gone. He said he needed to get away. I don't know where. He ran off. And he's not answering." Dominic's eyes are downcast with worry.

An icy panic creeps up my spine to my chest. We keep getting hit one after another. Now my baby brother is M.I.A. I put a hand on Dominic's shoulder and say, "We'll find him. I'm sure he'll be okay. Maybe he needs to clear his head. It's a lot to take in."

Victor saunters toward us, stopping when he notices Dominic. It's almost as if he can read my mind. He nods. "Some other day," he mouths.

I give him a nod. Dominic looks over his shoulder, watching him walk away. I know he's curious.

"We can talk about Victor tomorrow. Right now, I need to be with Rosa."

"Yeah, go to her. She needs you. I'll go outside and talk to Liam." I give him a bro hug before he walks out the front door.

Twenty minutes later, Rosa sits curled up next to me. The police have taken photos of the scene, the glass all over the floor, along with the blood on the floor and Rosa's face. As the minutes pass, my head goes heavy with what Rosa has gone through these last two years. There's no use for us to dwell on them; I'll forever think of the child we lost and always wonder, but now, with this that happened, I want it to end, for Ivan to be found so Rosa and I can move on from this. The house I have built for us should be ready in less than two months. I have considered bringing her to see it, but I believe it would be better to wait until they finish. Once it is done, she can decorate it however she pleases. I think this would be good for her to get away from this apartment and move out of the city.

Liam pulls out a chair and sets it in front of us, legs spread, leaning back. He grumbles something under his breath. "We're clearing out now. I'm having a car on patrol for the next couple of weeks or until he gets caught. I did some digging on him." With hooded eyes, Liam adds, "I'm sorry, Rosaline, that this happened to you, and I'm sorry you felt you couldn't confide in us. Santiago is right. I should have been a big brother and done a background check on him because he's the bastard son of one of the gang members of the Serpents."

Rosa stiffens beside me.

"I'm not sure if he was using you to get to me due to us killing his father, Pablo, or if he's just obsessed with you. I don't know how close he is to Marko, his stepbrother, the new head of the Cartel. What we found out is he has a dealer, and Ivan's been using for a while now."

My tongue darts out of my mouth to lick my dry lips. "So, you're telling me he was under your roof those times he came down while you were looking for his father? Do you think this is the reason he kept on pressuring her to date him and determined to do so to get back at you?" I ask Liam.

A couple of months ago, Liam almost died when they were hunting Pablo, the leader of the gang, for killing his father on duty. Pablo snuck up on him at his mother's house. They had a stand-off that left Pablo dead.

"Fuck, the thought of having him around has me feeling like a fool. I don't know how involved he's been with them. Marko is in jail," Liam says flatly.

Rosa looks from me to Liam. "I never spoke to him about anything private, and he didn't either. He just mentioned his mother."

Liam nods and adds, "I don't want you alone at home or at work, Rosa. Have one of us drop you and pick you up. I'm going to head out and hunt the fucker down. Call me if you need me."

ONCE IT WAS CLEAR, I grabbed a bag and packed the rest of Rosa's clothes, and we returned to *our* place. Turning the faucet on, I walk toward Rosa. A warm shower will help relax her a bit.

Gingerly, I strip her dress off, then my clothes. Together, we move under the cascading water from the overhead shower. I squeeze a generous amount of shampoo into my palm before lathering her hair. My fingers work gently, massaging her scalp as she closes her eyes and relaxes. I then use her flower-scented body wash to cleanse her body.

"Santiago," Rosa mumbles.

"Hmm," I say, washing my hair.

"I'm sorry I ruined your birthday."

Opening my eyes, I peer at her. "No, flower, don't be sorry. There will be plenty of birthdays. It's not a big deal. I turned thirty, sweetheart, and I'm not all that happy about it," I joke, earning a smile from her.

Turning off the faucet, I wrap her in a towel. She strolls to our bedroom and says, "Well, we should at least have cake," Rosa offers.

I know she is trying to salvage my night. "Yeah, I'll get it from the fridge. If you're hungry, I'll order us something."

She turns to glance up at me, her gaze rolling with heat—up and down my body as she watches me dry myself. Now is not the time for me to get hard. I try to think of other things so it can go down. She doesn't give me a chance to let my mind wander before she drops the towel.

Every hair on my scalp stands to attention, every skin cell tingles, every neuron fires. She beckons with a finger, and I obey—she's like a siren calling me: two steps forward, three more steps. I'm in front of her. Rosa shivers when her hands run down my chest until she gets to my dick… she strokes it. My eyes roll back, I force them open.

"Rosaline," I groan when she drops to her knees. "Not now, baby, you don't need to do this."

"Please, I need to, I want to," Rosa pleads, her warm lips wrap around my cock.

A rush of blood hits each nerve and pulsing vein on my dick.

The tip of her tongue lathers up and down, then takes me all in until I lose control and come into her mouth.

"Damn, Rosa. That was—"

She jumps on me, and my dick slides into her as if it has a mind of its own. "I need you. Please distract me."

Our lips collide, igniting a fiery passion that spreads through our entire bodies. We stumble backward, tumbling onto the soft sheets of the bed. I feel her bare skin pressed against mine, her breasts rubbing against my chest as we lose ourselves in a passionate kiss. Her nipples harden under my touch, and I eagerly take them into my mouth. She moans with pleasure. At this moment, all I want is to make her forget any worries or doubts by making love to her with every inch of my being.

I pound hard into her harder, faster, making her see that I'm never leaving her, but most of all, I want her to hear it in my voice. "I'll never let anyone hurt you. I'll protect you with my life, Rosaline, but one thing, don't ever fucking hide anything from me again," I say between thrusts. "You got it, sweetheart?"

"Yes," she murmurs, and her voice is scratchy and sweet with desire.

"Good girl, now come for me." I grunt my release while kissing her bruised cheek.

43

SANTIAGO

STARTING A FRESH POT OF COFFEE, I prepare breakfast for Rosa. She is still sound asleep. I couldn't sleep. I know Liam has someone on patrol out in front of our apartment, and she is safe with me. Those images keep flashing in my mind. When I parked at the house, my stomach churned with knots. Getting close to the door, I heard a man's shouts. He was standing over her, shouting at her. Rosa was on the floor, shaking—with her hands covering her beautiful face. I can't stop seeing it play on repeat in my brain.

The doorbell interrupts my concentration as I combine pancake mix, milk, eggs, and oil into a mixing bowl. Anger whips through me like a violent storm. I swing the door open, ready to beat anyone who threatens my girl. Instead, it's Liam, eyes bright red. His face mirrors mine, fucking tired. I step back and welcome him in then shut the door behind me.

"How's she doing?" Liam asks.

I walk back to the kitchen. He follows. Turning on the griddle, I reply, "She's okay," I give him a half-assed shrug. "Rosa's trying to be strong. She's blaming herself, but she'll be fine in time."

He nods, rubbing his stubble pensively. "I have to ask, why in the hell was she seeing him, if you guys are married? And you with women?"

I growl, "I wasn't with any other woman. The only reason I made it seem that way was because I didn't want you dumb fucks to question me about not screwing anyone, so I flirted, and Rosa thought I had a baby with Monica, and *you* told her I was sleeping with other women. Never did I touch or mess with anyone. Anyway, why in the fuck would you tell her shit like that?"

Liam's eyebrows pinch together. "For two people who have known each other their whole life, that is fucking stupid." Liam huffs.

Knowing Liam all my life, I can tell there's something he's not telling me. His eyes are downcast, avoiding meeting my eye. "You have that face, man. Tell me what's going on."

Liam leans back into the kitchen counter, ankles crossed.

"Did you go anywhere last night?" Liam asks.

"Yeah, went to get ice cream." After I made love to Rosa until my brother showed up. "Why?" I ask.

Liam peers at me right in the eye. "Alone?"

"Yes, Dominic came over to drop food for us and check-in. While he was here, I ran to the gas station to get us ice cream."

Liam slams a fist on the counter, shaking the granite. "Fuck!" he shouts. "Why in the hell would you go anywhere?"

Throwing my hands in the air, I shout, "Why not? You didn't say I couldn't."

"Because we found Ivan dead in his hotel room, beaten and strangled."

My eyes widen. Is it fucked up that I'm happy the asshole is dead and rotting in hell?

"They're pointing the finger at you, man."

"What!" I exclaim, my voice sounding raw and overworked from all the shouting.

"Why? Liam, why?" Rosa peeks into the kitchen with just my shirt.

Liam pulls on his hair. "When the police spoke to the neighbors here, a couple of them said they heard you shout, "I'm going to kill you."

My jaw clenches in frustration. "I may have said it in the heat of the moment, but that doesn't mean I would actually do something like that. You don't believe it, do you?" I glare at him with a pained expression.

Rosa moves to stand next to me, hands wrapped around my waist.

"No! Of course not, but the thing is, they're going by what happened yesterday, what the neighbors heard, and what the cop on patrol said when he saw you leave. I'm trying everything, bro. The thing is the surveillance camera shows you at the motel he was at. What happened? You need to tell me everything. I need to find who did it to prove them wrong, so you can be clear. I'm sorry, Santiago, but they won't listen to me since you're on the camera and you shouted a threat to kill him when you fought him here. It's enough for them to arrest and charge you and then build a case against you."

Fuck. I shouldn't have followed him when I parked at the gas station and saw him getting out of his car next to the motel he's staying at.

"When I was at the gas station, I saw him in the motel parking lot right next door. I didn't know he was staying there. I'll admit I was heated because of what he did to my wife. So I chased after him. I cussed him out, and we fought. He fell back and hit his head on the cement. I backed off. He got up and I told him to stay the fuck away from Rosa. Then I went back to the gas station to get ice cream. He was alive when I left, so it couldn't have been me."

Liam roars. "Why in the hell didn't you call me? I would have gone to arrest him."

"I was too heated and wanted to get home to my wife. I planned to call you this morning."

"Fuck," he shouts.

Rosa gets in Liam's face. "They can't arrest him, Liam."

He swallows and looks up at me sympathetically. My stomach dips with uneasiness. Something terrible is going to happen.

"The surveillance cameras from the motel are not clear. They're old and only show the area you were in. It doesn't show anyone else going to his place or you walking back to his room. The last person to see him was you. The gas station's camera does pick you up getting ice cream. The homicide investigators unit are on the case. We've been at the scene all night. The captain is giving me until tomorrow to find any other evidence to prove it's not you. We've been at the scene all night. Right now, you're the only suspect," Liam murmurs with pain in his voice.

"Fuck, Liam. This is ridiculous!" I roar. "I'll be honest. I'm glad the asshole is dead. But I didn't do it."

"This is all my fault, Liam. Tell them he would never do anything like this."

"I have, Rosa, but we need to cooperate right now, and I'll keep searching. I know it wasn't you. Someone else must have wanted him dead. I won't stop until Santiago is clear." Liam leans to kiss Rosa's cheek. "I'm returning to the station to see what's happening. I'll keep you updated." Liam walks out, shutting the door behind him.

Rosa holds on to me, my shirt moist with her tears.

Lifting her chin, I look into her beautiful eyes. "This is not your fault. How about I finish breakfast, then let's go cuddle in bed and watch your favorite shows?"

I kiss her tears and she whispers, "Sounds good."

Nothing sounds good because this could be our last time together if they charge me for murder.

As Rosa lays in bed, I followed Liam's recommendation and called our attorneys. Then I contacted Dominic, Reese, and Victor, asking them to come over later tonight. Despite my rising panic, I try to maintain a calm facade. Who has the energy to deal with this kind of nonsense and potentially end up in jail for something they didn't do?

Rosa canceled her classes until she was up for it. I tried calling Mark, but there was still no answer. Who knew where he went? I get him. Who the hell wants to be here with all kinds of shit happening? I want to do the same, take off with my wife, and relax on some private island.

Rosa furrows her brow and wrings her hands together, her voice trembling with concern. "What did the attorney say?" she asks, her eyes searching mine for any hint of news.

I move next to her and lift my shirt off from her. Fuck, she's beautiful, completely bare, a sight I want engraved in my mind and heart forever. "Let's not talk about that, Rosa. Let's talk about how you always turn me on, how sexy you are, how I love all of your curves, and how I love you." My tongue drags around her pointed nipples. "I love your tits," I tease.

"Santiago, now is not the time for this. We need to get to an attorney's office and figure something out. I won't let them take you."

Now *is* the time, I want to say, because I don't know how

things will go. How many cases are there when people get charged with something they didn't commit? I need to have that mindset as well—prepare myself.

"I need you right now, sweetheart." Her breasts are so full and perfect. Making my way down to her bare pussy, I take my time with her, wanting her to feel just how good we are together. She moans, then grabs a fist full of my hair. My dick is about to explode, hearing her call out my name. "Don't come yet, flower. Not until I tell you."

"Why?" she whines.

I laugh.

"Because I want you to come all over my dick. I want us to make a mess of ourselves." Sliding off the bed as she observes, I add, "Now, strip me, baby."

Without hesitation, she does. She pulls my sweats off and strokes my cock. Never would I have thought that getting a piercing would add so many extra bonuses to our sex life. My wife's thumb goes over the piercing, causing me to shiver.

"Ride me, Rosa."

Her body moves with fluid grace as she straddles me, matching the rhythm of the ocean's waves crashing against the shore. With each thrust, her hips roll, and her muscles clench. She rides my cock with fierce ownership. I can't help but buck my hips to meet hers. I'm lost in the sensation of her control over me. She feels so fucking good. My wife moans with pleasure as my finger slides smoothly into her wet heat. With each stroke, she arches her back and cries out in ecstasy. Our bodies move together in perfect rhythm.

"I need to—" She chokes on her words.

I flip us over and thrust into her fast and hard. "Not yet, baby."

I dive deeper than I've ever gone. I fuck her like it's the last time. Raw and untamed. A sheen of sweat rolls down our bodies. "You'll always be mine, and I'll always be yours, baby." I grunt and thrust. "I'll always reach for you." One last thrust. "Come with me." Our bodies shake wantonly, exploding into one another. This woman will always be my kerosene. I'll always light the match and will always set the world on fire.

WHILE DOMINIC and Mila speak with Victor, I pull Reese aside. I have already told him everything that happened.

"Hey, man, don't worry. I'll take care of everything at the shop, but I don't think they'll keep you after they question you," Reese offers.

"Liam texted me earlier that the police have enough information. The police department knows Liam well, they think he's defending me. Even Liam's close friends from work are vouching for me. The neighbor's ring cameras picked up on me, yelling, 'I'll kill you.'"

"So they think you went back to finish him?" Reese adds.

"Yeah, because we fought in the parking lot. Although I didn't follow him inside. The rest of the cameras that are angled on the opposite side of his room weren't working or not clear or something didn't pick up who went to his room so the only person of interest to them is me. They have no proof I did it, but the fucking homicide team or captain says it's enough to arrest me."

"This is all fucked up. We'll figure this out. What did the attorney say?"

I sit on the arm of the sofa in motion, my hands in the air. "Nothing yet, if I'm not charged. So when they come to arrest me, I call him."

Reese groans, sliding onto the sofa. Dominic, Mila, and Victor walk in from the kitchen. Victor had said he was going to have the same conversation with Dominic that he did with me.

So far, he's been around. He hasn't given me the vibe that he's full of shit.

"Santiago, I was thinking if they want to pin it on you, then I'll tell them I did it."

My head jerks, surprised and leery. Everyone in the room has that same expression.

"Why would you do that? If you didn't do it...unless you did do it," I drawl.

Victor grooms his peppered beard. "This is my way of showing you how deeply sorry I am for leaving you boys with Rachel. I love you three. I would do anything for you guys. You shouldn't be charged for something you didn't do. I won't let you do the time. You're young and have so much life ahead of you."

"I appreciate it, but there's no need to complicate things more. They wouldn't believe it, and there's someone who did it who needs to pay for it. It will just take time. I have faith in Liam. He hasn't slept a wink." I inhale the scent of wildflowers when Rosa emerges down the stairs in a flowing white dress. She comes to stand next to me. I glance at Victor and add, "Do you plan on sticking around? Because if you're here to cause trouble, you best leave. My brothers don't need it. As it is, Mark is gone, and I can't go looking for him until I'm out of this mess."

Dominic looks between us both, then nods at me. He agrees.

Victor strolls from the kitchen entry, where he is standing, to sit on the sofa near me. "I moved into a house I rented two days ago. That's why I stopped to let you know when I walked in on the fight." Victor pulls out his wallet from the back pocket of his jeans. Even after so many years, I can still smell his familiar scent from when I was a boy. He fiddles with his old leather wallet, tugging a photo out and handing it to me.

"I've carried this photo of us all this time. If you'd allow me, I want to be part of your lives. I would love to meet my grand-kids," Victor pleads, his voice trembling.

Dominic peers at me as I pass him the photo of Dominic at the age of three, Victor, and me at the age of eight, and I'm holding Mark when he was a newborn.

The bitterness and anger I've carried for Victor ebbs. Knowing he kept the photo has to mean something.

The only thing we can do is give him a chance.

44

ROSALINE

GUILT SETTLES in the pit of my stomach then spreads throughout my body. Had I known the outcome of all this, I would have done things differently. The consequences are mine to dwell in. The what-ifs play on repeat in my mind. What if I had told Liam when it first happened? What if I had gotten a restraining order? All the what-ifs pound in my head as I watch my husband on his knees, with flashing lights and police hand-cuffing him. They had said tomorrow, but they had tricked Liam, knowing he would tell us. Within seconds, Liam jumps out of his car and runs to us, yelling at the officer to uncuff him. Tears run down my cheeks.

"He did nothing wrong!" I yell.

Santiago keeps his head down. He won't look at me.

"Please," I beg. Mila holds on to me. If it weren't for her, I'd crumble on the ground.

Finally, Liam gets them to uncuff him. "It's fine. He didn't do shit. He's going to follow protocol. Santiago's not running. He's my best friend. He's like a big brother to me," Liam commands, his tone thundering with authority.

I run to Santiago, wrapping my arms around him.

"I'll find a way to get you out." I choke on my words. "Won't we, Liam?" I stare up at Liam for confidence.

"We will. I won't sleep, brother, until I find who did this."

Santiago whispers, "I know you will." Then he turns to me. "Don't cry, baby. I'll be okay. Promise me you'll take care of yourself?"

"Yes, I...I promise."

Liam guides Santiago into the backseat of the police cruiser. When they close the door and drive away with the person I love most, I collapse.

The thick teardrops cascading down my face like rainfall blur my vision. I'm not sure who carried me into the house. Probably Dominic. I rest my head on Mila's lap while she brushes my hair with her fingers. "He'll get out. Just wait and see," Mila says, voice low.

Dominic stands by a window, looking into nothing. His hand fists up, then relaxes again in a pattern. "Dominic, honey, come sit here," Mila calls to her husband.

He sighs and sits next to his wife. "I feel useless. How do I help him? He's my big brother, but he is more than that. He's always put us first. He's been a father to us, someone I admire."

"It feels that way, but what we can do is find him a damn excellent attorney. If the one he has sucks, then we find another. We keep fighting. I'm positive one of the gang members killed Ivan," Mila replies to Dominic.

Lifting my head, I sit back on the sofa to peer at them both. Mila and Dominic's heads prop on one another. I want to apologize repeatedly to Dominic, but I know what he'll say. It's not my fault, just like they've all been saying.

The front door swings open, and Sophie walks in with tears in her eyes. Her long blonde hair bounces as she speeds toward me. "Liam called me. He's been working nonstop. He'll get him out," Sophie assures, just like Mila had.

I nod.

Sophie wraps me in her warm, comforting embrace. "Liam asked me to pick you up, Rosa. He said to take you back to our place or your aunt's. Santiago doesn't want you to stay here alone."

My heart warms. Even behind bars, he's still looking out for me, but who will look out for him? We're supposed to look out for one another, and I failed him.

"I don't want to intrude. I'll stay at my aunt's."

Entering our bedroom, I inhale his woodsy aftershave and masculine cologne. I stuff a couple of outfits into a duffle bag along with Santiago's shirts to sleep in. Every fiber of my being prays he'll be out tomorrow. Zipping up my bag, I head downstairs.

Two weeks have passed, and Santiago is still in jail. They charged him for first-degree murder. Liam has been keeping us all updated. The bail is so high we would have to be millionaires to get him out. The investigators say that Santiago was the last person to see him before they found him dead, and Santiago had already physically attacked him, making him the primary suspect, even though he was trying to protect me from an abusive individual.

Several of Liam's co-workers believe it's Santiago. But he's not backing down. He knows Santiago, and he's fighting for them to keep searching for the right person. The chief of police took Liam off the case, but he's not paying them attention. Liam's been interrogating men who are part of the gang in jail and out.

They have been silent about it. Santiago has only called me

once, and it was a brief call. He changes the subject any time I ask how he's doing and asks me about my day. He sounded upset when I told him I hadn't gone back to work.

He said, "Baby, don't stop doing what you love. Never stop living. Will you do that for me? Will you continue going to work and making beautiful art for your next exhibit?"

I nodded, then said yes, not letting him hear the weakness in my voice.

The days have gone by in slow motion. When I get to work, the first thing I notice is Santiago's face in the newspaper. I gasp —how could they? *Like mother like son: Santiago Delgado accused of murder. It must run in the family*, it reads. My blood runs cold. He's nothing like his mother. How dare they insult my husband by comparing him to that monster? What the article fails to mention is the man who was murdered was a stalker and abusive psycho.

Ugh, I rear back, unprepared to go into my class when I'm all fired up. Instead, I head to a favorite coffee shop nearby. Walking in, I'm always amused. It's Alice in Wonderland themed with a long table. The Mad Hatter figure stands in a corner, and the Cheshire Cat peers at the doorway when you walk in.

The girl at the counter chews a wad of gum. "Can I take your order?" she says with a rough chew. Her jaw is definitely over-working.

"Yes, can I have an iced americano with a splash of cream and two sugars?"

"No, you may not."

I raise an unkept eyebrow. Mind you, I haven't had a chance to pluck. The girl with the wad of gum giggles. I'm not in the mood for her shit. I fix the shirt *Abuelita* gave me that reads: *Soy chingona*. I need a reminder of who I am.

"Joking, you said, 'Can I have?' and I said no. You get it?"

"Yup," I answer, not amused by her joke.

"I'll get that ready for you," the girl says, wandering to the back room. I run my fingers through my long, black hair.

"Hey, Rosaline. Is that you?" an annoying voice calls from behind.

Lack of confidence might have had me shrinking in years past. But not anymore. Marissa tried to ruin our lives, and I allowed it by listening to her bullshit. She made it believable because of the fallout Santiago and I had. I spin, my Converse making a squeak when I face her.

"Hey, Marissa." I muster a smile she doesn't deserve. She's holding the newspaper in her hand and waving at me.

"Just read this… I'm surprised to see Santiago accused of murder. The more I read, the worse I feel." She makes a faux expression, brows furrowed like she's about to bawl. "And this all started with you. He's always been defending you. You took him from me. I guarantee he wouldn't be in this"—she motions with her hands in the air—" if he were with me." She licks her glossed lips.

I straighten my stance. "My husband never wanted you. I'm the only one he's wanted to be with—the only one he ever committed to. The shit you pulled about Monica having a child with him was an immature move." Maybe it's not her fault I lost our baby, but I feel it is deep down.

She doesn't flinch at my words. She shows no emotion whatsoever. Zip. Zero. Nada.

Cold bitch.

What she does is smirk. Some people are just born natural cold bitches, and she's one of them. I'm already fuming. My blood is boiling. It was when I walked in here, but now it's boiling over the pot. With pulsing rage, I grab her blue silk blouse and pin her against the wall. I tower over her with a few extra inches in height and a bit more weight on my frame, giving me the advantage of a physical altercation. However, I refrain from using any force against her. The last thing we need is for me to get arrested while trying to help Santiago.

Letting go of her blouse, I step back. She's up against the wall, and luckily, the shop is empty. "Fuck off, Marissa. You're not worth my time. Stay away from my family."

"Your americano is ready," the girl says, amused.

Reaching for my coffee, I say, "Thank you." I smile and walk out the door without sparing Marissa a glance.

Walking to my car I hear someone shout my name. I turn back to the coffee shop, but no one stands in front of the door. I hear it again, and I turn to the children's clothing store next to the coffee shop where I heard my name. It's Monica. She jogs to me with her son and husband.

"Rosa, hey, how are you doing? I heard. Reese told me. I'm so sorry."

I glance toward her son who's holding his mom's hand. Well he certainly doesn't look like Santiago, and I realize he does look like his father next to him.

"I'm hanging in there," I answer, my voice low.

"Look, I know we didn't start off on the right foot. If I had known things would have turned this way for you and Santiago, I wouldn't have hung around. I apologize. That night, at your twentieth birthday party, Santiago told me how much he wanted you, and I'm glad he reacted to it. You see, my husband" — she looks up at the man with olive skin and smiles—" he's my child-hood friend turned lover. We dated in high school, but things went south." She grinds her teeth, and he gives her a sympathetic rub on the back. "We split up for so many years, but that night at your party, I drove back to my hometown. I went looking for him. He's who I've loved all these years. We talked and both missed each other. Weeks later, I found out I was pregnant. Look, Reese told me what Marissa did. I'm so sorry that bitch did that to you. Santiago loves you, Rosa. You two are perfect. I hope we can become friends at some point in our lives. If you need me for anything, I'm here for you both. If you need me to testify, letting them know Santiago is not a violent man, I will."

Every ounce of bitterness I've had for this woman brushes off me. "Thank you, Monica. That means a lot to me. I'm happy you found your happiness."

She nods. "Me too. And you'll have yours. Just wait and see. He'll get out. Don't lose that faith. Oh, and this is my husband. Sorry, I should have introduced you first. David and our son Anthony."

"Hi, I'm Rosa." I shake David's hand.

"Nice to meet you, Rosa. I've met your husband. He's a good guy."

"He is," I agree. The small boy waves at me, and I nudge his cheek. He's cute.

Monica gives me a hug, and they walk to their vehicle.

ANOTHER TWO WEEKS HAVE PASSED, and Santiago is still not free. The detectives who interrogated him believe he's hiding something. But it doesn't matter what they say. It's all in the evidence, and they are going by the bruise Ivan had on his face and stomach and of course, by the camera showing them fighting at the motel.

Even though he was alive when Santiago left, they don't believe it. The attorney called me, and I left my statement of everything that happened with Ivan. The attorney has been doing his part going through cameras and trying to look for witnesses who could have seen something at the motel. He's also been talking to a friend of Santiago's who owns a security company.

Santiago has called me. But when I ask to see him, he says to wait. I miss him. I've spent my time moping around my aunt's house.

"Rosita, are you up here?" Liam yells from downstairs.

"Yes," I answer. The heavy, clomping sound of his steel-toed boots echoes through the wooden stairs as he gets to my old bedroom.

"How are you doing?" he asks.

I shrug. Liam pulls out a red cushion chair from under the desk. I'm sitting crisscrossed on the bed. He looks just as bad as I do. Red eyes, bags under his eyes, sleep deprived.

"We haven't had the chance to talk about you and Santiago together. I wish you would have told us when you ran off to get married." He smiles, but it doesn't reach his eyes. "Then again, I would have overreacted. Falling in love with Sophie has taught me that love will come to you when it's the right time and the right person. In all, I'm glad it's Santiago. He's a good guy. Things happened when they needed to."

He's right. They do.

"It did, and I'm glad it was him. He's always been the one to rescue me from anything." Now it's time I do the same. "Tell me, Liam, when are they going to let him out? Be honest with me. He's my husband." His beautiful eyes gaze downward. "How can I help?"

He looks up at me, his eyes watering, and Liam is not the emotional type. Usually, he holds it in. He shakes his head and flexes with a hard swallow. "What will help Santiago is to see you holding up and not falling apart. Listen, Rosa. I'm trying so damn hard to find out more information. I've been on the streets searching for drug dealers to tell me something. I know it's drug, cartel, or gang related. Someone wanted that asshole dead. I'm glad he is, but not like this, not with my own co-workers ignoring my pleas. It makes me wonder how many people are falsely accused every day because that's the easy case.

I won't stop fighting for him. He's my big brother by heart. I promise I won't let you all down."

We both sniff, and Liam wipes my tears. "This is not looking good. We don't know until court, but it will all depend on what the charges are and what the jury decides. It could be ten, fifteen years or more. Or it might be less if they go for a lesser charge. It all just depends, and we don't know yet. That's why I need to find out who went after Ivan. My guess is someone was watching and must have followed him after Santiago left, or Ivan let them in because the door wasn't busted open," he whispers.

My heart leaps out of my chest, shattering into a million pieces. "No! Liam, please don't let them do this." I stand and lean into the rustic desk, trying to breathe.

"There's no way in hell I'll stop searching for evidence. I'm sorry, Rosa."

Anger, regret, and fear whip at me. I toss the ceramic pen holder on the desk to the ground. It shatters, just like my heart. Liam turns me around and lets me cry on his chest. If he wasn't holding on to me, I'd collapse, and my trembling legs would give out.

"Santiago wants to see you."

Stepping back, I peer up at him. "He does?"

"Yeah, I'm going to put you two in a private room to talk."

I nod because I'm too broken to speak, but one word slips out. "When?"

"Tomorrow at noon," he murmurs, his tone aching with pain.

45

SANTIAGO

"DELGADO!" the dick-head security barks.

I jump off my steel bunk. The stench of urine and shit lingers in the air, and it only makes my empty stomach queasy. Four weeks of being in this hellhole feels like months. In those weeks, I've dreamed of my girl. Those dreams are all I'll ever get.

For now.

The dreams are my anchor, keeping me from losing my sense of self. Her smile, laughter, and voice, even the taste of her, all inspire me to keep going. When other inmates try to provoke me into fights, I defend myself but always keep it from escalating. I stick with the guys who stay out of trouble because I know I need to get out for her.

The metal sliding door is cold and grimy, the paint chipped and rusted in places. The guard stands on the other side, his uniform crisp and his expression unyielding. He reaches for the handcuffs, the metal glinting in the harsh overhead lights from the small window. When he slaps them on my wrists, the cold metal presses, embedding into my skin.

"Detective Rodriguez is waiting for you," the guard spits out.

I didn't expect the guard to be chirpy, but fuck, you would think they had some decency in them. They treat you like rabid dogs.

He yanks me by the jumper. "Let's go!" he yells.

We travel down a couple of stairs. The surrounding noise— shouts, banging, and fights breaking out—fades as we step into an area where they take you in for questioning.

I sigh in relief when I see Liam standing in the room. The guard pushes me in.

"Watch it, Conner. He's like a brother to me. Treat him well. Or you'll hear from me." Liam's voice booms with authority as he commands him.

The door shuts, and Liam reaches over to uncuff me. I shake my hands to get the blood flowing again.

"How's she doing?"

He pulls out a chair for us and gestures for me to sit.

"She's managing as well as she can. I followed your instructions, just like you asked. I have faith and agree that you're making the right decision. Hopefully, she'll come to understand that as well." His words are filled with genuine concern and sincerity.

"Please keep an eye on her for me... Did you pack the moving trucks for her stuff in her apartment?"

"Yes, yesterday the movers packed everything. It's in storage. They're finishing up today." He looks down at his hands. "I'm so sorry, I'm trying...I promise not to stop. It's close, bro. I know it. My partner and I have been hunting them down, looking for clues. Whoever killed Ivan was clean, leaving no trace. I've been going over the camera footage and the street. That's how I know it's someone that has killed before. Expert—"

"Hey, you have been working your ass off. There's no one

else I'd trust. You're damn good at your job. You'll get me out. It might take some time, but I know you'll make it happen," I assure him with a tight squeeze on his shoulder. "Can you call Max? He's the owner of a security enterprise, and he can help."

"I will, I promise you. Rosaline is waiting in one of the rooms. I'll take you to her. There's no camera. I'll wait outside the door when you're done."

Rubbing my full-grown beard, I nod.

MY STOMACH COILS with anticipation at seeing her, of holding her in my arms, even if it's for a short time. I'll take anything.

Opening the door, my heart speeds like a racehorse. My wife's head turns the second she hears the squeak from the door. She's so beautiful, the type of beauty you dream of, the kind you worship. My gaze traces her body. She stands and takes two steps forward, then sprints into my arms. I hate she has to see me like this.

"Oh, sweetheart. I missed you." I kiss her like it's the last time, my lips lingering on hers before trailing down the curve of her neck. Inhaling deeply, I savor the sweet scent that is unique to her and embed it into my memory. Wet tears fall onto my cheek, trailing down from Rosa's leaking eyes. "Don't cry. It will all work out in the end."

"Santiago," she cries, the warm palms of her hands caress my face.

"You look stunning. Navy blue is a great color on you," I compliment her, trying to light up the mood. Seeing her cry breaks my heart more than it already is.

"How are you doing? God, I know it's a stupid question." She meddles with the bright orange jumper. "I miss you so much. I love you."

"I love you too, baby. Come on, let's sit." I pull a chair out, sit her on my lap, and toss the manila folder far from her reach. "As for how I'm doing, I'm living day by day. They let me keep a picture of us. It's the one Mila took on our date. It's the first thing I look at every morning and the last thing I look at before bed... Well, the food is great. I had a T-Bone steak the other night, medium rare," I tease, and my lips curve into a smile.

Ahh, there's the laugh I wanted to hear. "At least you still have your sense of humor. Don't lose it," Rosa whispers, her finger brushing behind my ear.

"I won't. Tell me, have you been working on those paintings for your next exhibit?"

"Kind of briefly," she admits. "You're my inspiration, Santiago. Without you, I feel dead inside."

Every fiber of my being wants to curse at the world for gifting us this cruel fate. We had plans, a future.

"You'll find your inspiration again, sweetheart. One day, it will come to you."

She shakes her head—my stubborn flower. It will take time, but she'll find something that inspires her to create a masterpiece. She's a lot stronger than she gives herself credit for.

The palms of my hands glide up her bare legs. I press a kiss on her lip. "Did Liam tell you anything?"

"Yes, he said they're going to charge you. I hate this. I can't believe they stopped searching for the rightful person, but we know Liam won't," Rosa replies, her voice soft.

My stomach coils into a knot. My heart beats angrily against my ribcage. I swallow the lump in my throat. "Not until some kind of evidence comes up. Then I'll be set free."

The day they interrogated me, they pressured me to confess. Liam came barging in when he saw them through the glass window getting in my face. That resulted in Liam shouting at the detectives. Nothing good came out because they asked him to leave.

"The attorney is fighting, searching for evidence himself.

Until then, I'll be here for weeks, months, or years. I don't know how things are going to turn out. Even if you testify about what Ivan did to you, it won't help the case. They would still accuse me of murder."

Her chin trembles, and my fingers twitch, stroking the fabric of her cotton dress between my thumbs. "I could be here for ten, fifteen, or more years if they charge me. Despite my constant prayers, I need to prepare for the worst-case scenario." Wiping her tears, I peck a kiss on the tip of her nose, then I continue, "The shop is under your name. The money will go to you. It's wired to your account. Reese will manage it, and Victor works there. The house is ready to move when you wish, or you can sell it. The title is under your name—"

"Santiago, no, don't think like that."

"Shh, I know, but I have to prepare myself. You know I love you, Rosaline, more than I could love anything. You couldn't have loved me better, and I'm grateful for all the years I've known you."

"I'm s-sorry, Santiago, this is all my fault. You can deny it, but it is—"

"No, and I'll repeat it a thousand times. It's not. If a man had tried to hurt you while we were grocery shopping, I would have beaten his ass, and it could have ended like this. This is the mother fucker's fault. He's the one who took advantage of you. I want you to stop blaming yourself. It's not your fault."

"I'll try," she compromises, rubbing her palms on my beard.

Have you ever done something you knew you'd regret, but it was for the best? I played this in my mind so many times. Overall, I knew I was making an unselfish decision.

I steel my nerves for the next part. This is what has to happen. "Remember when we spoke about going to London so you can study for your master's and have your art displayed in the best galleries?"

She nods. "I want you to go, Rosaline. Move out there, start a life, or anywhere you choose, just away from here. Could you please do that for me? You don't need to be here to see how it all plays out. I don't want you to lose yourself here. Starting fresh will help you."

She's about to open her mouth, but I shush her with a finger on her lips.

"I'm begging you, flower. I need you to move on and live the life you're meant to have. Liam spoke with the attorney, and it's fine. If they need you, they will get a hold of you."

"You're my life."

Fuck. She makes it hard. My fingertips dig into her waist. She's my everything, the oxygen I need to live.

"And you're mine. Therefore, I'm setting you free. I won't allow you to wither away, coming here week after week, year after year." A fat tear runs down my cheek.

She keeps shaking her head at me.

"I'm so fucking sorry things ended up this way. If I could go back, I'd change so much, but one thing I wouldn't change is falling in love with you."

I reach for the manila folder, sliding it in front of her. "Here are the documents to the house and copies of the divorce papers. I signed them. My attorney has the original, and it has been submitted." The pain in my voice is evident.

"No!" She thrashes in my arms, pounding on my chest. "You promised me."

Grasping her tight in my arms, I try to calm her and settle her so I can finish.

"You said you wouldn't make decisions without me."

I did say that, but I also said I would always do things in her best interest. A thunderstorm erupts in my chest. The pain in her eyes is ripping me to shreds.

"Listen to me, Rosaline. I had to make that decision for us, for you, baby. Because I love you enough to let you go. I know I'm repeating myself, but I won't allow you to live this type of life. Waiting on me for years. Staring at one another through a glass. You're young and goddamn beautiful. I won't rob you of your life. Go live, my flower, fall in love. Just make sure he treats you well. Grow a family."

"Stop that, please. I could never fall for anyone. It's always been you."

She will always be mine, but with time, her heart will be ready.

"I'm sorry, baby. I made you a promise, but how can I let you live waiting for me? How can I let you age day by day alone? This will be our last visit, Rosaline. I've taken your name off the list. I hope you understand I'm trying to do the right thing."

Then why does it feel like I'm drowning, and the angry waves keep knocking me down?

She sniffs, holding on to my neck for dear life. "I know you're trying to do the right thing. It's just not what I need. I want to see you, hear your voice."

"It's what we both need. You know it's going to pain me if I hear that you retreated back into your shell. Don't let that happen."

Silence fills the air for seconds, enveloping us, holding on to what we have left.

"What happens when you're out in months or years? Will you come find me?" Her voice is pleading.

I kiss the top of her head. "If I hear you're married with a family, no, Rosaline. I won't disrupt your life. If you're single, then yes, if you want me to." Thinking of her with someone else makes me want to flip this table over.

"I'll always want you to find me." Her soft, stained maroon lips run down my neck. "I hate we're not married anymore. I hate you kept the divorce papers I sent you. You should have burned them because I would have never signed if you handed me one." She mouths into my neck, then sucks gently.

"You don't hate me?" I ask. I figured she'd cuss me out, this is why she makes it hard instead she's nibbling on my neck.

"I could never."

Rosa is right. I should have burned them because now she's showing me how much she wants me. She's making it hard for me.

My fingers run up her thighs, pulling her thong to the side. I brush her pussy. "One last ride, sweetheart?"

She lifts her head to peer at me. Tears roll down, and I kiss each pain filled tear.

"Yes, please." Her voice is sweet as honey. She moans with just the tip of my finger. Then I add three that always makes her crazy. When I claim her mouth, we kiss, feverish and wild. She's always been intoxicating, like the finest wine. Thrusting deeper, she moans my name. I want to remember the way she calls my name. Her pussy clenches around my fingers. I want to say the hell with it and toss her on the table to lap and suck, then pound into her. But I meant what I said a while back to her. She is worth more than to be fucked in an interrogation room at the detention center.

"That's it, baby. I can feel you're ready to come. I've memorized your expression, how your cheeks turn red, your mouth gapes, and you clamp onto me."

She sucks on my neck so damn hard it feels good. It's surely going to leave a mark. "Now be a good girl and come for me."

Holy wetness, she drips all over me. I lick my fingers clean to have one last taste.

"Santiago," she breathes. Adjusting her underwear and dress, I give her a small smile. "I love you."

Liam knocks and yells, "Five minutes left!"

I forgot Dominic, Damian, and Victor were coming after.

"Me too," I volley back.

"My heart aches. Why us? Our lives were just starting out."

I nod. We have little time left. There's not enough time to tell her everything I'd like to. Like, will you think of me all your life? Will you take care of yourself?

"Maybe in another life, we will get to be together?" she whispers.

I grab her hand, squeeze it, and give her the reassurance she needs—or maybe it's me who needs it.

This sucks dick.

"Yeah, sweetheart, I'll find you."

She slowly stands. I want to grab and hold on longer. Without her, I feel empty already. My chest caves in. The heat from her body is gone. She's gone. I'm letting her fly once again, but this time, it might be for good.

"Then I'll be waiting for you."

TEN MINUTES HAVE PASSED since Rosaline walked out. The second time I've lost her. This time, it was for an entirely different reason. A dull ache in my heart resides where grief claws at me. Being locked up in a jail cell the size of a bathroom stall gives you plenty of time for your mind to play the same story repeatedly in your head. As it is, I abhor her seeing me in this orange jumpsuit. How would it be fair for me to have her visit me with a plastic transparent wall between us? Guilt would fester, knowing she had dreams. Rosa would do just that—wait. I love her more than words can describe. I could never do that to her. It would be selfish of me. Deep down, I know I did it for the right reasons, but why does it hurt so much?

I don't know what I did wrong to deserve karma's wrath. Since I was thirteen and doing odd jobs, I have been a good person who has taken care of my brothers and worked tirelessly. I defended my girl from getting beat, and they want to accuse me of that asshole's death. If I wanted him dead, I would have done it, and I would have taken the sentence with pride, knowing I saved Rosa's life along with others. Unfortunately, he died gang related, according to what Liam thinks.

"Hey, bro, you've been staring at the brick wall. Are you okay?" Dominic asks, a worried frown etched on his face when I turn to peer at him.

I shake my head. "No, I just got her back and let her go. I divorced her."

"For a good reason, Santiago. You're a better man than most. You put her needs first. She understands," Liam says, his back against the wall of the tiny room. The police badge around his neck flashes against his white button-down shirt.

"I think you should've waited until the trial to sign the divorce papers," Dominic adds, his head hung low.

I know this is the last place he wants to be. He's not taking it well. He was about to sell one of his restaurants to get me out. There would be no reason for it. They still plan to charge me falsely.

I sigh, running a hand down my face. "We all know Rosa. She'd go back to her shell where she's most comfortable. It's for the best. We don't know when the trial will be, and when they charge me, we don't know how many years I'll be locked up," I tell them.

Then I turn to Damian. "Will you do me a favor?"

"Sure," he replies without hesitation.

"What I'm asking is crazy, or maybe not. I know things are off the wall for you with your divorce. Do you think you could follow Rosa wherever she goes?"

He raises a brow, his messy brown hair covering one eye.

"Not like that. I want to know she's safe. I'm only asking you to do this because you're a private investigator. You have skills and could work from anywhere." Also, because I know he's desperate to get away from his ex.

"You want me to report to you?" His legs spread on the metal chair.

"I don't want to know if she falls in love or dates." That would wound me. "Just how she's doing. Don't let her see you."

Liam looks over at me. He thinks I don't believe in him. We all do, but it's the when.

"What happens if I fall in love with her since you have me following her?" he says with a smug look.

I roll my eyes at him. "Then treat her right."

He laughs at my response. "I'm joking, man. She's yours. I don't see Rosa in that way. More like a sister." I know that's true, or I'd ring his damn neck. "In all seriousness, you have my word. I'll make sure she's fine."

"Thank you."

I look at Victor, who's been quiet this whole time. His gaze pinned on me. I'm not sure what he's thinking. I don't know him well enough to read him. "How's the shop going?" I jut my chin at Victor. He stands in the corner dressed more laid-back today in a t-shirt and jeans with Nikes.

"It's good. Reese knows his shit and how you like to manage things there. He's been on my ass." His hand goes to his beard. One thing I have noticed is he does that when he's nervous. "I'm proud of you, boys. You've turned into prominent men… Santiago, let me help you."

Both Liam and I narrow our eyes at him.

"I'm close. I just need to find Ivan's mom and interrogate a couple of guys, maybe roughing them up a bit. Find a rat who's willing to score a deal with me. You'll only confuse and mess up the investigation," Liam explains to Victor.

Minutes later, the guard came to take me back to my hell hole of a cell. A painful tightening in my throat squeezes, knowing I'm going back to my cage, leaving my family, and every piece of her I'll engrave in my heart. She might find love one day, but me?

There was only ever one.

46

ROSALINE

THREE MONTHS LATER.

"DARLING, how's your masterpiece coming along?" my new dear friend Harvey asks.

He leans into his chair, legs crossed in his crisp Hermès pants, sporting it with a black leather coat. Everything he wears is Hermès and always looks good.

"You look a little more chirpy this morning," he adds.

I lean forward, my face inches from the canvas, and bite my lip in concentration as I fill in the remaining blank spaces. "You're going to dirty your expensive clothes. Don't blame me when paint splatters on them." I spin to look at him. He sighs dramatically. "And to answer your question, I'm almost done with this one. Then I need to move on to the next painting for the show in a couple of weeks."

"Wonderful." He clasps his hands. His blue eyes sparkle, and his blond hair is perfectly combed. "How about I take you out for some grub?"

My stomach grumbles at the mention of food. "I thought you said you had work?"

Harvey crosses his arms.

"Well, I did, but I was miffed today. I needed an out. And you're always my cup of tea, darling." He uncrosses his legs and adjusts his clean clothes.

My clothes are covered in paint—a fairly regular state. The sound of vibrant music fills the space of the three-story building of the art school. London has been a breath of fresh air.

"Of course, I needed to check up on you," he says, looking sympathetic.

I dab the brush into a different hue. "As good as I'm going to get, Harvey. Painting keeps me going. And now that I have an additional reason to paint, it has become my inspiration, a reason to keep moving."

"That's the spirit, Rosa. Now I'm hungry, and I'm sure our little pea is hungry." He rubs my tiny baby bump. "Fuck, now I'm full of paint," he sneers.

"Well, you little twat, I'm full of paint, especially my stomach. What makes you think you would not get paint on you when you're rubbing on my body?"

His head falls back in laughter. Even in my gloomy days, his laugh makes me smile. Harvey is a gorgeous man. I didn't know that British men were so damn sexy.

"You act like I was rubbing your arse. I mean, you do have a nice one."

I chuckle at him and unzip the jumper I use for painting.

The cobblestone streets of London glisten with the light rain, creating a symphony of soft pitter-patter as we make our way to a cozy restaurant. My umbrella shields us from the gentle drizzle, but the cool droplets still make it on my cheeks.

I've gotten used to the rain. My hair seems to be a mess most of the time because of humidity.

Aside from that, it has been an incredible experience living here. Everyone has been so incredibly nice to me. I look at my arm hooked into Harvey's. He's been a godsend, always looking out for me. I don't know what I'd do without him if we hadn't met. I peer up at his tall frame.

Loneliness greeted me with open arms on the day I moved into my beautiful flat. As I spent more and more time by myself, my thoughts spiraled out of control, leading to constant tears and wailing. I still can't comprehend why our relationship is forbidden. Nothing seems to go right.

Harvey found me walking out of my flat with swollen red eyes. The next day, he brought me treats. Trust issues had me unsure of making him my friend after what happened with Ivan. Then, when I saw him and Marvin together, they invited me over for dinner. At the end of the night, I spilled everything to them. Since then, they have taken me under their wing and designated themselves as joint uncles to the baby.

He gives me a boyish smile and winks. "Are you okay?"

"Yes," I assure with a small, lopsided smile, holding onto him tight to keep myself steady from falling into the slippery puddles.

I can't believe it's been two months since I came here. It doesn't feel that way; more like years without seeing or hearing Santiago's voice. It's only in my dreams that we're together. He's lying next to me, running the tip of his finger down my bare chest. Every night, it's different, but we're together.

"Darling?" I unhook my arms from Harvey to peer at him.

"I'm sorry. Did you say something?"

He sighs, and his shoulders slump. He pulls out a chair. I had not realized we arrived until now.

"Where did you go? Hmm?"

Air expels from his cheeks.

I take a seat. "You know." I rub my belly out of habit now.

Harvey pulls a chair next to mine. "We've been through this so many times." I'm sure I sound like a broken record. "You feel you shouldn't be here in London. You still blame yourself."

The last thing Santiago said to me before I left was if I could do him a favor. I asked what. He said to go to London as I had planned from the beginning. To me, those plans had changed. It was us together or not at all. I didn't intend to keep my promise. How could I leave him behind?

Warm hands cover mine. "How about some warm tea to help those nerves?"

"That would be great."

He gives my shoulder a light squeeze. "I'm going to get the waiter to get us some tea, then go to the loo. Remember, if you were there, you'd be a mess waiting for a trial. Here, you are keeping yourself busy. He knew you well enough. That's why he felt it would be better. Santiago seems like a good man. He let you fly and encouraged you to start a family with another man not knowing how long he would be locked up."

It took me a week to leave California. I crumbled on the ground, my heart in tatters, undecided about what to do. Santiago wanted me to accomplish my dreams, but how could I when he was a part of them? The MA program is for a year. I figured the least I could do was live up to his promise. Then I'd move back and wait for him. Santiago Delgado is wrong. I could never fall in love with anyone else. I'll wait for him all my life if I have to. Those divorce papers sliced me in half, but I knew what he was doing. That man always thinks with his heart. I'm not angry with him. It took a lot for him to do what he did. It would kill him to hear if I were to move on, but he did it so I wouldn't wither away waiting for him alone. Many might think it was a selfish or controlling act. It wasn't. He made a decision without me, but I understand why he did.

When I first arrived in London, I was a complete mess. My

tía was on the phone every night, checking up on me. Sophie's brother and wife live here. She called them and asked if I could stay for a couple of weeks until I got my own place. They are the sweetest, just like Sophie.

I tried to prevent my raging hormones from breaking down in their home. I wanted to go back to him. Although the energy was sucked right out of me, and I was out of fumes. The school did not appeal to me. I thought of getting a job, but in reality, I had enough money to not work. Santiago left me with so much money and a home. I'd never seen it, but it was our home. There was no way I'd step into it until he was back.

A few weeks after arriving, I puked, and Sophie's sister-in-law, Liz, came in to help me. She said, "Do you think you could be pregnant?" The bells in my head rang like church bells, and déjà vu hit all over again. This time, things would be different. Our baby is our inspiration, my reason to finish this school and get to my man.

"Your tea." The waiter sets it on the table along with Harvey's. "What can I get you?"

"I'll have the fish and chips."

"Good choice," the waiter says, writing it down.

"I'll have the same and another one for our friend," Harvey chirps in his strong, sexy British accent.

I raise an eyebrow at him. "Friend?"

He laughs.

"I'm not sure about our status. Yet." Harvey has been dating our neighbor. Well, to me, it seems like they're dating. They come out of each other's flat constantly. "I'm just not sure what Marvin wants from this."

"Have you asked? He's probably wondering the same thing," I prod.

He bites his lower lip. "Hell, I can't keep my hands off of him. You'd think he would know."

I take a sip of tea and savor it. I've never been much for tea, but for some reason, tea here is delicious.

"If I notice, then I'm sure he's noticed." That seems to make him happy. His blue eyes sparkle.

The sound of chatter fills the air as more people arrive for lunch. The restaurants buzz with energy. Everything I've eaten here is good. The rain has stopped, and the sun cascades through the window. Marvin arrives shortly, dressed in expensive slacks. Since Harvey is a designer, he likes to dress all of us.

"How are you feeling, Rosaline? Any kicking, honey?" Marvin asks, passing me the ketchup. They automatically know to get me ketchup since it's not really used here.

"Little flutters. Especially in the mornings." I wish Santiago could be here to rub my belly when the baby moves. If I had known I was pregnant before I left, I would have stayed and forced Liam to let me see him so I could tell him. A part of me wants to write him a letter and tell him in hopes it gives him hope, but what if he's charged? It will only make him feel horrible. My *tía* is the only one back home who knows I'm pregnant. Only because I'm waiting for that phone call telling me he's out. I want Santiago to know before anyone else in the family. I would like to tell him in person.

"I can't wait until he kicks," Marvin says with a glint in his eyes and a wide smile. He's adorable and very handsome. They both are.

Marvin adds, "I wonder if we will have a boy."

AFTER LUNCH, the guys walk me back to class. I spend part of that class period working on my painting and the second in a lecture class. It's close to five o'clock, so I walk down Kensington High Street to window shop. I come to a halt in front of a baby clothing store. My heart beats a little faster as excitement rushes through me when I step into the store. There are so many tiny clothes. I'll be four months pregnant next month. I'll learn the gender, but I'm debating on keeping it a surprise only because I would have liked Santiago to be with me at my appointment. While looking through baby clothes, I come across a cute onesie that says, *Daddy's keeper*. I toss that one in my basket along with booties, mittens, and blankets. Oh my gosh, I want it all.

My phone rings. I dig into my brown Chanel purse Harvey bought me. I give my purse a good shake in search of it. Found it. "Hello?"

"Rosy Posie. How's my girly doing?"

It's been weeks since I spoke with Jasmine. She thought I was mad at her for telling Santiago. She didn't trust Ivan, knowing he was in town, so she told Santiago because I was stalling. But when she learned the entire story with Ivan, she was upset with me for not telling Liam or Santiago sooner. It only made me feel like shit for Santiago being in jail. However, she said that part was not my fault. That's on the San Diego Police Department for falsely accusing him.

"Oh, I've missed your voice. I'm doing good. Just got out of class. How's Philip doing?" He turned three a couple of months ago. She switches it to FaceTime. I gasp when I see her hair. It's short, past her shoulders. "When did you chop it off? You look so beautiful."

"Me, beautiful? No, that's you. Rosa. Your skin is glowing, and girl, that outfit you have on is so stylish."

I'll have to thank my stylist who gifts me expensive clothing. I've never been the type to care about dressing up. I know nothing about clothes brands. Unfortunately, I've been schooled by Harvey. I'm wearing an eyelet belted denim dress by Louis Vuitton, and the only reason I know the name of the dress is because Harvey told me. When I looked up the price, I nearly passed out. It's more than any piece of clothing in my closet.

Well, not so much now because Harvey likes to dress me. He comes from a very wealthy family, and he works for some big-name brands. He has more money than I had pinned him for. And even though Harvey might dress like it, he doesn't act on it.

"Philip is doing good. I'm thinking of moving back to California within the next couple of months."

I continued walking around the store, shopping. "Why? I thought you loved Portland."

She makes a sad, droopy face. "No, not anymore. You're not here with me. I'm lonely. Oh, while I was down there, I ran into Reese, and I didn't have time to tell you. I was alone, and Philip stayed with Mom. He asked how I was doing. Can you believe the nerve of him to fuck me and then not bother calling me? Like I was some whore he slept with at a hotel. A part of me wanted to kiss him, and the other slap him silly." She walks to the fridge and pulls out deli meat and cheese. We are too much alike we need to stress eat.

"Then what happened?" I ask, tossing a burp cloth into the basket.

"He was getting all flirty. He was like, I missed you, kitten. How about we have some drinks, then we can sweat it off? I was so angry, partly because my pussy was like, yeah, get it, girl, and the other part was like, remember, he broke your heart."

I snort.

She shakes her head and takes a bite of her sandwich. "Wait, Rosa, are you at a baby store?"

I grin.

"Are you pregnant?"

I lower the camera so she can see my small baby bump.

"Why didn't you tell me?" she pouts.

"I'm four months. I found out when I moved here. The only person in the family who knows is *Tía*. I wanted to let Santiago know before everyone else. That's why. I'm sorry."

She has a big smile on her gorgeous face, and a tear skates

down. "Congratulations. I'm so happy for you. I understand, Rosa. There is no need to apologize. You take care of yourself. Remember to stay positive. Everything will work out."

We hang up when Philip wakes from a nightmare.

As soon as I step through my front door, I shrug off my coat and head straight to the bathroom. I turn on the shower, letting the warm water wash away the stress of the day. The beads of water cascade over my skin, leaving a trail of steam in their wake. I squirt body wash on the loofah sponge and gently start on my sensitive breasts. They have enlarged more than I needed them to. A moan leaves my lips as the sponge scrapes my engorged nipples.

I lean my head back on the marble tile. The knot in my throat loosens, and the tears I held all day fall like a monsoon-level downpour. I'm horny as hell because of my hormones, and I miss Santiago so much. I wonder if he's okay. Slowly, my legs give out, and I crumble on the floor. This has become my nightly routine. I wait until I get home to unshackle the pain barricading in my chest.

47

SANTIAGO

WHEN YOU HAVE nothing else to do but think, you detail every aspect of your life. You think about things you regret in your life and things you should have done to better your life or your decisions. One decision I could never regret was loving Rosa. Never in a million years would I have thought I'd fall in love with Rosa when she came to visit that summer. A night at the beach comes to mind.

"Come here, flower." I pat the blanket. She is wearing a swimsuit underneath her cover. I have not yet seen it. I'm dying, too. She fills the space next to me. I peel the long red shirt that hides her body. She's wearing that bikini I like. It only covers her nipples, revealing her large breasts spilling out from all sides. My gaze continues down to her pussy. The only thing holding the bottom of her bikini is the strings on each side.

I'm grateful for this spot no one can get to but us on the bike. I tug on each string until they're loose, then I tug it off. Fucking perfect. Damn, do I love her landing strip.

"Spread your legs for me, sweetheart. Better yet, baby, get on your knees. Ass up, let me eat you from behind."

She's so turned on that I can see the wetness between her legs glisten with the full moon. Rosa has such an amazing ass I could lean back and stare at it all day. She's a fantasy come to life.

Inserting a finger in her slick cunt, she moans my name. I'm so damn hard. I could skip lapping her up and go straight to fucking. My tongue seems to work its magic. I lick, then suck.

"Santiago, please."

I laugh. I never thought hearing my girl beg would turn me on. Her fingers dip into her wetness. I give her finger a suck while I'm down there.

"What do you want, Rosa? Tell me what you want. Let me hear you beg for it."

She moans as she rubs her clit. I swat her hands.

"Tell me." I bite her swollen lips. Her hands go right back. "Beg me, sweetheart, let me hear you."

"Fuck me, Santiago, please."

"That's my girl." My dick slides in where it belongs. My balls tighten when she clenches around my cock. The sounds coming from her mouth are goddamn hot. "Come for me, get me all wet."

She does. Rosa's a squirter. Nothing wrong with that. I love it. I grunt my release and give her one last hard pound before I come like a fountain.

It's been five months without her. Liam said she left for London a week after we saw each other. Knowing Damian is watching her gives me a sense of peace. It makes it hard to communicate with the time difference. When we spoke, he informed me she was doing okay. Not good, just okay. I know she's struggling. My poor baby. He said she goes to school. I don't ask who she hangs out with. Damian said she has friends.

I'm getting impatient with being here already. Liam has been keeping me updated. Max and his team have been checking security for the traffic lights. The ones from the motel were not clear facing the room where Ivan was staying at, but Max said he could get it. Liam's been hunting down the gangs and cartels.

I just want to wake up from this nightmare.

ROSALINE

"YOU'RE DOING GOOD. Baby is healthy," the doctor praises as she wipes the sticky stuff on my tummy. "Are you sure you don't want to know the gender?"

This is my second ultrasound. The first time, it wasn't clear because the baby had its butt on display and was not letting us see anything else. During this visit, the baby is active. I could've sworn I saw his penis flashing in the picture. If it's what I thought, he is his father's son. "No, I'll wait. Maybe I'll change my mind on the next visit." A smile springs on her face, and she takes my hand to help me up.

She prints me pictures of the ultrasound to take home. Walking into the lobby, Harvey sits with legs crossed, reading a magazine. He offered to drive me. I wish I had my own car. He glances up from his magazine. "Ah, darling, how are you two doing?"

My stomach has gotten a lot rounder, along with the rest of my body. "We are both healthy... Thank you for giving me a ride."

He waves his hand in the air.

"You're my bestie. Of course, I'm going to take you for your appointments." He reaches for my hand, lacing it with his. Others might think we're a couple, but to Harvey, this is his way of friendship.

Harvey parks the car at a shop, boutique, or warehouse.

Heck, I'm not sure where we are. "I thought you were taking me home? Didn't you have to work?" I ask, getting out. He walks around the car and hooks his arm in mine.

"We're at my work. You will be my model." He chuckles at my raised brow.

"What happened to your models, that you're so desperate you have to use me?"

"I think you don't give yourself enough credit," he scolds.

I gasp when we step in. This is not a store. It's a fashion design department. The furniture is luxurious. I'm not one to know about brands. I can only imagine since Harvey works here. As we walk through the room, my gaze is drawn to a plush sofa adorned with vibrant patterns in shades of crimson and teal. The end tables, made of sleek glass and metal, offer a modern contrast to the business setting. We go up an extensive set of stairs. When we get to the top, I gasp for air. Once I catch my breath, I peer around the room.

"This room is where we create sketches and technical drawings of garments." A couple of steps down. "Right here is the sewing machine, as you can see." He points to a long hallway. "And that's where all the material—fabric—is stored."

I nod, taking it all in.

"You see those glass double doors?"

"Yes."

"That's the editor's office."

I stare blankly at him.

"We are joint with Hugo Magazine." He sighs. "You really don't know diddly squat about fashion?"

"Isn't it obvious?" My hands go up in the air. "I'm an artist. I like to get messy and dress comfortably. It's not like I'm hitting the runway every day."

"Perhaps you're right." He frowns, clearly not happy. "Come, follow me. This room to your right is my office."

Wow! So many racks of clothes. "This is amazing. I'm speechless. You have an astounding job."

He hums in his environment. Harvey gets to work shuffling through racks of women's clothing.

"So, what are we doing exactly?"

He pulls out a black sequined dress, short in the front and long in the back. "We are getting you some outfits for your exhibit and auction in two weeks…Also, for my family dinner."

My eyes widen.

"Dinner? Why would I need to go?" I groan. "Don't tell me you want me to pretend to be your fake girlfriend and tell them we're having a baby."

He snorts. "My family knows I'm gay."

Phew

"*Cristo!* What a relief. I was going to do it for you only because you've done a lot for me."

He laughs and continues on his quest for outfits.

I lean in a furry soft chair to check my messages.

Liam: *He's doing good. Hanging in there. I found this guy who is friends with Ivan. I'm bringing him in for info. I think they got high together. The trial is set in a month.*

My heart thumps. My nerves skyrocket.

Me: *I'm going.*

Liam: *No, Rosaline. He doesn't want you to see if they sentence him.*

That's not happening.

Me: *I'll wait outside.*

Liam: *Okay. I'll let you know because the trial can always get rescheduled.*

Me: *Thank you. I love you and miss you guys.*

Liam: *Love you too, little sis. Stay safe.*

. . .

"HERE YOU GO." He hands me an armful of clothes. "Get naked, woman." He beams.

He's out of his damn mind if he thinks I'm going to get naked in here in front of him. I bite my lip, looking around for a dressing room. This room is quite large.

"Is there a dressing room?" My gaze goes back to his charming face. He has a lopsided smile that's too cute.

"We don't have dressing rooms. We are models. We are all comfortable in dressing in the same room."

"You're a model?" I ask.

He looks me in the eye. "Yes," he snaps, offended.

My hands go to my hips. "Well, excuse me. How was I supposed to know?"

Harvey says, "Because of this." He glides his hand from his chest down. Then wiggles his brow playfully.

I shake my head at him and smile. "Conceited much?" I joke. "No, but seriously, I didn't know you modeled."

"I used to while I was going to school for fashion designing," he admits, rustling through boxes. "Here are some shoes. Now, will you get dressed? It's not like I'm going to get turned on."

Well, that's nice to hear. I think. "I'm not sure if I should be offended or relieved," I mutter, taking a dress off the hanger.

"Oh, darling, If I were into women, I'd be all over those curves. You have the body of a model."

I don't argue with him. That will only get me scolded and lectured. I toss my shirt off, then my leggings, leaving me in my underwear and bra. When I turn to get my dress from the leather sofa, I set the clothes on. Harvey is in only boxers.

What in the hell? He was not wrong. This man has a body like a model. At twenty-eight, he looks younger than he is. "Why are you in your underwear?" He peers up from folding his slacks.

"What's wrong with me being in my knickers? I enjoy

walking around like this. Besides, I'm changing clothes to have dinner with Marvin tonight."

My body shakes with laughter. I fall back onto the peach leather sofa. It's been five months since I've laughed, and it feels good. The ridiculousness of us in our underwear is more awkward than anything to me. He's used to it, not me. Harvey grins at me. The only man who's seen me this way is Santiago. Instantly, my heart crumbles and tears fill my eyes. I'm going crazy, turning into a madwoman.

"Rosa, what's the matter? Come here, tell me?" Harvey tucks me into his side.

"I miss him. He's the only one who's seen me like this." I sniffle, toying with my hands. Harvey wipes the tears off.

"I apologize—"

"No, it's not your fault. I'm just emotional. You're my best friend. It's fine." I stand and pull him up. "Come on, let's get dressed."

I've changed into so many dresses, jumpers, skirts, boots, high heels, and different jackets. It's crazy. Harvey had me walking up and down, twirling as if I were on some runway fashion show. It lifted my mood up, especially the way all the styles he picked hug my curves and tighten around my ass and breasts.

Harvey parks his expensive car in the space next to the house. He carries all my boxes and bags up the stairs. Unlocking the door, I stumble inside, exhausted.

"Thank you so much. I had fun. I appreciate all you've done for me."

He waves a hand. "Lie down," he orders.

I do. My feet are swollen, and my back aches. He removes my shoes and socks and lifts a pillow under my feet.

"There you go. Get some rest."

I rub my belly and the baby moves. "Go on, I'll be fine. Your date is waiting."

He kisses my forehead and closes the door behind him.

Daydreaming before bed always leads to dreams of Santiago and the baby. I'll never be like the woman who abandoned me, and Santiago will never be like his father or mine.

48

SANTIAGO

ROSALINE and I have lost six months of our lives. During that time, I encountered a few guys who had been wrongfully accused. Some of them have been there for years, wasting time when they could be out living life. They don't have anyone fighting for them. Luckily, I have my private detective who didn't stop searching. You can see it on Liam's face how exhausted he is. The bright sun burns my eyes, and the light, cool breeze wraps around me. I sigh in relief when Liam's Camaro roars to life.

"Thanks, man, I owe you."

His eyes crinkle with a smile.

"Nah, you owe me shit. It's my job to get you out, and you're like a brother to me. You know I'd do anything for you."

I know. I knew he would get me out. It was just how long it would take to find who did it.

"You're a badass detective. Your father would be proud," I praise him, and he clears his throat and nods.

If it weren't for him, I wouldn't be going back home. Liam found out who killed Ivan. It was one of the drug dealers who followed him to his room that night. Apparently, Ivan owed him money, and the gang leader ordered him killed—his own stepbrother. Liam interrogated and threatened them until one squirmed and ratted on them. Liam also found out that Ivan had not known Rosa was related to Liam. He was obsessed with her.

"When are you taking off?" Liam asks, making a turn to where the apartments are.

"I need to take care of some stuff here first, then I'll split."

"Good bro, I'm happy for you two. By the way, I went to see the house you built." He whistles. "Damn, that's a fucking badass house. Holy shit. It's huge. It's a beautiful home. Five bedrooms. Dang."

"Yeah, man, I wanted a big house. I want a big family someday. I see how my brother's face lights around his, and I want that too."

Liam's smile reaches his eyes. "I know what you mean. I want that to someday."

"Yeah?"

He nods. "Yeah."

"Look at us, man. All pussy whipped," I say contentedly.

"Speaking of…I need to get to mine. Been trying to get your ass out. I neglected my woman," he teases, squeezing my shoulder now that we're parked at my place.

"Tell Sophie I'm sorry."

"Nah, Don't, bro. She's perfect. She told me not to come home until I got you out. We were all stressed. I'm relieved it all worked out, and you're free."

"Yeah," I say, running my fingers through my greasy hair. I can't wait to take a regular shower alone, not with a bunch of men. "Thanks again. I appreciate it. I owe you."

"How about you repay me by being my best man?"

I turn to him. "Really? I thought Dominic was?"

"You three are brothers not by blood, but you're all I have that resembles a brother's love. I want all three of you."

"We feel the same."

I reach for the door handle when Liam says, "I found Mark. You're not going to believe where he's at."

My blood pressure spikes.

"He's in New York. My guess is he's looking for his biological father. I asked Mila if Mark had called him. She said no. I hired a P.I. out there, and he sent me some photos. It seems he's not himself."

I take a breath. I am happy we know where he's at, but I am worried about him not being himself.

Shutting the door behind me, I inhale the musky scent of the closed-in house.

THIS IS the first time I've ever flown in my entire life. I know it's pretty pathetic for my age. It was a long flight. After I find my luggage, I search for Damian through the bustling crowd. He stands with a sign, waving at me. I laugh and walk toward him.

"Thank God you're out." He pats me on the back with a hug.

"Fuck, yeah." I sag in relief.

Walking toward the exit, I ask, "How do you like it here?"

"I love it. I'm not going to lie. I think I want to stay here. I met someone. We're not dating or anything, but she's cool. And don't get me started on the accent—it's hot."

I look around, and I don't blame him. It's gorgeous. I'm happy Rosa is experiencing all this. "Where is Rosa?"

He pops the trunk open. "Probably asleep at this time of night."

I roll my eyes at him. Smart ass. "Is there a pastry shop open?"

He cocks his head. "Why? Are you hungry?"

"No, I wanted to leave something for Rosa on her doorstep."

"Is she supposed to guess it's you?"

I frown. I would hope so. "Who else would it be?"

He starts the engine of his BMW. "For one, she thinks you're still in jail, and two, it could be her *Sancho*."

My jaw tightness. Her *lover*.

"You didn't tell me she was with someone—"

"If I remember, you said don't tell me if she finds someone." He parks by some pastry shop. "And I never said she was with anyone. I said it could be her Sancho or maybe an admirer." He shrugs. "Or a friend."

Goddamnit, I could squeeze his neck right now.

He orders three breakfast sandwiches, custard buns, and a semla. "Don't worry, I got it. This is what she likes." The fact that my best friend knows what she likes to eat here has my teeth grinding with a pinch of jealousy.

"Good to know you've come to know my wife well enough to know what she eats."

"Not your wife anymore," he says with a smug smile.

"The hell she isn't."

"No, you signed the paper, so technically, she is not."

I slam the car door shut while Damian takes his time nibbling on his sandwich.

"I don't need paper to call her my wife," I grumble. He passes me a breakfast sandwich. I want to smack it out of his hand childly.

"Take it, grumpy. You need fuel for when you see your girl. When do you plan to surprise her?" Unwrapping the sandwich, I take a bite. Damn, it's good.

"Later this afternoon at her exhibit."

He laughs. "Oh, my friend, the one surprised will be you."

I'm not sure what he means by that. A curling in my gut tells me I need to prepare myself for whatever it is.

MY BODY BUZZES WITH ANTICIPATION, and my heart rattles in its cage. Thump, Thump.

I stand in front of the tall, ornate doors of the historical art exhibit. The cobblestone entryway flows with colorful flowerbeds, and a small fountain trickles nearby. A line of people snakes along the sidewalk, eagerly waiting to get in.

It's been a while since I've dressed to impress her. I'm a little overdressed compared to what I'm used to, but it's a special occasion. I even brushed my teeth more times than a dentist requires. I run my fingers through my hair one more time before entering.

Swaying through the crowd, my heart drifts to the sound of her voice. I hear her, but I don't see her. Eagerly, I pick up speed, pushing my way to get to her. Coming to a halt, I stand five feet from where she's explaining her portrait to a group of interested people. All I can see is her back with just a glimpse of her round ass. I'm weak. She's in a dress way above her knees, so short that if my girl bent, her ass would show. Her knee-high boots are sexy. I gaze at her painting. Rosa is so talented. Everything she paints is a masterpiece. The portrait is of a father and son flying a kite. The child's head is peering up at the sky.

She turns, and our gaze collides like thunder and lighting, fire, and gasoline. My blood runs so hot that beads of sweat trickle down my neck. I'm fixated on her beautiful pregnant belly.

She watches me. Her chin trembles, and tears glide down. My legs are rooted to the ground. I'm in shock. She's pregnant. We are having a baby.

She takes a step forward. Then I run to her, drop to my knees, and wrap my arms around the swell of her stomach. It's like our child senses me… He or she moves. My smile grows.

"Santiago, you're here?" I stand and press my lips to hers.

"I'm here, sweetheart." Our tears mash together. "We're having a baby?"

"Yes," she muffles on my shoulder. "How long have you been out?" She cups my face.

"Three weeks. I needed to get things situated before I came." I brush a strand of hair to the side. "I missed you. God, I missed you." I kiss every inch of her gorgeous face.

"Same. You're all I thought of." She runs her fingers through my hair, and her breasts brush on my chest.

I groan with just a small fraction of her touch. She drives me crazy. "You didn't go and fall in love with anyone else, did you?" I tease.

"That was a horrible idea of yours. Luckily, I'm madly in love with you. And I don't listen to your shitty advice."

"It was shitty. Never again will I tell you that." I trace her lips with my finger. "We should go back to your place." I want to strip her down. I'm so damn horny, my balls ache.

She bites my finger, only making my cock hard, rubbing on the uncomfortable slacks I have on. "It will be a while. It just started." She gets on her tiptoes and runs the tip of her nose to my neck. "You smell good." She breathes, tickling my neck.

Letting go of her waist, I step back, and she frowns. "I just want to take a good look at you, baby. My God, you're stunning. Even more so carrying our child." My throat flexes with emotion. "How many months are you?"

Rosa grabs my shirt, pulling me toward her. "I'm six months. I found out when I moved here. He's due in November." She gazes into my eyes. "You're not going back, are you?"

My finger brushes her rosy cheeks.

"No, it's all over with. We can talk about it later. I'm staying with you until you're done with school. Then we can talk about whether we want to move back or go anywhere. I can start a shop anywhere." Wait. *He.* "You said he. Are we having a boy, flower?"

Her smile lights up the damn world.

"I'm not a hundred percent sure. I told the doctor not to tell me, but it seems like the baby was making it known. His penis was flashing me on the screen. He's definitely his father's son. And his hands were up like he was waving. I have the photos at home. I'll show you."

I rub her belly with tender, gut-fluttering affection. I'm going to be a father.

"I can't wait until he's born."

"Me too."

"Come on, sweetheart, show me your masterpiece."

I take her hand in mine, and we walk toward her portrait, and she tells me the story of a father and son who love each other to the moon and back. From a distance, I hadn't noticed that the person was me.

THE TAXI ARRIVES at Rosa's place, and I hand the driver some cash. Taking her hand in mine, we head toward her building and ride the elevator up to her apartment together. She fishes for her keys in her gigantic purse. I brush her hair to the side and press kisses on her nape. The door next to hers swings open, and a man steps out.

"Darling, you're home."

Excuse me. Darling?

He looks at me up and down. "You must be the stud muffin. Damian told me you'd be coming and that you were going to be at the exhibit."

Rosa giggles.

"Santiago, this is Harvey, my bestie. He's helped me get through this hard time."

I'm sure he has, and fuck Damian. He didn't tell me he's been chatty with her friends.

"Nice to meet you, Harold." I shake his hand with a tight grip.

"It's Harvey. It's nice to meet you finally." He turns to Rosa. "Breakfast tomorrow, you two?"

"Sure," Rosa chirps.

"Nah, I'm having breakfast in bed," I say flatly, moving my hand to Rosa's ass.

"Santiago," she scolds, her cheeks tinted red. "Harvey, I'll call you tomorrow. We can all have dinner or something."

"Great. Bye, you two." He winks at Rosa, slipping back into his door.

We step into her place. I take a quick glance. It's a nice place, but what I really want to know is who in the fuck the dude was. She tosses her purse on the sofa and then runs her hand on my chest.

"Darling, do you mind telling me who that was?" I say in a British accent.

All she does is smile and starts unbuttoning my shirt. "I told you his name is Harvey."

My wif—fuck, I hate it. I don't want to call her girlfriend. I want her to be my wife. She's mine. She unhooks the last button, and my shirt drops on her fluffy carpet.

"Why do you have so many shirts on?" In snap speed, she rolls the undershirt off of me "He's my best friend. Like I said."

She then licks my nipples. My dick chokes in my briefs. "Rosaline," I snap. "Does he like you?"

She then loops my belt off. Next, she unzips my slacks.

"I would like to think so, since we're friends."

I trust my girl. But I don't want him or any man around Rosa after what happened with Ivan.

"How about more than friends?" Roughness edges my question. I let my slacks fall to the ground and then kick off my shoes. Slowly, I turn her around and unzip her dress. Gingerly, I slide it off her body like butter. There are no words to describe how beautiful she is. Her breasts have tripled in size. The thin lace material barely covers her. I kneel and place kisses on her stomach. Pregnancy suits her well. She's flawless and sexy.

"He's gay," she moans.

Thank the fuck.

"Balance yourself with my head so I can get your boots off. I don't want you to fall and hurt yourself or our baby." Once her boots are off, I carry her to the sofa.

"Spread those legs. Let me see your pussy." With a tear, her underwear shreds off. Her landing strip is back just how I like it. Deprived for months of eating the best possible luxurious meal, I devour it with great satisfaction, with my tongue thrust, driving her wild. My girl wraps her legs around my neck, suffocating me. That's fine. Breathing is occasionally overrated.

I lift her ass with one hand and pull out my cock that's been ready since the second I saw her. I stroke it in the rhythm with her moans. "Cum on my face. Don't hold back." And she does. She gives me those five months of me not being here to satisfy her. I lick every drop to quench my thirst.

"Oh, my, that felt so good," she praises, gifting me an ego boost.

"I'll make you feel even better. The night is young. We have a lot of sex to catch up on. More than anything, I'm going to show you how much I've missed you."

The only material she has on is her laced bra, which shows her nipples. I need it off, so I tear it. Who has time to unhook bras and underwear when you could just rip them off?

"Santiago, that was expensive. Harvey gave me those from his work."

My eyebrows jog up, and I grab her hand, lifting her up. "Excuse me, did you just say he gifted you lingerie?"

"He's a designer." She licks her lips as I toy with her nipples.

"Listen to me, Rosaline, I don't give a fuck if he's a designer or a damn astronaut. Gay or straight, no one gives my girl lingerie but me," I growl.

Her eyes shine like a lighthouse. "You know, I like you being all possessive." She strokes my dick, almost making me forget I'm mad at her. "I'm turned on. You're sexy, all alpha male."

"You're about to see how barbaric I am." I toss a pillow on the floor "Get on your knees and suck my cock like a good girl. Show me how sorry you are, and you won't allow any man to give you things they're not entitled to give you."

"Such a gentleman," she sasses on her knees.

I laugh "Nothing but a gentleman, sweetheart. You're about to see." I then wrap her hair around my fist. Oh, hell, I thrust too fast, making her gag. That tongue of hers glides through sensitive veins, causing my dick to twitch. She takes it all in like the queen that she is. Those lips tighten around my cock like a rubber band, causing me to cum in under two minutes. She doesn't stop bobbing her head as the fountain of my release coats her throat and lips. She's hot.

49

ROSALINE

MY STARVED, greedy body wants a kaleidoscope of orgasms. I had not expected to see him at the art exhibit. It was the surprise of a lifetime. I'll never take it for granted. Right now, all I want is him all over me. His hands belong on me. Like now, his thumb swipes my lips, collecting the droplets of his release. Then he slips it in my mouth, and I suck it dry.

"That's my good girl."

Is it crazy I enjoy being called his good girl? Is it crazy I enjoy him being bossy in bed? I mean, who wouldn't?

My body heats as he scrutinizes me, biting his lip. His eyes darken with lust. It's beyond me how, all this time, he's disregarded the pouch of my stomach or the width of my hips, especially now that I'm pregnant. I feel the size of an elephant. He doesn't see my flaws. He sees me. His stare dances with desire. He lifts me up with his rough, hard-working hands cupping at my butt, carrying me to the bedroom.

"Get on your knees on the bed. I want to take you from behind," he instructs.

I do as he says. I want this as much as he does. The tip goes in, and he pulls out.

"Fuck, what if I hurt the baby?"

"You won't."

"I could. I'm so damn horny, I can't do it gently. I want to have rough sex."

Damn.

"Doctor said it was fine. I promise you won't hurt our kid. Just fuck me already."

He does and lets loose. By the way he pounds in me, I can tell he missed what we have. My breasts are so tender, they ache when I pinch them. But it feels so good. "You have a great ass," he confesses, taking a bite of my left cheek.

I roll over on my back. His body covers mine, not putting all his weight on me. Grabbing his toned butt, I push him deeper into me, making me arch. He tries to pull back, but I don't let him.

"Baby."

"It's fine. I need you deeper. Make me feel it to my bones."

Finally, he moves harder, making my toes curl. Santiago's lips press against my exposed skin, his mouth forming a perfect seal of one of my sensitive nipples.

His warm wetness sends shivers down my spine as he sucks and teases me with his tongue. Every touch, kiss, the sound of his grunts makes me wild with desire. I can feel the intensity building between us as he continues to pleasure me with his skilled mouth. Sliding my fingers in his silk brown hair, I keep his head in place. I love it when his mouth devours my breasts. He does it so well.

"I had so many fantasies of this."

He looks up, his mouth still busy. "Oh, yeah?"

"Let me show you." I flip us over now. I'm straddling him.

This is better. I'm in control. I rock back and forth, getting him worked up. His gaped mouth tells me I have. "Wrap your arms around me," I demand.

He lifts a sexy brow, and his lips curl. Our naked, warm skin presses against one another, sending spasms to my clit as it hugs his enormous dick. Now that I have him where I want him, I hold on to the nape of his neck for support and bounce. Our lips lock, tongues dancing. My kisses are feral, biting on his lips, sucking on his tongue.

"Rosaline." He groans as I bounce faster and harder.

Fulfillment engulfs me. His cock swells inside me. "Never forget how good I make you feel. Never ask me to leave you." I circle my hips. He watches me with hooded eyes, like he's intoxicated. "You belong to me as I belong to you. I only came here to keep my promise to you. I'll never leave you. I love you too much." I kiss his lips. "Now come for me, baby."

"Oh, Rosaline." The sound of his voice, filled with longing and desire, escaping in a low grunt. It's as if the world has disappeared, and all that exists is us, lost in each other's embrace. Our bodies move in perfect harmony, our breaths mingling as we come together. Nails digging into his back, I let go of the last orgasm I had built up, exploding like a grenade.

"Jesus, that was hot." He cups my face with both hands. "I'll never ask you to leave me. I just never want you to think I'm not putting you first. I love you more than I can express."

"I know I'll always be your first choice. I've known that for a long time. I understand why you've made the decisions you made. This is why I'm not angry about you signing the divorce papers. You did it out of love. We will be parents in four months, and you will no longer have the luxury of sending me away to protect me. We do it together. We're a team."

He nods, embracing me as we lay on the bed. Brushing a hair out of my face, he kisses my forehead. In his mind, he battles, afraid of making the wrong decisions that could affect me. He wants to make me happy. He wants to give me the world, even if it breaks him. I can't be angry at him for that. It only makes me love him more.

I've made horrible decisions that damaged our lives, but I will never again be so trusting.

"Don't ever break my heart again," I add.

"You're right. We're a team. I'll never leave you, Rosa, or our son. You have my word. I've lost you twice. I could never bear not having you in my life. You had me at that first kiss that scared the shit out of me." His thumb circles my nipple. "Sweetheart, we're going to be badass parents. I'm excited."

He smiles like he won a gold medal. Perhaps we did. I'm in awe of him.

"You're going to be a great father. He's going to be as handsome as you."

"Let's have five kids, maybe six. I can always add on to the house," he says, lying on his side, elbows pressed against the mattress.

"Sure," I say to his cock that still trickles, hard as a rock. Licking my lips, I peer at him. "How about another round?"

He laughs and flips back onto his back. "Hop on."

WE SPENT the weekend locked in the house. I only got up to eat and meet Harvey and Marvin for dinner. Also, I learned Damian was here the whole time when he showed up for dinner. I gave him the stink eye, only for him to ignore me and rub my back.

I'm worried Santiago might lose his mind here. He's used to working at the shop. While I'm in class, Santiago is with Damian, searching for a vehicle. The lecture seems to lag more than usual, probably because I just want to run into Santiago's arms. A text comes through, and I slide my phone out to read it.

Santiago: *Hey, baby. I bought a car. I'll be outside when you're ready.*

Me: *Yes, I hate walking in the rain.*

The bubbles come and go.

Santiago: *I know. I missed you all day.*

My heart explodes. He's so sweet.

Me: *Me too. I thought about you the whole time. You're very distracting.*

Santiago: *Show me when we get home.*

Me: *How do you know it's sexual?*

Even though it was.

Santiago: *Because I know you. And I thought about you in the same way.*

WALKING OUT OF CLASS, I find Santiago's back pressed on the car. It's a nice car, a dark royal blue BMW. I speed walk to him like a rocket is chasing after me.

"Slow down, Rosa, I'll get to you." It's too late. I get to him first and press my lips on his. Soft, warm kisses. Over the weekend, his stubble grew. I love that look. "Let's go have dinner."

"Okay, where?" He opens the door for me. The new car smell always gets me. I inhale. Santiago shuts the door on the driver's side.

"It's a surprise." That excites me.

"I love the car. It's so pretty."

He shakes his head and laughs. "Pretty?"

"Yes, black leather, seat warmers, vented seats, and a big screen." The back seats are nice. "There's so much room in the back." I wag my brows at him.

"I'm glad you fancy it, darling." He mocks Harvey's voice. My chest vibrates with laughter. "I bought it for you."

Wait what?

"For me?"

"Yes, you need one to go to school in and for the baby. You know I'm into big trucks and motorcycles. I'll get myself something later. Or I'll have the guys ship my truck."

"Thank you." My throat constricts.

We arrive at a vast, fancy restaurant. Thank God I'm wearing the designer clothes Harvey gifted me. Not that my clothes are a downgrade, but I don't buy clothes to dress up in, and this place must require them. Walking into the restaurant, I gaze at the crystal chandeliers. The tables are decorated beautifully with red tablecloths topped with porcelain vases and white roses. It seems expensive. While I'm taking it all in, Santiago speaks with the waiter.

I trail behind them to the marble staircase. Santiago holds my hand, helping me up the stairs. I realize I'm wearing sneakers. Oh, well.

The waiter guides us into a private room. My mouth hangs open. As I scan the room, my gaze lands on a floor-to-ceiling window that offers an expansive view of the bustling city below. It's breathtaking—like a work of art, a painting come to life. The room is sparkling, with a table like the ones we walked into, but this one has white and red rose petals all over it—on the floor and table. Bottles of wine and grape juice rest in a bucket of ice.

"Is this okay?"

I spin on my heels.

"God, yes. It's beautiful," I assure him. His gaze traces over my body, causing me to shiver.

He smirks. That smug asshole. "What a relief," he says, pulling a chair out, "because Harvey picked the location."

I scoot my chair in. "You and Harvey hung out?" I'm startled. Santiago had been jealous. He picks an invisible lint off his shirt. Wait. "Are you wearing Hermès clothing?"

His lips twitch, not meeting my eye. Harvey must have pimped him.

"I asked for advice on a restaurant, and he became invested

in helping me make it special for you. And the clothes he said you would like." He shrugs. "It's not my thing, but I'll wear it on special occasions."

"I love your style because it's you. I'm not really into expensive designer brands either. I do like to occasionally wear clothes that make me feel sexy though."

He reaches for my hand and scoots his seat close enough that our knees are touching. "To me, you are sexy in anything you wear. You are a goddess in my eyes." He clears his throat and then leans to press a kiss on my lips. "I was going to do this after dinner. But fuck it. I can't wait."

He drops to one knee and pulls out a ring. "Rosaline, I didn't get to propose to you the first time how I really wanted. I don't regret it because it happened like it should have. I'm lucky to get a second chance to do it all over. You changed my life. I never thought I'd experience what love was until you. You made it easy because it's you, and I'm crazy in love with you. I'm excited to spend the rest of our lives together with our kids. Will you marry me again?" His voice is deep and velvety, and his eyes glisten.

My hormones are already at their highest peak. I rub my belly and try to control my sobs. "Yes, I want to be your wife and nothing else."

He slips the ring on. It's not the same one. This one is bigger and more expensive. "What happened to the other one?"

A smile parts his lips. "Baby, it's in your jewelry box. I'm not going to take it, and then give it to you again. I wanted to start fresh."

My mouth forms an O. "Pregnancy brain fog, sorry. It's beautiful." He sits back in his seat, and I slide over onto his lap. "You know," I say, toying with his collar shirt. "I love what you did. It's romantic and all, but why don't we go home, change into comfortable clothes, order takeout, and cuddle watching a movie?" I know that's what he prefers. He loosens the top button of his shirt.

"Sounds good to me, but before all that, I have other plans with you."

We both stand. I glance up at his handsome face. His dimples deepen with his beaming smile. My hands wrap around his neck, and his arms wrap around my waist.

"I like how you think, Mr. Delgado. I want every piece of you."

EPILOGUE ONE

Three months later

As much as I love London, I miss home. With three more months remaining, Rosa will complete school and obtain her master's. Then we will head back to California. Our house, along with family and my shop, is waiting for us. I've been having zoom meetings for the shop with the team and trying as much as possible to work on my computer and do paperwork.

However, it didn't feel like enough. I needed to be doing something with my hands, moving around, and keeping busy. So, I do freelance work as a mechanic. It's worked out. I go to different shops that are short-handed. I make my own schedule and still have time to get to my wife. Weeks after I proposed like a gentleman, Rosa and I got married back home when she had days off from school. Of course, Harvey took her dress shopping.

That little fucker grew on me when I saw he wasn't sexually attracted to Rosa, and he means a lot to her and helped her when I wasn't around. I thanked him. If he's important to her, then he is to me.

I glance at my watch. It's close to four o'clock. Rosa should be out of school soon. I better clean up for the day. Grabbing my tool bag, I toss all my tools in when my phone rings.

"Hey, sweetheart. I was just cleaning up."

"Santiago, I'm having contractions. I need to get to the hospital. They're getting close."

Oh, hell. Don't panic. "I'm on my way. Wait, are you sure?"

"Yes, we're going to be parents today. Hell, it better be today. He better not keep me in pain until tomorrow."

"Okay, I'm on my way. I'm walking to the car."

Before she hangs up I can hear the pain in her voice.

I'm going to be a dad. My hands sweat, curled under the steering wheel. I know one thing for sure: I won't be like my parents, and I know Rosa will be an exceptional mother. We are not like them.

All the lost years with Victor still hurt, but he's back in our lives. Although he missed out on our childhood. He wants to be a father to us now and a grandfather. Dominic said he's been going around more playing with the kids. He even built Dante a tree house. He calls or texts me every day, checking in on us. He works at my shop, helping Reese.

I park and run out of the car to get to Rosa. She's leaned against a wall, a classmate with her.

"Baby, I'm here."

She grips my hand with Hulk's strength.

I get her in the car and speed off to the hospital. This is it. My dreams of having a family are happening. Pressure in my chest prevents me from breathing.

"Breathe in and out. That's it. Just like that." Rosa coaches me when it should be the other way around.

Damnit, Santiago. Get it together.

"I'm fine. I'm sorry. How far apart are the contractions?"

She cries in pain, arching her back and breathing like they taught her in a class she had me attend. I'm driving like a maniac, but cautiously. "They're too close."

When I see the hospital in view, I sigh in relief. I park on the curb and then run in for a wheelchair. I'm unsure how they do things here.

IT'S BEEN TWO HOURS, and Rosa has dilated four centimeters now. From my understanding, she's close. "You're doing good," I praise her. She does her breathing while I rub her back.

"Oh, I can't wait," she pants and smiles at me.

"Me too. I've been waiting for this moment for so long." Life happens when it needs to, and this was our time.

I texted everyone back home to let them know Rosa's in labor, and they're excited to hear from me. Rosa's aunt was upset. She wanted to be here, so I bought her a ticket to fly down to see her grandson next week.

"Call the doctor. I need to push. I feel the baby low."

Oh, shit.

Frantic, I run out to find the doctor. "My wife…she's ready," I shout.

She calls the nurses in, and they prepare for birth. I'm holding onto Rosa's hand and leg as she pushes.

"Almost, honey, push," the doctor calls out. Tears run down Rosa's cheek, and she screams, then pushes. "One more last push. Come on, I see the head," the doctor encourages her.

With one last earth-shattering push, our baby is out.

"It's a boy!" the doctor announces. It's like time stands still. They bring the baby to Rosa and hand me the scissors to cut the umbilical cord.

That first cry did something to me. I lost my breath and watched him take his first. My chest caves in with warmth as my wife kisses our son, and he looks up at his mom with his big brown eyes.

"Hi, honey. I'm so happy to finally meet you." His little lips perk up at the sound of his mom's voice. "Your dad is here. You look just like him."

She pats the bed. "Come meet your son." She flashes me a huge grin.

I'm rooted to the spot, taking in the most precious view.

Sitting next to her, I lean in and kiss his soft skin. He's perfect. He sticks his fist in his mouth and sucks. Rosa passes him to me. He's so tiny.

"Hey, buddy. I'm your daddy. I love you. We're going to do a lot of things together." He gazes up at me and continues sucking. Grunting and stretching. "I'm going to teach you anything and everything, especially how to ride a motorcycle."

"Santiago," Rosa scolds.

"Mama's already a killjoy," I joke.

She laughs.

"Can I take him for a second to get him washed up?" the nurse asks.

"Sure." I pass him to her.

"What's his name?" she asks.

My gaze goes to Rosa. We had come up with so many names.

"Sebastian," Rosa replies.

While Sebastian's getting cleaned up, I sit next to Rosa. She's so gorgeous. Who would have thought that the toothy girl on my doorstep nineteen years ago would be the woman to complete my life and give me everything a man can dream of?

"He's perfect. You did good, sweetheart. I love you, wife." I kiss her sweet, plump lips.

"I love you too." She leans back into her pillow, gazing up at me. "I'm so happy… Answer me this: did the king get his happy ending?"

I swipe my tongue, trying to hide my smile. Even after so many years, she still remembers the story she begged me to tell her. A story I made up only because I never thought I would find the perfect person for me.

"Mrs. Delgado, you're my salvation. You've given me more than just a happy ending. You changed my life. You have given the king in his story his kingdom." I peer at the nurse putting a diaper on Sebastian. Then back to Rosa. "You gave me a family and your love."

"You're too sweet."

"That's because you turned me into a cheesy guy." Although I'd only be it for her. And because it's true. She is my salvation.

The nurse brings our son back and hands him to Rosa. I take out my phone and snap some photos. "You can feed him now, dear," the nurse presses.

Rosa breastfeeds him, and I lay next to them.

Liam, Mila, Sophie, Dominic, and the kids FaceTime us. They all radiated with happiness over the new addition to our family. The only one missing is Mark. It kills me he won't answer my calls. Once we get back to the States, I'm going to go find him. I just need to see for myself he's fine.

The door swings open, and Harvey and Marvin walk in with balloons, flowers, and a teddy bear. "Darling, where is my baby?"

"He's not yours," I grumble.

He waves his hand at me, dismisses me, and sets the flowers down. "Listen here, Stud Muffin. It's like we all three conceived him."

He's ridiculous. I roll my eyes at him with my lips curled into a smile. He leans in and presses a kiss on Rosa's forehead. Marvin follows behind.

"He looks so much like you," Harvey says.

I take great pride in what Rosa and I created.

"He does, doesn't he?"

Once Harvey leaves and we end the call with the family, I stand next to my wife.

"Take a nap, sweetheart. I got him."

She yawns and hands him to me. Her eyes close, and within seconds, a soft snore leaves her lips.

"Hey, little guy, you wore your mama out." I press a kiss on his soft cheeks. "I promise to always be there for you and your mom. I'll never leave you or your mama. You two are my world." I kiss him, and he stares up at me. He smells of baby and his mama. "We love you."

All the shit I went through to get here was worth it, and I'd do it again in a heartbeat to have Rosa and our son. To have the life we created.

EPILOGUE TWO

RosaLine
Five Months Later

Peering out the window, I study the enchanted landscape. The river flows in a tranquil rhythm. Wildflowers of different hues scatter along the banks, and lilacs dance in the hills.

It's beautiful. I still can't grasp this is the home my husband built for us. Three months ago, we moved back home from London.

Santiago showed me the house when we came down for our second wedding. My heart soared when he surprised me with the art room he designed for me to work in. Since we moved here, I've been trying to spend as much time as I can painting when Sebastian goes down for a nap or when Santiago is home.

I bite my lip, concentrating and dotting petals on the canvas. My paintings in London sold for ten thousand. I know it's not much, considering paintings sell for millions, but for a new artist like me, I was stunned.

"You're absolutely gorgeous, Mrs. Delgado." I jump, startled by Santiago's husky voice. He leans against the pillar of the entryway. His gaze caresses my body. Even though I have more stretch marks from having Sebastian, he always looks at me with heat in his eyes. I've come to love my body, especially since I had my son.

I smile at him. "What are you doing here? You're home early?"

He strolls toward me, gaze pinned on my eyes. He lifts my chin with his index finger. My lips part with his tender kiss.

Every day, I fall deeper in love with my husband. "That was nice," I mutter into soft lips. His strong arms hold me tight. "You're going to get paint all over you."

"Paint mixed with oil and grease is considered a masterpiece, and that's what we are together. Sensational." He pecks a kiss on my nose and looks over at our son. "How long has he been asleep?"

"An hour. He should wake up in thirty minutes."

"Let's shower. I have something to show you once Sebastian wakes up," he whispers in my ear, causing goosebumps.

"What is it?" I moan when he picks me up and carries me to the bathroom. His tongue glides on my neck.

"It wouldn't be a surprise if I told you, sweetheart."

I set the baby monitor on the counter and strip eagerly. His gorgeous eyes darken with lust. He kicks his boots off, then his shirt and pants.

We stand in the wide brick shower. The way Santiago designed it is like a paradise with a showerhead waterfall cascading over us. Beads of warm water roll down from the waterfall showerhead as our lips lock into a passionate, desperate kiss. He lifts me with ease as if I'm as light as a feather. Wrapping my legs around his waist, I grip his hair. Santiago backs us into the wall, my back hitting the red brick.

My hands run down his broad shoulders and over his sculpted body. "I missed you. You and our son are all I think about." His index finger runs up and down my clit. "You're the most beautiful woman I've ever laid eyes on. I'm going to show you, just how much I missed you. And then I'm going to show you just how much I love you by taking you to see your surprise."

I'm not sure what it is, but I love everything and anything he does for me. He has a heart of gold. "Show me how much you missed me, baby,"

He smirks. "Gladly, wife."

He aligns his hard cock into me. I moan, tightening around him. God, he always feels so damn good.

"Moan my name, baby." He groans, hitting all the right spots. His mouth captures my nipple.

"Santiago," I pant.

"That's my girl," he picks up speed, and my eyes roll back. "You're sexy, sweetheart. I love how you look when you're about to come on my cock."

His dirty words always make me tongue-tied. "I-I need—"

"I'm right behind you. Come for me."

I let out a cry of pure euphoria. He keeps pumping in me like a never-ending fountain. His jaw tightens at the end of his release, eyes locked with mine. Life with Santiago is beautiful. Being parents is the icing on the cake. He's an amazing father.

"I love you," I tell him. The softness in his eyes melts my heart. My hands run through his wet hair.

"I love you more," he says worshipfully.

My eyebrows lift. "I loved you first, so that means I love you more."

He laughs, sliding his cock out of me, and I unwrap my legs from him. "That's not how it works, beautiful. You gave me all your firsts. I fell harder for you, and I was desperate to make you my wife. That was my way of keeping you."

Washing his chest with body wash, I muse. "I'm glad we

made impulsive moves, then. We both have made horrible decisions. Even through the time apart, I was always yours."

He groans, squirting shampoo into the palm of his hand. "I don't like to think of those times. I never want to be apart from you." He turns me around, massaging my scalp with shampoo.

"I think it made us stronger."

"Maybe, but I can't live without you and Sebastian. You're the air I breathe. You complete me in ways I never thought possible." His voice fills with emotion.

Facing him, I kiss his cheek and then wash his hair. We've been through so much together, but our love for one another could never fracture.

Once we're done washing, he turns off the faucet and hands me a towel. Sebastian coos through the monitor. Santiago rushes to put on shorts and a shirt. "I'll get my little guy. I missed him like crazy. Take your time getting ready, sweetheart." In a flash, he runs out the door to our son.

LOCKING THE FRONT DOOR, diaper bag hanging on my shoulder, I walk toward the truck. Santiago is putting our chunky monkey in his car seat. "Hi, baby," I tell Sebastian, who is babbling while sucking on his teething ring. "Daddy dressed you so handsome. He even parted your hair."

Santiago laughs. "It's a special occasion."

He's grinning. I can't imagine what the surprise could be. I already have everything I've dreamed of. It could be a romantic dinner, but we have our son with us. Once Santiago's done, I get in the backseat with Sebastian. At five months old, he's still small enough that I sit with him in the backseat. Driving out of the two-acre lot, I glance at the shovelhead motorcycle I bought my husband. When all the shit went down with Ivan, I asked

Liam to store Santiago's gift until things got better. When we moved back from London, I gave it to him.

"How's the Shovelhead running? I noticed you took it to work."

His hand reaches to the back, and his thumb rubs my knee tenderly. "She's a beauty. It's running like a beast. Thank you for the gift."

He's thanked me so many times. Santiago has always been the giver, so when I give him something, he doesn't know how to handle the gratitude.

"You deserve it and so much more." My voice comes out velvety.

Getting into the city, Santiago passes me a shirt.

"What's this for?"

"To blindfold you. That's all I could find." He laughs.

When I put on the shirt as a blindfold, my son starts to laugh. It's the cutest giggle. I must look funny to him.

"All right, we are here. Don't move, baby," Santiago pleads, jumping out of the truck. He opens the back door, helping me out. "Stand right here. Let me get our son out."

My husband takes my hand and walks me up to wherever he's taking me. The crisp air is soothing. My stomach flutters with anticipation. He removes the blindfold. However, I can't see anything because he's standing right in front of me, holding Sebastian.

"Are you ready, sweetheart?"

"Yes," I whisper. He steps to the side, and my heart swells.

Tears burn my vision, and my chin trembles. It's beautiful—a two-story building that reads Rosaline's Studio. I have dreamed of this my whole life.

"F-for me?" That's all I can manage to say. I'm so overwhelmed with emotions.

"For you, my love. You deserve it, flower. You've accomplished so much and been through so much. I'm proud of the woman you've become, the mother you are to our son, and the wife by my side." He lifts my chin. "Let's go inside. You can redecorate however you like. This is your studio."

He takes my trembling hand in his and leads us through the front door. I gasp in shock. It's gorgeous. It has a high cathedral ceiling, my art hung on the cream walls, white leather sofas, and a side table with a ceramic vase of flowers.

"Santiago, it's beautiful." My hand goes to my chest.

"Upstairs is a small kitchen and bedroom for when the kids are here." His lips twitch.

"Kids?"

"Yeah, I want a big family."

"Oh, I'll give you a team of kids."

He grins even wider. "Go check out the place. I'm going to show our son how talented his mother is."

Making my way to the wooden stairs, my eyes widen at the vast kitchen. Marble countertops, a stainless-steel fridge with a matching stove. I walk into the bedroom. It's simple: a playpen and a small twin-size bed. It's like a small studio apartment.

I notice the big wooden chest I had at my *tia's* is here. I've had it locked. It seems someone busted it open.

"Your aunt had me pick it up. She said you stored your art in here. When I busted it open, my eyes literally popped out. I was looking for pictures to hang up."

I roll my eyes, take Sebastian, and kiss my baby. He looks so much like his father.

"If you weren't my wife, I would think it's borderline creepy how many paintings you made of me in your teens." He grins. "Obsessed."

I swat him on the chest. "I call it infatuated."

"Uh-huh. Call it what you want. I love the one of me shirtless with us kissing."

Yeah, that was the first kiss.

"Santiago, thank you for this." I wave my hand around the

studio. "It's amazing. You do so much for us. You really didn't have to."

"Rosaline, remember, *your* dreams are my dreams. *Your* happiness is mine. I'll give you the world."

A tear rolls down my cheek. He makes me whole. *He* deserves the world. I'll do the same—always make sure my king is happy and loved.

Gingerly, I take a few steps until we're chest to chest. His brows rise, and his lips twitch. "What are you doing?" he asks.

"You have a bug on your cheek," I tease. His head goes back in laughter, remembering our first awkward kiss.

"You know that's the worst line to kiss someone, but it worked. You got what you wanted, and so did I." His fingers feather on my cheek. "Allow me to kiss you, wife?"

My mouth parts, and our tongues clash. It's tender yet desperate, but it only lasts a few seconds when Sebastian grabs Santiago's cheek, trying to push him away.

We both laugh, admiring the life we have created. We had a rough start, but it all worked out in the end. Our love can't shatter to pieces because it is filled with every piece of us. Love.

AUTHOR NOTE

Thank you for reading Every Piece of You. I hope you enjoyed
Santiago and Rosaline's story as much as I enjoyed writing it.
These two took me on a wild ride. These two taught me that we
make decisions that might not be the best, but we do the best we
can. Santiago made his decisions with love and did the best he
could for a man who had no guidance in his life. He raised his
brothers and taught them how to be men the best way he could.
His love for Rosa was special; he made decisions that were not
the best, but for her, he would do anything. He pushed her away
to go to college to give her a better life and, at the same time,
worked on building a life for them together.
Santiago handing Rosa divorce papers was an inspiration and
an idea I had from an event that happened with a family friend's
son. He had to serve twenty years. He was young at the time,
and his wife was pregnant. She went week after week to see
him. He then served her with divorce papers. He did it out of
love. He wanted her to have a life he couldn't give her. Marriage.
A family. This reminded me of Santiago because it was
something he would do for Rosa. Santiago wanted Rosa to
experience life at the expense of his own.

Readers, if you read this as a standalone and feel confused. *Every Piece of You* is the third book of *The Delgado Brothers Series*. I highly advise reading the first two books *Always You* and *Recklessly You* first to become acquainted with the characters and backstory. It cannot be read as a standalone.

Every Piece of You does follow the timeline, although <u>Part One</u> begins prior to *Always You* (Mila and Dominic's story) and <u>Part Two</u> continues with the present time with the end of the *Recklessly You* timeline. *Please note if you read as a standalone, you will come across events that will be answered by reading the first two books.*

You can read Dominic and Mila's story here Always You
Liam and Sophie's story: Recklessly You

<u>What's next</u>
We have two books left in *The Delgado Brothers Series.*
Mark's book will be next in the series, followed by Reese and Jasmine

You can follow me to get the updated news by following me on social media and

J. Morales Spoiler group
Newsletter signups

<u>Connect</u>

Scan QR code to connect with J. Morales on social media.

ACKNOWLEDGMENT

To my readers, thank you for your support in this series and for being interested in Santiago's story. I hope you loved it as much as I did.

Elizabeth, thank you so much for all your help. You have been a huge lifesaver. I appreciate you.

To my husband, thank you for your continued support and for being my cheerleader throughout my new journey. To my kids, who are always interested and ask what I'm writing about, even if it's romance, thank you.

To my beta readers and ARC team, thank you for your help. I appreciate the time you put in. To the editors who have helped me through this series, thank you so much. I appreciate all your help. It means the world to me.

To my mom, thank you for all your prayers and interest in my writing.

Thank you all so much.

J. Morales

Printed in Dunstable, United Kingdom